Azerick did not hesitate. Using the training Master Ewen had instilled in him, he ducked low, pivoted on his right heel, and slipped behind his assailant. As the man staggered and held his hands over the fresh wound in his belly, Azerick drove his newly acquired blade into the man's right kidney. Azerick knew from his studies that the kidney was especially vulnerable and caused an enormous amount of pain when struck or pierced. He was quite familiar with anatomy, and he knew the location of most of the body's tender parts.

The man seemed to choke on the scream trying to escape his lips as agonizing pain lanced up his back, completely overriding the bite of his original wound. He dropped to his knees in front of Azerick while trying to reach behind him and put his hand over this newest source of agony. Azerick thrust forward once more, stabbing the man high in the back. The knife skipped off the bottom of the man's shoulder bone, and the blade slipped between the upper ribs just below it, piercing his heart.

Azerick paused for a few moments, thinking about what he had just done as the man slumped forward onto his face. He stood over the body, bloody knife in hand, and processed everything that just happened. Not only had he killed a man, somehow, he knew it would not be the last life he would take in the years to come. He looked at the knife and the droplets of blood dripping off the tip to spatter onto the ground. His life was now irrevocably defined by death.

The Sorcerer's
ASCENSION

BROCK E. DESKINS

FOREWORD

For most of history, the races existed as a scattering of destitute settlements, the largest of which could barely be called cities. Dragons ruled the lands and oppressed the races for their masters, faceless gods whose existence has been forgotten through the ages. Two thousand years ago, the elves discovered how to wield the Source, a mystical energy which allowed a few to weave powerful magic. Sharing this knowledge with those who possessed the ability, the races united to cast off the shackles of oppression and live as free people or die trying.

The brilliant dwarven blacksmith, Dundalor Ironforger, crafted five magnificent suits of armor and gifted them to the greatest warriors amongst the races. Imbued with the magical ability of rune carving, Dundalor enchanted the suits to be able to withstand the dragons' awesome might and terrible magic. The races banded together and, led by their heroes, fought for their freedom in the Great Revolution.

Decades of slaughter cast a black pall over the land, but the races would not relent. To surrender would invite their destruction as punishment for challenging the old gods and their dragon overlords. With the aid of the new gods, a time of freedom grew from the ashes of their sacrifices.

No longer united in a cause greater than their differences, the races became strangers once again. The elves withdrew, fearful of the rapid growth of the human realm. The dwarves sought sanctuary beneath the mountains, and the humans hailed their first king, Magnus Ollander. With the aid of Dundalor's magnificent armor, Magnus led the humans during a tumultuous time, putting down those who wanted to divide the new kingdom and claim power for themselves. Magnus created a bloodline legacy, tying his progeny to the throne for all time. One of those descendants, fearing another bloodline could use the armor to usurp the throne, ordered the armor scattered to the farthest corners of the land and the records of its existence destroyed.

Today, a new Ollander, Jarvin, bastard son of Harlan Ollander, clings to a precarious rule. Unhappy with Jarvin's rule, many of the wealthier and more influential nobles plot against the bastard king but none with more fervor than the powerful duke of Southport. The overwhelming support of the common people keeps the traitors from seizing the throne by force, so Duke Ulric searches for the fabled armor in hopes of using its influence to take the throne with minimal bloodshed and establish a new bloodline.

CHAPTER 1

Captain Darius Giles oversaw his crew as they loaded the last of the precious cargo aboard his ship, *Storm Runner*. The trinkets, jade statuettes, ivory carvings, animal pelts, and gold jewelry, as well as local pieces of art and other exotic goods, would bring in a small fortune even after he paid taxes and salaries. He cast a wary glance at the two men approaching as he supervised the loading of his cargo. Despite being a clear, warm night, they wore the hoods of their cloaks pulled up, concealing their faces.

"You are the captain of this vessel?" the taller of the two men inquired.

"I'm Captain Giles. What can I do for you gentlemen this evening?"

"We require transport for a piece of cargo," the hooded stranger replied.

Darius looked from the men to the laden cargo net stretched taut with the last of his heavy, wooden shipping crates. "I'm afraid I've a full hold, sir. Perhaps another ship will call to port and they can help you."

"It is expected in Southport as soon as is possible, and yours is the next ship departing. I assure you, it does not require a great deal of space, only the discretion of an honorable man," the enigmatic stranger continued, undeterred. "I have been told that you are such a man."

"I like to think so. I would have to inspect this cargo myself so I know it contains no contraband. I'm a loyal king's man, and I'll break none of his laws, especially those that could mean the loss of my ship, cargo, crew, or life."

"That is precisely the type of man we seek." The hooded stranger reached into his cloak and produced a scroll. "Look upon the seal, sir, and you will note it is the king's own. Inside, you will see that our request is made with His Majesty's authority."

Captain Giles examined the seal and found it was either authentic or a forgery of exceptional quality. He broke the seal and read the missive by lamplight. In simple terms, it requested the services of a reliable ship's captain to deliver a small container of cargo to Southport with the utmost speed and discretion. The cargo was a state secret and not to be opened by captain, crew, or customs. A second group of men would meet the captain upon arrival in Southport where he would be provided with a similar document as proof of receipt of the aforementioned cargo. Any evidence of tampering discovered by the receiving party would be cause for charges of treason and espionage, both of which were punishable by death.

Darius furrowed his brow as he finished reading. "This is not the sort of thing I like to get myself or my men embroiled in, but if it is His Majesty's command, then I am honored to be of service. Bring the crate, and if it is small enough, I will secure it in my berth."

"That will do just fine, Captain," the man said, handing him a purse heavy with coin. "This should be more than sufficient payment for transport of such a small piece of cargo and your personal assurance of security."

Twenty minutes later, the two men returned bearing a wooden crate with handles on two sides. They carried their burden to the captain's quarters and secured it in a chest after Darius made room. They left without another word and disappeared back into the darkness of the foreign city's streets.

Captain Giles decided to remain in his cabin instead of celebrating with his crew on their last night in port before catching the morning tide. He was in possession of the king's property, and he would not relax his vigil over the special cargo.

Storm Runner set sail in the morning the moment they were able to clear the shoal. The large, three-masted ship caught a favorable wind and pushed steadily out to sea. The blow held true and propelled the ship along the gentle swells of the sea at a respectable clip for several days. Captain Giles said a quick prayer of thanks to Serron, god of the seas, for their continued good fortune.

This had been a long and circuitous voyage. It was going on three months since they had sailed out of Southport, and he was eager to be home again with his beautiful wife, Celeste, and his son, Azerick, just as he knew his crew would be anxious to return to whomever or whatever was greatest in their own desires.

Darius let his mind drift to thoughts of his family. He conjured a mental image of Celeste and longed to hold her again. Although she had been his wife for fifteen years, she still captivated his heart as strongly today as on the day they met.

Azerick was thirteen and as smart as any boy he had ever known. Darius decided he would spend some time at home and let the other captains he employed take care of the shipping duties of his maritime trading company for a while. He needed to stay at least a couple of years on shore duty, and if the gods willed it, give his son a little brother or sister. It was not as if he hadn't tried on his previous stays between voyages, but this time he would devote some real time to his family instead of his work.

After all, the business was doing well and could almost run itself without his constant attention for a time. He would have to find a good captain to take over his flagship, *Storm Runner*, while he stayed landlocked. Maybe it was time to reward his first mate by promoting him, as he deserved. Zeb was a good man: honest, hard-working, loyal to a fault, and kept a tighter ship than any captain he employed, including himself. Besides, Zeb had been a first mate since Darius himself began his sailing career. As he leaned on the aft railing looking out over the ocean, a call from the crow's nest took him out of his reverie.

"Sails, four points off port abeam!" cried the lookout.

"Heading?" Captain Giles called up to the sailor on watch.

"Cutting across on an intercept from the looks of it, Captain," came the answer a full minute later.

"Arm the catapult and ballista, man the scorpions, and draw weapons. Prepare to defend the ship," Darius ordered as he stalked across *Storm Runner's* rolling deck.

Zeb chased after the sailors, ensuring every man was armed and at his station. The crew cranked and loaded the ballista on the aft deck and its smaller counterparts, the scorpions. They wound the catapult on the foredeck, locked its swing arm into place, and seated jars of flammable oil in the basket, which they would light just before launching them at the enemy vessel if forced to defend themselves.

Pirates had been the plagues of the seas for centuries, especially this far out where Valaria's meager navy did not patrol. His was a paranoid, aggressive response but for good reason. Few merchants risked this dangerous voyage, which is what made his cargo so valuable, and Darius would not lose it without a fight.

"Tack three points to starboard. We'll see if we can outrun them."

"Unknown ship tacking to match new heading, Captain, and still on an intercept course," the update came about ten minutes later.

Captain Giles cursed their ill luck. "That's all the proof I need to call them pirates, boys. If we can't outrun them, fire as soon as they come within range and send them to Serron if they choose not to let us pass."

The captain's proclamation was met with a loud huzzah of support from his crew. The chase continued for most of the day before the other ship came within range. The crew of the *Storm Runner* could see the pirates on the deck of the pursuing ship now aiming their own foredeck catapult. The ballista had a greater range than the small catapult, and his men started launching its two-meter, steel-tipped shafts at the advancing vessel.

The javelins cut through lines, sails, and any man unfortunate enough to be in the bolts' paths. One of the bolts found purchase when the bow swung wide and presented a flat plane and it punched through the hull, but the wound was well above the waterline and presented little risk. The pirate ship was now within range to use its own catapult and began flinging chain to tear sails and foul the rigging. It also stripped men out of the rigging, perched there with loaded crossbows, ready to unleash their quarrels on the pirates as they came within range.

"Load incendiary pots in the ballista!" Captain Giles ordered.

His faithful and fearless crew obeyed his commands without hesitation, replacing the heavy ballista bolts with the oil-filled flasks. They launched the flammable jugs as soon as one of the sailors lit the wick. The clay pot sped through the air in a moderate arc and shattered as it struck. The incendiary burst into a spray of liquid fire, wreathing the front of the boat, but the sea spray from the rising and plunging bow washed the oil and flames away.

The sailors manning the heavy weapon raised their aim and fired a second shot, which shattered into the deck of the pursuing vessel. The crew of the *Storm Runner* cried out in triumph as the deck of the enemy vessel caught fire. Their elation was short-lived as the pirate crew smothered the flames with buckets of sand. The enemy ship may have been crewed by degenerates and scum, but the pirates were an experienced lot. It was apparent they had soaked the deck with salt water before engaging, and the burning oil did little damage to the wooden structure before they extinguished it. Chain shot and fist-sized stones continued to tear into the rigging and rain down upon the deck and heads of Captain Giles' ship and crew.

"Damn these pirates! Just our luck to get a pirate ship with a first-class crew! Zeb, have some of the men bring up a few barrels of that demon fire from the hold," Captain Giles ordered.

"Demon fire?" His first mate paled. "Are you sure?"

"Damn it, man! If I wasn't sure, I wouldn't have issued the order! Now move it!"

"Aye, aye, Captain!"

It was unheard of for Zeb to second-guess his captain, but fire was one of the greatest fears on a ship, and demon fire, or dragon's spit as some called it, was the most flammable substance known to man. It burned so hot it could reduce a man to ash and bones in moments and could not be extinguished by water. Minutes later, Zeb and several sailors had four barrels of the volatile liquid brought to the rear of the ship.

"I want a plank strapped to each side of the stern at a downward angle to create a trough. When we pour this stuff out, I don't want any of the infernal concoction to touch my ship," Captain Giles ordered.

Zeb and his fellow sailors lashed a six-foot-long, one-foot-wide plank at the rear of the ship on each side to create a track for the heavy liquid to follow in order to keep it off their vessel.

"Open up those barrels and pour 'em down the runnel. Quickly now! You men, grab torches and *carefully* swab a bit of that mess onto each of them. Lash them to a ballista bolt then throw the casks over the side as soon as they're empty! "

The pirate vessel had done significant damage and was overtaking the wounded *Storm Runner*. The pirate crew ceased launching chain into the rigging and sails and now flung small stones and shards of metal in an attempt to clear the deck before boarding.

Only Captain Giles, Zeb, and a handful of sailors, hidden behind the ballista and the aft railing, remained on deck after ordering the rest of the men below, but they were all prepared to rush back topside to defend against a boarding party.

His ballista crew used the empty, floating barrels as reference points to time their attack. Darius let the pirate vessel get near the first barrel before ordering his men to light and fire the ballista bolt into the shimmering, oily stretch of ocean between them and their pursuers.

The flaming brand arced across the water before falling into the sea. The combustible liquid floating on the surface of the water burst into flames when the torch struck the oily sheen. The pirate vessel now plowed through a blazing river of fire flowing atop the rolling swells of the sea.

The conflagration stretched several feet in the air, adhered to the hull of the attacking ship, and ignited the wood above the waterline. Left to its own devices, the demon fire would even burn below the water. The pirate captain realized the mortal danger he and his vessel were in and ordered his crew to swing hard to starboard to get out of the narrow channel of deadly fire.

"All hands on deck! Man the catapult. You men resume firing the ballista. Zeb, bring us broadside to that ship!" Captain Giles ordered as his men scrambled from below decks.

The pirates attempted to extinguish the flames lapping up the side of the ship as the *Storm Runner* tacked alongside them and unleashed a volley of bolts, stones, and crossbow quarrels at the now struggling pirate ship and her crew. The pirate captain realized that between the fire and the vengeful crew of the *Storm Runner,* his ship was lost. He ordered longboats to be cast over the side as far away from the all-consuming fire as possible and prayed the merchant ship's crew would have pity on them. The instant the longboats hit the water, the pirates leapt from the sides of their doomed vessel and swam to catch them. Unfortunately, two of the longboats hit at a bad angle and capsized.

"Bring the ship around to those longboats," Captain Giles ordered.

"You want us to finish off the pirate scum with crossbows, Captain?" a sailor asked.

"I'll not murder a helpless foe, even a pirate. But I won't go out of my way to help them much either. Throw a grapnel to right those capsized longboats and float three barrels of fresh water over the side." Darius scowled down from the railing of his ship to the men clambering into the longboats. "Who's the captain of this filthy crew?"

"I'm the captain of what used to be the *Insidious*," volunteered a heavyset, mustachioed man standing at the prow of one of the longboats.

"I am Captain Giles of the merchant ship *Storm Runner*. Remember the name of the man who gave you and your men a chance to live. Zeb, order us on our way as soon as you get those longboats righted. I want men repairing that rigging and replacing those damaged sails immediately."

"Aye, aye, Captain! And may I be the first to say 'HUZZAH!'" Zeb shouted and pumped his fist in the air.

CHAPTER 2

Storm Runner arrived in Southport early in the afternoon five days after the attack. After nearly three months at sea with only a few short days of shore leave between runs, the men were impatient to get ashore. But they were required to wait at anchor several hundred yards from the dock and would remain there until customs officials finally deigned to perform their mandatory inspections of the cargo.

The customs official and a handful of city watch would scour the ship for signs of smuggling and appraise the value of the declared cargo for the customary taxes and fees. Once that was done, the harbormaster would then grant them permission to dock when there was room and according to his schedule. They ended up waiting for four long hours before customs finally made it to their ship.

Two officials and their guard complement of ten soldiers from the city watch boarded his ship and went immediately to the hold to inspect *Storm Runner's* cargo. The taxmen tallied up the value of the goods, wrote down the amount, and figured the tax to be applied in a ledger.

"Do you have anything else to declare, Captain?" the official with the ledger book asked.

"I have a crate in my quarters that is a special shipment, but it is granted customs immunity by His Majesty," Captain Giles said as he pulled out the special writ.

The second official read it over before handing it back to the captain. "Very well. Everything seems to be in order, Captain. If you will give us just a few more moments of your time, I'll give you the tax receipt, and the harbormaster can then clear you for docking so you can unload your cargo."

The two officials and their guards made a final cursory inspection of the rest of the ship to ensure there was no hidden cargo stashed away before handing Captain Giles the tax receipt.

"Since you are registered to the City of Southport, you have seven days to make your payment at the tax registrar's office. You are a local merchant, so I assume you know where it is."

"Yes, I know all too well where it is located," the captain replied with an exaggerated wince.

The officials left with their guards, and *Storm Runner* was given leave by the harbormaster to dock within the hour. The crew spent the rest of the day and early evening unloading *Storm Runner's* cargo onto wagons and from there to the warehouses where it would be stored until it was either sold to local merchants for resale or sent off with caravan traders to be hauled across the kingdom. Captain Giles' own company would commission several of those caravans. Profits from those ventures were the mainstay of his trading company.

He gave his crew leave once everything was safely unloaded and stored. However, Darius himself could not yet depart the ship despite his eagerness. He waited impatiently on the deck for whoever was supposed to pick up the mysterious crate in his cabin. He fervently wished they would hurry up and relieve him of his burden so he could surprise his family with his early return. As the hour grew later, his anxiety increased. It was nearly midnight when six cloaked and hooded men approached the boat.

"Hail, Captain! I understand you have a delivery for us," one of the men called up.

"That would depend on your ability to prove who you are, sir," Captain Giles replied.

"Drop a basket and I will send up our credentials, Captain."

Captain Giles lowered a bucket by a tether down the side of his ship to the men waiting below. The man who had spoken dropped a folded sheet of paper into the bucket, which Darius reeled back up. He compared the seal to the missive already in his possession. They were identical. He broke the seal on the new writ and read the contents. The writ identified the bearer and also authorized him to take possession of the crate and its contents immediately. As with the first writ, it was signed and stamped with the king's seal. Captain Giles extended a gangplank from his ship to the dock. Two of the cloaked men secured it in place before all six crossed over.

"Welcome aboard *Storm Runner*, gentlemen," Darius greeted warmly. "I'll show you to your cargo so you can take possession of it. I don't mind telling you, I'm glad to be rid of it. I don't care much for this secrecy stuff, but a man's got to do what he's asked for the betterment of the kingdom, I guess. I nearly lost it to pirates, but we were fortunate enough to get away."

One of the cloaked men brought out a pry bar from the folds of his cloak and rammed it into the seam where the top of the crate was nailed into place. With a screeching of nails being drawn out of the wood, he wrenched the top off. Captain Giles stood near the door with three of the cloaked men behind him while the other three busily pulled aside the straw in order to examine the contents of the box.

"This is it. Arrest him!" the man who appeared to be leading the group ordered.

"What is going on? What's the problem?" Captain Giles asked as his arms were seized and forced behind his back.

One of the men standing near the crate turned with a clinking of chain mail. "Captain Giles, by order of the king, you are placed under arrest for attempting to smuggle illegal artifacts into the kingdom. By my authority as a member of the king's Blackguard, you will be held in a detention cell while a special magistrate is summoned from the king's court."

"There must be some kind of mistake! I have a document signed with the king's seal requesting the transport of that box," Captain Giles exclaimed.

"Release one of his hands," the king's guardsman told the man holding him. "Produce the document, slowly, and give it to me."

Darius carefully reached inside his vest, drew out the missive, and handed it to the guard. As soon as the man touched it, the paper burst into flames, incinerating itself in an instant. The guard immediately released the burning paper and withdrew his hand. Only a large, smoking flake of ash floated to the deck to show any evidence that it ever existed.

"Vile magic!" the guard cried out.

Darius barely registered the blow that caught him in the back of the head and plunged his world into darkness.

"Your Grace, the ship's captain hired to transport the item your men located in the wilds of Lazuul has been arrested by a contingent of the king's Blackguard. The ship and your property have been impounded," Master Alton informed his liege.

"What of the forged document authorizing transport?" Duke Ulric asked, masking his outrage with iron discipline.

Duke Ulric Stanbury was the ruler of Southport, a once wealthy city and still one of the more prosperous in the kingdom despite the economic turmoil that several years of war with their southern neighbors had caused. He was of average height, but solidly built for a nobleman. His hair was inky black without a hint of grey on his head or in his short, neatly trimmed beard.

"It was consumed by fire the instant one of the arresting guards touched it, as it was enchanted to do," the old, stooped chamberlain answered.

Duke Ulric nodded thoughtfully. "That is good. That would be a rather damning piece of evidence, and it would not do to have the king's men gain possession of it. Tell me of this captain."

"His name is Darius Giles. He is a reasonably wealthy merchant who has recently come into his fortune. He has many loyal friends within the shipping business, but most of the nobles and the affluent are little more than customers, so he lacks any sort of real power or support. He is said to be loyal to the king, however, and is known as an honest businessman," the chamberlain dutifully reported.

"What is the disposition of the captain at this time?" the duke inquired as he paced about the room, his hands clasped behind his back.

"He is currently being held in the city magistrate's jail, awaiting the arrival of one of the king's magistrates," the old chamberlain responded.

"He must not be allowed to speak with the magistrate. It is unlikely that he knows anything about us, who gave him the artifact, or who was to receive them. However, if he could deflect guilt away from himself, it could help point the king's Blackguard toward our agents in Lazuul, or worse, here. That would not do at all. Contact the Black Tower and have them send the Rook to take care of the captain."

"Your Grace, the Rook is very expensive, particularly on such short notice. Could we not just send in one of our own men to kill him?"

"No, we must divert attention as far away from us as possible. Let the king think he was working as a courier for a wizard trying to bolster his own power and was killed because he failed to protect his master's prize from discovery," the duke responded shrewdly. He paused his pacing and clenched his fists. "The loss of the gauntlets could set us back years! Now that the king is aware that an effort is being made to recover the armor, it is going to make it that much harder to acquire the other pieces and complete my plans. Have General Baneford recover my artifact at once. Jarvin must not get his hands on a single piece."

"Of course, you are wise, Your Grace. I shall contact the Black Tower and the general immediately."

Darius awoke in a dark but reasonably clean and dry cell. The only light came through the narrow, barred window set in a heavy, iron-bound door, cast from a torch flickering just outside. The floor of his cell was covered in straw that was beginning to mildew. A chamber pot sat in the corner. From the smell, he could tell that it was emptied occasionally, but it was never washed out. His head was throbbing with pain, and any movement caused his vision to swim and made him slightly nauseated. He lay back down on the stone bed built into the wall and let sleep retake him.

Darius stirred sometime later when he heard a noise at the door, but he had no idea of how much time had passed. A clay bowl full of something resembling stew was slid through a small hole at the bottom of his door. He rushed to the portal, nearly toppling the bowl in his haste, and called out to whoever had brought his meal.

"Where am I? Why am I here? Please tell me!"

The only sound was a heavy door clanging shut farther down the hall. He picked up the bowl and sat back on the bed. They had given him no utensils to eat with, so he simply tipped the bowl up to his mouth, drank the broth, and then ate the bland bits of stew.

Hours passed before he heard someone outside his door once again. As before, he ran to the door, pounded on the barrier with his fists, and shouted hard enough to make his throat burn.

"Where am I? Why have you detained me?"

"You are in the magistrate's jail. You are here for smuggling an artifact of power into the city," the voice whispered through the door.

"Who are you?" Darius demanded.

"I am Chief Constable Lazlo, the chief constable of Southport."

"How long am I to be held?"

"Until your trial."

"How long will that be?"

"That I cannot tell you. A magistrate from the king's court has been sent for to interview you. When he arrives, you will be questioned. I can tell you no more and neither can anyone else. The king's Blackguard has ordered that no one may speak to you until the magistrate arrives, so please do not bother any of my people again. They cannot speak to you and neither can I," the chief constable said with finality.

Darius listened to the constable's footsteps recede down the passageway and was once more left alone in his cell. He lay back down on his bunk, closed his eyes, and covered his face with his hands. He should be home with his wife and son, but he was rotting in a cell for some terrible mistake. He could only pray that it would all be cleared up when the king's magistrate arrived.

CHAPTER 3

The duke's chamberlain, Master Alton, shuffled out of his patron's study and back to his own room. Once inside, he bolted his door, crossed the room, and sat at his desk. He produced a black gem half the size of a hen's egg from the top drawer and focused his will upon it. After a moment, the gem vibrated slightly in his hand and produced a tinny voice.

"What is your need, Master Alton?" the voice from the gem asked.

"Magus, my master requires the services of the Rook immediately," the chamberlain insisted.

"Something must have gone seriously wrong for someone to be willing to pay for his *immediate* services," the voice responded with amusement.

"There has been a complication with the transport of the Lazuul item. My master needs the Rook to contain the damage already done."

"Very well, we will contact him and inform him of your urgent need."

Master Alton always felt disconcerted when talking to the mysterious wizard through the gem, but that discomfiture paled in comparison to how he would feel when he had to face the Rook once again. Alton returned the gem to the desk drawer and returned to his lord's study.

"It is arranged, Your Grace," the chamberlain informed the duke as he entered the room.

"Excellent! At least that is done! This setback is going to cost me a great deal, and not just in gold. Other factions will certainly use this to their advantage and try to steal my prize out from under me."

"None have a strong claim to the throne, Your Grace. You will certainly be successful, and the kingdom will be better for it, grateful even, I am sure."

Three nights after contacting the wizard through the gem, Chamberlain Alton awoke to the touch of cold steel on his face. His eyes snapped open and locked onto a pair of ice-blue orbs that seemed to glow with an unnatural light beneath a dark cowl. The hooded stranger pinned the chamberlain to his bed with nothing but the weight of fear he cast from those merciless eyes visible in the pale light of a dimly lit oil lamp. The cold steel of a wickedly curved blade caressed the chamberlain's slack jowl.

"M-master Rook?" Alton stammered.

"Were you expecting another master assassin? I do give multiple target discounts and may have been able to save you some gold if you needlessly hired another," the Rook said with twisted humor.

"No, no! Of course not, Master Rook! I was expecting only you. As well as anyone can expect someone of your legendary skills, that is."

"Have you finally decided to hire me to assassinate your beloved king? I long to savor such a delectable target once again."

"No, the king must not be assassinated! It would not suit my lord's plans for the king to die in that way," the chamberlain exclaimed, sitting up as the Rook stepped away from him.

"Neither of you were so squeamish when you had me kill his father."

The chamberlain sighed. "At the time, we were unaware the king had an heir. Duke Ulric was the most logical choice for the succession. King Jarvin has managed to endear himself to the commoners far more than his father did. If you killed him now, you would have to kill his children as well. Then the people would almost certainly turn against whoever tried to claim the throne if they were ever implicated in the king and his family's death."

"Politics is such a sordid affair, not like the clean execution of a proper assassination. What is your urgent need of me then?"

"There is a prisoner held in the magistrate's jail who must be silenced immediately."

"That sounds like a rather simple task, and I do so find simple tasks insulting and beneath me, Chamberlain."

"Evidence must point to a killer with the ability to wield magic, Master Rook. It must be done with the utmost speed and competence. There is far too much at stake for my master to risk any more mistakes, no matter how slight, which is why we must have you. My master knows you are supremely reliable, and he would not dare ask you to undertake a task below your skills if it was not extremely important."

"You are trying to flatter me, Chamberlain. Fortunately for you, I am able to appreciate flattery when it is true. How many prisoners and guards are with or near the target?"

"He is held in isolation with no visitors. Only the guards who bring the prisoner his meals and empty his waste bucket go near him. Even so, they are not allowed to speak to him for any reason."

"Good. Your prisoner will be dead by morning," the assassin assured the chamberlain. "You have my payment."

"Yes, of course. Allow me to get it for you."

Alton hastily crossed the room and swung open a small door in the wall, which was hidden behind a painting and false stonework. He retrieved a key from his desk which he inserted into the large lock of a steel strongbox situated within the cubbyhole. Once he had the strongbox unlocked, he pulled out a small sack of gold.

"It does seem a bit light, my Lord Chamberlain. I hope you do not expect me to work so cheaply," the assassin said mockingly, the hint of humor only heightening the threat laying beneath.

"Of course not, Master Rook. The other half of your payment is here when you have completed your task," Alton assured his deadly guest as sweat started to bead on his brow.

"My dear chamberlain, your prisoner is already dead. He just doesn't know it yet." The assassin's cool reply was punctuated with his outstretched hand.

The chamberlain handed over a second bag of gold, not wishing to argue with one of the most lethal men in the realm. Alton replaced the box, closed the false stone door, and hung the painting back up. When he turned around, the assassin was already gone without a single trace remaining in the room to show that he was ever there. Alton knew it was barely past midnight, but he got dressed anyway knowing he would get no more sleep this night.

A sound outside his door woke Captain Giles once again. He had no indication of the time since there were no windows opening to the outside of the cell where they were holding him. He watched the door, thinking that morning had come and one of the guards was bringing food with which to break his fast.

As he watched, the stonework around the door melted like candle wax and dripped onto the floor. With nothing to hold the bolt in place, the door swung open freely and a dark, hooded form glided silently into the room. Fear filled Darius' body as a wave of what could only be described as pure evil washed over him. He stood and tried to back away while calling for the guards, but he found himself locked in place with his limbs refusing his commands to move and his voice frozen in his throat.

"Do you know why you are going to die tonight?" the terrifying, hooded creature asked.

Darius tried to answer, but he could neither speak nor shake his head. He could only look into the luminous, ice-blue eyes promising his death.

"Of course you don't. Pawns never understand the greater strategies of the game they are forced to play. That is what you are, a poor pawn unfortunate enough to be caught up in a game much bigger than himself: a game of kings, queens, knights, and of course, rooks," the frightening figure said with a small laugh.

Darius did not understand the joke, but he did know this man was going to kill him, and there was nothing he could do about it. He thought about his family and what would happen to them. In that moment, he knew the pain of true regret, knowing that he would not see his son grow up, nor would he be able to give Azerick a brother or sister. Hundreds of thoughts raced through his mind as the dark figure advanced with a wickedly curved blade in his hand. He could not move, but he could still feel the steel as it pierced his heart.

The Rook disliked killing people of such little stature or power, but he was a professional, and he was paid to do a job. Normally he would draw out his executions, but this was just a merchant who, through no fault of his own, had been caught up in greater people's schemes. Since he took so little pleasure in this man's killing, he granted him a clean, quick death. However, it would not look that way when the body was found by the guards during their next rounds. The assassin finished his gruesome work within minutes and vanished as quickly and mysteriously as he had appeared.

Lord Crassus, the king's magistrate, arrived early that same morning and insisted on seeing the prisoner immediately. Chief Constable Lazlo and four guards led the king's magistrate to the isolation cell and immediately saw that the cell's door was ajar. The chief constable's first fear was that the prisoner had escaped. Then he noticed the stone around the doorframe was melted, and rocky slag was spattered upon the floor. Lazlo pushed open the door and gaped at the horrific scene.

The cause of death was obvious. A single thrust of a blade to the heart. Then the man had been opened from 'stem to stern,' as the sailors called it, allowing the entrails to fall in a pile onto the blood-matted straw scattered on the cell floor. However, it was not the manner of death that shocked every man looking into the cell. Most had seen far worse brutality in their line of work, including the king's magistrate. It was the placement of the body itself that was so dreadful. It was not laid out on the floor, nor was it on the bed. Instead, it hung from the solid stone ceiling in a horrific manner. The prisoner's hands and feet were spread wide and had been completely encased in the solid stone of the cell's low ceiling. It appeared as though the extremities had passed through the stone, as if it had been liquefied then made solid once again.

"How could such a thing have happened?" Chief Constable Lazlo asked in shocked awe and disbelief.

"Wizardry, obviously, but that is the least of my concerns. I no longer have a prisoner to interrogate, and the king demands answers! How could you allow a man to walk in here and do something like this without a single guard raising an alarm?" the magistrate demanded.

"If it was a wizard, and I think we both agree that it must have been, he may not have walked in at all," Southport's chief constable responded.

"I will speak to every guard who was on duty last night and this morning. No one leaves this building until I have spoken to them," Lord Crassus ordered.

"Of course, My Lord, I will see to it at once."

Lord Crassus interviewed every guard, jailer, and servant that day, but none had any idea how or when someone was able to get into the cell and murder Darius Giles. He was exhausted by the time he completed his interviews, but Lord Crassus needed to call on the duke to express the king's displeasure at the loss of his prisoner.

"His Grace will be with you shortly, Lord Crassus," Alton assured the impatient magistrate.

Crassus looked about the study in which he was waiting. He found it rather typical, adorned in hardwood shelves, tables, and flooring along with a small wine rack and a crystal decanter full of some amber liquid. The door to the study opened and Duke Ulric strode in, interrupting his observations.

"Good evening, my Lord Magistrate. I hope my chamberlain has made you suitably comfortable," the duke said as he shook the magistrate's hand.

"I am having far from a good evening, Your Grace. This debacle concerning the king's prisoner has left both His Majesty and me in a most uncomfortable predicament," the magistrate said with a scowl.

"Yes, a most unfortunate and disturbing situation," the duke agreed. "I assure you, Lord Crassus, I will spare no expense in rooting out the culprit behind this murder as well as the dead man's illegal activities. I have my men securing everyone who sailed on that ship for questioning. Once I have them in custody, I will get answers."

"The king is most appreciative of your diligence. Had you only displayed such attentiveness in the safekeeping of His Majesty's prisoner in the first place, perhaps all this would not be necessary."

Lord Crassus regretted the accusation as soon as he made it, knowing that it was somewhat unfair considering the manner of the man's death. Not to mention that, despite his own lofty position, Ulric was a duke of the kingdom and every bit his superior.

"I understand His Majesty's and your displeasure at the loss of the prisoner, but I did everything reasonable to ensure his safekeeping," the duke responded in a tight voice, obviously fighting to hold his temper in check at the accusation of negligence.

"Forgive me, Your Grace. I am exhausted and forget myself. Of course His Majesty will understand that you did everything within your power to safeguard his prisoner. Given the method and obvious determination of the murderer to carry out his dark deed, I doubt there is anything anyone could have done to prevent such a thing."

The king had enough troubles with his lords and nobles these days without him getting into a spat with one of the most powerful men in the kingdom.

"It is quite all right, Lord Crassus. I understand it has been a long day after an even longer trip. Please, allow me to offer you the hospitality of my castle and staff."

"Thank you, Your Grace, but I must decline. I have a nice room already prepared in town. I will retire there and send a pigeon back to His Majesty informing him of the loss. Please alert me once you have the ship's crew in custody so I may question them myself."

"Of course, Lord Magistrate. I'm sure it will not take long."

Half a dozen black-garbed men galloped down the moonlit road toward Brelland, the capital and seat of power within the kingdom of Valeria. As the king's Blackguard, they had access to fresh horses at several private stables for their and the royal messenger service's use. They were also authorized to commandeer any horse from any citizen in the empire in the line of duty. It would take the men less than two days to travel from Southport to the capital, a trip that would normally take more than a week by normal horseback.

The men were on their third change of mounts and had already covered over a quarter of the distance to Brelland. Their business was urgent, a matter of national security. The artifact they had discovered in the possession of the ship's captain was as good as a death sentence to anyone who possessed it. Whether the man was guilty or had been set up as a dupe was not their concern. Protecting the king from assassination and usurpation was.

None of the riders saw the thin rope stretched taut across the road between two trees, intentionally dyed in dark, mottled colors to make it nearly invisible in the pale moonlight. The two lead riders caught the rope at full gallop: one across the chest, the other, shorter man across the throat, crushing his windpipe and killing him almost instantly.

Both men were thrown to the ground as if they had been snatched out of their saddles by a giant, invisible hand and dashed onto the road. One of the men struggled to regain his senses while the other lay unmoving after issuing a few short choking sounds. The next two soldiers ducked low, sensing the type of trap that had been laid, while the remaining two reined in their horses before reaching the strung rope.

It was bad luck and poor judgment that the group's commander was one of the men in the lead as well as the one carrying the artifact. Given the importance of their mission, getting the artifact to the king was the only thing of importance.

Had someone else been carrying the ebony gauntlets, they would have continued riding hard without pausing for the fallen men. It was a duty of which each of them was fully aware, and not one man amongst them would view the others with anything resembling contempt or scorn for leaving them behind.

One of the riders reached down to haul their fallen captain onto his horse as dozens of men burst out of the trees on foot as well as on horseback. Seeing that they were surrounded and unable to retrieve the gauntlets from the dead man, the blackguards prepared to sell their lives for king and country.

Small hand crossbows appeared from under the guards' heavy black cloaks and filled the air with a sound like large, angry hornets. The small darts uncannily found their way into exposed throats and between helmet eye slits, dropping several ambushers.

The blackguards cast aside their hand crossbows and flung small throwing knives into the faces and exposed flesh of the ambushers. The brigands responded with the twang of a dozen light crossbows. Two of the blackguards disappeared from their saddles as the bolts swarmed past or stuck in the suddenly empty saddles of their mounts. The other two swept their thick black cloaks around and caught the quarrels within the heavy folds.

An instant later, the blackguards were once again in their saddles, vaulting back up from where they had been clinging to their mounts' sides as the other two flicked back their cloaks with the crossbow bolts dangling harmlessly from the heavy fabric.

Guiding their mounts with their legs and knees, the blackguards charged fearlessly into the mass of ambushers as they drew the swords unique to the king's Blackguard. Only slightly longer than a shortsword, the blades were wider and weighted to help them cut through armor and block heavier blades without fear of being snapped in half.

Such an ambush should have been an unqualified success against any opponent, particularly considering the numbers pitted against the ambushed men. However, these were not ordinary soldiers. These were the king's Blackguard. They were the best trained and most feared men in the kingdom. Even the king's elite house guards recognized them as their superiors when it came to small unit combat.

The ambushers used their greater numbers to surround the blackguards and came at them from multiple angles, but even that tactic was proving costly.

The blackguards seemed to almost dance upon the backs of their mounts, opening the throat of a man to their front then spinning around backward in their saddle to block a cut from an enemy to their rear and counterstrike, more often than not with lethal efficiency.

General Baneford saw his men being slaughtered by an enemy he had outnumbered five to one. With a savage cry, he charged through his own men to get within range of these agents of death. The outcome, despite the blackguards' well-earned reputation and skill, was never in question. They were mortal men despite their prowess. The only variable was how many men it was going to cost him to relieve them of the artifact they carried. Right now, it looked like the answer was going to be far too many.

Three of the blackguards were down, counting the one the rope had laid low, which left two still in the saddle and one afoot who was wreaking havoc on his men on the ground. The man had obviously shaken off the effects of his hard, painful dismount and was darting beneath the horses and ambushing the men on the other side, delivering savage cuts to the legs of the riders on his way past.

Baneford reached the fight just in time to see one of the blackguards open the throat of another of his men, only to dodge a spear thrust and a slashing sword by jumping into the air and turning a somersault over the head of a third man from the back of his mount. The blackguard landed nimbly behind the mounted man and stabbed him through the back before leaping onto the rump of another horse belonging to one of the tightly packed riders and cutting him down.

The general engaged the man now fighting from the back of one of his own horses and matched steel with steel. Like all blackguards, the man fought with twin blades, his off hand, if such men could be said to have an offhand, darted about as if it were being controlled by a completely separate man. The blackguard slashed at General Baneford, his blade ringing loudly against his shield, while simultaneously parrying the blade of another man behind him.

Gods, what I could do with a hundred men like these, the general thought to himself as he finally broke through the defenses of the blackguard and struck him down.

Given the side he found himself on however, he was profoundly grateful there were not a hundred such men in the entire kingdom.

The remaining mounted blackguard fell with a spear thrust through his lower back, leaving only the man on the ground still fighting like a dervish despite the numerous wounds soaking his heavy cloak and armor with his blood.

General Baneford's trained warhorse lashed out with a fore hoof, catching the blackguard on the thigh. The crack of the man's femur was audible even over the shouts of battling men and the cries of the wounded as he crumpled to the ground. One of Baneford's men raced forward to finish the man off and received a sword through his chest for his enthusiasm.

Despite the blackguard's grievous injury, he defiantly cast one of his blades at the man rushing toward him. The blade pierced his heart and protruded from his back, knocking him backwards with the force of the impact. The guard's shattered leg sent waves of agony coursing through his body, but he responded to the pain with nothing more than a hiss.

General Baneford dismounted and pressed through the men that had the blackguard surrounded with their weapons nervously poised to strike at the slightest movement.

"You and your men fought well, Agent. It is unfortunate we find ourselves on opposing sides and I had to witness the truth of the rumors surrounding the fabled blackguard as a foe."

"To the abyss with you, you vile, treasonous scum!" the blackguard captain spat in anger, pain, and disgust.

"It is not I who commit treason. I am simply a soldier following the orders of the one I have pledged my loyalty to," the general replied. "Where is the artifact?"

The blackguard laughed despite his pain. "I'll never tell the likes of you. The only way you will get the gauntlets is off my corpse!"

General Baneford shook his head with unfeigned remorse. "Unfortunately, such had always been the only option available to us."

General Baneford stretched out his hand, took a loaded crossbow from one of his men, and put a quarrel into the kneeling man's heart. He found the artifact packed away in the dead man's small haversack, still strapped to his back. He examined the inky black gauntlets with their gold trim in amazement. Not a single scratch marred their surface, and they seemed to reflect no light despite their perfect ebony gloss.

General Baneford stood up and put the gauntlets into his own saddlebags. "Drag these men deep into the woods and strap our own fallen onto horses. We will leave no evidence. We will bury them far from here later."

He tallied the number of men who had fallen and shook his head. Out of three dozen men, only fifteen would be riding back under their own power. With any luck, two or three more may survive their wounds, but it would be a close thing. This was only the first battle in Ulric's fight for the throne, and already his general had lost nearly two dozen men to less than a quarter their original number. He wondered how much blood would be spent to purchase the duke's throne.

CHAPTER 4

As was usual, Azerick had his nose pressed into a book of mathematics. He had grown bored with his history and engineering studies earlier in the day and sought a greater challenge for his mind. He was a handsome lad with brownish hair that shone like polished bronze when the light struck it. He was slender but in no way weak or sickly. His hazel eyes were almost constantly buried in one book or another.

He wanted to keep reading until he was able to solve Garran's equation for ethereal entropy, but he was pressed for time. He looked at the expensive water clock on top of the polished ironwood bookcase in the study. It was time for his private weapons training. He wondered what weapons it would be today. He hoped it wasn't hand-to-hand fighting. Azerick did not care much for barehanded brawling. Being only thirteen years old, he hated the size and strength disadvantages he had against his instructor, even though Ewen would let him use the moves he taught him without putting up much more resistance than he could handle. Azerick figured a primarily all-theory lesson had its uses, but he looked forward to the day he could make old Ewen submit due to his own skill and power. However, that would be years off.

Azerick was the son of a successful merchant and of a caste that should have been beyond such a crude thing as actually engaging in any kind of melee outside of fencing. Those of his class hired muscle for that sort of thing, but his father had gotten his start as a sailor and then as captain of his own ship and considered a wide range of self-defense important for any man.

From there he had built a successful trading company that now consisted of six ships: five two-masted schooners and his three-masted flagship which was a large boat able to make the long journey's across the sea to exotic lands and bring back rare and sometimes never before seen curiosities and treasures. Azerick often heard tales of his father and crew having to fight off pirates and hostile natives of some of the unsettled lands across the sea: lands full of savages, rare spices, and strange, valuable trade goods for which the local elite paid handsomely. In fact, his father was due back in a few days from another such lucrative journey.

Azerick loved his father and wanted to make him proud, so he did not mind the martial training. His father said that a good man exercised his brain and his muscles, and any man who let either one go soft could not be truly successful. He actually enjoyed the training and change of pace, but not as much as his books. He would always be a scholar before a warrior, but it did not hurt to have a fallback. He had a sharp mind and remembered almost everything he read at a glance. More importantly, he was able to visualize what he read and understand the material at such a level that he could apply it in a practical manner with minimal review.

He closed his book with a sigh and left his beloved study. He walked down the wood-paneled hall and out into the marbled foyer. His martial training took place in the courtyard. The courtyard was a large flagstone enclosure surrounded by stone walls topped with mostly decorative wrought-iron spikes. The entrance to the courtyard was barred by a large wooden gate made of two halves that swung open on hinges to allow passage of carriages and delivery carts. A smaller postern door built into the wall just a few feet to one side of the larger gate allowed the usual foot traffic.

As usual, Azerick was a little late and his instructor was waiting for him with a look of impatience upon his face. He was a grizzled old man well past his middle years. What age had diminished in his reflexes and strength, Ewen made up for in experience and expertise. Ewen had served with Azerick's father for over twenty years, teaching not only him, but also almost every sailor serving on his ships, how to handle a weapon and fight with their bare hands. These were dangerous times, and any ship not prepared to defend itself likely would not be plying the seas for long. Azerick's father had been fortunate enough that he had yet to lose a ship to pirates and had lost only one to a nasty northern storm after it had begun its return trip from one of the far coastal villages.

But Ewen was mostly retired now, teaching a few private weapons classes to the more affluent families. Duels were not entirely unheard of, and a man of breeding should be ready to defend his honor when hired muscle would be unseemly or cause the family to lose face. Anything less than honorable combat was done in secret; "from behind the curtains" was the popular saying.

"Well, well, the young scholar finally pulled his nose outta his books long enough to grant me the pleasure of his pasty lordship's company," came Ewen's usual sarcastic remark. "So what was the topic today, eh? How to comfort oneself when a sissy bookworm gets beat up by a girl?"

"Actually it was an alchemic treatise on plants that, when mixed with certain earth elements, will cover and prevent certain offending body odors. In fact, when applied in sufficient quantity and concentration they may even do something to mask your pugnacious odor of fish, cheap gin, and silver-piece prostitutes. Although I imagine it would take a truly adept alchemist to create something of that potency."

Anyone observing this exchange might have seen a cantankerous old man and a precocious, spoiled, rich brat verbally assaulting each other. However, the reality of it was that both were equally fond of each other and almost always started their sparring with words before drawing their practice weapons.

Ewen had drilled into his training early on that if you could get into your opponent's head, you could get into his arm. What that meant was that if you could psych out your opponent or get him angry to the point of distraction, you could get him to make a mistake he might not normally make, and you needed to be prepared to strike when he did. The reverse held true as well. Ewen told him repeatedly never to let emotion fuel your fight. Anger burned hot and fast and would burn out of control if you let it. Control was everything.

Smiling, Azerick asked, "So, what is it going to be today, Master Ewen: swords, knives, staff, or bow?" Azerick left out the brawling option, not wanting to give Master Ewen any ideas if he had not already thought about it.

Ewen taught a myriad of weapons and fighting styles. His motto was to be prepared to use whatever you could get your hands on and use it effectively, whether it was a weapon, chair, crockery, or even your opponent or an innocent bystander.

"I think a bit of staff work again today, young sir. You seem to have a real knack for it, and I think I'd like ya to get proficient in one weapon before we try to get more than a passing familiarity with the others."

Azerick was glad to hear it. Given his youth and size, he felt much more comfortable with the staff than many of the other weapons. He also enjoyed it more than any other weapon he had trained with thus far. Swords were heavy, and his young body tired quickly swinging them around. Knife training was all right, but Ewen was able to use his greater reach and strength to do whatever he wanted, and the bow left Azerick's fingers and hand aching to the point it made writing difficult, and that was totally unacceptable.

"Do ya want to warm up first, or are ya ready to begin?" Ewen asked.

"I'm ready. The benefits of youth, you know. I do not have to work the dust and rust out of my old bones first like some salty old sailors. How about you?"

"I knew you were gonna be late, so I took advantage of your usual tardiness to warm up before ya got here. Wisdom of experience, ya know. Now let's see how that smart mouth of yours works when I swell your lips to thrice their size."

They took up their weapons and slowly started circling each other, each one throwing out a few sensing blows and parrying each other's strikes and counterstrikes. Ewen swung his staff down in a standard ten o'clock strike that was aimed for the side of the youngster's head. Just as Ewen had taught him, Azerick brought up the end of his staff, blocking the blow. However, instead of returning to the guard position as he had been taught, Azerick continued to push his opponent's staff nearly to the ground. He then took a step forward, then snapped the same end of his staff behind his opponent's right knee. Azerick braced the other end of his staff between his body and left arm while pulling the far end toward himself with his right hand and pivoted on the balls of his feet. Using his hips to maximize leverage, he flipped the old weapons master onto his back.

Ewen let out a whoosh of expelled air as he hit the flagstones. "Bah! Where'd ya learn that, boy? That ain't nothing I taught ya!"

"I read a book written by a monk of Thelmos on martial exercises. It had a really well-illustrated section on staff techniques. I have been practicing some of them on my own. There's a lot more to books than just being a sissy," Azerick replied, smiling.

Azerick grinned down at his instructor and offered him a hand up. Ewen grasped the boy's proffered hand and allowed himself to be helped to his feet.

"That's a clever move. Nice to see you're studying something other than egghead books and not leavin' everything to me." Ewen returned to the guard position. "I think maybe I've been takin' it too easy on ya. Let's step it up a bit."

Ewen came at him again, this time with considerably more speed, feints, and blows. The clacking of wood striking wood reverberated throughout the courtyard. Once again, Ewen struck at the boy with an overhand blow aimed for the top of his head, and once again, instead of ducking or blocking, Azerick caught and forced Ewen's staff toward the ground and stepped forward, setting his instructor up for another trip to the hard courtyard floor. As Azerick swept his staff toward the back of Ewen's knee, the crafty old fighter lifted his right leg up high then swiftly brought it down with perfect timing to crush Azerick's staff to the ground, trapping it between the stones and his foot.

Had Azerick been stronger it may well have snapped off the last two feet of Azerick's staff. But since Azerick lacked the strength to maintain his grip, the staff was stripped from his hands and clapped loudly onto the flagstones. Another instructor, perhaps a gentler one, may have let the disarmament serve as the lesson. Ewen knew Azerick was headstrong and often needed a firmer hand to drive a point home. Besides, Ewen did not coddle his students like some fancy upper-class tutors. Azerick had just enough time to see the triumphant grin appear on Ewen's face before the weapons master finished his disarmament with a swift clout to the back of Azerick's head.

Azerick went sprawling with a curse, face first onto the flagstones. It was a good, hard strike, and Azerick knew he would be walking away from this sparring match with a nice goose egg, but that was not unusual. The stars cleared from his eyes in just a second, and he rolled over onto his back and glared up at his instructor's grinning face.

"Never assume your opponent is so stupid that he'll fall for the same trick twice," Ewen chuckled as he reached down to help up his floored student, "and never let your mother hear that kind of language or she'll likely whack you twice as hard as I just did."

Azerick's petulant look evaporated as he grinned at his instructor and allowed himself to be helped up.

"I think this will do for today. Next time we'll go at it with blades. Every gentleman and sailor should know the fine arts of fencing and sword fighting."

"Great! I've been studying Master Ellaina DeMarco's book of fencing!" Azerick exclaimed.

Ewen shook his head. "Boy, is there a book you haven't read?"

"Oh sure, lots of them, but they are all in the Academy library. I hope I can enroll next year." Azerick frowned as he thought of all those books that were out of his reach.

"I'm quite sure you'll be there next year. Your father's done real good these last few years, and he's made a lot of friends with some influence. Why, I'll bet you'll have all them books in that library read too in just a couple years," Ewen assured him.

"You think so? That would be so great! I bet I will read them all, too!" Azerick turned to leave. "Bye, Master Ewen! Thanks for the lesson!" he shouted over his shoulder.

Ewen raised a hand in farewell to the retreating youth, chuckling to himself as he gathered up the training equipment. Azerick was probably the only boy he taught who would thank him for putting a lump on his head that likely would have sent most of his students crying to their mommas.

Not a bad kid for a rich boy, Ewen thought once again.

Azerick's next tutor was also waiting impatiently for his student in the foyer. Unlike Ewen, there was no love lost between Azerick and his etiquette tutor, Master Astrallia. The boy disliked him immensely, and the feeling was mutual.

Master Astrallia was a fat, pompous, overdressed popinjay in Azerick's opinion. He was a regular court sycophant who never failed to miss a court ball or function. Through gall and guile, he had managed to worm his way deep into the aristocracy's social network. Master Astrallia found Azerick crude, lazy, and precocious. His job was teaching etiquette, court protocol, and the finer points of mingling with the upper class so as not to embarrass oneself. This, Master Astrallia felt, was an exercise in futility when it came to Azerick. He knew the boy was not stupid in the slightest and that Azerick was a devout reader who could be a preeminent scholar if he kept to the path he was on.

Nevertheless, he was utterly illiterate when it came to proper social behavior. In fact, he was sure the boy went out of his way to frustrate him. He had taught proper etiquette to many children from wealthy families who had a fraction of this boy's intelligence, but in this case, he was utterly flummoxed.

Master Astrallia figured it was probably the trouble with being low-born. There simply was not any noble or high-class blood in him. His father was nothing more than a glorified fisherman or some such thing. You cannot make a silk purse out of a sow's ear, or so the saying went. Take the king. Bastard born, his blood was watered down by a commoner, and look at what was happening to the kingdom. It was being torn apart because he pandered to the peasants, ignored his nobles' advice, and incurred their scorn.

There was a considerable amount of prejudice within the upper classes against those of "new money." Azerick's family held no titles or positions of power. Technically, they were at the lower rung of the upper class, and those who mingled with the long-established families looked down on those who were coming up. Nevertheless, it was good, steady pay and he needed it. Traveling in elite social circles required a hefty amount of gold to keep him in the latest fashions.

"Well, if you are done brawling like some common thug," Astrallia drawled, "we can once more attempt to teach you how to act like a true gentleman."

"Even a gentleman may find the need to defend himself and what is his." Azerick looked pointedly at his tutor's ample girth. "Even you may find a foot of steel hard to digest."

Astrallia's face colored in blotchy shades of red. "An educated gentleman can always use his wits and words to settle any confrontation. Only an uncouth hooligan who lacks the ability to form complete and coherent sentences has to resort to violence. Violence is the solution of the ignorant and stupid. You would do well to remember that since you are not stupid, and I will hopefully cure you of your ignorance."

That was another thing Azerick found incredibly annoying about his tutor. Astrallia was not an idiot, and he could easily match him in a contest of words. Instead of paying attention, Azerick daydreamed about catching *him* behind the knee with his staff and sending all that blubber falling hard to the floor, flailing and rolling like a landed fish as he tried to regain his legs. This image brought a smile to his face and kept him in a good mood for the rest of the boring class.

"Did something I say strike you as amusing, Azerick?"

The youth shook off his glazed expression. "No, sir, you are correct in your argument, at least within the circles you travel."

"Good, I am glad to hear that it is possible to get through to you despite your inferior breeding."

Had Azerick known that this was going to be his last class with this snob, he may well have tried to lay him out. However, no one could have foretold the horror that was soon to befall him and his family, that he would have nothing to lose because everything he had was about to be taken.

CHAPTER 5

Three days later, a contingent of the Watch and a court official called on Azerick's mother. He was in the study once again reading a tome on mechanical applications when he heard the commotion outside. He went to a side door and spied upon the proceedings, wondering what could draw such a crowd. His worst fears sprang to mind: that his father's ship had been lost at sea. But it was summer and the seas rarely posed much of a threat to an experienced captain and crew. Unless it was pirates! Had his father and his ship fallen prey to pirates? The truth, as he was about to find out, was far more horrible than he could have ever imagined.

"What is this, sir? What brings you to my home with these armed men?" Celeste demanded.

She tried to remain polite despite the sudden pang of anxiety that made her hands shake and her voice quaver.

The official gave her a look completely devoid of expression or emotion as he unfurled and read loudly from a scroll embossed with the duke's seal. "Let it be known that due to the treasonous acts perpetrated by one Darius Giles, all rights, titles, and properties of the aforementioned are hereby declared to be in forfeiture to the crown and are to be seized by the local authority. Forfeitures are to include and encompass those belongings of direct family members. Those in residence will vacate the premises within thirty minutes of this notice: to include family, guests, and household servants. Non-family members of the convicted may take their personal belongings. The family of the accused may take only clothing, personal items lacking real monetary value, and a purse of no more than ten gold crowns or equivalent currency. Anyone still residing within the premises thirty minutes henceforth will be arrested, signed by Duke Ulric of Southport." The official rolled the scroll back up and turned an hourglass that he produced from a satchel. "Your time starts now."

"I do not understand! What has happened to my husband? There must be some mistake!"

"I assure you, madam, there has been no mistake. Darius Giles committed an act of treason and forfeited his life as well as his property," the official coldly replied.

"My husband is dead? You killed him?"

"No, madam. Unfortunately, the traitor escaped My Lord's justice." Celeste let out a sigh of relief, but that relief was replaced by renewed sorrow as the official finished his statement. "He was murdered in his cell by one of his accomplices. Time is running out, madam. I suggest you see to yourself and your son."

Azerick's knees trembled and his stomach felt like a fish was flopping around inside him. He cried out and ran to hold onto his mother who was also weeping tears of utter anguish.

Celeste consolidated her courage and turned to her son. "Go, Azerick, collect your things, and hurry now."

Azerick's mother rushed him inside to collect some clothes. Tearfully, Azerick grabbed a sea bag he took with him on the occasions his father took him out on a voyage. The smell of the bag and the thought of his father brought back fresh tears. He filled the bag quickly, but on an impulse, he took half his clothes back out and ran with his half-empty bag to the study.

His heart was tortured on which books to take and which ones to leave behind. He finally made up his mind and deposited his chosen books into the bag. Some were not the most enjoyable to read; many of those he had to leave behind, but the ones he took he knew he would need so that he would still be able to advance his education.

As he and his mother returned to the courtyard, the compassionless official had one of the soldiers do a cursory search of their possessions. The guard set aside a jewelry box of his mother's. Celeste let out a small cry of protest, but she held herself back from lunging at the man or engaging him in a verbal altercation she knew was hopeless. The guard held up the books Azerick had packed, flipped through them to see if anything was hidden within the pages, and then looked to his superior for instructions.

The small, weasel-faced official took one of Azerick's books from the guard, read the cover, and seemed to ponder whether or not to allow him to have them. Books, particularly books of this quality, were rather valuable. Azerick did not know what he would do without his books. He was sure that if the man told him he could not have them he would attack him. He swore he would die before living without his books. He looked from the official to the guard and eyed the dagger at the man's belt. He would snatch that blade and kill this man with it if he could, or with tooth and nail if need be.

Perhaps the man saw the look of potential fury in the young boy's eyes and did not want to be forced to restrain and possibly hurt him. He was sure the mother would come to the boy's rescue if he had to put hands on him, and that could lead to unnecessary bloodshed. This was distasteful business as it was, family of a traitor or not, and he lacked the stomach for such things. Whatever his reason, Azerick could care less. What was important was that the man tossed his book back to the guard who stuffed it into his sack and returned it to him.

The soldiers ushered Azerick and his mother out of the courtyard and onto the streets. Word had circulated quickly, for there were already several people in front of the manor. Some wore accusing stares, and scorn was evident on their faces. Others had looks varying from pity to indifference. Regardless of what any of them felt, none spoke up in either condemnation or defense. The last thing Azerick saw was a few servants standing by as the guards inspected their possessions before ushering them out of the gates.

Those who they had called neighbor or friend made no offer of shelter to the widow and her son. Celeste did her best to hold back the tears and be a beacon of strength for Azerick. She was unsure where to go, but given the small amount of coin they were allowed to keep, their options were severely limited. They soon found themselves in the common quarter where they took shelter at an inn.

The duke's men worked quickly, and within a few days, nearly every man who had sailed into port on *Storm Runner* that night was brought in for questioning. Unfortunately, the magistrate's questions produced very few answers. None of the crew claimed to know anything about the secret cargo. Apparently, the captain had not told a single man on his ship about it, and none of them had seen it brought aboard. Even his first mate knew nothing about it being brought on board much less who was to receive it once they reached Southport.

Duke Ulric promised the king's magistrate he would continue his inquiries and send a courier with any news he discovered. Lord Crassus did not envy the crew of the *Storm Runner*, but it was not his concern. Perhaps the interrogations would turn up some new details. He decided he had done all he could, called for his coach, and set out for Brelland to report what had happened to the prisoner and his subsequent findings to the king in person.

The magistrate fell asleep in his coach almost immediately, and by the time he awoke it was morning again. The city of Southport lay nearly a hundred miles behind him. The trip took just over a very uncomfortable week before he reached the gates of the grand city of Brelland.

Lord Crassus went straight to his home, took a long, hot bath, dressed in his court clothes, and went to inform King Jarvin Ollander of everything he had learned, or had not learned. His manor house was thankfully close to the castle and he was shortly waiting for his liege in the king's audience chamber. He started to kneel as King Jarvin Ollander strode into the chamber.

"Please stand, Lord Crassus, it is only us today," Jarvin insisted.

"Thank you, Your Majesty. I have returned from Southport with as much information as I could gather, which unfortunately is very little," the magistrate explained. "The ship was carrying the artifact, as was suspected. It was intercepted by your blackguards, and the captain detained as ordered. He was kept in solitary confinement, allowed no visitors, and two guards were always posted on the outer door. However, when I arrived, the prisoner had been recently murdered by either an assassin with the assistance of a wizard, or a knife-wielding wizard working alone."

"A wizard you say? Why say you a wizard?"

"The stone around the doorframe was melted away as if it were made of wax. The man was suspended face down from the roof, his hands and feet completely encased in the stone as if the stone had been molded and baked like clay around them."

"This is very disturbing, Lord Crassus, very disturbing indeed."

"I am doing everything in my power to find out who is behind this."

"Half the nobles in my kingdom are likely behind this, or at least support it. If it were not for the favor of the commoners and the fear of rebellion, they would likely have forgone such trouble and had my head mounted on the walls already."

"Have your guards brought the artifact to you yet?" the magistrate asked.

The weary king shook his head ruefully. "No, and they should have returned with it days ago. I fear it may be lost again and in the hands of my enemies. As morbid as it sounds, I hope my blackguards were waylaid and killed. I shudder at the thought of being betrayed by those most sworn to me."

"All of that trouble, the ship's captain, probably an innocent man from everything that I have heard, dead, and we do not even possess that for which men have died. It is very distressing, Your Majesty."

Jarvin stared intently at his chief magistrate with his penetrating gaze. "I want you to assemble a team of my own special guard, and send them out on expeditions to locate the armor before my enemies do. I want them sent immediately."

"At once, Your Majesty," Crassus replied with a quick bow.

"Alton, what is the status on the recovery of my missing artifact?" Duke Ulric inquired of his chamberlain.

"Your Grace, I just received a missive from General Baneford. He reports that his mission was successful, although the cost in the lives of his men was quite high. He is waiting for further instructions at the prearranged location."

"The cost is of no concern. That is what the general and his men are paid to do," the duke replied without remorse or compassion. "I will write to the general myself."

Ulric penned his letter in neat, flowing script, sealed it with wax, and sent it off in the hands of a special courier. He was relieved to know General Baneford possessed the gauntlets. It was the first bit of good fortune he had achieved since he began plotting the overthrow from the day Jarvin's existence had been declared. It was but one of several pieces of a puzzle he needed, and he would stop at nothing to get the others. The armor was the key to replacing Jarvin and his bloodline without sparking a revolution. Without it, he and his future offspring would always be the target of assassins displeased with the death of the Ollander line.

General Baneford was inspecting his men's equipment at the camp they set up in the woods away from any of the main trade roads when his rider returned with Duke Ulric's response. He took the missive inside his command tent before breaking the unmarked seal and reading its contents.

He examined the parchment with interest. Crushed grains of crystal glittered in the reflected light of the brazier like hoarfrost upon the frozen ground. The general knew the granulated crystals were part of a magical spell cast upon the sheets that would cause them to burst into flame at the touch of anyone other than the intended recipient. Even with that precaution, the duke avoided using names or specifically referencing the artifacts.

> *General,*
>
> *Congratulations upon the success of your mission. Continue to search for information in regards to that which I seek. I understand that it is likely to take some time to recover the scattered pieces, but do not delay or slacken in your efforts to locate them. You may use the*

pieces you recover to further aid you in the recovery of the rest. It would not do to have one of the king's agents find any such items anywhere near my person until it is whole and I make my final move. I currently have other sources scouring archives across the kingdom and beyond, and I will send you any information I believe will aid in your duty to locate what I seek. I trust in your loyalty, discretion, and competence. Do not disappoint me.

General Baneford dropped the message into the brazier's flames and stirred the ashes. Now his mission had turned into a scavenger hunt with little information to help guide him toward the target of his quest. Missions suffering from an acute lack of intelligence rarely ended well for the men charged with their success; however, he would do his best, just as he always had. Men rarely attained, and never earned, such a vaunted position as his by doing anything less.

CHAPTER 6

In the weeks and months following the death of Azerick's father and their subsequent eviction, his mother waited tables, took in laundry, and performed any menial task she could. She did whatever it took to care for her son: the only family she had left. When Azerick was not reading, he was running with other youths in the streets where he learned how to pilfer bites of food he then took home to share with his mother. He was now the man of the house and he would take care of her no matter what.

The streets were his life now, and the street children his friends, not friends precisely, more like cohorts or partners in crime. Azerick did not keep friends much beyond the necessity of committing the petty thefts that helped him and his mother survive. He was clever and educated, and he took up something of a leadership role scouting targets and devising clever distractions to maximize the gain while minimizing the risk of being caught.

Although his mother worked hard, times were tough for them and she was not paid much. What little she made was barely enough to pay for their room and board. The fat innkeeper charged his mother an unreasonable fee considering the amount of work she did, and he took part of her earnings to pay for things like broken mugs, plates, and the food she and Azerick ate at the inn.

What Azerick did not know was that sometimes she did not make enough from working to ensure there was enough to eat and make the room payment. She sold what little jewelry she had when they were evicted, and when this money ran out, she had to offer another sort of compensation to the innkeeper. Fortunately this was not often, and only under the most dire of circumstances. Each time she did, Celeste died just a little bit inside. Azerick saw the changes in his mother, but he thought it was only grief and sorrow. He could never have guessed the truth, and she would die before telling him.

The days, weeks, and months plodded on in seemingly grey monotony. What had once been a world full of color, life, and happiness now took on the dullness of simply existing and scavenging to survive. It was a typical, overcast day in the coastal city, and Azerick was scouting out the crowds and tables in one of the market corners when he spied a familiar face.

"Master Ewen!" Azerick yelled and raced across the square, all thoughts of the day's foraging forgotten. "Master Ewen, I thought I'd never see you again. Where have you been? Why didn't you come for us? I thought we were your friends. More than friends. My father called you brother. I know I heard him say it many times." Azerick was barely able to keep his voice from cracking.

Ewen glanced left then right before fixing his former protégé with a hard look. "Quick, run over to that alley and wait for me. No questions, now go!" Ewen whispered harshly. "Get away from me you little sneak thief!" he yelled at Azerick's back as the boy ran to do what he was told.

Ewen wandered around the trade booths for a few minutes before slowly making his way toward the mouth of the alley to which he had ushered Azerick. He looked briefly over his shoulder then ducked inside.

Two buildings three stories tall formed the alley. Its brick and stucco walls cast the narrow passage in a perpetual gloom. Trash heaps were piled along its entire length. A stray dog picked through one pile while a cat chased a rat out of another. About a third of the way down its murky length, Azerick waited partially hidden in the deeper shadows against one wall. Ewen walked down the filth-strewn alley and let out a loud sigh as he looked down at his former pupil.

"What's going on? Why do we have to stand in this waste-soaked alley to talk?" Azerick asked his old instructor and friend.

"Listen, son, I'm sorry it has to be like this, but you don't understand what's going on. Quite frankly, I don't either. Please believe me that I tried to find out. I would'a taken in both you and your mother in an instant, I'm sure you know. I went to the constable and demanded to know what was goin' on. He told me I'd best mind my own business if I knew what was good for me. Well, if I always done what was good for me instead of what I knew was right, I wouldn't be worth a damn. You remember that, boy. By your father's honor, you remember that real good."

Ewen paused and took a deep breath before continuing. "I know damn well your father ain't no traitor to the crown. Fact is he was more loyal to the bastard king than most these high snobby nobles ever were. So I started askin' around, mostly near the docks where me and your father are well known, and where I knew I could trust some folks. He was taken by the king's Blackguard after they found some things on his ship, and they stuck him in one of the local jails. Then they sent off for an official questioner from the king's court. Next thing you know, he's found guilty of high treason and…and was gone.

"Apparently, word got back to someone that I was askin' questions, because the next thing you know I'm dragged off to the castle and thrown in a cell. Some muckity muck official and about half a dozen guards came to see me a couple days later, askin' me if I was in league with your father. They told me I shouldn't get myself worked up over a traitor or his family, plus a few other less than respectful things about your father. Well, this got me pretty riled up, I can tell you, and quick as a wink, I snatched a truncheon off one of those lazy-eyed guards. I bet they didn't expect an old man to have that much gumption or move that quick." Ewen let out a short bark of laughter at the memory.

"I took that club and bopped that smart court sissy right upside his powdered face. This woke them guards up pretty quick and they came at me, but I was ready for 'em. I surprised 'em again by chargin' right into the mess of them and we went at it for a bit. I gave 'em hell pretty good, but there were a lot more of them than me, and I fell to their numbers in pretty short order, but I bet at least two of 'em didn't feel like comin' to work the next day! Well, that official was screeching like a cat caught in a mousetrap as the guards worked me over real good.

"They left me in that cell a few more days before they came back. Different guards, a couple of them were anyway, and the same official. He had a nice shiner still, I can tell ya. He said to me that if I so much as spoke the name of your father or had anything to do with you or your mother, I'd hang for treason or at least conspiracy. My wife, kids, and grandkids would be out in the street just like they'd done to you," he said, his voice dropping off to a remorseful tear-choked whisper.

"I'm sorry, boy. I'd do anything, give anything for you and your mother, I hope ya know. If it were just me, I'd say to hell with the duke, his slimy official, and his threats, and I'd do as right as I could. But I can't risk my family. Their lives don't belong to me to put them in that kind of jeopardy. I hope you understand, son. Please tell me ya do."

Azerick embraced his friend and former tutor. "I understand, Ewen. I really do. It would not do any good to take those kinds of risks, especially with your family."

"Here, son, take this," Ewen said, handing Azerick a small pouch of coins. "It isn't much, but it will buy a couple meals at least. My loyalty to your father cost me several of my clients, but I'm still gettin' by. I'm better off without their kind anyway. I wouldn't work for 'em for all the gold in the kingdom." Ewen spat on the ground. "You take care of yourself, boy, and take care of your mother. If there is ever anything I can do for ya, you know I'll do it. I just can't risk my family."

"I understand. You take care of yourself and yours too. We'll make it. I know it."

With a final farewell, Azerick left the alley and wandered the city for hours thinking about the injustice of it all. He thought about who might have been responsible and the revenge he would exact for the loss of his father, home, and friends. He thought about what Ewen had said about the duke's actions. They certainly seemed strange. If the duke was involved in some nefarious scheme or conspiracy that made it necessary to sacrifice his father, what could Azerick do about it? He would have to be able to prove it.

Azerick knew he would kill any man, even the duke, if he were responsible for murdering his father. However, he could only act on proof, not suspicion alone. If he did find that the duke had his father murdered, how would he get to him? Azerick was just a street urchin now. How would a common sneak thief ever be able to take on a man of power like the duke? Azerick decided it did not matter. Somehow, someway, and some day he would get his vengeance, even if it took the rest of his life. He would take down the king himself if he had to.

Celeste was making her usual rounds serving mutton stew, ale, wine, and spirits to the evening crowd at the less than reputable inn where she worked and lived. It was a boisterous night bordering on rowdy. Several ships had called into port today and unloaded a large amount of cargo, and the ship crews were blowing off steam as well as their newly earned coin. One table in particular had been giving all of the serving women a hard time: groping, pinching, and making lewd comments. Celeste was at this moment fending off the advances of a large, besotted sailor.

"C'mon, love, show old Harlow what you got under them skirts," the heavily built, drunken sailor urged as he pulled her down onto his lap, his breath reeking of powerful spirits.

"The only thing I have for you, sir, is what you see on my serving tray or behind the bar," Celeste said firmly but politely as she tried to extract herself from Harlow's groping hands.

"Oh, listen to the pretty tongue on this one, lads. She sounds like a right lady, don't she?" Harlow brayed, his breath making Celeste's eyes water. "I bet she knows how to use it for more than just talking too!"

His loud guffaws were accompanied by the laughter of his friends as one of them joined in on his harassment. "You got it right, Harlow; you got you a real lady there. I heard she was the wife of a noble or some such before her man got hisself killed for treason."

Harlow's eyes lit up with renewed interest. "Is that right? Well I never had me a real lady before. What say you and I go upstairs and have us a bit of fun?"

"I will do no such thing, sir. Now unhand me!"

"Oh come now, I just got paid and I know all you serving gals are just whores with a side job. Now let's go." Harlow stood and began pulling her toward the stairs.

"I said no!" Celeste upended a large flagon of ale over the belligerent sailor's head.

Harlow's face turned red at her rejection and the public humiliation as the other patrons laughed at his plight. "Teasing whore!"

He threw her to the floor, upending her tray of food and beverages. The food and drinks came crashing down, much of it landing on her, soaking and staining her clothes. Harlow was reaching into his vest with a look of pure wrath in his eyes when Delbert, the fat innkeeper, intercepted him.

"Here now, sir, leave her to me and I'll take care of you and your friends," the innkeeper said, gently laying a restraining hand on the furious sailor. "The next round of drinks is on the house. Celeste! Get upstairs and clean yourself up, and when you come back you had better treat my guests with a hell of a lot more courtesy! And the contents of that tray are coming out of your pay, you can be assured."

Celeste fled up the stairs to her room and was in tears as she stripped off her soaked and soiled dress. She cursed Harlow, Delbert, Duke Ulric, the king, and the gods themselves for the plight in which she and her son found themselves. She knew Delbert would make good on his threat of making her pay for the spilled contents of her tray as well as those that were "on the house." She was barely able to make ends meet by taking in laundry, and this would put her in debt to that fat pig.

Her body gave an involuntary shudder at the thought. She had been able to fend off most of his lecherous advances for nearly a year already. Celeste did not like the idea of being in debt to the man, and she knew what he would demand to pay it. She felt a hard, calloused hand clamp over her mouth and pull her back toward the bed. No one heard her muffled struggles, just as no one except Harlow's friends ever noticed the big man leave his table and stalk up the stairs after her.

Azerick had been chewing on Ewen's words and the conspiracies he imagined for most of the day. Someone had framed his father then murdered him. He refused to believe his father would ever knowingly commit any crime, much less treason. The more he thought of it the angrier he got. At least now he had something upon which to focus other than the insubstantial gods, terrible luck, and fickle fates. Azerick swore he would find out who had done this terrible thing and make them pay. With the purpose and direction of revenge now in his life, Azerick headed back to the shabby inn and up to his and his mother's room. At the top of the stairs was a group of people. Three city watchmen, the innkeeper, and one of the other women who worked at the inn were gathered outside his room. The woman spied Azerick as he crested the top of the stairs. She broke ranks from the group standing outside his room's open door, gently grabbed him by the arm, and turned him back toward the stairs.

"What's going on?" Azerick asked as she hustled him back down the stairs.

"Just wait down here, boy, and someone will explain it all in a bit," came the woman's curt reply.

Azerick did not know what was happening, but he thought he had glimpsed something through the open doorway that looked like blood. The sight made his mind run wild with thoughts that turned his blood to ice. He was left alone with his thoughts to imagine the absolute worst possible scenarios for nearly an hour before he heard the group tromping down the stairs. The same woman who had brought him downstairs approached with a look of sorrow on her face.

"I'm sorry, kid, but there has been a terrible accident, and your mother was hurt very bad. I'm afraid she's gone."

"Gone? I don't understand," Azerick said weakly, blinking away tears before they could escape and run down his dirty face.

However, inside he did understand. He just refused to accept it. His brain blocked out the possibility of him losing the only person in the world he had left. It was simply too much of a shock for him. It had been less than a year since he had lost his father, and now his mother was gone too.

"I'm sorry, boy, but done is done, and there isn't anything you can do about it now," the fat innkeeper said without a hint of compassion as he dropped Azerick's bag at his feet. The bag carried what appeared to be all of Azerick's clothes but little else.

"What about my books?" Azerick asked in a quiet voice.

"The constable said everything else had to be left untouched so they can investigate and see if anything is in there that can help them find out who cut up your mother. Now you just move on and go wherever it is you gotta go. I'm not running an orphanage here."

"Delbert, have some compassion. Ain't you got no heart under all that blubber?" the serving woman said.

"I'm just an innkeeper! There's nothing I can do for the boy. Are you going to take him in? Are you gonna feed him and clothe him outta your pay?"

The woman's silence answered the question. Azerick picked up his bag, left the inn, and walked out onto the street. He did not know where he was going, just that he had to keep moving and thinking. Sometime after midnight, he found himself in an alley in a part of the city that made the common quarter look as grand as the park within the palace grounds. Azerick thought living penniless in a shabby room in a run-down inn was as bad as it could get, but now he was truly homeless: homeless with no one to care for him. He was completely on his own at the age of thirteen, or was he fourteen now? He was not sure, and he really did not care.

He thought about Ewen and his promise. He wondered if he could go to him now. Surely the duke would not send his men after him for taking in a homeless boy just because of his father, would he? What if he refused to take him? Could he handle the rejection after all he had lost? No, Ewen would likely take him in regardless of the danger to himself, or his family. Azerick was sure of that. But did he have the right to put that kind of burden on his friend? Was Azerick's life worth jeopardizing the life of his only friend in the world and his family? He did not know, so he decided to sleep on it. He was exhausted from walking, weeping, and the sorrow threatening to destroy him.

The only consolation was that it was summer and not raining. He curled up in a ball against the filth-littered wall of the alley, surrounded by trash. He used his bag of clothes as a pillow and fell into a restless sleep. Azerick did not know how long he had slept. He figured it could not have been long before the sound of footsteps alerted him to the fact he was no longer alone. He came fully awake when hands grabbed him roughly around the waist and strong arms lifted him from the ground.

"Well, what have we here?" a voice asked, carried by the foulest of breath. "A wee cully all by his lonesome, left out like a present just for me."

With the exception of being caught by the Watch for stealing or freezing to death in the winter, predation was the greatest danger facing the city's street children. Azerick's initial fear was that slavers had grabbed him, likely to be sold in Sumara far to the south. But a completely new kind of terror coursed through Azerick's body as he tried to fight the hands that were now grabbing roughly at the laces of his breeches. Azerick fought his rising panic and forced himself to think quickly but calmly.

He caught a brief reflection of light from the belt of the man attacking him. He reached back, grasped the hilt of a knife or dagger, and pulled it out. Reversing his grip on the handle of the blade, he thrust it behind him into the soft flesh of his attacker. The man let out a bellow of pain and surprise and released his grip.

"You done stuck me, ya little bastard!" the man bellowed as he pressed his filthy hands against the profusely bleeding wound.

Azerick did not hesitate. Using the training Master Ewen had instilled in him, he ducked low, pivoted on his right heel, and slipped behind his assailant. As the man staggered and held his hands over the fresh wound in his belly, Azerick drove his newly acquired blade into the man's right kidney. Azerick knew from his studies that the kidney was especially vulnerable and caused an enormous amount of pain when struck or pierced. He was quite familiar with anatomy, and he knew the location of most of the body's tender parts.

The man seemed to choke on the scream trying to escape his lips as agonizing pain lanced up his back, completely overriding the bite of his original wound. He dropped to his knees in front of Azerick while trying to reach behind him and put his hand over this newest source of agony. Azerick thrust forward once more, stabbing the man high in the back. The knife skipped off the bottom of the man's shoulder bone, and the blade slipped between the upper ribs just below it, piercing his heart.

Azerick paused for a few moments, thinking about what he had just done as the man slumped forward onto his face. He stood over the body, bloody knife in hand, and processed everything that just happened. Not only had he killed a man, somehow, he knew it would not be the last life he would take in the years to come. He looked at the knife and the droplets of blood dripping off the tip to spatter onto the ground. His life was now irrevocably defined by death.

Azerick shook off these thoughts, stripped the belt and scabbard from the body, grabbed his bag, and ran from the alley. It was unlikely anyone would bother calling the Watch in this section of the city, but he wanted to put as much distance between himself and the dead man as he could just in case the Watch may have heard the man's scream and felt either duty-bound or simply bored enough to investigate.

Once again, Azerick stalked through the city as he planned his next move. He needed a place to stay, somewhere that would offer him some sort of shelter from the weather, the opportunists, and the predators of the city's darkened streets and alleys. He knew that if he was going to survive he would have to contain the despair that threatened to overwhelm him. The adrenaline and fury brought on by the recent attack helped him compress the torment of his recent loss and the anguish manifesting as he thought of his mother.

All these emotions burned inside him hotter than the fires of a blacksmith's forge. The flames would have consumed a lesser man, but Azerick's resolve to avenge his family turned that searing heat into a tool he would use to temper himself like a finely crafted sword: a sword he would thrust into the bowels of his enemies. But first, he would get back his books.

He returned to the common quarter of the city and the less than respectable inn that had been his home. Just a few hours ago, it was the place where his mother had been alive and trying so desperately to take care of him. Now she was gone, and a familiar fluttering once again entered his belly. Azerick pushed those thoughts aside and focused on the problem at hand. He shoved aside his emotions, pain, and loss, burying them so he could focus on surviving the days ahead.

He was on his own in a world that cared not one bit if he lived or died. But he would live, he vowed, and when he found those responsible for his torment, he would make them wish to the gods he had not survived his life in the streets. He would never be a victim again, and anyone who tried to hurt him would pay dearly.

He knew the fat, heartless innkeeper would have barred the door this late at night. Any resident of the inn caught outside when he closed up would have to find another place to spend the remainder of the night or just sleep on the stoop.

Azerick pulled the clothes out of his bag to make room for his books and then slung the satchel over his shoulders. He went around the back and climbed the small, slanting porch roof hanging over the door leading into the kitchen. From there, he pulled himself up onto a small ledge separating the second floor from the first. Pressing himself against the wall, he sidestepped around the tiny ledge until he reached the window to his former room.

He slipped the bloody knife blade between the two sides of the window shutters and lifted the latch securing them shut. He stepped from his narrow perch into the room and froze, listening for any sounds of disturbance. He heard nothing, but he could smell the blood that had seeped into the old floorboards which the soap and water used to clean it up had failed to reach.

Azerick looked around the room and saw nothing but bloodstains. Everywhere he looked he saw the remnants of what had happened in this room. Even in the wan moonlight, the dark stains were visible on the floors, walls, and ceiling. This room would have to be completely repainted before it could ever be rented out again, probably in a dark shade of paint at that.

He pushed all these thoughts from his mind. His cursory glance showed that his books were no longer here. Azerick was unsurprised to find they were gone. Anything that may have held any value had been stripped from the room. Azerick knew where he would likely find his books. He silently crept across the floor to the room's single door and pressed an ear to it. He heard no sounds in the hall, and quietly opened the door. With equal stealth, he slipped down the corridor to the door at the far end where the innkeeper lived in the best room the inn had to offer.

Again, he pressed an ear to the door and listened. The sound of snoring lightly reverberated through the door. He tried the handle, but it was locked. This was not unexpected either. The innkeeper, being an untrustworthy man, never trusted anyone else. He probably assumed everyone lived by the same greedy standards he did. Azerick pulled his knife out and slipped it in the doorjamb to see if he could pry open the latch. He worked the catch with a light scratching and scraping of the knife tip on metal and wood, but he was unable to trip the lock.

Azerick made his way back to his old room, slipped back through the window, and out onto to the small ledge. He hugged the wall and slowly sidestepped his way around the building until he reached the window that opened into the innkeeper's room. The window was already open to let in the cool evening air during these hot summer months. He slipped his legs over the sill and silently dropped to the floor where he paused and surveyed the room.

In the center of the chamber against the wall immediately on Azerick's left, just a few feet from him, was the occupied bed of the innkeeper. The middle of the large lump in the bed rose and fell with the rasping snores reverberating through the room. In the far-right corner, he spied uniformly stacked objects. He carefully crept across the room and saw that it was indeed his beloved books. He slipped the bag from his shoulder, set it on the floor, and packed his books away. It took only a few seconds to stow his last book and begin to make his way across the floor to exit through the door on the opposite wall.

As his foot set lightly down upon the aged wood floor, a floorboard gave slightly under his weight and creaked loudly. Azerick froze in mid-step and listened as the snoring ceased to fill the room. The innkeeper came awake with surprising suddenness. He turned the wheel of an oil lamp on the nightstand next to his bed and cried out when he saw the intruder in his room.

"You! What are you doing here, boy?" he demanded as recognition dawned on his face. "Thief, you came back to rob me! I'll thrash the hide off you, boy!"

With that promise, the innkeeper rolled off his bed and onto his feet, his nightshirt flapping in the flickering light of the oil lamp.

"They're mine. You stole them first, you fat bastard!"

The eyes of the portly innkeeper filled with rage as he lunged with his arms outstretched and his hands grasping for the throat of the boy who had not only broken into his home to rob him but also cursed and insulted him!

Equal rage filled the young man he intended to throttle. Azerick swung the heavy bag of books at the innkeeper's head and clipped him hard in the temple. Delbert dropped in a heap as the laden bag continued its barely controlled arc and hit the corner of the nightstand, upsetting the oil lamp and its flammable contents. The pool of rapidly expanding oil burst into flames, licking at the floor and the overturned table. Azerick ran for the door, turned the lock from the inside, and threw it open.

He paused a moment to consider the unconscious man in the room now on fire, wondering if he should do something. Did the evil man deserve any help? Not from him, Azerick decided and ran for the stairs. His only effort at helping the innkeeper and anyone else unfortunate enough to live in the inn was shouting "Fire!" at the top of his lungs. He raced down the stairs, lifted the simple bar securing the front door closed after hours, and raced into the night. He paused long enough to scoop up the clothes he had left next to the door and stuff them into his bag before darting down the street.

Azerick peered around the corner of a distant building and looked back at the inn. The roof was now nearly engulfed in flames. He spied the cook, a barmaid, and the woman who had told him of his mother's death, now standing outside in their nightclothes and looking on at the burning building along with a few citizens who lived nearby and had come out to see what the commotion was.

He saw nothing of the innkeeper, and he was only slightly disturbed by the fact that he had a hard time giving a damn.

CHAPTER 7

A zerick knew there were several abandoned buildings in the old industrial district. Years ago, this had been the center of the industrial war effort and the city's manufacturing hub, but over the last couple of decades, the economy of the nation had been continuously declining and fewer goods and trades came into and went out of the city. Once Jarvin ended the war with Sumara, there was nothing to keep it going. The district was a sore reminder of better times, and many of the abandoned warehouses and trade goods shops now served as shelter to the city's many homeless.

As Azerick picked his way down the dark, deserted streets, he noted several burned-out buildings. Sometimes an entire block would show the ravages of past fires. Fire was always a real fear of those who dwelled within the city. The Watch kept close tabs on the abandoned buildings, and chased out and sometimes arrested anyone they found residing within them. Everyone feared that a vagrant's cookfire, or a fire built for lifesaving warmth during the winter, might set the buildings aflame and spread to the more inhabited sections of the city. Azerick found these fears did not lack merit as he passed by another fire-scorched building.

He spied an abandoned tannery that looked promising. Unfortunately, there was a man standing in the darkened doorway, apparently keeping some sort of watch. Azerick studied him from the safety of the shadows for a few minutes before another man appeared in the doorway, and the two began a quiet conversation of some kind. With the anxiety of what had happened to him in the alley still fresh in his mind, Azerick decided it was best to avoid everyone and was about to move on when his ears picked up the sound of marching feet.

The men loitering in the doorway came on alert, and one ducked back inside. Several people scurried out of the building. At least three or four men, two women, and a couple of children abandoned the building and ran off into the night ahead of the approaching city watch. As the Watch came upon the building, they spread out to cover all avenues of egress. Four circled around the side and to the back, probably to check and guard any rear exits, six stormed inside, while another four guarded the front from anyone who might try to sneak past the invading guardsmen and escape that way.

In a few minutes, the guards reappeared and regrouped. Since they had no prisoners in tow, Azerick figured everyone who was in the building must have already fled. As the guards went on their way to check another building, seemingly chosen at random, Azerick continued to watch the building from a small alley across the way. After about twenty minutes, he decided the original inhabitants had been properly chased off by the Watch, and the guards themselves would not return to a building they had already cleared.

Azerick slinked across the street and ducked into the dark opening of the doorway of the now vacant building. He looked carefully around the dusty, cluttered room to ensure that it was indeed unoccupied. The building appeared to be a long-abandoned tannery given the many barrels that probably once held various oils and chemicals used to treat the hides of animals. He thought he could even detect a faint lingering odor even after so many years of disuse.

Azerick crept across the large room and went through a doorway on the far side. He came to a smaller room that had a single closed door in the far end. He crossed the chamber and slowly pulled it open, holding his knife firmly in his grip just in case the building was not as empty as it appeared.

Behind the door was a small storage room. Shelves lined the walls and wooden barrels occupied a good portion of the floor. He figured this was as good a place as any to sleep for the remainder of the night. The newly orphaned boy cleared a small area behind the barrels which he hoped would provide some concealment just in case someone did take a cursory glance into the room. Azerick laid his bag on the floor and rested his head on the clothing-filled half. His stomach growled ferociously, but exhaustion won out and he drifted off to sleep, silently weeping for his newest loss.

Azerick, the voice called softly from within the blackness.

Azerick barely heard the voice calling his name and saw only darkness before his eyes. It was faint and feminine. For a moment, he thought it was the voice of his mother.

Azerick, be my hand. Be my hand of vengeance and bring death to those who have wronged you. Give death to all who deserve their fate, the voice whispered.

"Who are you? I can't see you," Azerick called out into the darkness.

I am your fate, I am your future. Embrace me. Be the hand of Sharrellan.

Someone was playing tricks on him. Sharrellan, goddess of death, vengeance, and all things dark did not talk to street rats.

"Who are you? What do you want? What do you mean?"

Be Sharrellan's hand, the voice repeated before fading to nothingness.

"I'm having nightmares," Azerick said aloud. "It was nothing but a nightmare."

The last few hours of darkness passed while he slept in the small storage room. Not even the horrors his nightmares brought were able to wake him from his exhausted slumber. The sun was just beginning to burn away twilight's veil when footsteps and voices woke him once again.

Azerick went on alert and listened intently from his hiding place. He could hear low, muffled voices and footsteps shuffling about in the rooms outside the door. The voices cut out, but he could still hear the footsteps coming closer to the door of his hiding place. His hand flew to the hilt of his knife as the footsteps stopped right outside the door to the small storage closet. As the door was slowly pulled open, he swiftly pulled the knife out and held it in front of him. Standing in the door, silhouetted by the waxing morning light, was a large, bearded man. Azerick could just make out two other figures beyond the open door in the gloom behind him.

"Well, well, what have we here?" the man rumbled in a deep baritone voice. "You thinking to cut us all down with that pig-sticker in your hand, boy?"

"Your life will be the least you'll lose if you think to put hands on me," Azerick replied, breathing in quick, shallow breaths. "Just ask the previous owner of this knife if you think I do not speak the truth!"

"Oh, I believe you, boy," the large man said. "You're lucky the Watch didn't come return. Sometimes they like to double back to try to catch us sneaking back into a place they already checked. Now put away that knife, boy. You don't need it against us, and I'm no more intimidated by it than the guards if they would'a caught you here. I give you my word, we'll treat you a damn sight better than they would have."

"Why should I trust you any more than the rest of the alley-born I've run afoul of?"

"I'll pardon your insult to my good character and intentions and tell you true. Whether you were alley born or a cast-off prince like your high-born way of talking marks you don't matter. From the looks of you, you're one of us now. Me and my group take care of our own. Come on out. I got a bit of bread and some cold beans I'll share, and don't try to tell me you ain't hungry. It was your rumbling belly that led us right to this closet you're hiding in."

Azerick pondered his options a moment then sheathed his knife. The man sounded honest enough, and the odds were not exactly in his favor regardless. If they turned on him, he only hoped he could count on their underestimating him enough that he could break free of them. The nervous boy slowly walked toward the small group with his hand still on the handle of his knife. They parted ranks and made way for him to leave the tiny room unmolested. He followed the big man into the large room he had originally entered a few hours earlier.

There were a couple of men, two women, and three children already sitting in the room as he and the three men entered it: about a dozen people in all. The large, bearded man bade him sit down near the wall and took up a seat next to him. He then offered Azerick the piece of bread and cup of beans he had promised. Azerick mumbled a brief thanks to the man and devoured the proffered meal. As he finished off his breakfast, using the bread to wipe the inside of the tin cup clean, the man spoke again.

"I guess I'll start the introductions now that there's a little something other than air in your belly. My name's Jon Locke," he said, and then pointed around the room introducing everyone else in turn. "That's my wife Margaret, my oldest boy Patrick, and my younger boy William, or Will for familiarity. That's Maggy over there with her little girl Beth and her man Steven. Ryan is out foraging." He continued introducing the others around the room, and then he looked pointedly at Azerick when he had made the last of the introductions.

Margaret was a comely woman with auburn hair. Patrick looked to be maybe two years older than Azerick, and Will about two years younger. Maggy was a tiny woman with dark brown hair and a severe look. Her daughter, Beth, had light brown hair and was perhaps four or five years old. Maggy's husband had dirty blond hair and was whipcord lean.

"I'm Azerick, and I thank you for your hospitality."

"I think ya got it right when ya called him a lost prince, Jon. Just listen to the pretty way he talks!" one of the men crowed, eliciting a round of soft laughs from the group.

"Don't you mind him none. Like I said, it don't matter where you came from. It's where you're at that matters. You can tell us your story, if you've a mind to, whenever you're ready. You still look rather tired out. Why don't you go back and get some sleep? A couple of us will stay here and keep watch over you while the rest of us go take care of some business."

Azerick was indeed exhausted from all the activities of the last day as well as the stress and pain of his newest heartbreaking loss. He excused himself, thanked them all again for their kindness, and went back to sleep in his closet. Perhaps it was the food or maybe knowing someone was looking over him, but Azerick's sleep was far less fitful this time around.

It was late afternoon by the time Azerick once again awoke to the sounds of people talking and milling about the abandoned tannery. He left the tiny room serving as his sleeping chamber and joined the others in the main room where he had met them earlier in the day. Jon hailed him and called him over. Several others gave him a short greeting as he entered.

"Just about everyone is back from their forays," Jon informed Azerick as he took a seat on the floor. "We always meet back here or wherever we're camped at the time. We share everything equally amongst us from whatever we're able to scrounge up, whether it's food, clothes, coin, or anything else of use or value we come up with."

Jon looked at him seriously and continued. "I've talked it over with the group while you slept, and if you want, and if you can abide by our rules, then I'd invite you to stick with us for as long as you like."

Azerick thought about it for a moment, thought about not being alone and having someone else watching his back. The streets were not a safe place when one was alone, especially when one was still just a boy.

"I would like that very much, sir," Azerick replied.

Jon nodded his big, shaggy head. "All right, first rule is you call me Jon, none of this sir business. Likely go to my head and I'd make everyone say it, then I'd be tossed out on my arse. Second rule is we are all family and we treat each other as such. We have our squabbles from time to time, but in the end we always stick together. Third rule, as I already told ya, is we share what we find. So if that's agreeable to you, then welcome to our little family."

"That's all fine with me, sir, um, Jon."

Azerick remembered his accidental run-in with Ewen and pulled out the small coin purse his tutor had given him. He had completely forgotten about it until now. He did not even know how much was in it.

"I have this pouch of coins a friend gave me. I don't know how much is in here, but I'm sure it can be of some use."

Jon took the small leather pouch and turned up a satisfied grin at the weight of it as he hefted the purse in his big, calloused hand. He opened the drawstrings, poured out the contents into one beefy palm, and his eyes opened wide in surprise.

"My goodness, lad, you certainly earn your keep quick," Jon said as he looked at the coins of copper and a few silver. "This'll do well, lad, this'll do very well, especially with winter comin'. Some things are just too darn hard or risky to pilfer, and this will come in right useful. Thank you, lad."

"I'm glad I could contribute. I am afraid I am not much of a pickpocket, and I really have not stolen much more than a piece of bread or a meat pie. I imagine I'm going to have to learn how rather quickly if I'm going to make it out here."

"That you will, but not to worry, we'll train you up real good before we throw you out of the boat and into the water," Jon said with a grin. "We're just waiting for Steven to get back before we settle in to eat, and then maybe you can tell us what exactly brings a boy of your breeding to living on the streets."

Jon had just finished speaking when Steven strode into the building carrying a sack from which something heavy bulged out of the bottom.

"What luck today, Steven?"

"Only the best kind of course, the good kind," Steven replied and pulled a large smoked ham out of the bag.

"By the gods, how'd you manage to pinch that thing?" Jon asked as everyone scooted closer to take a better look.

Steven's eyes lit up as he grinned widely. "It was the darndest thing. I was in the butcher's shop hoping to pilfer a small sausage or something. I knew it'd been a long time since we had meat, but I was about to give up and leave because that butcher is an eagle-eyed penny-pincher, you can bet. Then the ugliest mongrel dog you ever did see runs in and snatches up an entire chain of those linked sausages."

Steven was doing a good pantomime of the actual event. "Now, the butcher sees this and vaults the counter like a thoroughbred jumpin' a hedgerow and starts chasing the dog around the shop. This woman had just gotten this nice smoked ham all wrapped up and was just about to pay the butcher when the dog made his move. She starts wailing as if her knickers are on fire and runs out of the shop, followed shortly by the mutt chased by the butcher. So I grab the bag with the ham in it and walk out like any good payin' customer!"

"That's good to hear. For sure we haven't had a good piece of flesh in some time. Here, look what the boy has chipped in," Jon said as he passed the coin purse to Steven. "We should be able to get mittens, scarves, and decent blankets for the winter this year."

"That's fantastic! Thank you, kid. You know we almost lost little Beth last winter when the cough caught her something fierce," Steven said.

"I'm glad I could help, and I'm glad you got that ham. I'm starving."

Everyone had a good chuckle as they passed around the meager fare. As they finished their meal, Azerick began his tale of the misfortunes that had brought him to such a low point. He told them of his happy life and fine home in the wealthier part of the merchant district, his murdered father, being forced from his home, his past year running the streets while his mother worked to provide for them.

His voice caught and he was barely able to talk of how his mother had been killed, but he managed without shedding fresh tears. He finally told them about the man he had gotten the knife from and killed. Everyone was silent as he told his tale. A few even had tears glistening in their eyes as the boy told his tragic story. Jon finally broke the silence.

"Now don't you worry about that man in the alley, son. You did what you had to do, and he got what he had comin' to him. That inn you were living in, was it in the common quarter?"

Azerick confirmed that it was with a nod.

"You wouldn't happen to know anything about the fire that took an inn over there last night, would you?"

Azerick swallowed hard and stared at the floor before answering. "He wouldn't give me my books back. He said the constable needed them for evidence, but he was going to sell them. I know he was! He had them in his room. The fire was an accident."

"Son, you've had some hard times and been through some rough spots, and nobody holds anything against you. But you need to know when to pick your fights and when to let alone. You go chasin' down everyone who wrongs you, and you're going to be chasin' and runnin' all your life. Sometimes revenge may come at a price too high to pay," Jon said wistfully while shaking his head.

Azerick just responded with a "Yes, sir" and let the conversations pick up amongst the group. Will, Patrick, and Beth came over and talked with him, and soon all four youngsters went into the smaller room that held the door to Azerick's closet and talked.

"Why did you go back for your books, Az?" Will asked, shortening the unusual name for simplicity's sake.

"They are very important to me. They are like my family, the only family I have left," Azerick replied.

"Well I guess I just don't understand 'cause I can't read. Besides, now we're your family, so you have more than just books to keep you company."

"You can't read?"

Will and Beth both shook their heads and Patrick said he could read only a little. This shocked Azerick because he could not imagine not being able to read. In fact, he could not remember a time when he was not able to read.

"I'll teach you if you like. I remember most of the lessons my first tutor gave me that got me started. Most of the books I have are pretty advanced, but I have a book of stories my mother used to read to me to get me to go to sleep. That should be easy enough once you get your letters down. Then we can start on ciphering!" Azerick exclaimed, thoroughly excited at the prospect of being able to share his love of reading with someone.

"Really? That would be so great, Az. Can we see your books?" Patrick asked.

"Sure, I'll even read a story or two from my storybook."

Azerick scrambled up, went into his private sleeping area, dragged out his bag, and showed off all of his books to his eager audience. They all loved the storybook and the history book. Patrick and Will were amazed with the drawings on engineering. The last two were well beyond the comprehension of Beth, but she played along and was excited as well.

Such became the routine for the next several months. The winter came all too soon. It was cold and wet and with seemingly endless rain. It snowed only a few times. This being a southern land and lowly elevated, it simply did not get the frequent winter storms that dumped several feet of snow in the northern cities.

On days that were too miserable to go outside, Jon and the others taught Azerick how to pick pockets and lift small items necessary for their survival, first from a dummy made of old clothes stuffed with rags. They tied bells near the spot that carried the pretend purse and eventually on the purse itself. Once Azerick had mastered the dummy, he practiced picking the pockets of various members of the family.

They also taught him how to avoid the Watch and pick locks. They showed him how to blend in with a crowd and hide when need be. While he learned the tricks of the trade, they all said he was a very fast learner, he taught Will, Patrick, and Beth to read. Beth surprised them all with how quickly she caught on and was soon reading Azerick's storybook to everyone else in no time at all.

CHAPTER 8

Spring came and started to roll into summer without anyone catching a serious illness thanks in large part to the blankets and clothes Azerick's money had purchased. Such was not the case for some of the more unfortunate homeless people. It was not uncommon for a body to turn up in an alley or near one of the abandoned buildings. People died of exposure as often as a blade thrust between the ribs.

Azerick and the others did not always steal to support themselves. They took jobs whenever they could find work, but with the large number of conscripts returning now that there was peace on the border, there were far more people than jobs. This great imbalance between supply and demand reduced the already pathetic wages unskilled labor brought. While most men congregated about the docks hoping to get jobs scraping barnacles from hulls, sanding and calking ships, unloading cargo, or stacking it in warehouses, Azerick, William, and Patrick split up and looked for any work opportunities around the middle and upper-class sections of the city.

It was pure luck that found Azerick walking in front of a fine manor house, not so dissimilar to his own former home, when a fat man wearing the apron and the tall hat of a cook shouted to him from behind the iron bars of a gate closing off a flagstone courtyard.

"You there, boy, come over here!" the man demanded sharply.

Azerick crossed the clean, well-maintained street to see what the man wanted. He had to be wary. Youths his age were prone to disappearing, favored by the slavers who hunted the streets and lured victims into their clutches with promises of work. They would often awake aboard a ship heading south to a Sumaran slave market or tied and gagged in the back of a wagon after getting clubbed over the head or drugged.

The fat man was on the other side of the closed gate, and it was broad daylight so the risk was small. Besides, he could not afford to pass up the opportunity to earn enough coin for a few loaves of bread.

"You are just about the right size, I think," the man said as Azerick drew near. You are looking for work, yes? You certainly do not live around here."

Azerick ignored the implication and look of disdain. "Yes, sir, I'm looking for work."

"Excellent, I have recently discovered a rat problem within the manor that must be taken care of before the master realizes the severity of the infestation. I will pay you a copper for every rat you kill— discreetly. You do know what that means, don't you, boy?"

"Yes, sir. It means to judge or act on one's own initiative while displaying judicious reserve or acting without pretension or ostentation," Azerick replied before remembering that people like the cook did not appreciate excessive wit or intelligence in the help.

The cook narrowed his eyes at the boy. "Yes, quite right. You will need to slither through the crawl space in the ceilings as well as hunt down the vile vermin in the cellar. I hope you do not take issue with dark or enclosed spaces."

"No, sir. No problem there."

The cook motioned to a liveried man nearby, and the gate opened wide enough to admit Azerick inside. He followed the sweating, waddling cook to the kitchen entrance where the man handed him a burlap sack and a long wooden rod slightly shorter than his own height and as big around as a man's thumb.

"I suggest starting in the cellar where you may remain out of sight."

Azerick descended the wooden stairs into the cellar armed with his stick, bag, and an oil lamp. Rats scurried away from the light and squeaked their protests at his intrusion into what they considered their domain.

Azerick hung the lantern from a peg in a ceiling beam and began chasing after the swift-moving rodents, laying them out with his stick whenever he got within reach or was able to corner them. The work was brutal, slow, and exhausting, but Azerick's bag was filling and getting heavier by the hour. He was often forced to sit perfectly still for up to an hour, waiting for the vermin to work up the courage to come out of their hiding spaces and renew the process all over again.

By late evening, Azerick had earned twenty-eight copper pieces and was told to return first thing in the morning. There was indeed a severe rat problem in such a fine home. Most people not living in the streets would scoff at the handful of copper, but it was enough to buy bread for the entire family. The cook had also fed Azerick from the kitchen. The food alone was worth the work. The bits Azerick stuffed into his pockets when the cook was not looking were a bonus as far as he was concerned.

Azerick returned to the mansion in the morning. He had set out several improvised traps designed after similar setups he had read about in one of his books written to educate someone on the tricks of wilderness survival. The guard at the ornate wrought-iron gate was expecting the rat-catcher's return and let him in with instructions to go around to the kitchen entrance. The smell of freshly baked bread, fried sausage, and eggs hit Azerick's nose like a physical force as he neared the kitchen door. The door swung open when Azerick was only a few feet away as the cook burst through to dump a pot of dirty water out onto the ground.

"Good, you're back. Come on in then," the cook commanded.

The cook saw the rat boy, he did not remember his name nor did he care to, eyeing the small loaves of bread he had just pulled out of the oven for the master and his family's morning meal.

"You'll be fed when you get some work done, not before," the cook said brusquely, handing Azerick his stick and sack.

Azerick did not comment on the cook's rudeness. He had learned the man did not possess a kind disposition and seemed to enjoy abusing the position of power he held over most of the other servants.

He lit the lantern using a burning twig from the kitchen stove and crept down the cellar stairs. A smile split his face as he looked upon the success of his traps and snares. Snares made of fine wire strangled the creatures when their heads passed through the loop. Drop traps crushed rats beneath a heavy object that fell when the rat pulled on a piece of bait tied to a lever holding a weighted object directly above it. Simple box traps captured rats beneath them.

Azerick had almost half the number of rats he caught yesterday before he even started work. By noon, he figured that the cellar was nearly clear with only a few left in hiding. He set up several traps before leaving the cellar and dumped his haul outside under the watchful eye of the cook who kept careful count, certain the rat boy would cheat him if given the chance.

After a simple lunch, the cook showed Azerick to a ceiling hatch giving him access to the crawl space above. It was dusty and only afforded about two feet of space through which to work. Since swinging the stick in these confines would be nearly impossible, Azerick constructed a small, trident-like gig using a large fork attached to the end of his whacking stick.

The young exterminator found that, unlike the wealthier manors in the city, this one's walls and ceiling were made of wooden slats plastered over and sometimes covered in a thin veneer of marble or granite to imitate the higher-class mansions. They were cheaper to build and held the heat better in the winter, but the hollow walls and ceilings provided excellent homes for rats and other vermin if not kept in check.

It was difficult to chase the rats down in an area that was far better suited to their size than Azerick's. He was going to have to set several traps up here tonight to have even the slightest hope of clearing the creatures out. At least it was not cold like the cellars had been. Heat from the rooms below penetrated the slat and plaster ceiling, trapping the warmth in the crawl space.

Azerick knew the cheap construction would provide little protection from the summer warmth like the homes built of stone did and would turn the crawl space into an oven. The mild spring weather was already trapping enough heat to make it uncomfortable as the day neared late afternoon.

Azerick began setting numerous noose traps along the most likely trails the rats marked with their scent and baited drop traps made of heavy, flat stones he hauled up. It was getting late, and he could hear the master of the house entertaining dinner guests just below in the dining room. As he lay on his back running a cord over a beam for one of the noose traps, an ominous cracking of wood sounded directly beneath him.

Azerick went perfectly still and held his breath. He let out a sharp bark of surprise as the beams below him gave way and sent him plummeting in a shower of rotted timbers, chunks of white plaster, and dust. He struck the top of the long dining table with enough force to knock the breath from his lungs, but he was otherwise uninjured in the fifteen-foot fall.

"I'm okay," Azerick wheezed to the wealthy guests all staring in disbelief at the sudden intrusion of the filthy boy, "I think the roast goose broke my fall."

The fat cook ran into the dining room as the master roared, "What is the meaning of this?"

Azerick sat up, looked from the large hole in the ceiling to the crushed goose, and then to the master of the house. "Sir, I would recommend leaving the rats alone and hope they eat the termites that have invaded and seriously undermined the integrity of your home."

The lean, well-dressed master with his quill-thin mustache quivering in livid anger shouted at the red-faced cook. "Get this creature out of my home, and have him whipped!"

Azerick tried to roll off the table and flee, but his battered and bruised body protested and resisted his sudden movement. Moreover, the cook was rather swift despite his great bulk. Azerick felt the cook's vice-like grip encircle his upper arm, drag him off the table, and force him through the kitchen. The cook frogmarched him to the stables where a slovenly, gap-toothed man in filthy leathers was pulling a bale of hay from the loft with a long gaff to feed the horses.

"Baldric, the master demands this boy be whipped. See to it," the cook commanded. "I would take the pleasure myself, but I am far too busy at the moment."

The stableman grinned with cruel delight at the cook's order and grabbed a set of leather reins from a peg in one hand, and Azerick's arm in the other. To ensure the groom properly carried out his order, the cook lingered despite his assertion that he was busy. Azerick tried to pull away and cursed both men with every foul expletive in his considerable vocabulary, but the groom's grip was every bit as strong and unbreakable as the cook's had been.

The thick length of leather whistled as it cut an arc through the air and cracked like a bolt of lightning when it struck Azerick's back, buttocks, and legs. Fire erupted in thin lines across Azerick's body as the groom gleefully lashed him repeatedly. Azerick changed tactics when he realized he was not going to be able to pull away. Seething anger inundated Azerick's soul and a strange tingling walked featherlight fingers over his skin. The static continued to build until a bright blue arc of electricity sent a jolt up the groom's arm. He released his hold with a bark of surprised pain.

No longer constrained, Azerick lunged toward the leather cord-wielding man. He lashed out with a hard kick to the man's groin and sent him to his knees. The leather lash dropped uselessly to his side as he clutched his abused privates with both hands and vomited from the intense pain.

The cook reached for the rat boy, but Azerick dove forward out of his reach and scooped up the set of reins in one hand. He spun around and lashed the cook across his enraged face with the leather straps. The cook cried out as the leather raised a bright red welt across one corpulent cheek. Azerick darted past him and raced across the courtyard toward the gate.

The cook shouted to the lone guard watching the gate and ordered the man to stop the fleeing urchin. The guard drew a shortsword from the sheath at his hip and stood before the gate, feet spread in readiness to arrest the boy's flight. Azerick skidded to a stop a few feet from the guard and whipped the stout length of leather at one of the man's legs. The reins wrapped around the guard's ankle like a bullwhip. Azerick yanked on his end of the cord with all his might and dumped the surprised guard hard onto his rump. Before he could recover, Azerick sprinted past, threw the catch on the iron gate, and disappeared into the streets.

Once Azerick felt certain he was beyond any pursuit, he slowed to a walk and fumed in anger at the abuse he had suffered through no fault of his own. Now that his mind had time to relax, his aches throbbed even more, which only added to his fury.

Whip me will you? I will make you all pay for this! Azerick swore as he returned home empty-handed.

The realization that the cook had cheated him out of a full day's pay made Azerick even more determined to enact his justice against those who had wronged him. Jon's words regarding the price of revenge rang hollowly in his young, stubborn head. Had he not been so lost in his anger and humiliation, Azerick may have pondered the strange electricity that had coursed along his body and expended itself on the stableman. However, logic and introspection vanished in the wake of his anger and thoughts of retribution.

CHAPTER 9

Azerick returned to the abandoned building he and his adoptive family were currently calling home. It was after dark, and he was the last one to arrive. Patrick was just outside the door standing watch when Azerick stomped toward him.

"Hey, Az, working late again, eh?" Patrick called out as his friend approached.

"Yeah."

Azerick entered the large room where everyone sat eating whatever meager fare they had scrounged up. They each glanced up from their bowls and greeted him warmly.

"Out late again, lad?" Jon said. "Did ya bring us a good bit of coin again then?"

Azerick sat cross-legged on the floor, scooped up a bowl of stew, and replied, "Not exactly."

"What happened, lad?" Jon asked.

"I did not get paid."

The others looked at the boy sympathetically. It was not the first time one of them had been cheated out of their earnings. Unscrupulous men knew there was little recourse a vagrant could take against them, so it was not an unheard of event. Ryan and a couple of others muttered curses under their breath.

"It happens, lad. Don't let it get you in a twist. We'll be fine," Jon assured him.

Azerick did not tell the others what happened. He was angry and embarrassed by the beating he had received and did not want to talk about it. He especially did not want any of the others to try to avenge the wrong and get themselves into trouble. Azerick would take care of it himself in due time.

He knelt next to his pallet and prayed to any god that would listen to give him the strength and the courage to avenge the wrongs inflicted on him. Azerick fell into a fitful sleep that night, waking up every time he rolled over and aggravated the welts crisscrossing his back and legs. Again, that mysteriously seductive voice called to him.

Azerick, you must not let them get away with this. How many times will you allow others to hurt you, punish you, before you strike back?

Azerick bolted upright and hissed into the darkness of his small room. "Who are you, what do you want from me?"

You know who I am, and I want what you want—blood. Blood for blood, that is our way. Blood owed your father, blood owed your mother, blood owed to you.

"What am I supposed to do? How?"

Kill them, kill them all! The voice faded from his mind with a gleeful laugh.

Azerick was shaking. He was far too lucid to be dreaming. Was the voice really Sharrellan? Why would the goddess of death and vengeance be speaking to him, a street rat? Sleep did not easily return, and when it finally did it was not particularly restive.

The weeks rolled by, but time did little to cool the heat of his anger. The cook and the rich man would get their due, but Jon and the others came first. Azerick was returning late from a mostly fruitless day of scavenging when he rounded the corner of one of the abandoned buildings to find Jon arguing with another man he had never seen before. The man was lean but obviously not weak. He carried himself with an ease that marked him as a very dangerous person. Azerick stayed hidden around the side of the building across the street and listened to the two men's heated discussion in the darkness.

"I've been working these streets for years now, and I haven't had any run-ins or conflicts with the guild in all that time. I've avoided the guild and your kind with good reason," Jon said in a tone clearly showing he did not like this man or what he had to say.

"Look, Locke, it's simple. If you're not part of the guild then you're going to pay a tax for the privilege of working in guild territory. It's not a request, Locke, and be glad Daedric has even given you this chance to get in line," the wiry man said with a threatening undertone.

"I barely make out with enough to feed my family and keep them through the winter as it is. How am I supposed to do that and still pay your guild boss his extortion money?"

"That's not my problem, Locke. You don't want to make it my problem either, trust me. You better figure it out and damn quick, or else." With that final threat, the dangerous-looking man glided off into the night and disappeared into the shadows.

Once Azerick was sure the man had gone and was not coming back, he crossed the street and hailed his unofficial leader. "What was that about, Jon?"

"It's complicated, son. Let's go inside. I'll have to talk to the whole group about this."

Azerick followed Jon into the building they were currently occupying. The structure had once been a large, industrial smithy that turned out worked iron for fences, gates, and other large items. Azerick had located a small room toward the very back of the building, this time constructed of thick stone with a heavy iron door.

He was mystified as to what the room had held that was valuable enough to warrant such strong walls and door. He liked his new family greatly, but he still preferred to sleep alone and sometimes just to find solitude within his own room to read.

He and Jon settled themselves amongst everyone in the main room of the building to explain what had taken place. Jon told the group about his run-in with the guild man and what the encounter portended for the family as a whole.

"So, basically, we either join the guild or pay their 'tax' as they like to call it. You all know how I feel about the guild. Once you throw in with them, you belong to them completely. You do what you're told when you're told no matter your feelings on the subject. If they tell you to rob a widow of her last coins, you do it. They tell you to break in and rob a merchant and kill him if he objects, then you do it or you'll be found floating in the harbor."

Everyone was quiet for several moments. Maggy broke the silence and asked, "What are we going to do then?"

"We'll do what we can as best we can, like we have always done. We'll pay their tax if we can, and if we can't, well, I seriously doubt they'll waste too much effort on the likes of us. We're not even small-time thieves. We're just some folks trying to survive."

"I hope you're right, Jon," Ryan said, "because I don't swim very well, especially with my throat cut and my pockets full of ballast."

They all went off to sleep in their corners while Azerick bedded down in his tiny stone-walled fortress. He thought about what the hard-looking man had said and felt a strong sense of unease course through him. He was certain this was not the last they would hear of this situation.

Word was out on the street that one of the wealthier families of the city was going to go on holiday or visit relatives outside of Southport or some such. Azerick investigated the rumors and found that it was the same manor from which he had been unceremoniously thrown out several weeks earlier.

Azerick watched the comings and goings of the manor for three days before he saw the coach leave with the master, his homely wife, and fat son. The disgusting stableman looked to have scrubbed himself clean and was dressed in something resembling livery for his secondary role as driver.

He still looks like a pig no matter how fancy you dress him, Azerick thought as he watched the coach depart.

Azerick darted down the street and into one of the small alleys created by the tall stone walls of a couple of nearby mansions where he had stashed some things he would need. He pulled several tightly woven oilcloth sacks from under piles of refuse. Even with the treated canvas, dark stains seeped through and a foul stench emanated from the bags. He carried them the few blocks to the wall surrounding the manor and threw them over, making four trips to retrieve them all.

He then strode casually up to the gate where the same guard was again acting as gateman and sentry. Azerick was confident the man would not recognize him. Few people committed the faces of the homeless to memory, and the man was not exceptionally bright.

"What ya want, boy?" the guard asked lazily.

"Sir, the master ordered Baldric to muck out the stables, but he din't get 'round to it and told me to have it done b'fore he got back or he'd beat me somethin' fierce," Azerick told the man in a low-class drawl.

The guard rubbed his stubble-covered chin with one rough-nailed hand. "I don't know. I weren't told nothin' about anything like that."

"Please, sir, Baldric said he din't want nobody to know lest word got back to the master that he was shirkin' his duties. I gots to get inside and get it done. You know how he likes to take the leather to a boy," Azerick pleaded. "I'll give ya half what he paid me if you'll let me pass. I get good work here, and I want to keep it without fear o' Baldric's lash."

The guard's eyes lit up at the mention of a bribe. "How much he give you, boy?"

"Two silver swords, sir. One I got now that I'll give to ya, and the other I'll get from Baldric when I finish the job and he gets back and pays me."

"Let's see it then."

Azerick fished the coin out of his pocket. He hated to give up the sum he had held back from his earnings and pickings of the past weeks, but it was a justified means to an end in his mind.

The guard snatched the coin from Azerick's hand through the bars quicker than he would have given him credit for before opening the gate a crack. Azerick went straight for the stables, examined the loft, and formulated his plan.

He lifted a stall door from its hinges then tried to muscle the wooden half-gate up a ladder and into the loft, but it was too heavy. He found a block and tackle, used to lift the heavy bales of hay on a wooden platform dangling from a series of ropes attached to a rafter beam. Azerick used it to hoist the door into the loft. He then set the door down flat across two bales of hay like a tabletop, with the bale closest to the loft opening barely under the edge of the stall door.

Once the door was in place, he returned to the stalls and began scooping piles of horse dung into a small cart. When the cart was full, he wheeled it to the hoisting platform and dumped as many droppings as he thought he could lift onto it.

Azerick scrambled back up the ladder into the loft, tied a couple of bales of hay to the pull rope, and rode it down to the stall floor where he tied the rope off to a ring set in the floor. He climbed back up into the loft and scooped the dung onto the door lying atop the hay bales. He repeated the process several times until he had a couple of hundred pounds of manure deposited on the stable door perched precariously across two bales of hay.

Once he had as much filth piled up as the gate would hold, he stacked the bales of hay back into the loft, placing them out of reach of the gaff so that the only bale within view was the one holding up the front half of the stable door. He then used the cart to retrieve the oilcloth sacks and wheeled them up to one of the servant entrances.

After checking that the coast was clear, Azerick grabbed a few of the laden sacks and carried them up into the crawl space. Once inside, he untwisted the wire holding the sacks closed and almost retched at the horrid stench wafting out. He remembered the perfumed kerchief he had swiped from a woman in the market square and tied it over his nose and mouth.

The smell of the decaying carcasses of the dogs, cats, and rodents inside the sacks still threatened to make him vomit before he finished his work, but he forced down the bile that rose in his stomach and dumped the remains between the walls of several rooms within the manor. It took several trips before he emptied the last sack between the slat and plaster walls.

Seeing he still had a bit of time for more mischief, Azerick took a bucket and filled it several times at an outside well used to fill the horses' water troughs. He liberally soaked the dung pile concealed in the loft then covered it with loose straw before leaving by way of the gate, and tipping a make-believe hat to the guard while whistling a jaunty tune.

The wealthy family returned three days later from their short trip enjoying the warmth of the early summer. The guard opened the gate at the approach of the carriage. The horses' hooves clopping on the flagstone courtyard alerted those inside the manor to the return of the master and his family. The cook stood in the courtyard wringing his hands in his apron. The sweat pouring down his bloated face had little to do with the heat of the day.

Baldric climbed down from the carriage's driver's bench and opened the door for his master and family, extending an arm for the missus as she exited the coach.

"Bring in the luggage after you have seen to the horses, Baldric," the master drawled as he strode toward the house.

"Aye, milord, won't be but a moment," Baldric replied and led the horses toward the stables.

"My Lord," the cook said as he intercepted the master, using an honorific the master was not technically entitled to seeing as how he was not actually a nobleman despite his pretenses.

"What is it?" he snapped irritably.

"It is the manor, My Lord. There is a foulness we have not been able to locate," the cook replied nervously.

"What sort of foulness?"

"I do not know, My Lord. The servants have left every door and window in the house open in hopes of airing it out, but it has had little effect."

The wind shifted and the putrid scent wafting out of the open windows and doors struck them full on as they approached their home.

"Oh, what is that horrible smell?" the master's homely, dim-witted wife asked as she pressed a scented silk kerchief to her nose.

The family walked into the house only to bolt back out seconds later. The missus and her fat son vomited most undignifiedly upon the flagstones as the master cursed and gagged.

Baldric parked the carriage under an overhead cover to protect its glossy paint from the sun and elements and led the horses to their stalls. He glanced at the empty stall lacking a door. He was certain there had been one when he left. He scratched his head in confusion, but he lacked the desire to tax his brain to devote the necessary energy to the mystery.

Baldric grabbed his gaff, snagged a hay bale with its iron hook, and gave it a sharp tug. He watched the bale fall and guided it away from him so it would not land on his head, something he learned after clobbering himself more than once with the fifty-pound bales.

The moment Baldric pulled down the hay bale, the soggy, dung-laden platform tilted downward and dumped its entire load onto the head of the stableman. Before he could fathom what had befallen him and utter a curse, the heavy stall door slid down from the edge of the loft and crashed onto the top of his head, knocking him senseless into the muck.

CHAPTER 10

The decaying carcasses inside the walls of the manor had turned into a rancid mess of entrails and bones under the assault of the summer heat and soaked into the wood and plaster. The vile taint had so infested the insides of the home that the entire structure had to be razed and burned after several failed attempts to clean it out. Azerick watched from across the street, smiling at the orange flames and greasy black smoke curling into the air like his personal banner of triumph.

Azerick had almost forgotten the lingering unease in his gut after hearing the conversation between Jon and the thieves' guildsman. It had been more than a week since the threat, and none had seen the man since. Perhaps Jon was right and the guild had better things to worry about than them. Azerick had little to show for his day's work again due to his vengeful activities, but that was over and he could now devote his full attention to their subsistence once again.

They all sat around the common room, as they called it, and waited for the return of Ryan and Steven. They were long past due to return, and there was talk of going out to search for them. Maggy was certain something bad had befallen the pair. Margaret was comforting her when the man guarding the door yelled in and said he saw them coming up the street. The two men stumbled into the room a moment later, bruised and battered.

"Steven, Ryan, what happened to you?" Jon asked, his voice thick with concern.

Maggy ran to help Steven sit down, held him, and dabbed at his split lip and cut brow with a damp rag.

Steven pulled away from his wife's ministrations and replied, "Several men jumped us on the street a few blocks from here as we were returning. They took what we had pilfered and told us what we had wasn't nearly enough to pay the guild's tax, and that we had better pay them in silver by the end of the week, or we would all be paying them in blood."

"Damn it, Jon, I'm not going to end up dead because you don't have the guts to do what needs to be done! I'm leaving tonight. I'm sorry, Jon. You're a good man, but I don't have anyone here but myself, and if I did have someone I'd get out and take them with me, and you all should do the same. I'll not cross the guild. You see what they'll do, and this is just the start," Ryan exclaimed before getting up to pack his few belongings.

"Ryan, please, we'll pay their tax. We'll come up with something tonight," Jon swore.

"I'm sorry, Jon. I don't mean to insult you all, but you're just not cut out to do what's going to be required to please the guild. I hope you do, but I'm not willing to risk my life on it." That said, Ryan left and disappeared into the night.

Jon turned sullenly back to the remaining group. "Okay folks, we have some planning to do. Anyone have any ideas?"

They all argued back and forth, debating the merits of different schemes long into the night. Azerick decided this was not his area of expertise and had little to offer, so he decided to wrack his brain on his own back in his room without the distraction of competing voices. Alone with his thoughts, he summoned a bird's-eye view of Southport in his mind. He noted the primary and secondary routes through the multiple districts, the traffic for various times throughout the day, and the Watch's typical patrolling routes. They needed a respectable score to appease the guild. That eliminated their usual petty thefts, which left the market square and the upper district. Jon would vehemently oppose any sort of burglary, so that meant his best option was the bustling market square. Azerick only realized he had fallen asleep when dawn woke him in the morning. He went out to the common room where Maggy was sitting with Beth and William.

"Where is everybody? Have they all gone out already?" Azerick asked as he found a piece of bread and some cheese to break his fast.

"Aye, Jon and the others put some half-baked plan together to get their hands on some real coin and left early this morning," Maggy replied, clearly unhappy with the plan.

"What are they going to do? Why didn't they wake me?"

"Jon said to leave you out of it, that you were too young and too inexperienced for this kind of job."

"I'm almost as old as Patrick and twice as quick!" Azerick insisted.

"I know, but that was what they decided, and you're probably better off not going. I hope I'm wrong, but I got a bad feeling about this."

"I'm going out then, Maggy. I may not be able to help them on their run, but I can do something," Azerick announced as he got up and left Maggy and the two younger children.

Azerick traveled throughout the city looking for an opportunity that would make a significant difference. He had a half-formulated plan put together last night before he fell asleep, but it was hours before he found his opportunity. The young thief found himself in the largest of many market squares throughout the city. This one was located just inside one of the better districts. That meant there were better goods being hawked, but also more city watch.

Merchants of all sorts plied their wares while hawkers yelled over the loud droning of hundreds of shoppers and merchants. Azerick spied a jewelry maker's stand at the base of a small rise in the street. Perhaps ten or fifteen yards up the sloping avenue was a cart laden with leather belts, bags, and other adornments. One wheel of the cart was chocked to prevent it from rolling down the hill and into the crowd below.

Azerick sidled up to the leather worker's cart and waited for the artisan to become preoccupied before making his move. A large woman in fine wool and cotton garb asked to try on the belts to determine which one went best with her outfit.

The merchant had several belts slung over one arm as he handed them over one by one for the woman to inspect. When the vendor stepped away from the cart to help the woman wrap a belt around her prodigious waist, Azerick kicked behind himself like a mule chasing off a stableboy and knocked the wedge holding the cart out from under the wheel. The cart began to move slowly at first, but it quickly gained momentum on the far side of the crest.

Seeing his livelihood rolling away, the merchant dropped his belts and chased after the cart, bellowing for help. Azerick also ran after the cart shouting for all he was worth to get people to notice the runaway wagon so they could get out of the way. He feared that the errant cart would strike a pedestrian, but he had risked it anyway. He would never get another chance like this, and he meant to make the most of it.

As luck would have it, the people were rather alert today and dove away from the rampaging, leather-laden carriage. Azerick was surprised at the force with which the cart slammed into the jewelry maker's stand. The runaway cart knocked over tables, sent wood and glass display cases crashing to the ground, and scattered jewelry and leather items everywhere.

Azerick raced ahead of the leather merchant and was the first one to reach the cart and overturned jewelry stand. Before the jewelry seller could recover from the shock, Azerick scooped up several pieces of shining loot, along with shards of broken glass which sliced into his fingers, and shoved them into his pockets. He made a second grab at a few more items and dashed out of the square before anyone realized what he was truly up to.

Azerick ran for several blocks, ducking in and out of alleyways and side streets to put as much distance between him and the accident scene as he could. He decided to duck down one more alley then take a rest before he made his way back to the others. He turned into the alleyway and ran into a large youth about three or four years older than himself and twice as big.

Both boys went sprawling from the impact, and a few pieces of stolen jewelry went ringing onto the cobblestones. Azerick looked up from where he lay on his back and saw two other boys already helping the larger young man back up. The other two youths were perhaps a year or two older than Azerick, but they were not nearly as big as their friend was. All three glared at Azerick as he got his feet back under him.

"Hey, Hugo, this little squirt just knocked you down!" said a lean, red-haired boy.

"No kidding, Carrot. Gee, I hadn't noticed," Hugo said, clapping Carrot on the back of his bright orange head.

"Hey, look at what he dropped," exclaimed the other boy, Rolly, as he reached down and started picking up the bits of jewelry.

"That's mine, give it back!"

"What else you got, worm?" Hugo demanded as he advanced on Azerick.

"Nothing, now give me back my stuff."

"Hand over everything you got, or you're gonna get pounded real good," Hugo threatened, smacking his fist into a meaty palm.

"Yeah, hand it over, chump, or we'll pound you real good," Carrot parroted.

Before Azerick could respond, the three boys lunged at him and tackled him to the ground. Azerick rolled with the hits and sprang back to his feet. He launched a quick right jab into Carrot's nose and landed a solid kick into Hugo's stomach. Hugo's mass trapped Rolly beneath it as the larger boy went sprawling back onto the ground.

Azerick fled as fast as his feet would take him with the three thugs in pursuit. He ran down alleys, through buildings, and even across the rooftops at one point, but he was unable to shake his pursuers.

Azerick was not familiar with this part of the city, but it soon became apparent that his assailants were. They seemed to anticipate his moves and were often able to cut off his retreat. It occurred to him that the thugs were herding him like a sheep, but he did not know to where. The answer was soon revealed when he found himself at the end of a dead-end alley.

"He's trapped in the alley," Azerick heard one of the boys call out.

Azerick looked around, but the few doors that emptied into the alley were solid and locked. The cornered street rat searched desperately for another way out. The three thugs ran into the now empty alley and looked around in bewilderment.

"Where'd he go?" asked Carrot.

Hugo looked up then down before pointing to a sewer grate. "There, he went into the sewer. Let's get him."

"Are you sure you wanna go down there?" Rolly asked, "We already got what he dropped. Maybe that was all of it."

"No, he's got more or he wouldn't have run. Now let's go."

The three followed Azerick down into the sewers, which reeked as badly as only a sewer could, and looked around in the darkness.

"It's really dark down here. Carrot, climb back up and find something to make a few torches," Hugo ordered.

Carrot came back a few minutes later with several planks of dry wood, some discarded burlap, and strips of canvas. Hugo took the material and wrapped it around the pieces of wood before lighting it with his tinderbox. The torches gave off a weak, flickering light since they had no pitch or oil on them, but they worked well enough for their purposes.

"All right, come on. He couldn't have gotten far without any light," Hugo insisted.

Rats scattered at the approaching light of the flickering torches and the noise of the three young men as they traversed their way through the muck. Meanwhile, Azerick made his own way down the pitch-black sewers, running a hand along the slime-coated walls and feeling his way down the dark, dank passageways. He kept track of each turn he made and how far each run was between any changes in direction, cataloging the number of steps he took in his near-perfect memory.

The concern of getting lost was predominant in his mind. Azerick ran his hands along the wall and discovered he had reached a dead end. He turned back the way he had come but heard voices and saw a flickering of light.

He walked to the very back of the tunnel hoping they would not come down the passage he now occupied, but he had no such luck. He could just make out the trio of goons at the open end of the corridor he was in, and they were coming closer.

Azerick began to feel blindly along the walls in hopes of finding a ladder and climbing out. He felt nothing but smooth, crud-covered stone, and the three thugs were getting closer. He was just about ready to set himself to fight when his hand touched a stone that gave a little. He tugged on the stone hoping he could pry it out of the wall and throw it behind the boys to distract them and maybe send them along a different route.

Azerick pulled on the stone, but he couldn't dislodge it from the wall. He realized it was attached somehow, so he gave it a twist hoping to break it free from whatever was holding it. He twisted the stone, but instead of breaking off, it rotated in his hand and he heard a scraping noise and felt a slight breeze on his face. He twisted the stone some more and a very faint light shone through a now revealed doorway. Azerick pushed the stone back into place, and without even pondering his good luck, dashed through the doorway and found an iron wheel on the other side of the door. He turned the wheel and the door slowly swung shut and closed with a light click.

A faint, yellowish-green light glowed from some sort of lichen growing on the damp stone walls. He made a small slash with his finger through the glowing substance. A dark line was now visible on the wall and his fingertip glowed. The light was very dim and did nothing to illuminate the passage. Still, it was better than the blackness of the sewer. Azerick carefully made his way along the narrow corridor, following the wall since he could barely see his own feet.

He had crept forward only a few paces when he felt a small section of the floor shift under his weight with an audible click and the grating of rusting metal. Instinct drove him to the ground as a snapping sound preceded a clash against the wall just a couple of feet over his prone form. He felt something light but solid ricochet off the wall and drop onto his back.

He reached with his hand, plucked the object off his back, and sat up. It was a rusty crossbow bolt with a shaft made of solid iron. Wherever he was, it was set to dissuade visitors, with lethal intent.

There was no way he could continue without risking being killed by one of these traps. He needed light, but he had none nor anything with which to make it. He supposed he could wait out the three thugs and go back into the sewer, but he was unsure if he could find his way out from there. There was also the possibility that they could also find the secret door and then they would have him trapped.

Azerick knew he needed to proceed and find another way out. He looked at the glowing substance on his hand wondering if there was some way he could use it. He did not see how. Even if he scooped up a handful of the stuff it would not produce enough light by which to see.

Use it.

Azerick's body tensed at the unexpected command. "Who's there?"

Use it.

It was then Azerick realized the voice was not coming from within the passageway but from inside his own head. He did not recognize the voice as he replayed it in his head. At first, he feared that it was the same voice from his dreams—Sharrellan, goddess of death. But this voice was different. It was neither male nor female, and it held no malice.

"I don't know how. How can I use it?"

Look and you will see.

Azerick stared at the lichen for a minute. He held it closer to his face and looked harder. On instinct, he stopped focusing on the glowing substance and looked past it.

Beyond the visible illumination, Azerick spied silvery threads no thicker than a spider's web and the feeling of power lying somewhere unseen. If he could feed some of that power into the lichen, maybe he could get it to glow brighter. But how? Azerick kept his eyes unfocused and tried to grab one of the silver threads, but his fingers passed harmlessly though it. On a purely instinctual level, he willed the thread with his mind and watched as it began twisting and writhing like a tendril of smoke in a faint breeze.

He grabbed more of the threads with his mind and gently attached them to the glowing moss. As the threads found purchase within the azure aura, the lichen began to glow more brightly. It was mentally taxing, and several times Azerick lost focus and was forced to start over. He had no idea how much time had passed since he began, but all thoughts of Hugo and his lackeys had vanished, and his stomach began rumbling.

His hand now glowed in a bluish light with the intensity of a candle. He could see for several yards down what appeared to be a rather long passageway. Once he overcame his amazement at what he had done, Azerick continued his exploration on his hands and knees, carefully crawling along the floor, looking and feeling for any more triggers.

Azerick had found three more trapped floor plates by the time he reached the first intersection. Each time he discovered a trapped floor stone, he wiped a bit of glowing lichen onto it to mark its location. He did not know how long the lichen would continue to glow after it was scraped from the wall, but he hoped it was long enough for him to avoid the booby traps when he made his way back out. He came across more than one sprung trap, where either time or an intruder had snapped the trip wire. He guessed it was likely the former as he saw no skeletons or traces of anyone injured.

In the few hours he had been exploring the place, he was able to find three side rooms, a main chamber about thirty feet long on each side, and two cleverly hidden doors leading to a narrow corridor holding the crossbow traps that fired into the hallways.

Unlike the crossbows, some of the traps were powered by a strong, tempered-steel spring and were still active. Tar and grease coated the springs and kept them functional long after the wood and sinew parts of the others had rotted away. It was these that had tried to skewer the young explorer.

Azerick had no way of knowing how long the place had been abandoned much less how long it had been here, but he knew it was a long time, years at least, probably stretching back several decades given the amount of dust and the condition of some of the more degraded items he found.

The entire subterranean complex was mostly empty. Only a few tattered and rotted wall hangings, carpets, and empty wooden crates littered some of the rooms. He was certain there were more rooms but figured it was time to go back to the family, tell them what he had found, and show them the loot he had stolen.

Azerick left the hidden complex using a trapdoor he located at the end of one of the halls instead of departing by way of the sewer entrance. The trapdoor was bolted from the inside and he was able to work it free and slowly lift the door up just enough to peer out.

Azerick could see nothing but darkness all around. He made out the shadow of a wall just a few feet to his left and was just able to see a wall about forty feet ahead of him. Azerick lifted the door completely and quietly climbed out of the hole. He was now standing in a distant corner of what appeared to be an abandoned warehouse.

He wiped the glowing lichen off his hand using a discarded piece of cloth. Azerick was not ready to try and explain why his hand was glowing. He then found an opening where a door once stood and carefully ducked outside and into the night. Thankfully, the abandoned warehouse was located in the squatters' district where he and the others made their home, so it would not be much of a walk.

As he worked his way home, he noticed the smell of smoke and an orange glow from farther within the district. His stomach clenched and heaved in horror as he ran toward the orange glow, which looked very close to where his home was.

The anxious lad pumped his legs as hard as they would go, fear fueling his weary muscles. Azerick was about four blocks from where his home was when he saw the first licks of flame. A few seconds later, he realized his worst fears were borne out.

His home was on fire along with a couple of nearby buildings. Dozens of people formed a bucket brigade and threw pail after pail of water onto the fire. Men and women passed the empty buckets back along a second line and refilled them with water from a horse-drawn cart bearing a massive, water-filled cistern strapped to its bed.

A team of horses tore down nearby buildings to prevent the spread of fire. Azerick looked through tear-blurred eyes at all the people hauling buckets, tearing down adjoining structures, and at those just watching the spectacle and waiting perhaps to relieve someone on the bucket brigade. But he could not see a single face he knew.

Of his foster family, there was no sign, but he did recognize one face in the crowd. It was the hard, evil-looking man, the same man he had seen threatening Jon a few weeks ago. He tried to creep closer, but as he did, the man turned, walked away, and disappeared beyond the crowd and into the night.

The fires were put out by early dawn, but nothing could extinguish the anguish in Azerick's heart. People began to walk home, all exhausted from their night's toils and muttering about the "damn squatters" starting fires.

Azerick could do nothing but sit and look at the smoldering ruins after everyone had gone their own way. He heard one of the guards say that the constable would be out later in the day to inspect the area for the cause of the blaze.

Once everyone had left and the ruins had cooled down, Azerick began to walk amongst the remnants of his former home. Another home and another family lost. Why was he cursed like this? What had he done to warrant such continued loss and pain?

He saw an object in the burned-out rubble and walked over to inspect it. It was a doll scorched nearly beyond recognition. As he stooped to pick it up, he saw the bones, also burned beyond recognition. Azerick shifted a large plank of wood and discovered more bones beneath it. Intertwined with each other, he could tell, were two sets of grisly remains, one set much smaller than the other. Azerick was certain they belonged to Maggy and little Beth. He fell to his knees and began to sob once again as sorrow filled his soul and threatened to tear him apart.

The heartbroken boy knelt in the ashes of the burned-out building, holding the doll for what seemed an eternity. The sun was nearly overhead before he picked himself up and wiped a soot-stained hand across his tear-stained eyes, creating a black smear across his face. He walked to a large section of wall that had burned and fallen but was not broken up. Like a lean-to, it was propped up against another structure that had somehow survived the blaze.

Azerick crawled beneath the wall and saw that it was leaning against the stone room where he had slept. The door was shut tight, and for just a moment, a flicker of hope touched him that perhaps not all was lost.

He grabbed the iron handle and pulled his hand back due to the heat remaining in the metal. He inspected his hand, but the metal had not burned him badly. Azerick pulled the sleeve of his shirt over his hand and grasped the handle again. He could still feel the heat through the sleeve, but he was able to withstand it enough to turn the handle and pull open the solid door.

Azerick stepped inside the stone-walled room and looked around. The wooden shelves showed signs of scorching but were intact. He spied his bag toward the back in the center of the room. It too was intact with only a few signs of burnt fabric around the frayed seams at the top of the bag. He opened it up and pulled out his books, carefully inspecting each one and placing them reverently back inside. His clothes and books smelled strongly of smoke and probably would continue to do so for a long time, but they were otherwise unharmed. At least one god took pity on orphans it seemed.

Azerick hefted his bag onto his shoulders and stepped out of the ruined building. Before he left for good, he turned, bowed his head, and said a prayer for the second family he had lost.

As he stared at the ground, Azerick spied another object lying in the ashes where the front door had been. He bent down and scooped it up with his free hand. It was a large iron spike. Azerick thought it an odd thing for he had not seen any around their home before. He looked at the still standing doorframe and saw uniformly shaped indentations in the charred wood. He walked back to where another door to the outside had once stood and sifted through the ashes until he found more identical iron spikes.

Jon and the others could not get out. The doors had been wedged shut.

Seething rage replaced his sorrow. "Jon, I know what you said about seeking revenge, but I promise you, they will all pay for this. I hope you understand and will forgive me."

That promise made, Azerick found the warehouse and the trapdoor it hid and slipped down into his new home beneath the streets of the squatters' district.

Azerick expected the nightmares that once again filled his dreams. First, the face of his father seemed to hover around him, almost lost in the darkness. The image of his mother replaced it before shifting into the form of Jon, Margaret, Patrick, and all of his dead friends and family. Even Beth's cherubic little face called to him from the inky void, and all spoke the same message.

Seek your vengeance. Become the hand of Sharrellan, and bring death to those who deserve their fate.

Cold sweat beaded on Azerick's brow as he shouted at the faces before him. "Who are you? What do you want?"

I am Sharrellan, goddess of darkness and death. I want what you want—vengeance. Be my hand and deliver death to the worthy, the voices called out in a strange, discordant harmony.

Impossible, Azerick thought. *The gods do not speak with mortals, much less orphaned street rats.*

"I will get my revenge," Azerick shouted at the faces. "I will kill them all, but I do not need you to do it! I don't need anyone!"

CHAPTER II

Azerick fenced his jewelry and was able to buy oil and lamps he then attached to the walls of his new home. He purchased a bedcover that he was able to fill with straw and made himself a decent pallet upon which to sleep. He also bought himself several tools that he was not able to steal and made a shelf for his books. He then bought some carpets and stole a couple of others along with materials to begin fixing and replacing the various traps throughout his underground lair. Azerick made sure he was able to bolt the doors from the inside so no one else might stumble upon one of the entrances and invade his newest sanctuary.

He had found five exits leading out into the city. Two opened into the sewer: one into the warehouse he first used to exit, another, surprisingly enough, opened into the old tannery where he had first met Jon and the others. This brought back a fresh feeling of loss and loneliness, but he did not weep for them again. From now on, he would wear his pain like armor, and he would let no one and nothing hurt him again.

The last exit was a small door he had to crawl through on his hands and knees to navigate. It opened into the dark basement of one of the shabby inns in the common quarter that butted up against the squatter's' district. He liberated several bottles of wine and a small cask of ale, along with a couple of mugs, and got thoroughly drunk for the first time.

Azerick awoke with a splitting headache and decided that drinking was not as enjoyable as some people made it out to be. He did not like the way getting drunk interfered with his ability to think, and it made him sick the next day.

As his muddled brain began to function once again, he turned his thoughts to the future, a future of vengeance for those he had lost. He would avenge his father, mother, Jon and the others. He did not know where to begin concerning the murder of his father and mother, but he did have a lead on at least one person he was sure was responsible for the death of his foster family.

Just thinking about the man from the thieves' guild, with his hard face and cruel eyes, sent a shiver up his spine and set his stomach to tingling. Anger replaced his fear and Azerick was determined to get his justice from the man and all those responsible.

Once he settled into his new shelter, he once again started plying the streets. He became increasingly good at lifting a purse and even breaking into homes in the dead of night. He usually made off with silver serving dishes, small rugs, and anything else small enough to make off with that might bring him a few silver coins from the fences. It was on one of his fencing jobs that the fates stepped in once again.

"Good morning to you, Azeel," Azerick said as he walked into the seedy-looking store at the edge of the merchant quarter.

Azeel was a swarthy man originally from one of the cities located in the Great Desert, or Great Wastes as most called it. Azeel had dusky-brown skin, a great black mustache, and eyes as black as coal. He wore a red silk vest over a white linen shirt and always had a smile for his customers.

"Ah, if it isn't my favorite customer," Azeel replied. Everyone was Azeel's favorite customer, Azerick soon learned. "What do you have for me today?"

"A bit of the usual silver, but very nice."

"Hmm, more silver. My shop is full of silver, but for you I will give a good price anyway because you are my favorite customer."

"Azeel, you know darn well you are going to offer me a terrible price, the same terrible price you offer all your *favorite* customers, so let's cut to the chase."

"You wound me, young sir. I am an honest businessman, and where I come from haggling is not only a courtesy, it's almost the law.

It is not my fault most of you northerners don't know how to do business."

Azerick dumped his bag on the counter and out of it poured two silver goblets and enough silver flatware to make six place settings.

"Now, I know this is worth at least fifty silver swords to you, but because you are my favorite fence, I'll let you have them for forty-five."

Azeel looked over the silver adorning his counter with an appraising eye. "No good. The goblets are both stamped with the household crest. They'll have to be melted down. They're only worth their weight in silver. The flatware looks like it was made of the same low-quality metal, maybe even worse. Twenty-five swords is all I can give, and that is being generous because I like you."

"You may think I am no more than a boy you are trying to take candy from, sir, but I know good silver when I see it, and I've even supped from such fine silver often enough and not so long ago. Because I like you and would not want people to say 'there is that Azeel, watch out for him, he steals from poor homeless boys and kicks puppies,' forty pieces of silver."

Azeel's hand flew to his chest and he reeled back as though physically struck. "I am insulted! I have never kicked a puppy in my life. Nevertheless, I will not have my fine reputation tarnished by a young man's slander even if I have to take the food out of my family's mouths to pay his extortion. I will give you thirty-two silver swords. Even now, I hear the stomachs of my children rumbling from their missed meals. Too bad I cannot feed them your greed; they would be as fat as noblemen."

"And I can see the honest folk crossing the street before they walk in front of your store so that they will not be robbed whilst they pass by or have their beloved pets booted like a child's rag ball. I think thirty-five pieces of silver will be sufficient to make you an honest man and lover of small, furry puppies."

"It is slander of the highest sort and blackmail of the worst kind. Very well, you will have your extorted coin. I do not know how you sleep at night," the merchant said, finalizing the deal.

"I will sleep with a full belly thanks to your unwavering honesty and generosity," Azerick said as Azeel counted out the silver coins bearing a sword stamped on the face.

"It looks like not all you northerners are so ignorant in the ways of honest business and good haggling. Good days and profitable nights to you, young sir. I look forward to the next time we conduct our business."

Azerick turned toward the door as someone was pushing his way in.

"Pardon, sir," Azerick said as the man barged past him.

"Watch out, you little street rat, before you get eaten by the big dogs," the man rudely snarled.

Azerick glanced up and looked straight into the eyes of the man from the thieves' guild. He was shocked into immobility as he stared into those hard, angry eyes—the eyes of a killer.

"What's the matter, boy, you deaf or just dumb?" he growled. "Must be both," he answered himself and pushed past Azerick, striking him with his shoulder hard enough to force him to take a couple of steps back.

Azerick pulled the door open and raced blindly down the street. He ran several blocks before he stopped to think. *It was him! I can't run from him. I have to watch him.*

He forced himself to turn and run back the way he had come. As he reached the street of Azeel The Fence, he approached cautiously, keeping a wary eye out for the guild man. Azerick continued to walk down the street toward the fence's store but on the distant side until he came to an alley just across from the storefront. He ducked inside, cloaked himself as best he could in the shadows, and waited for the man to emerge.

He did not have to wait long. The hard-eyed man emerged from Azeel's a few minutes later, tucking away a coin purse. Azerick had not seen him carrying anything in to fence, although it could have been something small like jewelry. More likely, it was protection money or some tax the guild forced the shopkeepers to pay. Azerick followed the man, but not so close he would spot him. Not that he was likely to notice even if he followed him as close as his own shadow. He walked the streets with the confidence of a man who knew no one dared lay a hand on him.

Azerick shadowed the man the entire day and into the evening. He watched as the man entered various shops and always walked out with a purse of coins. He was definitely collecting some sort of payment from these merchants and service providers like smiths, potters, coopers, and wainwrights.

As the day waned into dusk, the guildsman entered a seedy, smoke and noise-filled tavern. A few minutes later, Azerick slipped into the same tavern as unobtrusively as he could. It was clear that stealth was not necessary. No one would have noticed him if he set his clothes on fire until half the common room was ablaze.

Azerick stepped away from the door and followed along the back wall, scouring the crowd with his eyes until he saw the man sitting at a table with two other men. One looked as hard as the man he had been tailing, but he carried half again the weight and about eight extra inches of height. His nose looked to have been broken numerous times and a heavy, brutal-looking cudgel hung from his belt as well as a long knife.

The other man looked like a shaved weasel with human legs. He had a thin, ratty mustache and darting eyes that seemed to look everywhere at once. All three seemed to be enjoying themselves with the coin his man had procured from the merchants. They drank cup after cup of wine and ale. Just the thought of drinking wine made Azerick queasy as he vividly remembered the awful hangover he had the morning after his own indulgence a few months ago.

A large man staggered past their table on his way up to the bar, interrupting their revelry. Whether he tripped over the weasel-looking man's foot or the man had tripped him on purpose, Azerick did not know. What he did know was that there was going to be trouble—big trouble. The hard-faced man and his two friends jumped up as the large man went sprawling across their table, knocking over their drinks and nearly the entire table as well.

The man Azerick had followed and the big man he was with grabbed the inebriated oaf by the collar, hauled him up, and pushed him backward into the bar.

"Watch where you're going, you big dumb bastard!" the guildsman cursed as he shoved the drunken man toward the bar.

"Your rat-faced friend needs to check his overgrown feet! I ought'a break his skull for that!" The clumsy man squinted at the guild man and recognition dawned on his face. "Oh, it's you, Merik. I thought I smelled Daedric's men. Either that or someone lost control of their bowels in here."

Azerick watched this confrontation with great interest and finally learned a name to put with the face of his quarry.

"You had best watch your tongue, dog, lest my friends and I remove it for you," Merik threatened as the weasel-faced man reached inside his short coat with an evil grin of anticipated violence.

"Best you remember where you're at, Merik. This is Night Raven territory and don't forget it, or we'll be feeding your tongues to the dogs."

Merik gave an imperceptible signal to his henchmen. Quick as a striking snake, or maybe a mongoose, the weasel-faced man pulled a needle-sharp stiletto from the inside of his coat and stabbed the drunken man in the back of his knee. Merik's broken-nosed bruiser whipped his cudgel into the rival guildsman's gut and sent him to the floor gasping for air.

Quick as that, the fight was over. The tavern patrons went back to their drinks and conversations as if this was a normal occurrence, which it likely was, Azerick figured.

Merik grabbed the fallen man by his greasy hair and glared down into his face. "Nothing lasts forever, fat man, and Daedric's Demons is looking to expand its territory. Night Raven is weak and ripe for the plucking. You tell that popinjay you call a guild leader it might be a good time for him to pull up stakes and move on out while he still has the option."

Merik threw the man's head down, and he and his cronies walked out of the tavern. Azerick waited a few moments before following them out into the night. Just before they disappeared into the night's gloomy darkness, he spied them walking up the street and carefully resumed his stealthy pursuit.

Azerick followed the trio just close enough to keep them in view. When they turned a corner, he lost sight of them for a few moments. He increased his pace so he would not lose them down more than one street at any time. The small group turned another corner, and Azerick had to quicken his steps before they rounded another building and escaped.

As he peered around the corner of the building, he feared for a moment that he had lost them anyway until he saw the back of the large man disappear into a three-story structure about halfway down the far side of the street.

Azerick studied the building as best he could from where he was, not daring to draw any closer. Two men guarded the door Merik and the others had entered and kept a vigilant eye on the street traffic. He only had a moment to study the men and the building before he felt the sharp edge of a knife press against his throat. Azerick held his breath and froze in place.

"What are you looking at, boy?" a voice hissed in his ear.

The knife pulled away from his throat, and a hand grabbed the front of his shirt and pressed him hard into the side of the building he had been using as cover. The knife reappeared, its point pricking the soft flesh under his chin.

"Answer me, boy, and you best answer good, or I'm going to be giving you the first and last shave you'll ever get. Who are you, and why were you following us?"

Azerick stared into the beady eyes of the weasel-faced man who had been with Merik and realized his mistake. He saw the back of the big man and just assumed that the other two had preceded him through the door. He thought quickly, and it was a good thing he was better at thinking fast than he was at shadowing guild thieves.

"Sir, I'm just a street rat, but I'm pretty good. At least I thought I was. I was just looking for someone to talk to about joining the thieves' guild, but I didn't know who to approach. That's what I was doing in the tavern. I knew that Night Raven men hung out there, but when I saw how you handled that big oaf, I knew I wanted to talk to your guild instead," Azerick stammered out, only half acting the part of a terrified boy.

The weasel-eyed man cuffed Azerick on the side of his head. "Stupid boy, lucky for you, Daedric's Demons is growing and expanding its territory. At least you're smart enough to see that and come to us first." The thief took the knife out from under Azerick's chin and released the front of his shirt. "We're always looking for new men, especially young men that can be trained proper and have quick hands. Convince me that it's in my house's best interest to let you live, and maybe even take you in, instead of making you bleed out right here for spying."

"I have your purse, sir," Azerick said as he lifted his hand and showed the small coin pouch dangling from his nimble fingers.

The weasel's face split into a grin and he let out a wheezing sound that must have passed for his laugh. "Well, ain't you a clever lad, and you can work under pressure. I think we may have a use for you after all. Come back during the day, tell whoever is at the door you're a new recruit, and that Slyde sent you."

"Yes, sir, I will! Thank you, sir."

When Slyde turned and stalked away, Azerick sprinted down the street as fast as his legs would carry him. He ran clear across the common quarter, into the squatter's' district, and all the way to the hidden entrance to his lair under the old tannery. He easily avoided his own traps, even moving as fast as he was, and dropped down into a pile of pillows he used as a chair. Azerick lay on his back puffing like a blacksmith's bellows and wiped at the sweat pouring down his face.

Now that he knew who and where, the only question remaining was how. He knew the why. His adoptive family was murdered because of greed and as an example to the other freelance thieves within the city who profited and stole more than they needed to survive. Jon's group were more like subsistence farmers, stealing just enough to get by. What little tax the guild could extort from them was a pittance; it surely was not enough to kill for, but what they took from Azerick was.

He would burn them. He would burn theirs like they burned his. Azerick wracked his brain for ways to accomplish his grisly revenge. He searched through every shred of knowledge it contained. He pulled his history and alchemy books from their place on the shelf and scoured through them, looking for historical precedents and forgotten formulas. He found several alchemic formulas for poisons and one to create a type of fire that stuck like honey to whatever it was cast upon, even water.

It would take several gold crowns to purchase the necessary ingredients to make what he needed, but he only had a few silver swords. The only crowns he had even seen were a few that had changed hands between his father and a customer with a large purchase.

He would have to make a score and a good one at that. He would buy only the ingredients, not the services, to mix the components. That alone saved an enormous amount of gold. But the components themselves would be expensive, and he would have to buy the equipment to mix them. Mortar and pestle, retort, scales, beakers, flasks, condensers, and several other glass items would come to a significant cost.

Azerick had the method of his vengeance formulated; now he must think on how to finance his operation. The estimated costs of his revenge were staggering and could keep him in comfort for a year or more, but he would place no limit on the price of justice.

CHAPTER 12

The gruff voice of an old sea dog greeted Azerick the moment he stepped through the door. "Welcome to Peg's Sailing Emporium."

Azerick looked across the room at a grizzled old man sitting behind a long counter running nearly the entire length of the left wall of the store.

"What can old Peg do for you today, young sir?"

"Good morn to you, Mister Peg. I am in need of some materials for my work."

"And what work might that be?" peg asked. "You're far too pasty for a sailing lad."

Azerick smiled and shook his head. "No sir, I haven't been a sailor for a couple of years now. I'm a chimney sweep. I need some strong but light rope and few other odds and ends."

The old shopkeeper nodded and described the various types of ropes, their advantages, and disadvantages. One in particular drew Azerick's eye.

"How much does this one cost, Master Peg?"

"Buttering me up with fancy titles won't get you in my good graces, lad, and it won't make me any more charitable in my price. It's fifty copper a foot, and that's a firm price."

Azerick looked downcast. He loved the look and feel of the rope, and the lighter his equipment the more loot he could carry out of the manor.

"Please, sir, I must have that rope or the master won't take me as his apprentice, and I need the training and the work," Azerick pleaded, giving the storeowner the sorriest waif eyes he could manage.

Unfortunately, the old sailor was unmoved. "Times are tough all around, son, and it would be even tougher if I went and gave out my merchandise to everyone with a sad tale. You said you were a sailing lad once. Why not go back out to sea? It's an honorable profession. Who did you sail with before?"

Azerick thought a moment, pondering whether he should use his father's name. He knew his father was a well-liked and respected captain, but that was before the false charge of high treason against the crown. He rolled the dice and took a chance.

"It was with Captain Darius Giles, sir, a good man, and no matter what anyone says he would never betray the crown. He was an honest and loyal man."

"Aye, that he was, lad. I knew him well. I sailed with him a bit before I retired from the open ocean. He gave me the loan to start this store and only charged a pittance in interest just to make it legit. I don't remember any lads as young as you would'a been on any of his boats even as a cabin boy. What was he to you that makes you speak of him with such devotion?"

"I'm his son, sir, and I did sail with him from time to time before…before he was murdered and they took everything my mother and I had and threw us out onto the street."

Azerick saw his words crack the stern façade in Peg's countenance. "That was a bad bit of business, lad, I can tell you. Bad enough business to chip a bit of charity even out of me. Where is your mother now, son? How does she fare these days?"

"Also gone, sir. Just over a year now."

"Damn it, boy, you're going to give me a reputation for softness I can't afford!" barked the old salt but with pity plainly evident in his voice. "How much coin do you have, and how much rope do you need?"

Azerick gave Peg the rest of his money and walked out with fifty feet of the remarkable silk rope and old Peg's best wishes on his "chimney sweeping." He had a feeling the old deckhand knew he would not be sweeping any chimneys with his new rope but had wished him luck anyway.

Azerick considered it a rather successful day as he carried his purchases in the bag he had bought at the clothing merchant's shop. His good fortune failed to hold though as a familiar voice accosted him.

"Hey, Carrot, Rolly, look what we have here," came Hugo's malicious voice.

"You broke my nose, you little runt," Carrot said, scowling at the young thief.

"And you made Hugo fall on me! Nearly crushed me he did! May even have busted a rib or two," accused Rolly.

"Shut up, Rolly, you idiot. What's in the bag, runt?"

"Nothing important, now leave me alone."

"I'll decide what's important. Now hand over the bag and we'll only beat you a little bit."

With a sigh, Azerick slid the bag off his shoulder and set it down behind him. He turned as if to open the bag but instead grabbed the strap with both hands and swung it as hard as he could into Hugo's face, catching Carrot right in the nose on the follow-through. He slung the bag back onto his shoulder and ran, hitting Rolly with his shoulder and spinning the youth around as he sprinted past.

With a curse from Hugo, all three ran in pursuit with Carrot holding his now twice-broken nose. Once again, Azerick found himself chased down the streets and alleys of the common quarter toward the old industrial district. He knew he could not run straight to his hideout, not only because he was afraid of giving away his best-kept secret, but because the three thugs were rapidly closing the lead on his slight head start.

He needed to either slow down his pursuers or lighten his load, so he slipped the bag off his shoulder as he sprinted around the corner of the next alley, stopped, and extracted the pry bar from the bag. He listened as the pounding footfalls drew closer and readied his weapon. Azerick lashed out with the pry bar, just as the three rounded the corner, and caught Rolly, who was the thinner and faster of the bunch, across the shin with the heavy length of steel.

With a loud cry of pain, Rolly tumbled face first onto the cobbled street, barely able to cushion his fall with his outflung hands. Hugo came next, tripped over Rolly's prone form, and crushed the already injured boy's face into the unyielding stone. Azerick swung the bar into

Carrot's stomach as he tried to jump over his two friends to avoid tripping over them while still holding his nose in an attempt to stanch the flow of blood.

The pry bar caught him in mid leap dead in the midriff and blasted the air from his lungs. The force of the expulsion created a spray of blood from Carrot's brutalized nose as he too plowed helplessly into the hard cobblestones. Hugo was on all fours trying to regain his feet and got a heavy wallop across the kidneys with the pry bar for his effort.

"Next time you see me, I strongly suggest you leave me the hell alone," Azerick warned the trio.

Azerick slipped the steel bar back into his sack and hoisted it onto his shoulder. He made for home with only curses and threats now chasing him as he ran down the alley, thinking to himself that one day those three were going to make him pull sharp steel, and not everyone would be walking away then.

He finally made it back to his home, tired but none the worse for wear, and took stock of his inventory. He pulled out the stiff metal wires, worked them with the tools he had, and made them into a set of acceptable lock picks. He practiced with them for hours on a couple of old locks he had scrounged up on one of his many forays until he could open them in a matter of seconds. In the evening, he put on his new clothes and scouted out the homes of the city's wealthier denizens trying to decide which ones had the most promise with the least risk.

Magus Aegir Illifan was sitting in his tower within Castle Stonemount studying an ancient tome about long-dead kings, queens, wizards, and conquerors in hopes of discovering a clue to the location of another ancient artifact when a luminous falcon flew through his open window.

Magus Illifan was in his mid-sixties with shoulder-length grey hair shot through with traces of brown, but he still moved and sounded like a man of middle years. He had once taught at the Academy, but he had decided to travel and study for several years before King Jarvin appointed him as one of his leading counselors and court mage.

That is Alleel's sending. They must have discovered something, the wizard thought.

The magus extended his arm for the magical messenger bird to land. As soon as the falcon lit upon his arm, it burst into tiny motes of light that drifted to the floor before disappearing, its message transferred to the recipient in a series of vivid images as soon as they touched.

"This is not good, not good at all," the wizard muttered to the empty room and rushed out in search of the king.

It took the wizard nearly thirty minutes to find King Jarvin. He eventually flagged down a serving maid who had just sent hot wine and bread to the king's library. He rushed toward the library to deliver his news to his liege. When he burst into the room, he found King Jarvin sitting in a high-backed chair across from Bishop Caalendor.

"Ah, Magus Illifan, please join us. The Bishop and I were just discussing some rumors of Dundalor's armor he was able to uncover within some scrolls in the church's archives. Have you any news of Captain Brellion's progress?" Jarvin asked his court mage.

"Yes, Your Majesty, but I fear it is not at all good. Captain Brellion and his party fought their way through to the citadel's vast underground caverns. They found the sorcerer king's deep chamber where sat a large suit of armor, the central piece comprising Dundalor's breastplate."

"So the sorcerer king had the breastplate all these years. Fantastic!" the bishop said, interrupting the wizard's oratory.

Aegir continued, "When Captain Brellion and his party approached the artifact, it, along with several other suits of armor, became animated and attacked his party. Several men were slain including the Sumaran, Khalar."

"That is most unfortunate. He was a good man and Captain Brellion's close friend, if memory serves," Jarvin said, bowing his head in a silent prayer for the fallen man.

"Your memory is correct, Your Majesty. They were able to defeat the magical constructs, including the one wearing Dundalor's breastplate, but not before Magus Alleel was severely injured. They interred the dead in the great chamber and carried their wounded as well as the artifact back to the surface; however, they were ambushed by a large group of unknown men barely a mile from the citadel. Magus Alleel regained consciousness just long enough to see Captain Brellion and several others fall and send me this message. I fear the breastplate has been lost," concluded the wizard.

"Damn it all to the abyss and back!" Jarvin shouted as he sprang to his feet and paced the room. "That is the third group I have lost on these expeditions. Are you sure it was humans and not orcs or goblins from the fortress?"

The magus shook his head. "Alleel was confident it was men and not beasts, sire. I was able to see what she saw in the last few moments of her life and concur with her observations."

"I haven't the men to spare on these hunts without anything to show for it. We must find a way to recover at least part of Dundalor's armor. If we cannot control it in its entirety, we can at least prevent my enemies from acquiring the complete suit. Gentlemen, we must obtain that armor at any cost," the king insisted.

"Of course, Your Majesty, but who else can we send? Your special guard is already severely short on men, and the Blackguard is in even more dire shape. It will take years to train and replace the slain blackguards, and their numbers were never great to begin with. I fear if we send any more of your personal guard your enemies may send an assassin," the hawk-faced bishop warned.

The weary king scratched at his beard before speaking. "I must think on this. Thank you for bringing me news, Magus. Allow me to ponder this alone for now, but if you conceive of any way to alleviate this problem, please come to me immediately. You two are my closest advisors, and I need your good counsel now more than ever."

The king dismissed his advisors and slumped back down in his chair, swirling his wine, and thinking on the unfortunate report just brought to him.

CHAPTER 13

Azerick identified three splendid houses that often had the shutters open on the upper floors to let in the evening air, had fences low enough to scale with ease, and few guards. They each had a great deal of flora growing in the manicured lawns the wealthy took so much pride in but also provided excellent concealment for would-be burglars.

Now he needed to find out when the inhabitants of the elaborate homes would be away for at least a few hours in the evening so he could complete his audacious raid. Some daring thieves would break in even when the owners were at home, and the most heartless would slay them without a thought if they were unfortunate enough to wake and confront the intruder. But even in these hard times, that was a rare occurrence.

You could not have too many of the wealthy or noble families being murdered, or that would cause a great crackdown on the thieves' guild, and the guild masters were not about to let that happen. More than once, justice for a slain noble or rich merchant came not from the Watch but from the guild itself. The overzealous thief's body would be found dead, hanging from the statue outside the Watch's headquarters or the elaborate iron gate of the dead man's manor itself, often with a note of confession and apology written in the hand of the thief, or a guild boss if the murderer was illiterate.

This was of no concern to Azerick. He would run like the wind before confronting anyone within the house. He continued to case the fine homes and kept an ear to the streets.

Azerick frequented the taverns in the area and offered himself as cheap day labor to the houses. It was by doing this that he was able to determine the perfect time to pull off his heist.

A stable boy had come down too sick to muck out the owner's stables, so Azerick was able to get hired on by the house's majordomo to clean them out.

While eating a lunch provided by the kitchen staff, he listened to their gossip hoping to learn something useful. Azerick had tired of hearing about the latest tryst of the master or of the mistress when the scullery maids finally brought up a topic of interest.

It seemed there was a ball or gathering of some kind next week at the duke's castle, and the mister and missus would be attending until late in the evening. This was interesting indeed. Today was his last day of work. The regular stable boy would be back tomorrow, which would be plenty of time for everyone to forget all about him.

Azerick cased the manor house from the outside as best he could until a staff member chased him back to the stables. He knew the layout of the kitchen and even the hall and a few rooms beyond it by "accidentally" taking a wrong turn to use the privy. At the end of his workday, he collected his few coppers and returned to his own home beneath the streets.

He had slept in the stable for the three days he had worked and took special care to study the movements of the six guards patrolling the outside grounds. The master of the house, who was a sportsman, kept several hunting dogs on the premises. This could be a problem and a gamble he would not normally take, but he knew this house as he knew no other and so decided it was still worth the increased risk. He thought of how he could neutralize the threat of the dogs then lay down on his pallet and slept, reasonably certain of his solution to the dog problem.

The week passed, but far too slowly for Azerick's taste. He spent nearly the entire time reading and practicing his lock picking skills. He made no forays into the streets, not wanting to risk being caught, injure himself, or in any way jeopardize his plans.

Azerick stole from his dark den about an hour before midnight, which should have put him at the eastern-facing fence about a quarter to the hour. He had to make a couple of detours and hide in the shadows of an alley or building a few times to avoid the Watch and other pedestrians.

Upon entering the lower nobles' quarter, he avoided everyone, city watch or not. He found it ironic that he was in the very quarter he had once lived in, its inhabitants his equals, only to return in order to rob them. Dressed in his new clothes, he was just another shadow gliding down the street or across the side of a building.

Azerick had just made it to the manor house as the distant bell toll sounded the hour. He watched the fence until he saw the house guard stroll past. A few minutes later, he was over the wall and on the grounds of the manicured lawn. He darted between sculpted hedges toward the side of the grand house itself.

Plastered smooth, the walls gave him nothing to grip to climb up. Instead, he skulked along the side of the house until he came to a mature maple tree that brushed up against the wall. Azerick made the easy climb nearly to the top, which still left him a full story below the mansion's roof. However, it put him close enough to try to loop his silk rope over one of the decorative crenellations.

It took him nearly a half dozen tries before he was able to lasso one. Once he knew his rope was secure, Azerick swung out of the tree and landed lightly on the side of the house. That was the plan anyway. Instead, he twisted in mid-flight and struck the wall solidly with his left shoulder.

Azerick had just begun his careful climb up the side of the building when the second guard reached the spot where he had scaled the stone and wrought-iron fence. Unfortunately, this guard had one of the master's hounds with him, which instantly perked up at the new scent running across the lawn.

"What is it, boy? What do you scent?" the guard asked the hound as it followed Azerick's trail.

The hound followed the unknown scent from the fence, around the fancy hedges, and along the wall to the big maple tree, and was now sniffing along the base of the tree Azerick had just vacated a moment before.

The young intruder had prepared for this contingency. Fortunately, he was also clever enough to have coiled the excess rope around his neck and shoulder instead of leaving it to dangle down the wall for the guard to see and the hound to smell.

Bracing his feet against the wall and wrapping a loop of rope around his hand, Azerick slowly worked the drawstrings loose on the pouch hanging from his belt and reached inside. He grabbed a small fistful of finely ground red powder he had purchased with his last few coins and several promises to Azeel, and tossed it out toward the tree and the dog beneath it.

The hound continued to circle the tree, snuffling loudly until it found some of the powerful spice Azeel actually put on his food. It was so strong, just carrying it in the bag nearly brought tears to Azerick's eyes.

The hound got just one whiff of the powder up its super-sensitive nose and went into a sneezing fit, running and rubbing its muzzle and face in the grass.

"What is it, boy? What'd ya get a hold of?" the guard asked, running after the dog as it pawed at its nose to no avail.

Once they were sufficiently distracted, Azerick continued his ascent up the side of the house. It took less than a minute for him to reach the summit and pull himself over the decorative crenellation and onto the roof. Sweating profusely, he took a minute to rest with his back against the stone.

Azerick caught his breath and wiped the sweat from his brow. Unfortunately, it was with the same hand he had used to throw the noxious spice at the dog. With his eyes burning and watering, he cursed Azeel and his devil spice from the abyss, though only halfheartedly, knowing it had saved him from the dog and may well save him again if he ran across more dogs inside or on the way out.

Azerick wiped his stricken eyes clean with his untainted sleeve and made his way across the roof once his eyes cleared enough to carry on with his mission. He went to a trapdoor, but he found it locked with no keyhole for him to attempt to pick.

He took his piece of flat steel, jammed it between the edge of the door and the wall and worked it around the thin gap of the trapdoor. Azerick located the simple bolt holding the portal shut, but he had no room to work the bar back. The thief gave up this approach without remorse, not expecting for an instant that access would be so easy.

Azerick hunched over as he ran to the wall opposite the side he had climbed. He came to a corner where a series of rooms expanded from the main structure, forming a separate wing.

Azerick fastened his rope to the roof once again and climbed down the L-shaped corner. He stopped at a shuttered window and looped the rope under his thighs and made an uncomfortable but stable seat that left his hands free to work. He took out his slim length of steel once again and slipped it between the two shutters. With an upward flick of his wrist, he tripped the latch that secured them and climbed inside.

It was dark, but the well-lit streets allowed enough light for his night-adjusted eyes to make out the larger details. The room was well kept and the bed perfectly made with no personal effects left out. He pulled his rope into the room and left it coiled on the floor below the open window. He thought about closing the shutter as he had found it, but that would put the room into total darkness. Azerick paused a moment to listen for any sounds or alarm that he may have raised by his intrusion. He heard nothing but the pounding of his own blood through his ears. He took several deep breaths to calm himself before making a closer inspection of the room.

Azerick stepped quietly across the bedchamber to a large wardrobe. Slowly opening it, he peered inside and found nothing but empty space. He opened several drawers of a dresser and found the same.

It must be a guest room. Just my luck.

A truly lucky thief would have climbed right into the master's bedroom and found piles of jewels that had not matched the lady's evening attire laying on top of the nightstand just waiting to be plucked up and dropped into his bag. Nevertheless, Azerick had never considered himself terribly lucky, and it continued to hold true tonight.

Azerick crossed the room and listened at the door. Still no sounds emanated from within the house. He pulled the handle down ever so slowly and eased the door open. The ornate, solid-wood door opened on well-oiled, perfectly balanced hinges without a sound. Azerick darted his head out and checked both directions of the hall. The floor was clear as far as he could see.

He stepped out into the carpeted hall, silent as a ghost. The young thief closed the door behind him but did not latch it. With his luck, it would lock behind him and he would have to take precious minutes picking the lock. Azerick looked at the lock and was reasonably confident he could pick it if he had to but would rather not find out. There were two more doors on each side of the hallway with a large set of double doors at the end.

He slipped past the two sets of doors on the side figuring the double doors to be the master and lady's bedroom. Once again, he gently pulled down on the highly polished brass door handle. It was locked. With a quick glance over his shoulder, Azerick went to work on the lock with his picks. Unlike the locks he practiced on, this one was of a better quality, but it was just a bedroom door not the king's treasury.

In a few minutes, he heard the satisfying click of the lock surrendering to his picks. Azerick gently closed the door behind him as he entered the large, elaborate bedroom. Dim light filtered through the ornate plate-glass window. The window alone would pay for everything he needed with a fair bit left over.

Azerick spied the decorative jewelry box sitting out on a bureau made of rich mahogany. It was an impressive affair made of gold and silver with elaborate scrollwork swirling between polished stones affixed to a lid inlaid with ivory. Azerick reached his trembling hands out to take the entire box then stopped.

Something felt wrong in the air. He could feel a sort of static making the hairs on the back of his hands stand on end. His brain conjured the memory of the strange feeling he got just before the strong shock jolted the groom. He turned his head left and right, looking at the fancy box out of the corners of his eyes. He could just make out a faint, glowing, swirling pattern of light similar to smoke, twisting and writhing like snakes around the box.

He tried to study the strange emanations coming from the box, but his eyes failed to decipher its mysteries. Just as he had done with the silvery strands of energy before, he closed his eyes and focused on the strange swirling webs of energy surrounding the box. He reached out to it with his thoughts but did not touch it. It was a strange sensation similar to what he felt when he made the light in the dark passage of his home, only this filled him with an enormous sense of unease. He closed off all of his other physical senses: seeing, hearing, and feeling. He saw, felt, and heard only with his mind.

With his hands held out before him, he slowly began to unravel the smoky webs of energy without ever touching them. Azerick could not fathom how he was able to see and feel the emanations from the box, but he knew he somehow possessed some intrinsic understanding for unraveling its mystery even though he did not really understand what it was. He knew it was a trap of some kind, magic to be sure, but he went about unlocking it like he would a lock made of common iron, only his mind was the pick and of far better quality than the crude set he had fashioned out of metal.

After what seemed an eternity, he knew he was done and that the box no longer posed a threat. Azerick thought of stuffing the whole thing in his bag, but it was large and he did not want to take anything so bulky on a run like this. It had a small lock built into the elaborate wood and silver front.

Azerick slid his knife blade in the tiny gap between the box and the lid and gently pried it open. The top popped open with a slight cracking of wood. He lifted the lid and stared for a moment at the glittering jewels set in gold.

Rings adorned with rubies, emeralds, and diamonds winked at him, reflecting even the tiniest light within the room. Necklaces of elaborate designs and of varying lengths and thickness lay coiled in felt-lined nooks.

He lifted out the top shelf and poured the contents into his bag, then pulled out each of the three drawers and did the same. He looked around the room but saw nothing else within his immediate view worth taking that was small enough to carry in his bag.

Azerick made a quick circuit around the room but still found nothing of interest. He did take a moment to stuff a handful of silk shirts and well-made trousers into his bag as well as a fur-lined cloak he found in the master's large standing closet.

He crossed the room back to the big double doors and slowly pulled them open, more than eager to make his escape. As Azerick opened the door, ready to duck back into the hallway, he found himself face to face with the stubble-bearded countenance of one of the house guards.

With a look of utter surprise on both of their faces, each reached for a weapon at their hip. The guard drew his short sword, but Azerick was faster. He flung another handful of the fiery red powder straight into the eyes of the unfortunate guard.

The surprised man let out a loud curse, dropped his blade at his feet, and fell back, wiping at his eyes with his hands as he shouted an alarm that was repeated throughout the house. Azerick darted past him and ran down the hall and into the guest room where he had made his entrance.

The stricken guard burst into the room behind the intruder just as he reached his rope. Azerick did not bother to even slow down on his dash across the room toward the open window. He grabbed the rope at a dead run, his momentum swinging him out of the window and into the darkness beyond.

The guard, with his eyes still burning and nose running profusely, loped to the window ledge. Azerick caught him dead in the chest with both feet as he swung back through the window and brutally cut short the man's shouting.

The impact drove the guard back into the guest room, rolling him halfway across the chamber, and leaving him sprawled in a heap. Azerick slid down his rope so fast it burned his hands. He hit the ground and performed a somersault before springing back onto his feet. With a skillful twist and tug, his rope let loose from where it was anchored at the top of the mansion. Azerick slipped the bag off his shoulder and stuffed the rope inside before tearing off across the yard.

The angry shouts of men and the braying of hounds issued from around the corner of the manor house. Men and dogs rounded the building and took up a hasty but determined pursuit. Azerick tore the bag holding the rest of the red spice from his belt and upended it behind him, covering his tracks and slowing the dogs. He came to the stone and wrought-iron wall and scaled it like a cat treed by dogs, which was not far from the truth.

He paused for just a moment before jumping down the opposite side onto the street and saw that the hounds did indeed get a snoutful of the powder that wreaked so such havoc on their sensitive noses. With a grin of triumph, he dropped lightly to the street and sprinted down the cobbled avenue then turned down the dark alleyways. In just a matter of moments, the shrieking whistles of the city watch grew fainter as he made his way back to his hideout.

Azerick sat on his pallet with the glittering pile of jewels between his legs. He knew he could get a good price from Azeel, if the merchant had that much money on hand. He was certain the fence had it despite the constant lamenting about his dire financial straits. He would have to. Azerick did not know how much everything he needed was going to cost, but poison like the one he required did not come cheap, and neither did the alchemic equipment needed to make it.

Azerick had considered buying the poison outright, avoiding the cost of the equipment and saving a bit of gold, but he feared leaving a trail of any kind that someone could follow back to him. If the thieves' guild ever got so much as a hint that he played a part in what he was going to do, his life would be forfeit, assuming he even succeeded.

Exhaustion came on with surprising suddenness now that the rush of excitement, and maybe just a bit of fear, had worn off. He scooped the loot back into his bag and instantly fell asleep.

CHAPTER 14

Morning came quickly, and Azerick rolled off his pallet to start the day. At least he thought it was morning. He really needed to get an hourglass or clock of some kind. He decided it was best to wait a few days before seeing Azeel with last evening's haul. His stomach reminded him that he needed to get some food. Azerick decided to take one of the more simple gold necklaces to sell and get himself enough money to stock his larder for a few days.

He went to the merchant's shop, and Azeel broke into a big grin as soon as Azerick entered. "Ah, my favorite customer has come back. I heard your late evening meal turned out especially well."

"I am sure I have no idea what you're talking about, Azeel."

"Oh really? I thought maybe it was you who dined on some minor lord's fare last night up in the rich quarter. I heard the meat was especially fine, but the guards and their dogs found it a bit too spicy for their taste. But you wouldn't know anything about that, would you?" Azeel asked under his bushy raised eyebrows.

"As it so happens, I found the food especially tasty once a little special seasoning was added. In fact, I found it so good I brought you back an appetizer," Azerick said grinning and handed the gold chain over to Azeel's awaiting palm.

"Hmm, that does look good."

Azeel brought out a small balance scale, placed the gold chain in one of the brass disks, and started placing small iron weights on the other. Once the scale reached its balance, Azeel gave him a price.

"It's a nice chain, decent weight, good gold if somewhat plain. I'll give you three gold crowns for it."

"I'll take it, but that makes us square for that horrid spice you sold me."

"Bah, that's a hard bargain for good spice, but all right. So this is just an appetizer you say, and from what I've heard, a tiny little bite it is, eh?"

"Yes, it is a very tiny bite and rather plain in flavor compared to the rest. Do you think you will have the money to cover it, or will I need to see someone else?"

Azeel frantically waved his hands. "No, no, don't go anywhere else with it! Just wait a couple weeks. I already had a constable asking about it when I opened up, but don't you worry about old Azeel being short of coin. I want that meal and every course served. I am the only one who will come close to giving you a fair price. What are you going to do with that much gold anyway, if I may be so bold to ask?"

"I have to buy some equipment for my studies, and it is going to be quite expensive. The rest, if there is any left, will get me through the winter in reasonable comfort."

Azeel's face took on a very interested expression. "What kind of equipment is going to cost that kind of gold? If you tell me, perhaps we can come to an agreement that will benefit us both, eh?"

"I need a complete alchemic set. I have a book on alchemy, and I wanted to start working with it. I don't want to be a thief forever, and anyone who can brew some decent potions can make a pretty good living for an honest man."

"Mayhap I can get you this and we can make a good deal. Maybe with less coin leaving both of our pockets, eh? You come back in about ten days and we show each other what we got and make a deal."

"Sounds good to me. Take care, Azeel. Oh, Azeel, not one word to anyone about the jewelry or that equipment, right?"

"The only thing greater than Azeel's honesty is his discretion, gods be witness if I am lying," the fence replied.

Azerick left the pawnbroker and pondered his words, unable to determine if they were reassuring or not. After a few minutes, he gave it up as a mystery that only time would answer. With a coin pouch heavier than he had had in some time, Azerick headed to the market district. Once there, he stocked up on enough food to warrant buying another bag to carry it all.

He stuffed the bag full with a smoked ham, several loaves of fresh bread, wheels of cheese, fresh fruits, and a few vegetables on top. He also bought a kettle, tea, coffee, sugar, salt, pepper, and a few other seasonings he was not familiar with but which the merchant assured him were necessary for decent food. Definitely none of Azeel's spicy red pepper made its way into the bag, however.

Azerick took all this back to his home, following a circuitous route and constantly looking over his shoulder. Occasionally he would duck into an alley or a doorway and wait to see if anyone passed by who may be trailing him, but no one ever did. Over the next several days, he turned it into a routine he maintained with exceptional vigilance. No one must ever discover his lair.

Once safely ensconced in his home, he packed the cupboard he had made full with the food he had bought. There was a small stove built into the wall that vented its smoke into the sewer. Azerick found it rather clever as it was the best place for a chimney with the least likelihood of discovery. He would really need it come full winter. It was already starting to get cold in the evenings. He boiled some water in his new kettle, made some tea, and settled in for a couple of weeks of routine boredom while the Watch's aggressive investigation of the break-in slowly ground down to a crawl and was eventually filed as unsolved.

Azerick let two weeks pass before he brought the rest of his cache to Azeel. He had stopped by on occasion and was assured by the merchant that he would have what he was looking for when Azerick brought in the jewelry.

He made his way through the city once again, picking his way randomly through the squatters' quarter then navigating through the common quarter to Azeel's with his precious prize stuffed inside his shirt. Azerick found it remarkable that so much wealth was so easy to conceal and transport. He wondered why people would place such value on what were essentially useless items. Gems were nothing more than pretty bits of glass and gold was useless for forging blades or armor. They were valuable to him only because he would be able to get something of true worth—revenge.

Azerick finally reached Azeel's shop and went inside once he saw the last customer leave. Azeel flashed him his usual friendly smile, walked past him, and bolted the door.

"You have it today, don't you boy? Let's see what you have for Azeel, eh."

"You have what I asked for?"

"Of course, my friend, of course. What Azeel says he will get he gets," the fence said with an incredulous look, as if anyone should ever doubt him. "Here, it is a very nice set," he said and placed a small trunk on the table.

The trunk was about thirty inches long, twenty inches tall, and eighteen inches deep. Some sort of reptile skin covered the case, silver cusps protected the corners, and an elaborately engraved ivory handle was secured at the top.

"Behold every alchemist's dream," he said as he popped open the silver clasps holding the two sides together with a flourish.

Inside was the grandest set of glassware Azerick had ever seen. A crystal-clear retort, beakers, glass rods, three sizes of hourglasses, some clear glass containers, opaque ceramic flasks, a small balance scale with counterweights, oil-fueled burners, rubber hoses, glass tubes, and a marble mortar and pestle. It took Azerick all of his will to resist showing his amazement and giving Azeel the upper hand in their inevitable negotiations.

"I think it will suffice, although it is a bit more than I was thinking of, cumbersome-looking really," Azerick said and even managed a yawn just for effect.

A broad grin stretched across Azeel's swarthy face. "Oh ho, you have started the duel already, have you? Very well, let me see this paste and tin you call jewelry. Mayhap you will have to do a second run to earn this magnificent glass and crystal."

Azerick pulled the bag of jewels out of his shirt and spread them on the counter. He had spent several hours polishing the gold and silver and the stones they held to a brilliant shine.

"It is fortunate we are inside your gloomy shop and not outside lest the brilliance of these dazzling jewels burn out your eyes. Might be that you will have to take out a second mortgage on whatever shanty you call a house to even make me a fair offer, even with the scullery maid's cookware you have in that fish-scaled box."

"A shack you say! Azeel is no street rat taking shelter in whatever shipping crate he can drag off to an alley to sleep in! I own, own mind you, a beautiful home of stone, plaster, and marble. Why, Azeel's neighbors are none other than Counselor Trant and Barishan the moneylender!" Azeel squealed with indignity, his face coloring brightly.

"Good, then you should have no problem meeting my price for this rare collection. I bet your wife is looking forward to wearing a few of the pieces herself," Azerick slyly replied.

Azeel turned even more scarlet as his eyes crossed and his heavy brows drew together before he burst out in loud, raucous laughter. "You got me, boy, right in the pride! Oh the humility, the great barterer Azeel is brought down by a lowly street rat not old enough to shave."

"I could shave if I wanted to!" Azerick declared with indignation and rubbed the soft hint of stubble on his chin.

"Yes, yes, lad, sure you can. Maybe in a year or two Azeel will gift you with a nice razor, eh?"

Azerick and Azeel haggled over the price he would pay in addition to the fantastic alchemic set. The crafty fence finally relented, agreeing that the jewelry was all of exquisite quality and gave Azerick an amount that was close to what he had wanted, which was very good haggling on the youth's part.

Azerick left Azeel's shop with an impressive amount of coin, lugging his newest and finest acquisition. He took a route back to his home that was far from direct, but it kept him away from the general populace. The last thing he wanted right now was to run into Hugo and his band. He would defend his precious cargo with his life although preferably with someone else's life. He would gut all three of them rather than give up the alchemic set. However, luck was with him for a change. He made it safely back to his lair, using all his guile and security sense to ensure no one followed him.

He spent the rest of the day and much of the evening setting up the equipment and studying his book, reminding himself what each piece was and how to use it.

The next day, he went to a bazaar in another section of the city and found a shop called the Hedge Witches' Cauldron. Strange scents and sights accosted him the moment he entered. Eyes, insects, and unidentifiable objects floated in some kind of preserving agent, and purportedly magic charms to bring luck, love, or good fortune lined shelves and hung from pegs. An old crone sat in a corner stroking a cat (a black one of course) and studied him through cataract-impaired eyes as he entered.

"What brings you in, young sir? Is there a young lass you wish to have fall in love with you, or maybe you want a charm to bring you great wealth, hmm? With wealth, a man has no need for a charm to get a girl to lay with him." The old crone burst out in a cackle of wild laughter at her own satirical bit of wisdom.

"No, old woman, I need neither fake charms nor any other snake oil potions you might sell one of the local rubes. I require dream lily, blackwort, and clove extract." Azerick also named several other compounds he needed for his work. "Can you supply them?"

Azerick had a great distaste for people who were stupid enough or gullible enough to think that some bit of bone, wood, metal, or strange liquids were the answers to all of their woes. A man had to find his own answers and create his own solutions, and those solutions were found in hard work and education. Answers were found in books of knowledge, in one's imagination, and by possessing the determination to make those images come to fruition.

"Fake charms and potions, eh, that's what you think, eh? What do you know about magic, boy, about power?"

"Power is found in a person's heart and mind. It is within themselves if they have the courage to use it," he answered shortly.

"Aye, you're partly right there, but the problem with being partly right is that you are also partly wrong," crowed the old woman as she hobbled over to him, spilling her cat off her lap and onto the floor. "But there are other sources of power, sources that do not take heart or courage to wield. Many a cold or cowardly man has wielded such power and still does."

Azerick narrowed his eyes in contemplation. "You mean wizards. Yes, there are wizards, but they are at the Academy or hiding away in the Black Tower. They are not out crafting tokens and talismans and hawking them on street corners like some fat baker selling his meat pies. I have no interest in wizards or their foul sorceries. Do you have what I need or no?"

"Aye, I got what you want. Give me a moment to fetch it. I hope you have a lot of coin, boy. Many of those are rare and expensive things you ask for. Powerful too if used correctly. Deadly if used wrong," the witch warned.

"I have enough gold. Please fetch what I asked for."

"Oh, it's please now, is it? Such a gentleman you are," the crone cackled as she shuffled away into a back room.

The old woman appeared nearly twenty minutes later. Azerick was beginning to wonder if she had suffered a bout of dementia and had forgotten what she was looking for when she shuffled back into the main room with several paper-wrapped packages.

"Mind you know what you are doing, boy; powerful and deadly, I warn you."

"I know my business, madam, and am quite familiar with the dangers."

Azerick paid for his reagents, which cost a good portion of his wealth although he was not particular taken aback. He had researched his plan and knew it would be expensive, and he was determined to put it to use no matter the cost. He turned and walked to the door and was about to take his leave when the old woman spoke to him one last time.

"There is more power in you than heart and mind, boy, and it will set you on a path of great knowledge and danger. Best be prepared. Some people take the path, but sometimes the path takes them."

"What do you mean by that?" Azerick asked, turning to face the crazy old crone, but there was no one there, just the black cat sitting on the chair belonging to the old woman.

He turned back around and was starting to walk out when he saw the black cat lying in the window catching the warm rays of sun streaming through the glass. He looked back at the cat in the chair and then to the cat in the window. Azerick convinced himself that the crone must have had two cats, walked out, and went back home feeling just a bit unsettled by the entire event. Once back in his personal laboratory, he went to work grinding the dream lily and blackwort and firing up his burner. He took painstaking care to follow the directions in his book. It was a complicated process and the slightest mistake would create an unusable concoction or an undesirable result.

Azerick worked late into the night preparing as much as he could. Distilling the dream lily required it to simmer for several hours before he could continue, so he set his burner and went to work on his makeshift water clock. He took a glass tube and filled it with water to the hash mark that indicated four hours and placed it on the pan of a large, homemade balance scale. He weighed down the other side with a few weights to counterbalance the weight of the water-filled glass tube and placed a small bell beneath the weighted end. As the water slowly ran out of the tube, the weighted end of the scale would drop, ring the bell, and with any luck, wake him up in time to continue his work. Once all was prepared, he went to his pallet and fell asleep.

What seemed like only an instant later, the ding of the small bell placed under the balance scale woke him. He was pleasantly surprised to find that it had worked, although when he glanced at the hourglass, he saw that it had gone off about twenty minutes later than he had anticipated. That was fine since he had given it nearly an hour for margin of error.

He checked his equipment and brewing potion and saw that it still had at least forty minutes before he could move on to the next stage. Once satisfied everything was proceeding well, he fixed himself breakfast.

Azerick continued his work for another three and a half days, checking and rechecking his figures, measurements, and processes, verifying at each stage that his brew matched the color and consistency of the descriptions in his book. He maintained his strict routine and diligence throughout the mentally fatiguing brewing process. He could see why alchemists and poisoners charged such an exorbitant sum to create substances like this.

CHAPTER 15

A zerick fired up his alchemic set and went to work on the second type of brew he needed. This one was especially dangerous in that it was extremely flammable, and any mistake could incinerate him, his precious laboratory set, rugs, books, and just about everything else in the room. It was an extraction of common lamp oil, distillated coal tar and other ingredients to make it more viscous. The powdered dragon stone made it burn with a heat that would melt iron, crack stone, and be impossible to put out with water.

The work was ten times as nerve-wracking as making the sleep poison had been. Azerick dared not rely on his makeshift alarm clock and sleep, so he stayed awake the entire night, not taking his eyes off the bubbling brew. He made some strong tea and passed the night away formulating the plan for his first revenge.

By the next night, his combustible concoction was finished. He had brewed enough of it to fill four earthen mugs. Azerick slept the rest of the night and well into the afternoon the next day. When Azerick awoke, he had no idea what time it was. He glanced at his large hourglass, but when it had run out only the gods knew.

"Fat lot of good that did," Azerick grumbled as he went to check the hour.

He poked his head out of the trapdoor leading into the old, burned-out tannery and saw it was late afternoon. He then went back inside and fixed himself some coffee and dinner. Azerick found himself lost in reminiscences as he sat and stared at his home-brewed liquids. His mind conjured images of his parents, Jon Locke, and the others. He thought about how they died for no reason other than someone else's greed or cowardliness. Were his motivations any better? What about the dreams he had, urging him to take revenge?

"I don't care," Azerick growled. "If this makes me no better than their killers, then so be it. I never claimed to be better."

At around two in the morning, Azerick loaded a packsack with some small candles, the earthen jugs of demon fire, and the iron spikes he had found at the burned-out ruins where his friends died. He strapped on his knife and slung the wineskin over his shoulder. Before he left, he doused his shirtfront with untainted wine, then struck out into the night, his mind filled with thoughts of vengeance and his heart full of justice, although some might call it murder.

Azerick moved slowly and stealthily across the city until he occupied the alley across from the house in which he had seen Merik and the other thieves enter. Once again, two men stood in the doorway watching the streets for anyone who did not belong there or thought to cause trouble.

"You are going to see someone tonight, friend. You can bet on that," Azerick whispered under his breath.

Azerick looked around to make sure no one saw him before he wanted them to, carefully stashed his bag of equipment, headed back into the alley, and circled the block until he came out up the street from the guild house. He slipped the wineskin off his shoulder, took it in hand, and staggered down the street toward his target, walking a swerving path that took him right by the men guarding the door.

"Hey you, boy, what are you doing out here?" demanded one of the men at the door.

"Hmm, what here? I'm just walking, taking in some air," Azerick slurred.

"Damn, boy, you smell like a tavern. Give me that." The thug snatched the wine from Azerick's hand. "You've had enough, I think. Besides, you're too young to be drinking like that anyway."

"Hey, give that back, that's mine," Azerick complained as he made a lurching grab for the wineskin.

"Get out of here before I give you a lot worse than my boot, boy!" the guard threatened, pushing him to the ground.

The other thief kicked him in his backside as Azerick tried to regain his feet, which sent him sprawling once again into the street.

"Bastards," Azerick mumbled as he staggered away.

He circled around the block, ducked back into the distant end of an alley, then crept up to the entrance just down and across the street from the guild house. Azerick had just gotten back into position when the guards slumped to the ground, one with his back pressed against the doorjamb, the other laid out with his head propped against the door.

Azerick walked across the street and recovered the wineskin still clutched in the hand of one of the comatose men. He then slipped along the side of the house down a narrow passage toward the back of the thieves' den, certain there was more than one entrance needing guarded. As he turned the corner at the back of the house, he felt a knife pressed into his ribs.

"What are you doing here, boy?" came a voice hidden in the deep shadows.

Azerick replied nervously but confidently, "Slyde sent me, sir. Said he found this fine wine in some uppity lord's house and thought you might want a taste on this cold night."

"Why didn't he bring it hisself?" the man asked.

"Said he and Merik had a thing tonight, he did. He didn't tell me nothin' though. I just run errands for them, but he and Merik says they are gonna teach me everything they know and take me with 'em on jobs," Azerick answered.

"Well you done as you were told, boy, now get outta here with ya," the man ordered with a lazy swipe of his boot.

Azerick ducked around the corner and waited. Within minutes, he heard the thump of the thief's body hitting the ground. He retrieved his wineskin from the unconscious door guard before crossing back to the alley for his bag. Azerick pulled out the iron spikes before hefting his bag onto his shoulder.

He stayed in the alley for a few minutes studying the street and the house. After seeing no sign of activity, he crossed back to the house with the unconscious guards. He shoved an iron spike between the door and its frame, wedging it closed so no one could open it from the inside.

Azerick then made his way to the back of the house and secured that door with a second spike. He gently set his bag down and pulled out one of the clay jugs of liquid fire. He pulled the stopper and sloshed its contents upon the door, wall, and sleeping guard. He pulled out two of the other pots and emptied them along the side of the house in the alley.

The building next to it was made of brick and did not appear to be a dwelling of any kind. Azerick hoped it would not burn, but if it did, it did not look like anyone lived in it. In fact, most of the buildings appeared to be workplaces of some kind. He guessed not many people wanted to live next to a den of thieves.

He went back to the rear of the house, pulled out a small candle, broke a bit off the end, lit it, and set it on the iron spike wedged in the door. When the flame consumed enough of the candle, it would touch off the liquid, incinerating the house and every thief in it. They would all burn just like Jon, William, Patrick, little Beth, and the others.

He set the same sort of candle-type fuse on the side of the house then made his way to the front. He poured the contents of the last clay jugs around the front of the house and set his candle fuse before disappearing back into the alley across the street.

Azerick waited and watched the little flame burn on the candle for several minutes before it finally reached the deadly liquid now soaked into the wood and brick of the house. The instant the flame burned close enough, the entire street lit up in a brilliant glow of orange light. The fire was so intense it made him night-blind for several minutes.

Flames raced across the wooden door and porch while the brick started to crack under the intense heat. A moment later, another whoosh of super-heated air sounded in conjunction with a second flash of light from behind the house followed almost immediately by the ignition of the demon fire in the narrow alley.

White-hot flames consumed the two guards who had stood watch at the door. The slight evening breeze blew the smell of smoke and charred flesh to Azerick's hiding place, but to him it was the sweet smell of vengeance, although he had not thought that justice would nearly make him gag.

A few people were now walking up the street to see what was happening. In the distance, Azerick heard the cries of 'Fire!' Hellishly intense flames nearly engulfed the entire house as the porch collapsed in on itself, burying the remains of the two men who had been guarding the door. Azerick imagined a similar fate had befallen the guard at the rear of the house as well.

A crowd was now beginning to form. People watched the dancing flames, several running to nearby inns, or perhaps homes, and coming back with buckets. A horse-drawn wagon with one of the large cisterns in it that Azerick had seen trying to douse the flames of the fire that took his friends and home came racing down the street, a bell clanging in warning for people to clear the way. It stopped on the far side of the street directly across from the burning house.

Men jumped off, opened a valve, and started filling buckets and thrusting them into waiting hands. The crowd threw pails of water onto the flames in hopes of extinguishing them. However, this was no ordinary fire. When the water struck the flames, instead of smothering them, it only served to cause the fire to flare up and spread. Now, thin rivulets of fire were crawling out into the cobblestone street.

One of the men operating the fire wagon called for the bucket brigade to stop throwing water on the flames at the same time a scream and the shattering of glass sounded from a second-story window. A man, his back wreathed in flames, struck the ground rolling. Like out of a nightmare, the burning man jumped to his feet, and in a panic, started to run right toward the alley from where Azerick was watching the chaos unfold.

The crowd cried out in horror as they jumped out of the terrified man's path. Two of the firefighters grabbed heavy leather cloaks and rushed after him in hopes of smothering the flames enshrouding the man's form.

Azerick stared at the horrifying sight rushing toward him and knew in an instant the man was Merik. Without pausing to think, he ripped off his own dark cloak and ran at him even as Merik and the two firefighters ran toward him.

Azerick shoved the cloak out in front of him and wrapped Merik up within its folds as they collided. He slowed the panicked man long enough for the two men with their leather cloaks to catch him from the rear. Merik was already on his way to the ground when the two men threw their cloaks atop the burning figure, smothering the flames beneath the heavy leather.

"That was a brave thing you done, boy. Might be that the constable may have a small reward for you," one of the men told him as he held his cloak over Merik's smoldering form.

Azerick did not meet the men's gazes. Instead, he grabbed his scorched cloak, ran down the alley, snatched up his bag, and retreated into the night leaving behind the shouts of the firemen telling him to come back.

The people in the streets saw a hero risk his own safety and tackle a burning man to help smother the flames, but no one saw the knife Azerick was gripping in his other hand, or how that blade had come away bloody when he ran off.

Azerick ran until he thought his lungs would burst before he even started to slow down. With heavy breaths, he walked along the docks, stuffed his cloak and several stones into his bag, and tossed the entire bundle into the harbor.

He turned and started to walk back home, slinking through the shadowed streets and alleys that were such a natural part of his environment. The young assassin had just gotten control of his rapid breathing and racing heart when an arm wrapped around his throat with a vice-like grip and pulled him into one of the buildings near the docks. A hand clamped over his mouth with equal force.

"Not a peep, boy, if you want to live longer than the next three seconds," came the raspy voice of the man who now had him at his mercy.

The hand dropped away from his mouth as the man slipped a heavy canvas bag over his head and secured it around his neck with a cord. "One noise and I'll pull that cord so tight it will pinch off any words you got before they escape your lips. You got that?"

Azerick did not bother to answer with words; he just nodded his assent, following the man's words in a strict literal sense. When the man was satisfied his captive was going to obey his commands, he took his arm from around Azerick's throat and shoved him out of a door and into the street.

They navigated their way through dozens of twists and turns for nearly an hour before Azerick felt the surface under his feet change from stone to wood. He could smell smoke and lamp oil and knew he was in a house or a building.

The man shoved Azerick into a chair and removed the hood from his head. Azerick blinked rapidly as his eyes tried to adjust from the total blackness within the hood to the brightly lit chamber in which he now found himself.

A well-dressed man sat behind a large desk in a plush, high-backed swivel chair with his fingers steepled before him, the fingertips resting just below a thin, dark mustache. He gazed at the young boy in front of him like a man studying a mysterious and exotic animal. Dozens of questions danced within his eyes, whether or not to allow the boy in front of him to live being the preeminent one in his mind.

"Let me see if I have a proper tally of your night's activities. You have poisoned men of the thieves' guild, set fire to their chapterhouse, stabbed a man in the middle of the street in front of dozens of witnesses, and killed nearly everyone, including the local guild boss of said house, by burning them alive. Is this correct?"

Azerick simply nodded in affirmation.

"So, you see, I know what you have done. What truly confounds me is why you did it, and just who in the blazes you are?"

"Who are you? What do you want with me?" Azerick demanded.

The dandy behind the desk wagged a finger and a large man who had been behind Azerick stepped forward and slapped him hard across the face.

"That is a reasonable question, but impertinent. I asked a question, two in fact. I will continue to ask questions, and you will answer them until I have no more questions. If I decide to let you live, I may then grant you an answer to a question or two of your own. Right now, your odds are about fifty-fifty of being alive long enough to ask your question, and only because I am extremely curious about you and your activities tonight," he said in an almost pleasant tone.

"Actually, I think I have just answered your question to why you are here, so I will go ahead and grant you a boon and conduct introductions like a gentleman should do when he has guests. I am Andrill, guild boss of the Night Ravens. That man behind you, who set your cheek to stinging, is Braxis. And you are?"

"Azerick, sir."

"Azerick sir! How wonderful. It is rare to find a boy with manners these days, especially one who just murdered two score of men,"

Andrill said joyfully. "Now, Azerick sir, why on earth do you risk the wrath of the entire city's guild of thieves by murdering so many of their men, a boss, and burning down one of their chapterhouses?"

"They killed my family in the squatters' quarter. They wedged the door shut and burned to death the people who took me in, as well as the children I read to and who were my friends," Azerick answered, his voice still filled with the hate his vengeance had failed to purge from his soul.

"And how are you so certain it was the guild, and that chapter in particular, that committed such a terrible deed?" Andrill asked as if they were discussing nothing more important than the weather.

"I saw Merik threaten Jon, and I saw him at the fire. I saw him one night and followed him to that house. I drugged some wine and gave it to the men guarding the doors, wedged the doors shut with the same iron spikes I pulled from the ashes of my home, and then set the building on fire."

"Oh, the irony! You used their spikes against them. I so adore the symbolism. It's almost artistic in its application," Andrill squealed in delight, clapping his hands.

Azerick was certain this man was most likely insane and that his chances of getting out of here alive were slim to none, but he resolved not to show him any fear.

"And when that beast, Merik, ran out into the street you stuck him like a pig. Incredible, just incredible. But as a guildsman myself, what am I to do? I'm afraid I can't let the murder of over a score of my brothers go unavenged, can I, Azerick sir?"

"No, I suppose you can't. I certainly would not," Azerick answered.

"No, you most certainly would not, would you?" Andrill burst out in another wave of laughter as he came around the desk and advanced on Azerick with a wickedly sharp blade in his hand. "It really is such a shame. I find you most remarkable."

Andrill bent low and peered intently into the doomed boy's eyes. "Would you look at this, Braxis? He murders nearly thirty men, is sentenced to death, the executioner stands right in front of him, and yet not a single bead of sweat breaks upon his brow. His face is neither flush nor pale; he does not tremble, nor beg for his life. Simply remarkable. What I wouldn't give for a dozen men like you. Hells, I'd take a dozen boys like you. What am I to do with you though?"

"You could let me go," Azerick suggested.

"Let you go? To tell the truth, I should reward you for your services. Finally, I am able to break that deathly calm façade!" Andrill exclaimed as Azerick's face twisted in confusion. "I see I have confounded *you* now. Wonderful, I thought I was losing my touch. You see, boy, Daedric was looking to expand into my territory. In-house fighting is fairly common when one house smells weakness in another. Daedric's Demons have been bolstering their strength for months, and it was only a matter of time before there was all-out war between Daedric and myself with little chance of yours truly coming out on top. So, Azerick sir, how would you like to join my merry band of thieves? You could go very far, I promise you."

"With all due respect, I would not like that in the least."

"Braxis, did he just say *no*?"

"I believe he did, Andrill," Braxis answered.

"To *me*?" Andrill asked in disbelief.

"I'm quite certain it was to you that word was directed, yes."

"Remarkable. Simply remarkable. What if I gave you no choice in the matter? What if I were to say that your life belongs to me and it is me whom you shall serve or you will die?"

"I would say that I hope you enjoy a warm fire in the evenings—a very warm fire," Azerick replied, his voice thick with intent.

"Indeed, you would set me a blaze to ward off the evening chill, I wager! All right, this is the deal; the reward I give you for destroying my rivals is your life. It may not seem like much, but you defied me and my generous offers, so I feel it is a fair balance struck. In return, when you hear in the streets, and I assure you that you will, of how I single-handedly destroyed Daedric's Demons, you will not raise witness against me. If I hear one word of how a mere boy started that fire and destroyed a guild house, I will have you flayed and hung in the square. You will also pay the tax due every non-guild associated thief in the city to me. Do you understand?"

"Yes, sir, on one condition," Azerick challenged.

Andrill threw his hands in the air. "Even now the stripling sets conditions! Remarkable, amazing, unbelievable! What is it? What are your demands? This is truly going to be interesting." The guild boss sat back down, cupped his face in his hands, elbows resting on the desktop, and stared at the impertinent boy.

"I have lost three homes in as many years, each to murder, and I do not wish to lose another. I ask that you command all of your men and any others you have influence over to never attempt to track me to my home or enlist others to do so in their stead. I will defend my home to the death, both their lives and mine. Should I survive the invasion, I will seek vengeance on as grand a scale as I can dream up and carry out. You have seen the least of what my imagination can devise," warned the young thief.

"Very well, that is a reasonable demand." Andrill turned to his henchman. "Braxis, issue the order that any man on guard duty caught drinking anything other than water drawn from the house will be whipped and hanged, and I want no less than five buckets of sand in every room. Please escort our young friend from the premises."

Once again, Azerick found his head encased in the heavy canvas sack and enveloped in darkness.

"And, boy, I will issue the same warning to you as you have given me. Do not show your face within three blocks of my chapterhouse. To do so will negate our treaty and your life will be forfeit. One of my men will approach you when your taxes are due, and I suggest you have the coin on you."

The guild lieutenant pushed Azerick through the halls and into the cool night air and hurried him down several alleys and streets for what must have been a half hour before the bag was pulled off his head and he was shoved roughly forward. Azerick stumbled, his arms windmilling for several steps before he regained his balance. He turned to face his escorts but saw nothing but a faint light at the end of the alley and dark shadows all around him. It took him over an hour to make his way home due to backtracking and the circuitous route he used to ensure that that no one followed him.

When Azerick finally climbed down into the relative safety of his home, he could still not shake the feeling of being vulnerable. It was a concept he loathed more than any other. His nerves would not let him go to sleep until he was certain he was safe from the thieves or anyone else who might want to do him harm.

He had traps set throughout his home, but a decent thief was adept at neutralizing such things. Azerick knew he needed more, and his mind kept taking him back to the jewelry box, particularly the magical ward that had been cast upon it. He pictured those strange, silvery strands in his mind, recalling their appearance and the obvious pattern in which they were laid. If he could undo such a thing, he should be able to remake it as well. But how?

Azerick grabbed a charcoal stylus and a piece of parchment and began drawing what was in his mind's eye. Over and over he scribbled until he was certain he had it exactly right. He then sat beneath one of the trapdoors leading into his sanctuary and willed himself to see the wisps of silver energy once again.

Willing those strands forth was far more difficult than seeing and unraveling those that were already present. Azerick was about to write it off as impossible when he glimpsed a glimmer in the corner of his eye. He did not try to look at it head-on, certain it would vanish if he did. Instead, he gently coaxed it to come to him as if it were a shy animal and he had a scrap of food for it.

Azerick drew the silver thread to him and gently tugged it out of the ether, lengthening and shaping it with his hands and mind. Once he was able to grasp that first strand, the others came much more easily. He shaped and twisted them into the form he remembered and had drawn out on the parchment. Several times the form broke apart like smoke in the wind and he had to start over. After hours of drawing and shaping the magic, he managed to complete the ward and the form held true.

By the time he was finished, Azerick was soaked in sweat and thoroughly exhausted. He could probably get to sleep now without a problem, but there was far more work to do. Azerick went to another of the entrances into his lair, sat down, and began all over again.

CHAPTER 16

Months passed and Azerick was able to settle back into his usual routine of running the streets and searching for clues to his father's murder. Despite Andrill's threatening tone, the thieves left him largely alone as promised. Azerick imagined this was due in part to always keeping his tax payment current.

He was presently sitting in one of the seedier taverns near the port district, drinking watered wine and listening for rumors that might point him toward a profitable venture, when he overheard a rough-looking, foul-smelling, drunken sailor bragging about how he had gutted a whore who was once a rich merchant's wife. Azerick drew a few curious looks when he choked on his wine, understanding the event to which the man was referring.

Harlow regaled his tablemates with how he took her on her bastard son's bed and how when she refused him, he had bled her out with a couple of dozen cuts and stabs. He laughed as he waved his blade around in the air in a macabre reenactment of the grizzly event.

Azerick thought quickly and flagged down a serving woman. He whispered a quick message into her ear, glanced toward the men at the table, and slipped her five coins of silver. Azerick left the tavern as the wench delivered the large man's drink and an invitation to meet her in the alley.

The woman disappeared into the kitchen as Harlow walked out to the alley next to the tavern thinking she was slipping out the back to meet him. It was not unheard of for a whore to service a man in the alleys of a tavern that boasted no rooms.

Murder in the streets was so common in the lower wards that it scarcely drew anyone's attention unless you were the one who was killed. However, when Harlow's body was found the next day, the manner of his death was so gruesome that word spread throughout the district.

Azerick's revenge nourished his soul, but he was far from satiated. His ability to avenge his mother served to strengthen his resolve that if he kept searching, he would find all the people he sought. Azerick continued looking for clues of his father's murder and his true involvement with these alleged artifacts, but he was able to find out surprisingly little. The king's Blackguard had boarded his ship and found something aboard they deemed treasonous. The guards had arrested him, and someone had snuck into his cell and killed him.

Two years of investigating had gotten him no closer to finding the murderer of his father. Discovering the sailor who had killed his mother had been a fluke encounter, but despite the satisfaction he received from taking his revenge, he still felt hollow inside. His desire for justice still gnawed deep in his stomach, and the more time that passed the more the hunger grew.

Azerick was unable to find anyone who had been sailing with his father on that trip. He knew he had crossed the sea for the exotic goods that made him popular amongst the wealthy. Other than that, the trail was cold and no one knew anything. If they did, they were not talking about it. Days, weeks, and months went by as he did what he must to survive, hoping to one day pick up the trail of who had set up his father. For now, it was all he could do to eke out a living and feed the normal sort of hunger plaguing him.

He was currently staking out an open market in the common quarter that catered mostly to food vendors. Farmers had set up tables laden with crates of fruit, vegetables, and all variety of tubers, each proclaiming that theirs were the freshest and most succulent.

There were an annoying number of city watch strolling the grounds, and Azerick was about to give up on the food market and go elsewhere when a boy and a girl, maybe a couple of years older than Azerick was, caught his eye. The young man was handsome and broad-shouldered with dark hair. The girl was pretty, maybe even beautiful if she were to comb her long brown hair and wear better clothes.

The two were trying to look inconspicuous and not together but failing badly at both. Azerick watched the pair pick their way through the crowd and amongst the tables of produce, seemingly perusing the wares but actually looking for an acceptable target.

Azerick already knew how they would play it out. The girl was going to cause some sort of accident or scene and the young man would grab as much food as he could and make a break for it during the confusion. The couple trying not to look like a couple soon chose a stand and made their move.

The girl pretended to stumble over something in the street and fell heavily onto the corner of a produce stand, sending an entire crate of fruits and vegetables crashing to the ground. The young man scooped several of the pieces into a bag as they rolled across the ground and made to sprint off through the crowd. Unfortunately, the proprietor was no more fooled by the farce than Azerick was.

The farmer grabbed the girl by the wrist and hauled her to her feet. "I got you, you little thief!"

The girl tried to pull away, but she was unable to break the farmer's grip. "No, it was an accident!"

"You think I'm stupid, girl? You don't fool me, and you won't fool the Watch," the man snarled and began yelling for the nearby Watch.

"Bran, help!"

Her cohort had only taken a few steps and turned back when his accomplice cried out. Seeing his friend in danger, Bran dropped his bag of pilfered goods and lunged at the man gripping her wrist.

"Andrea!" Bran yelled as he ran back to her.

Seeing the look in the large boy's eyes, the farmer released his grip and backed away, holding his hands defensively in front of his face.

Bran grabbed Andrea's now free hand and pulled her after him as the owner of the stand continued to shout for the guards. It took only seconds for the Watch to give chase, blowing their shrill whistles as they ran.

In a spur of the moment decision, Azerick darted through the crowd, snatched up the bag the young man had dropped, and chased after the thieves and guardsmen. There was a limited number of avenues through which to escape, and it did not take Azerick long to gain the lead on both groups.

Running across the rooftops, often across rickety boards precariously spanning the gap between buildings, Azerick managed to get ahead of the fleeing pair.

"Hey!" Azerick called down to Bran and Andrea. "Run down the next alley on your right!"

Both young people looked up at Azerick with startled expressions plastered on their faces. The boy named Bran nodded and nudged his girlfriend to make the next right.

"Climb the rope at the end of the alley," Azerick shouted to the fleeing couple before turning back the other way.

Azerick found the guards pursuing Bran and Andrea less than a block away, and they were closing in. He reached into the bag Bran had dropped and pulled out the pieces of produce. He needed to buy the two thieves some time.

"Hey, kettleheads!" Azerick shouted and began pelting the Watch with produce from above.

Intent upon catching the fleeing thieves, the guards ignored the bombardment of fruits and vegetables. Frustrated at his attack's lack of success, Azerick picked up a brick and hurled it after launching his last potato. The brick struck with a resounding clang that sent the hapless guard staggering and his helm flying from his head.

The effect was sufficient to shift the Watch's ire squarely onto Azerick. One angry guardsman lifted a light crossbow and snapped off a hasty shot. Azerick ducked away from the ledge of the building and let the quarrel zip harmlessly past. He peered back over the edge, flashed a rude gesture to the shouting guards, and raced along the rooftop, drawing the Watch away from Bran and Andrea.

Azerick made certain not to get out of the pursuing guardsmen's sight for long as he led them on a short chase down several streets and alleys. He wondered if the guards even realized the futility of pursuing someone who was completely out of their reach. It was obvious to him that the Watch did not hire people based upon their intelligence.

Deciding the chase had gone on long enough, Azerick skimmed along the edge of a roof that ended in a dead end—for the guards anyway. The city watch pulled up against the brick wall blocking off the end of the alley and shouted impudent curses at the boy grinning down at them.

"You guys really are incredibly stupid," Azerick taunted. "How did you ever think to catch me from down there?"

The answer came in the form of a barrage of crossbow bolts. "Let me catch you on the ground, you little rat, and I'll show you who's stupid!" one of the men shouted.

Azerick carefully peeked back over the ledge. "Well that was just rude. As fun as this all is, I really have better things to do. Goodbye, kettleheads."

Azerick leapt a narrow span between buildings and raced back toward the alley where he had last seen the hapless thieves. He spotted the pile of rope they had pulled up after themselves and found them only two buildings over from where they had climbed up. They were hiding behind a large chimney, apparently waiting to see if their young rescuer was going to return.

Azerick smiled and waved at the couple as they stepped away from the chimney. Although Bran was considerably larger than Azerick was, he still approached the younger boy with a measure of caution, never releasing the hand of the girl with him.

"Thanks for your help," Bran said.

"Yes, thank you so much," Andrea added. "I have never been so scared in my life!"

"Yeah, it looked like you needed some help."

Bran finally released his grip on Andrea and stuck out his hand. "My name is Bran and this is Andrea."

Azerick gripped the proffered hand and shook it. "I'm Azerick. You two do not look like you have been doing this for very long."

Bran's face reddened in embarrassment and a small amount of anger at what he perceived as a slight against his abilities. Andrea spoke up before he became defensive.

"We haven't. My father used to drink when he wasn't out fishing, but now he goes out fishing when he isn't drinking. Unfortunately, that is not very often these days. I had a job cleaning up at an inn, but I was fired after I broke a mug against a man's head for pinching me. We were getting desperate for food, and that's what brought us to the marketplace today."

"I'll get better! I just need some practice," Bran responded.

"You won't get much practice if you get caught up by the Watch," Azerick replied. "I know a fair bit about running the streets, and working as a team can have some benefits if you want to work together and learn a few things."

Andrea enthusiastically accepted Azerick's offer of help, but Bran's pride took some reasoning and an outright threat from Andrea before he accepted. Azerick wasn't certain he had made a wise decision, but he liked the idea of working with someone again and having friends to talk to. It reminded him a little of Jon and the others, but that also brought back the pain of their loss as well. Was he setting himself up once again for more pain? Azerick decided he would chance it while doing what he could to shield himself from any more loss.

CHAPTER 17

A zerick, Bran, and Andrea were staking out the market square, watching for inattentive shoppers or purveyors from which they might be able to relieve a few items of value or at least a morsel or two of food.

He had been friends with Bran and Andrea for a little over a year now. Although Azerick was technically the only homeless one amongst the three friends, the line of distinction was hair thin. Bran and Andrea lived at home with at least one parent, but they were every bit as poor as he was, and quite honestly, Azerick would not trade homes with either one of them for anything.

Bran was sixteen, just a little more than a year older than Azerick was, but a fair bit larger. Despite being bigger, Bran made no qualms about recognizing Azerick as their unspoken leader. The younger boy's strategies were often what made them successful in their urban forays.

Andrea was an attractive girl bordering on womanhood. She was closer to Azerick's age, which put her at one of the most vulnerable periods in her life. Running the streets made her particularly susceptible to illegal slavers who would snatch street children in the night, the bolder ones even did it in broad daylight.

She was nearing the age where she would have to find her own way in the world, and being unskilled, uneducated, and poor left her with few prospects. Being poor, she lacked any sort of dowry, which meant the only marriage prospects lay at her own economic level leaving her in the same pit she had grown up in and married to a day-laboring drunk like her father. Being uneducated, she could not hope to get any sort of skilled work or apprenticeship. Her work options were limited, leaving her with the choices of washing clothes, working in a bar or, most often, prostitution.

Azerick knew she was desperate to move out of her home and away from her father. He felt guilty not offering her a place to live with him in his own private sanctuary, but he prized his privacy above all other things and still felt the painful loss of Jon and the others. He could not bear the responsibility and risk losing someone else if he allowed them to get close.

The plan for their current operation was simple. Bran, being and looking the oldest, would buy a loaf of bread from the stall a baker had set up. Using the finger of one hand, he would dig a small hole into the bottom of the loaf out of sight of the baker or other customers and slip a dead mouse into it. Bran would then break open the loaf in front of the baker and as many customers as possible and raise a cry of shock and revulsion at "discovering" the dead mouse that had, by all appearances, been baked inside the bread.

Bran, along with most, if not all, of the other customers, would demand a refund after dropping their potentially tainted loaves upon the counter in disgust. Azerick and Andrea would slip several loaves from the counter amidst the upheaval and demand a refund as well. If they were lucky, they would even walk out with some bread.

Bran moved in as the crowd looked to be as thick as it was likely going to get and pushed his way to the front. He ignored the glares he received, and dropped his few copper pieces onto the counter in exchange for a small, round loaf. The frenzied baker swept up the coins and replaced them with the bread. Bran picked up the loaf and had the dead mouse inserted with the deftness of a street magician.

He turned and made eye contact with a few of the other patrons as he broke the loaf in twain, and just for added effect, brought the piece with a dead mouse sticking out of the end inches from his open mouth.

Just as he expected, a woman saw the dead mouse protruding from the bread moments before an apparently unsuspecting customer chomped it, and screamed. Customers followed the horrified woman's eyes to the loaf Bran held near his face. He looked at the piece of bread in front of him and added his own curse to the chorus of shouting, gagging, and retching sounds of the crowd.

The baker, a balding, rotund man wearing a customary checked apron, stood in shocked disbelief at the mouse-tainted bread and the disgusted and angry crowd. He was jolted into motion by people pressing against the counter, hurling bread at him and demanding refunds. Word quickly spread, and customers who had already purchased and departed began returning, also insisting on their money back.

The baker was helpless to defend himself against the angry crowd, emptying his purse before the crowd became a mob. Azerick and Andrea received refunds for seven loaves they had not purchased and still managed to walk away with six more tucked under their shirts and arms.

Once his stomach was full, Azerick almost felt bad for the cruel manner in which they had swindled the baker. He and the others would begin spreading rumors throughout the district that the baker had been the victim of a cruel hoax. None of them had the desire to drive a man out of business, even one that obviously never lacked for food as they so often did. It was not a swindle they could pull off very often otherwise people would become wise to it and would set the crowd against the perpetrators.

The trio of friends had a reasonably successful week, enough so that Azerick was able to spend a few days reading and tinkering with his alchemy set, brewing potions with various reactions. His latest resulted in a stench so foul he had to open the hidden door to the sewer to bring in a fresher source of air.

The pungent concoction convinced him to climb out of his hole and find out what Bran and Andrea had been up to lately. Azerick crossed the market square and saw that the bald baker was back in business, thanks largely in part to the success of their counter rumors proclaiming his innocence in the matter.

He spotted Bran's tall form navigating his way through the crowd and noticed that his older friend was not moving with the careful grace that would indicate he was looking for a mark to pickpocket. In fact, his normally carefree face was shadowed with a look of concern. Azerick wondered if he had gotten into some trouble recently.

Despite the fact that it did not look as though Bran was currently working the crowd, years of habit caused Azerick to move smoothly and quietly up to Bran's side instead of shouting to get his attention.

Bran realized Azerick was near before his friend had a chance to say anything. "Azerick, have you seen Andrea in the last couple of days?"

Azerick sensed the tension in Bran's voice and knew something was not right. "No, I was going to ask you where she was. I have not seen her since the last time all three of us were together a few days ago."

Bran's lips disappeared into a thin line as he clamped his mouth closed. "Damn it!"

"I'm sure she is all right. Maybe she got a job or something and has been busy." He wilted under Bran's frustrated glare. "You're right, I was just hoping. Have you gone to her house?" Azerick asked, already knowing the answer to that question too.

Bran shook his head. "Naw, you know her old man and I don't get along."

"I think we need to though."

"Yeah, let's go."

The two young men walked to the docks and headed toward the rows of shacks mostly owned by fishermen and sailors who often spent weeks and months at sea. They were shabbily built and intended primarily as temporary shelters just to keep them through the winters until the ships sailed out once more.

Andrea's father, when he did manage to sober up enough to work, usually managed to attach himself to a fishing boat hauling in nets or unloading cargo from the merchant ships. He was one of the few people who made Sailor's Row his year-round home.

Azerick and Bran approached the house, which was little more than a one-room fishing shack with a small iron stove used to cook and fight off the winter chill and the many drafts that found their way in through the single-ply walls.

Azerick knocked on the door while Bran stood behind him. He had to knock three more times before they heard the sound of movement within. Azerick could smell the alcohol fumes through the door. Andrea's father jerked it open with a scowl on his face. His grimace deepened when he saw who had interrupted his breakfast, which sloshed about in the bottle in his hand only half finished.

"What do you two vermin want?" he demanded through squinted eyes.

Azerick ignored the barb as he physically recoiled from the fumes erupting from the man's mouth. "We are looking for Andrea. Is she here?"

"No," he replied and began swinging the door shut.

The slovenly drunkard glared when Azerick blocked the door with his foot. "We have not seen her for a few days. When was the last time you saw her?"

"Huh, I thought she'd been with you little pukes." A lewd grin spread across the man's grizzled face. "Maybe she finally made herself useful and whored herself out. Ought'a make a good bit of coin if that one ain't ruined her already," he slurred and looked pointedly at Bran.

Before Azerick could issue a retort, Bran's fist sailed over Azerick's shoulder, past his ear, and smashed into the foul-mouthed man's nose, sending a spray of blood across his face. Andrea's father reeled back from the blow, dropping the half-finished bottle of cheap booze on the floor next to several empties.

Bran shoved violently past Azerick into the shack after the staggering drunk, murder evident in his eyes. The tall lad hit the surprised man twice more, sending him sprawling backward onto the floor. He reached down, grabbed one of the empty bottles by the neck, and broke it against the stove in the corner before lunging toward the fallen man's throat with the razor-sharp edge.

Azerick and Bran both liked Andrea, but Bran's affection was of a different sort, a kind that went deeper than mere friendship, although neither of them had really spoken of it. Bran was going to kill her father for what he had said, but Azerick could not let him do that. Not because Andrea would be particularly upset over the matter, but because Azerick knew Bran was not a killer, not like himself.

Azerick knew what it was like to kill a man. He knew what it did to a person's soul, and he felt he was a harder sort than Bran was. Bran had a light heart and gentle nature. Azerick did not want to see that destroyed in an act of rage like his had been. He grabbed his friend by the wrist just before Bran was able to bring the bottle across the vile man's throat.

"No, Bran, don't! He's not worth the cost," Azerick shouted, barely able to restrain his friend.

Bran turned and looked at Azerick's pleading eyes before dropping the broken bottle and standing up.

"If you ever say anything like that about her again, nothing will keep me from killing you," Bran warned Andrea's father in a strained voice before spitting in the man's face and kicking him in the jaw.

Azerick had to walk swiftly to keep up with Bran as he practically ran from the house, needing to put as much distance between himself and Andrea's father as he could. Azerick knew Bran's violent reaction was only partly due to her father's vile words. The other part was what his ignorance of her whereabouts portended.

"Don't worry, Bran, we'll find her," Azerick swore.

Bran surprised Azerick by spinning about, grabbing him by the front of his shirt, and shoving his back against one of the rough-boarded shacks. "How are we going to do that? You know those gods-be-damned slavers got her!" he shouted, tears streaming freely down his face.

Azerick wanted to deny Bran's angry assertion, but he knew he would be lying to them both. "We'll still find her. If she is still in the city, we will find her, free her, and make them pay."

"How are we going to find her? The king has men who do nothing but look for slavers within the kingdom, and he can't find most of them much less stop them. Hell, he can't even keep his own nobles from buying slaves right in front of his face!"

"I do not know, Bran, but I will find a way."

It took some time, but Azerick had an idea and was putting it into effect now that the sun had gone down and those who were most active at that time were out. He darted from shadow to shadow keeping a sharp lookout for two types of people: the ones he was looking for, and the ones who might be looking for him, or at least the category he fell into that made him their prey.

It was past midnight when he finally found one of the people he was searching for. Azerick was not exactly on friendly terms with the men he sought and needed to be very careful in his approach. He crept as quietly as he could toward the man standing at the darkened corner of a building. He appeared to be doing nothing, but Azerick knew he was working, on what was anyone's guess.

Azerick got within ten yards of the man before he felt the tip of the knife poke through his thin shirt and draw a bead of blood which trickled down his side. Azerick cursed under his breath. The ease with which the man had snuck up behind him reminded him that he was little more than a glorified street rat and not a real thief like the man now digging his blade into his side. Unless Azerick found a master to train him, and not being a guild member made that very unlikely, he never would be.

"Three seconds," the man growled.

"I need to speak to Andrill," Azerick replied without hesitation.

"I don't think he wants to speak to you."

"Braxis, please, it is urgent. I need his help, and I need it fast," Azerick told the Night Raven lieutenant.

"Andrill does not like the idea of you being around the guild house."

"Then ask him to meet me somewhere he feels comfortable."

Braxis could tell that whatever the boy needed was important, possibly valuable. He removed the point of his knife from the young man's back.

"All right, go to the Salty Sailor and wait. Someone will tell you whether Andrill wants to talk to you or to go stuff yourself."

The thief disappeared before Azerick could even turn around. He looked back at the corner but the other man was gone as well. Azerick knew the Salty Sailor; it was the same tavern he had followed Merik from to his chapterhouse.

Azerick made his way down the dark streets, narrowly avoiding a couple of men who seemed to have taken too much of an interest in him. He may not be a master thief, but those who failed to learn how to hide or lose a pursuer did not last long on the streets.

He walked into the tavern, and the noise hit him like a physical force. He found a small table where he could sit by himself. He noted the looks of more than one set of eyes following him as he sat down. Azerick knew that if one of Andrill's men did not come for him, he was going to have to run a gauntlet of potential trouble on his way out.

He ordered watered wine from the serving woman with a few of his remaining coins, nursing it for all it was worth since he did not know how long he would be waiting. Azerick looked at the many faces within the tavern and found a few pairs of eyes still watching him. Night Ravens? Slavers? There was no way to tell. A good thief would not be so obvious in his observations. Slavers, if he was to hazard a guess.

Perhaps he could follow these men and find out where they went if they were indeed slavers. Azerick discarded that plan almost immediately. His earlier encounter reminded him of the level of stealth he possessed, and slavers were a type of thief; they just stole people instead of property. He would likely wake up on a ship headed south before he knew what hit him.

Despite his small sips, his mug was nearly empty now. He was just coming to the conclusion that Andrill had decided he had no interest in speaking to him when three men got up from their table and walked purposely toward him.

The men grabbed chairs and sat down without invitation, pressing Azerick between two of them while the third looked at him from across the table.

"Don't say a word, boy," the man said. "All four of us is gonna get up and walk on out like we was the best of chums. You got it? If you think anyone in here is gonna come runnin' to your rescue because you make a fuss, all it's gonna get ya is a good thump on the noggin. Now stand real calm-like."

Two men appeared behind the one who had issued the orders. "Sit your asses back down," one of the men said, punctuating his command with a poke from a blade hidden in his hand.

"This don't concern you, friend," the slaver growled but followed orders.

"That's where you're wrong. This boy has a prior appointment with us, slaver scum. You and your girlfriends had best keep your seats for a good long while and hope we don't find you out on the streets tonight."

"You got us all wrong, friend. We were just talking to the lad, that's all. No harm in talking, is there? We needed a new cabin boy, thought maybe he'd like a job, that's all," the slaver replied.

"Remember what I said, slaver. I know your faces, and I'll be looking for you. Come on, boy, Andrill don't like to be kept waiting."

Azerick slid past the slavers and fell in between the two men. They left the tavern and walked down the dark streets and alleys. Azerick lost sight of the man in front of him several times when he disappeared into the shadows of a building. He was not intentionally trying to lose the young man following him but was simply moving as he always did out of a habit that had become his natural form.

"Where are we going?" Azerick asked as he exerted himself to keep pace.

"King's Coffer, an inn in the upper district."

"Why did Andrill not meet me at the tavern?"

The man in front of him gave a snort. "Andrill don't frequent places like the Salty Sailor. He has a higher standard that he don't break for anyone."

"I am glad you came when you did, or I would probably be tied up in a sack right now."

"Will and I'd been watching you and them for better'n half an hour. We just wanted to see what they were going to do before we moved. It was more fun that way." The thief spat on the ground. "Filthy slaver scum."

Azerick was surprised and gladdened to see that there was no love lost between the guild and the slavers. It made Andrill much more likely to help him. He had feared that the guild and slavers might have a mutual agreement of some sort. Seeing now that that was very unlikely would make his job a lot easier.

The upper ward was nearly the entire way across town, and it took over half an hour of swift walking to reach the King's Coffer even though it stood at the nearest edge of the district. Azerick was impressed. The building was in excellent shape with fresh white paint covering the exterior and a large, shingled awning stretching across the entire front of it. Several panes of amber glass let out enough light from the interior to illuminate the porch and boarded sidewalk beneath it.

It was crowded inside and filled with the noise of many voices but much more subdued than the raucous, obnoxious shouting filling the common rooms of the inns and taverns he had been at in the lower wards. Polished tables with nice chairs were organized about the large common room; a long polished bar with clean, clear glass mugs stacked behind it served patrons sitting on the tall stools before it, while others sat at tables lit by glass fluted oil lamps: good ones with oil that did not reek of fish.

The inn smelled of wood smoke, good food, beer, and wine that had not gone sour. The two thieves crossed the room to where Azerick saw Andrill sitting with Braxis at a table in the corner.

Andrill stood up and extended his hand. "Ah, Azerick sir, how interesting it is to meet you again. You are a little late. I hope you did not run into any trouble. The fire crews are busy enough as it is."

"Couple of slavers were about to move in on him. Will and I set them straight," one of the thieves answered.

Andrill grimaced and washed out his mouth with a sip of wine as if the very mention of a slaver had left a foul taste upon his palate.

"Mmm, Azerick sir, you must try the wine," Andrill insisted, pouring the young man a glass from a dark green bottle resting in a silver pail full of chipped ice.

Azerick picked up the delicate glass, brought it to his nose, sniffed it as he had seen Andrill do, and took a small sip, then a larger one. The wine left a pleasant trail of warmth from his tongue to his stomach and a slightly sweet aftertaste in his mouth.

"How is it?" Andrill asked.

"It is very good," Azerick replied honestly.

Andrill laughed as if Azerick had just told him the best joke he had ever heard. "It is *good* he says! My boy, that is the last winter wine, made of the finest grapes of the finest vineyard in Brightridge. The grapes for the wine must be picked within four hours of midnight on a full moon of the very last day of harvest. Marrying a beautiful and wealthy woman is *good*. Not dying from a stab wound is *good*. Even stealing the most prized treasure from your most hated rival is *good*. This, my boy, is divine!"

"Precisely what I meant to say. I simply lack the vocabulary to do it justice," Azerick returned in an attempt to save face.

Andrill roared in laughter again, slapping the table with his palm. "Oh, I am so glad I decided to ask you to join me. I knew you would not fail to be entertaining, my quick-minded young friend. However, we must eat before discussing business since I doubt this is purely a social call. Do not look so frightened. Your wit and humor have already paid for your dinner, which I have taken the liberty to order. I doubt you could afford a glass of water in this place."

As if on cue, two attractive serving women brought out large round trays bearing several plates laden with different meats, bowls full of potatoes cooked at least four different ways, vegetables that Azerick was helpless to identify, and three types of bread. It was a banquet that would feed a king's court, and Azerick looked around to see if anyone else was going to join the three of them.

"I must apologize," Andrill said as the two women began loading plates up with food and setting them in front of the diners. "I imagine you are feeling a bit out of place here. I should have sent a set of finery along with my men so you could change. Do not fret. Most of the people you will find here are exceedingly polite and will not stare, and the rude ones are smart enough not to, so enjoy your meal."

Andrill surprised Azerick with his seeming ability to read his mind. He was feeling extremely underdressed and out of place. Just his inability to appreciate the wine properly showed how far out of his element he was, but the guild boss' words put him at ease enough to enjoy the food. He did not know what half of the items were, but every one of them was delicious.

Azerick finally had to push his plate away, too full to consume another bite. He had not wanted to overindulge, but he had been unable to help himself, and he sensed that his obvious pleasure in the food pleased his host.

"So, now that we have gotten the preliminaries over with, what is it that has you so concerned that you would seek me out even though you are behind on your taxes?" Andrill asked, sipping another glass of winter wine.

Azerick blushed having completely forgotten his debt, but Andrill cut him off before he could respond. "Do not lose focus, lad. That is another sort of business, not tonight's business, and I do not like to mix different topics at the same meeting. Concern yourself, and me, with the topic that brought you here."

"I am looking for a friend. She has been missing for several days now, and I think she may have been taken by slavers."

"I would have to agree with you, Azerick. It is very likely she ran afoul of those cretins," the guild boss replied, very businesslike now. "The problem is that they are a very secretive bunch, and even with my resources, are hard to track down, much less locate a single individual they may have taken."

"I was not sure you could or would help me. I was afraid the guild might work with the slavers, but I did not know who else to turn to."

Andrill's look grew dark at the assumption. "Hardly, though many people think otherwise. They steal from our city and feel they have no need to pay taxes or report to the guild, not to mention many of the guild come from the very streets these men use as their hunting grounds. The only reason we do not drive them from the city is that such open warfare would be very costly, far too expensive given the fact that the ones in the most danger are simply street rats. No offense."

"So you cannot help me?"

Andrill sighed as he stared into his wineglass as if he were seeking answers within the amber liquid. "As interesting as I find you, I am a businessman first and foremost. What do I stand to gain compared to the level of risk I would take by seeking out this information you desire?"

"I would owe you a favor. It is all I have to offer. I have no wealth, no power, nor any particular skill, so a promise of a returned favor is the best I can do."

Braxis looked dubious but Andrill leaned forward, stared Azerick in the eye, and actually sniffed. "Do you smell that, Braxis?"

Azerick thought Andrill was making sport of him or commenting on his hygiene, but the guild boss looked deadly serious.

"Do you know my mother was a Traveler, a seer at that? No, of course you do not, how could you? You carry the scent of destiny, fate, or a god's touch—whatever you want to call it. Sometimes, if it is strong enough, even I can sense it, although the skill is always stronger within the female bloodline. I have a sister that could probably tell me a great deal of what I might expect in return for accepting your proposal, but I believe I know enough that such an arrangement could be a wise investment. Very well, I will see what I can discover in exchange for a favor at some future point of my choosing."

"Thank you, Andrill, this means a great deal to me," Azerick replied.

"Do not thank me yet, young man. I have not collected my fee. The cost of such deals can sometimes make one feel like a fool when it comes time to pay. Remember that for the future."

Azerick felt a chill run down his spine at the warning, but at this point he had nothing else to offer. The only important things he ever had had already been taken, and he doubted the master thief wanted his books.

Azerick recognized the dismissal and made his way back to his lair, managing to avoid the Watch out of habit and, out of necessity, the numerous shady-looking characters skulking about the dark streets. He tried to go to sleep, which considering the amount he had eaten and the potent wine he had drunk, should have come easily, but his concern for Andrea and his anxiousness to hear back from Andrill kept him awake until the early hours of the morning.

CHAPTER 18

He awoke well after the sun had risen and went in search of Bran. His first instinct was to go looking for him around one of the several market squares throughout the city, but something told him that his friend was probably not staking out their usual haunts. His gut led him to the docks where he eventually found Bran in one of the taverns looking warily over the top of the clay mug gripped tightly in his hands.

At first glance, Azerick was afraid his friend had fallen into a depression and was trying to wash away his sorrows with cheap ale, but on closer inspection, Azerick saw he was watching and listening to the sailors and laborers around him.

Azerick pulled up a rickety chair and sat next to him. "You hear anything yet?"

"No. If the slavers are operating, they're not talking about it openly, at least not where I can hear them," Bran replied without taking his eyes off the patrons of the tavern.

Azerick saw that his friend was taking Andrea's disappearance hard. He was sullen and withdrawn, a polar opposite of his usual genial self. "I have some people looking into it. If anyone can find something, it's them."

Bran simply nodded as he continued to scan the crowd as if at any moment someone might stand up and confess to the abduction.

"I am going to go and look around. I will let you know if—when I hear something."

"I'm going to find her, Az. If it takes the rest of my life, I'll find her."

Azerick laid a hand on Bran's shoulder, giving it a squeeze before walking out of the tavern and into the salty seaside air. He paused just outside the door, listening to the complaints of the seagulls and the shouting of dockworkers a block away. Azerick headed toward the docks and walked into Peg's store, figuring the old sailor was likely to see and hear a great deal of what went on around the docks.

"Well, if it ain't the young chimney sweep," Peg called out from behind the counter as Azerick entered. "So, did you manage to get the job done?"

"Oh yes, I got it cleaned out real good," Azerick replied. "I wish I had been able to save enough to repay you for the value of that rope, but more pressing debts soaked up most everything I made."

"Well I hope you're not sniffing around for any more handouts. I liked your father, but I gotta eat too, and I ain't gonna be able to do that if I give away all my merchandise."

"No, I'm just looking for information this time, Peg. It will not cost a thing. I am looking for a friend of mine, a girl, about my age, brown hair about this long, kind of pretty. She lives on Sailor's Row with her drunk of a father."

"How long she been missing?"

"A few days."

Peg rubbed the grey stubble on his chin. "Good chance slavers got her if she was foolish enough to run about after dark."

"I was thinking the same thing. Have you heard anything about any slavers lately?"

"Too often to tell the truth. Fat lot of good it does to make it illegal if it ain't enforced. All the king did was make it more profitable for those that don't worry about getting arrested. A ship came in last week, not much cargo to unload, just a few odds and ends from Sumara. It left port about four or five days ago without taking on much more cargo than it dropped off."

"That does not sound like a very profitable trip."

"Nope, not unless they loaded up some cargo they didn't want nobody to see."

"Thanks, Peg," Azerick said and walked back out onto the docks.

Peg had told him enough to strengthen his suspicion but nothing that could help him find out who took Andrea or where they had taken her. He assumed slavers would transport her south by ship, although a few captives were hidden in wagons and taken to private estates outside the city. Either way, it would be nearly impossible to find her if she had been taken from the city already.

A sailor approached him and interrupted his thoughts. "Hey, boy, can you read?"

"Yes, I can read," Azerick warily replied.

The sailor pulled out a scrap of parchment and handed it to him. "Good. Andrill said you were clever, but clever don't necessarily mean literate. He says this is the best he can do, so don't come asking for more help. You won't be able to afford it anyway."

The guild thief, Azerick knew now he was no sailor, left without giving Azerick a chance to ask any questions or make any comment. He unfolded the parchment and saw there was a set of instructions and a small, crude map drawn on it. It told him of a warehouse Andrill's men had been watching last night. Several men were always present, but there was little activity around the place until well after dark. Men carried large sacks in on their shoulders and moved wooden crates out by cart to be loaded onto an unregistered ship, and always after midnight.

Azerick returned to the tavern and was glad to see that Bran was still there although the time had done nothing to improve his mood. In fact, his lack of success made him look even surlier than he had before. Azerick hoped his news would lift his spirits some.

"I have some information," Azerick said as he sat down.

Bran's face lit up with hope. "Did you find her?"

"Calm down and listen. First, promise me you are not going to go charging off the instant I tell you what I know."

"Fine, just tell me you found something out!"

Azerick told Bran about the warehouse and showed him the map, describing the security and movements of the men around the building.

"So what are we waiting for?" Bran asked after Azerick told him what he knew. "Let's go get her!"

"And do what, Bran? Charge in and take on a dozen or more slavers, just the two of us? And with what weapons? Do you have a ballista in your pocket you did not tell me about? We need a plan, preferably one that does not get us killed," Azerick shouted back then lowered his voice when people began to stare.

"We need to rescue her before they take her out of the city," Bran urged.

"She may already be out of the city. We do not know for certain she is there, but if she is, us going in with swords waving, if we could even get a sword, is not going to free her."

"Do you have a plan?"

Azerick rubbed his eyes and pinched the bridge of his nose. "I will have one tonight."

Azerick told Bran to meet him later that night and to bring whatever weapons he could get his hands on, although he hoped that whatever plan he came up with would avoid, or at least minimize, any physical confrontation with the slavers.

He returned to his home and took stock of the potions he had created during his numerous experimentations and formulated a plan as he determined what he had to work with and how it could help him and Bran in their mission. Azerick dismantled one of the many crossbow booby traps that he had painstakingly refurbished and which was guarding the halls of his sanctum. Fortunately, the steel bows had avoided significant corrosion and had lost only a small amount of their strength. He had spent the past two years carving new stocks and replacing ruined strings.

Azerick counted the beads flicked over on an abacus indicating how many times he had turned his hourglass and saw it was nearing the time to meet Bran. He loaded several stoppered glass bottles into a padded rucksack, grabbed up his crossbow, and left through the warehouse entrance of his lair.

The squatters' district was not far from the docks and the warehouse where Andrill suspected the slavers were holding their prizes. Even moving carefully through the streets, it took Azerick less than thirty minutes to reach the rendezvous point. He was not surprised to find Bran already waiting and he looked as if he had been here for some time.

"Have you seen the place yet?" Azerick asked, confident that he had.

"Yeah, I've been watching the place for a couple hours. I couldn't stand just sitting around waiting. I made sure I wasn't seen though."

"So, what have you found out?"

"Come on, let's get closer and I'll show you."

From a dark area between two buildings, perhaps thirty yards away, Bran showed Azerick the warehouse and explained what he had seen so far.

"You can see the main door there," Bran said, indicating a large panel that slid on metal rollers and rails. "They lit the lanterns as soon as it got dark, and my guess is they'll stay lit until morning. There's a small door on the side and another larger set of doors at the rear. One man guards the small door while the big doors have two men each, and that is just on the outside. I have no idea how many are inside, but I have seen at least four men enter and three leave, but one of them was not the same person as went in. Two slavers take a walk around the outside of the warehouse, and sometimes they'll wander around some of the surrounding buildings."

Azerick blew out a breath in a soundless whistle. "This is a big operation. It sounds at least as big as a thieves' chapterhouse." He understood why Andrill did not want to have a direct confrontation with the slavers if this was any indication of their usual numbers.

"So how are we going to get inside?" Bran asked.

"You say there is no door on the other side?"

"No, just a solid wall."

Azerick nodded, a plan forming in his mind. "All right, that is the way we will go in."

"You got a saw in that bag? It'll make way too much noise."

"We won't be cutting our way in, but we will need to create a distraction." Azerick looked at a few of the surrounding buildings and inclined his head toward one. "Let's get over there."

Azerick and Bran walked swiftly between the buildings, keeping out of sight of the warehouse until they had circled around and hid in an alley that opened opposite from where Azerick planned to breach the wall.

After a quick check on the guard standing in front of the smaller single door, Azerick pulled two flasks out of his rucksack and concealed them under bits of rubbish several feet in from the end of the alley and close to the walls.

He handed Bran a small metal vial plugged with a cork. "When I say 'now', pour that into the flask. As soon as you pour it in, we need to get our butts over to the back side of the warehouse."

"What is it?" Bran asked, shaking it next to his ear.

"It is a catalyst for the stuff in the flasks. As soon as you pour it in, those flasks are going to smoke like a bonfire made of green leaves. It should bring most of the guards over to investigate and give us time to get into the warehouse."

Bran nodded and stood next to one of the flasks while Azerick stood near the other. "Do it."

The instant the liquid from the vials was added to the contents of the flasks, thick, white smoke billowed from the bottles. The two boys darted further down the alley and around to one side of the warehouse just in time to see the smoke blowing out of the alley.

The smoke gained the attention of the guard on that side of the building. The man looked left and right before running across the street to find the source of the smoke. Assuming it must be from a fire; he ran to the corner of the warehouse and called for help, shouting that the alley was on fire. One of the other guards yelled something through the door, probably a warning, before running toward the source of the disturbance.

Azerick and Bran ran around the building they were hiding next to until they reached the back side of the warehouse. They paused before darting across the narrow throughway between them and the warehouse wall. The two boys pressed their bodies against the rough, worn wood as Azerick pulled out another glass flask containing a liquid whose viscosity was close to that of lamp oil.

Azerick unwound the waxed cord sealing the glass stopper in place and sloshed the substance onto the warehouse wall. The wood began giving off an oily, acrid smoke. Bran watched in amazement as the wood dissolved as if it were in a swamp, aging decades in mere minutes. The wood became spongy and began crumbling into a sodden pile of pulp.

"Watch that stuff!" Azerick warned as Bran impulsively stuck his head through the growing hole. "You definitely do not want to get that on your clothes."

Azerick used a stick to knock a larger hole into the wall, big enough for them to walk through if they hunched over. Dim lamplight showed through the hole from lamps barely lighting the interior. There were several large crates stacked haphazardly within the massive interior but little else.

They heard the sounds of voices and whimpering cries coming from their right near the far wall. Using the crates as cover, Azerick and Bran stole stealthily toward the sound of people. Peering around a crate, they saw four adults, three of them women and none more than twenty-five years old or so. There were also close to a dozen children ranging from perhaps five to sixteen years old, but the light was too poor to tell if Andrea was amongst them.

Rope or leather cords bound the captives' hands, and the oldest had gags in their mouths. All sat with their backs pressed against the wall, looking fearfully at each other or the three men playing dice using an empty crate for a table.

Azerick looked at Bran and pointed at the sling he had looped through his belt then at the light crossbow he himself carried. Azerick had seen his friend hit rats and pigeons at thirty yards or better with unerring accuracy. The twenty feet or so separating them from the three slavers would be no problem for him.

Bran quirked an eyebrow at Azerick, jabbing his finger at their two weapons then pointed at the slavers and raised three fingers. Azerick gestured to the knife hanging at his belt. The blade had never failed to take the life of anyone he had used it against so far, and he hoped his luck would hold.

Bran nodded once, stepped out from behind the crate, and whirled his sling over his head; a heavy lead shot fishermen use to weigh down their nets cradled in its leather pouch. All three men turned to look at the whirring sound Bran's sling made just as he released the lead ball. As Azerick had expected, the heavy bullet struck one of the men square between the eyes with an ominous thud and the crack of splitting bone.

Azerick sprang up from the other side of the crate and put a quarrel in the second slaver before the one Bran brained dropped to the floor.

Azerick was no expert with a crossbow, but as close as his target was, missing would have been a difficult feat. The bolt struck the man just below and to the right of where his heart struggled in its losing battle to keep beating. Azerick dropped his crossbow and ran at the third slaver, pulling the knife he had acquired the night Harlow murdered his mother.

As sudden and efficient as the ambush had been, there was simply no way to prevent the man from shouting for help. Azerick grimaced, his hopes that the man would freeze for just a moment in panic dashed. He hurled his knife at the slaver and watched it tumble end over end. The blade struck true just above the man's heart, severing the aorta, but not before he was able to sound an alarm.

Azerick kept running at the dead man and retrieved his knife as Bran ran toward the prisoners, looking for Andrea and shouting her name. His gut churned every time Bran called out but received no answer, his cries becoming more pained and desperate with every recitation.

Azerick yanked his blade free from the slaver's chest and ran back for his crossbow. He could hear the pounding of feet across the wooden floor of the long warehouse, and they were drawing nearer.

Without pausing, he scooped up his crossbow and rucksack, taking a position near one of the crates, and set the two items on top. Azerick pulled another glass flask from the rucksack as several men charged out of the dim light toward him and Bran. He could just make out swords, clubs, and knives gripped in their filthy hands.

He hurled the bottle toward the men, aiming for a point several yards in front of them. The bottle burst, splashing its noxious-smelling contents across the floor. The putrid odor struck the men like a fist to the gut, causing them to clutch their stomachs and retch violently onto the floor. A few continued to stumble forward, gagging, but intent on not allowing their captives to get away. Even with those not completely incapacitated, it gave Azerick enough time to cock the crossbow, load another bolt, and send it flying into the gut of one of the men still rushing forward. He sent a second quarrel into another man's hip, spinning him to the ground.

"Bran, we need to get out of here!" Azerick shouted, pulling a heavily scented piece of cloth from his pocket and pressing it against his nose and mouth as the rancid stench continued to spread.

Bran came running up behind him, tears of anguish and fear streaming down his face. "I got everyone cut loose, but Andrea isn't here!"

"I'm sorry, Bran, but we have to get out of here, now."

Azerick could tell Bran wanted to stay and kill every slaver he found, but it would be suicide to attempt it. They needed to get going. Azerick retrieved another flask, this one full of lamp oil, and threw it against the wall where one of the lit lamps provided some of the meager light inside the warehouse. The flask shattered near enough that the oil caught and set the wall aflame.

"Come on, get them through the hole," Azerick ordered and began herding the captives toward the breach they had made to gain entry.

Azerick and Bran urged the captives to move faster as they heard the doors slamming open and men shouting in anger. There were shouts and curses of surprise when the pungent smell of Azerick's foul concoction reached their noses, but it was dissipating fast enough for it to cause little more than inconvenient heaving and burning eyes.

Azerick was the first one to duck through the hole in the wall and saw a slaver as he rounded the corner of the building. He began shouting at the runaways and to his comrades. Azerick fired his crossbow, but he missed and the quarrel skipped harmlessly off the side of the warehouse wall just over the slaver's head. It did serve to chase him back around the corner, but the arrival of nearly half a score of men bolstered his courage.

"Come on, people, move it!" Azerick shouted, fearful that his plan was falling apart.

The captives fled through the hole and chased after Azerick while Bran followed behind them shouting warnings of more men joining in pursuit. The rescuers led their freed captives down the small alleys created by the warehouses and fisheries that comprised the majority of the dock ward, desperately trying to lose their pursuers. The shouts of men continued getting closer and soon came from beside as well as from behind them.

"Bran, get up here!" Azerick shouted, frustrated at not being able to lose their pursuers, largely because they were limited to the speed of the youngest and slowest child. The adults were carrying the smallest, but they were still slowed enough that he had to do something, or many of them would soon be caught, especially those who would not leave the smaller kids behind and save themselves, and he knew there was going to be at least one of those—him.

Bran ran up next to his friend and gave him a worried but determined look.

"Bran, I have to try and slow them down or lead them away. I need you to get everyone to safety. Find a patrol or run all the way to a Watch office."

Bran wanted to argue, but he knew Azerick was right. If one of them did not do something soon they would all be caught, and at least a few would die fighting or be killed as examples to the others. Bran nodded his understanding and hoped his friend would be able to buy them enough time to get away.

Azerick dropped back and fished through his rucksack. Judging by touch alone, he found he had four flasks left: two smoke, one acid, and one stench pot. He removed the acid flask and waited until they crossed an intersection of four buildings before throwing it down and shattering it upon the cobbles. He threw the stench pot a few seconds later at the next intersection and readied the smoke pot for the next. Azerick shouted and charged to his left toward the sound of the pursuers flanking them.

"Hey, you fatherless, goat-loving sacks of goblin feces, you are too late! Your slaves are long gone thanks to me, so why don't you all go home and get in line to pleasure your mothers like everybody else in the city!"

Azerick's taunting had the desired effect. Men turned toward him, cursing and screaming the vilest threats they could imagine, and they certainly did not lack in imagination. Although he seriously doubted many of their threats were physically possible, Azerick definitely did not want to fall into their hands.

He sprinted away as fast as his feet could carry him, pouring the catalyst into the smoke pot and dropping it as he crossed the intersection where he had last seen Bran and the freed captives. The bottle broke upon the stone street, releasing a pall of smoke that completely obscured all four corners in an instant. The smokescreen ensured that Bran and the others were well out of sight as the slavers converged upon the intersection.

Azerick shouted again, making certain the slavers did not deviate from their course and discover he had lured them away from their prize, although he thought there was a good chance they were more interested in capturing him now than recovering their human property.

He nearly ran right into the arms of half a dozen men as he and the group unexpectedly converged at another four-way intersection. He leapt high into the air, kicking out at the lead man with his foot and catching him in the side of the head. The blow sent the man tumbling to the ground and he did not rise as Azerick continued running, his feet already moving the instant they hit the cobblestones.

Azerick was breathing heavily as he tried to shake the determined pursuers, certain he had led them far enough away from Bran that he and the captives should be able to reach safety. Instinct led him to the squatters' district as he darted down narrow alleys and through abandoned buildings, surprising the vagrant tenants of the occupied ones.

The slavers were intent on not letting him escape, and he came to realize that running into the squatters' district had been a bad idea seeing as how there was little chance of finding help or a safe haven in the area. He could scurry down one of the entrances of his lair, but that put it at great risk of discovery, and he was not about to lose the most secure home he could hope to find in the city. Not yet at least.

With the slavers now boxing him in on three sides, they began coordinating their chase and herded him like a pack of wolves. Azerick skidded to a halt as men appeared at the end of the alley, their black silhouettes blocking his path. He spun around in hopes of fleeing back the way he had come but his pursuers barred his egress from that direction as well.

Azerick's heart pounded as much from exertion as the realization of the predicament he was now in. His mind raced furiously for an answer to his potentially lethal dilemma, but for once, no answer was forthcoming. He was about to unhook his crossbow from the rucksack as the slavers stalked toward him, calling out taunts, threats, and jeers, but before he could loosen the thong securing the crossbow behind him, a rope dropped from the roof, nearly striking him in the shoulder.

He did not care who had thrown him the rope, figuring whoever was on the rooftop could not possibly be more hostile than those on the ground and he began climbing. Seeing their quarry escaping, the slavers rushed forward, but a hail of thrown knives and bolts launched from small crossbows dropped several in their tracks and chased the rest back.

A strong hand gripped Azerick's wrist as he neared the summit and pulled him onto the rooftop. Several men wearing dark clothing and wielding small but numerous weapons looked over the side of the building, watching the slavers flee from the lethal rooftop attack. Although the slavers possessed considerably superior numbers, they had no way of readily reaching the unknown assailants who whisked their prey away before their very eyes.

"Move it, boy, we can't keep to the roofs around here forever, and I have no desire to meet those scum on the ground," the man who had pulled him up said.

Without a word, Azerick followed the men as they leapt from roof to roof when the distance was not too great and ran across sturdy planks spanning the gaps of the more distant rooftops, which they secreted onto the roofs after they had crossed.

After the group had crossed several blocks by rooftop, Azerick said, "I am glad you saved my hide, but who are you?"

"Just someone Andrill sent to protect his investment. He decided the risk to the house was justified by the chance of future profit. I don't know what he expects to get outta you, but it sounds like it's gonna be more than I would want or even be able to pay."

Azerick and the small band of thieves dropped back to street level as the buildings spread too far apart to continue by way of the rooftops. In the more settled and developed parts of the city, one could traverse nearly the entire ward without ever stepping foot on the cobblestones. Of course, the Watch would give one a merry chase if they spotted you leaping through the open air or using a span to cross between buildings seeing as how few would have legitimate requirements for such a method of travel.

"All right, street rat, I think you can find your way from here. We lost the slaver scum, but I suggest you find a place to hide out at least until daylight," the man told him as they dropped from the roof and into a dark alley.

"Yeah, I have a bolthole not too far from here. Thanks again for saving my hide."

The guild men made no response and disappeared into the shadows, leaving Azerick standing alone in the middle of the alley. He carefully made his way deeper into the squatters' district toward one of the secret entrances to his subterranean home. He decided that he would use the one beneath the burned-out tannery.

Azerick moved with as much stealth as he could muster, keeping both his ears and eyes peeled for any signs of the slavers, but it appeared they had given up the hunt. He wished he could go and find Bran but knew it was safer for both of them if he waited until morning.

Despite the evening's exertion, both physical and mental, sleep came to him with great difficulty and only after a few hours of restlessness. Azerick was worried for Andrea and about how Bran was handling the fact she had not been in the warehouse. Had she ever been there or had something else happened? It was not unusual for a person, especially a young girl out at night, to be attacked and their body thrown into the harbor.

Azerick forced himself to push those morbid thoughts away. Andrea was bright and knew the streets and its dangers as well as any of them. Being a girl, she was even more cautious than him and Bran despite her near fearlessness and tenacity.

Tears crept into his eyes as he thought about her fiery spirit and unquenchable enthusiasm for life despite the lousy hand she had been dealt. Had she been born a woman of even moderate means she would have been a truly remarkable person. The thought of that bright spark of life extinguished by the selfish and greedy desires of another filled him with rage, which did nothing to help with his current bout of insomnia.

Azerick did not know when he eventually fell asleep, but when he finally awoke he recalled the disturbing dreams he had had. He had no way of knowing what time it was and prayed it was not too late. Bran would surely be looking for him this morning to at least find out if his friend had survived the night.

The restless and troubled sleep did little to reduce his exhaustion, so he decided he had time to make a strong pot of coffee before embarking on his search for Bran. His reflexes would need the energy-generating properties of the brew to help keep him alert. There was a chance the slavers had only been momentarily deterred. Given their numbers, it was quite possible they were as firmly entrenched and had comparable resources within the city as the thieves' guild.

It took Azerick about thirty minutes to heat the water for his coffee and boil the crushed grounds before using the tannery entrance to strike out into the city's surface life.

The sun was already far into the sky, probably not more than an hour or two before noon. Azerick hoped Bran was still running about the city and had not been captured or killed. Still wary after last night's events, Azerick moved cautiously through the squatters' district and toward the merchants' ward where he, Bran, and Andrea had always linked up in the past.

Despite his elevated alertness, Azerick didn't notice the man hunkered down inside the shadowy doorway of one of the abandoned buildings, watching the troublesome street rat slink through the quarter as he followed him at a distance into the merchant district and toward one of the market squares.

CHAPTER 19

Azerick nearly stabbed Bran when his friend came up from behind and grabbed his arm. "Damn it, Bran, warn a guy when you are going to sneak up on him the day after he narrowly escapes certain torture and death at the hands of severely irate slavers!"

"I'll try to remember. Listen, Andrea wasn't there last night."

"I know, Bran. I'm sorry, but we might still be able to find her. Maybe she is being held in a different building in the city or was sold to some rich guy as a maid or something."

"No, listen to me! I talked to some of the people we freed last night. A couple of them remember her because she spit in the eyes of a few of the slavers and managed to kick one between the legs so hard he walked hunched over for two days. They took her and a bunch of others away the same night the ones we rescued were brought in. They overhead the slavers talking about a ship sailing to Bakhtaran." Bran shook Azerick by his shoulders. "Don't you see? I know where she is! We can find her now!"

Azerick wanted to be excited along with his best friend, but what he said numbed him. "Bran, Bakhtaran is a major slave city a thousand miles to the south. Even the King of Sumara cannot control the emir of that city."

"So what am I supposed to do, just leave her there? Forget about her, give up on her, and go on with my life?"

Azerick felt the bile rise in his throat the instant he answered. "Yes. You have no money, no skills other than stealing bread and lifting a purse, and no knowledge of anything outside of Southport. You can barely read Valerian. Do you think you can just start walking south or hop a ship, show up in Bakhtaran like some knight-errant rescuing the princess, and live happily ever after? You will be dead within a week, and that is if you are lucky. You will starve in a month or end up a slave digging in a Sumaran mine."

Azerick did not see the blow coming. The next thing he was aware of was the clouds gliding lazily across the sky. It took him a moment to realize what had caused the sudden change in his orientation. He tongued a loose tooth and tasted blood in his mouth.

"Ow. Now help me back up, you savage," Azerick said and extended his hand toward Bran. Bran clasped Azerick's wrist and pulled him back onto his feet. "You know, you have gotten exceedingly violent recently. And coming from me, that should frighten you more than a little."

"I'm sorry."

"No you're not. All right, let's figure out how to give you at least a small chance of getting there alive and not in shackles. I will give you my crossbow and whatever coin I have, which is terribly meager as you well know. However, I may be able to get you an honest ship going south."

"That sounds better. Now I am sorry I hit you."

"You should be, you cretin. We'll go talk to Peg and see if we can get you on a boat. You better hope like hell I do not lose my tooth, or I may end up in Bakhtaran just to return the favor."

"In that case, maybe I should hit you again."

"Unless you want to swim all the way to Sumara, I would not recommend it."

The two young men walked into Peg's shipping supply store.

"Peg, I need your help again," Azerick said without preamble upon entering the shop.

"Why am I not surprised? You sure be callin' in a lot of favors you ain't even earned yet."

"Yeah, I seem to be spreading my credit around pretty thick lately. Don't worry though, this one does not cost you anything either. This is Bran. We need to find him work on a ship that is going south, preferably as far as Bakhtaran."

Peg looked Bran up and down and rubbed his grizzled chin. "Might be I can put the word out and find him a boat that needs hands."

"I know he does not look like much, but he is a decent sort when he is not punching me in the face, reasonably bright, and he is reliable."

"I know a ship that does a fair bit of trading in Sumara and travels that far south, though I don't rightly understand why anyone would want to be looking for passage to that den of wickedness," Peg said with a sour look.

"You remember the girl I was asking you about yesterday? We found out she was taken to Bakhtaran, and Bran is intent on finding her and bringing her home."

"She must really mean a lot to risk going after her down there."

"She does, at least to me," Bran replied.

Azerick was not sure if Bran intended his answer to be a slight against his decision not to go, but it still stabbed like a knife twisting in his gut.

"All right, Bran, you stay here with me, and I'll give you a crash course in knot tying and the basic rules of sailing so you are not a completely useless landlubber. I'll go have a word with the captain of the ship I got in mind later. Don't worry, lad, he ain't due to ship out till tomorrow. You won't miss your ride," Peg said as fear flashed plainly across Bran's face.

"Do you need me to get anything for you, Bran?" Azerick asked.

His friend shook his head. "Everything I have of any worth is either on me or waiting for me in Bakhtaran."

"All right, I will leave you here with Peg for now. I have a few things you might be able to use. I'll go get them and bring them back."

Bran nodded and Azerick left to go and retrieve a few things from his home. The sudden turn of events made Azerick forget the need for caution as he made his way back to the squatters' district and dropped through the hidden trapdoor in the tanner's shop. He returned to the surface several minutes later with a canvas bag slung over his shoulder and the crossbow tucked under an arm.

Hidden eyes watched his hasty return and departure for the second time that day then returned to the burned-out building the street rat had vanished into and reappeared from a few minutes later. The watcher decided the tannery was more important right now than following the boy and went to take a closer look at the building as Azerick passed out of sight.

Azerick returned to Peg's store with his burden and found Bran sitting on the floor amidst a pile of short ropes with various knots tied in them; Peg sat on a stool nearby giving him instructions.

"That's it, boy; you got most of the sailor's hitches down. Reach over and grab that round timber over there and I'll show you how to make a stopper hitch and a weaver's hitch," Peg was saying as Azerick entered the store.

Peg looked up at Azerick as he entered. "If I can trust you two lads to watch my store, I'll go see about getting young Bran here a berthing. If anybody stops in, tell 'em I'll be back in an hour."

"Don't worry, we got it," Azerick assured him.

"I never thought there were so many types of knots," Bran said, throwing down a length of rope with an intricately designed knot tied in the center of it.

"I brought you that crossbow I promised," Azerick said as he slipped the bag from his shoulder and sat down next to Bran. "There are about a half-dozen quarrels in the quiver. I did not have much ammunition made for it since it was a trap. I also have a coat and a spare set of clothes that are too big for me anyway. I scrounged up what few coins I had. They are in a small pouch in the bag with the clothes."

Bran looked at the weapon and bag sitting across from him. "Thanks, I'm glad you could at least spare that."

Azerick felt the familiar stab of pain Bran's snipe brought. "Look, Bran, I'm sorry I cannot go with you. It is just that—something tells me that going with you to rescue Andrea is not what I am supposed to be doing. I wish I could explain it but I can't. I feel like something is pulling me in another direction. Andrill said he felt that fate or something had its hooks in me. I don't know. I just know I am not supposed to go with you, and if I deny the fates, or whatever it is, then my going may just make things worse."

Bran looked up, his face flushed with either anger or shame. "I know. Anyone who has spent time around you can feel it. It's weird. It's just that you're the one who always has a plan. No matter how crazy something is or how bad the odds are, you are the one who figures a way out of it, or something completely random happens that lets you figure out an answer. I'm afraid, Azerick. I'm afraid because I am not as smart or as lucky as you. You know all these things, and whenever you are around things just seem to happen, and no matter how screwed up it is, you always find a way out. I love her, Az, and I am afraid I don't have what it takes to save her. I don't have the fates or the gods or whatever looking out for me like you do. I'm just a street rat, a useless street rat."

"You are not useless, and maybe the fates are watching you, guiding you to do this. How many people would even attempt to do what you are doing? Anyone who would risk their life, and worse, is special, special enough for the gods to take notice."

"Thanks, Az, I hope you're right—for her sake."

Peg came back in less than half an hour. "I got your boat, boy, but you better be prepared to work for it. Captain Zeb don't put up with no slackers or boys who can't follow orders."

Bran jumped to his feet. "I'll work hard and do what I'm told, Peg, I swear."

"I know, and that's what I told him. Zeb's an honest man. He'll do right by you and get you where you need to go. It ain't a straight run, mind you. This ain't no passenger boat. The ship's gotta hit North Haven before sailing down to Langdon's Crossing, and only then is she sailing for Bakhtaran, but it will still be a far sight quicker than any land-bound caravan."

"Thank you, Peg. When do I leave?"

"Zeb says he'll take you on right now. He can use some strong hands to finish loading up the stuff they're runnin' to North Haven."

Bran turned to Azerick. "I guess I better be leaving then. I'm going to find her, Az."

"I know you will. I can feel it. I will see you both when you get back."

Bran picked up his things, turned, and walked out the door, headed for his own destiny. Azerick was already walking after him but stopped with his hand on the door handle. His heart urged him to keep walking, to go with his friend to rescue Andrea, but something else, something profound and hidden deep within the shadows of his soul stopped him.

"Go to hell!" Azerick growled.

Peg raised a bushy salt and pepper eyebrow at his vehemence.

"Not you, Peg."

"Oh, I know who ya meant, and I'll warn ya to watch your tongue lest they decide to meet ya down there one day."

"Thank you for everything, Peg. I will pay you back one day for what you have done for me."

The old sailor scowled at the dejected young man. "They say a good deed is its own reward, and anyone who expects to be paid back for a good deed ain't done any good. Maybe you'll be in a position to help ole Peg out someday, and if ya are then you'll do him a good turn for the sake of doin' it, not for some sense of obligation."

Azerick nodded at Peg's sage advice and walked morosely out of the store and toward his home. He did not have a copper to his name and had nothing to eat but a handful of beans, but he was not in the mood to go foraging today. Instead, he took a direct route back to his lair and spent the next few hours wondering if he had done the right thing.

Was it really the pull of destiny stopping him from going, or was he simply a coward? Azerick was confident he was no coward, but if the gods had taken an interest in him, why was his life filled with so much misery and pain? What kind of destiny required him to lose everyone he got close to?

Azerick finally dropped off into restless slumber and dreamed a dreamless sleep. He awoke the next morning to a rumbling stomach and cottonmouth with nothing to satisfy either one. The beans were dry and would take hours to cook, and the water jug had a crack that left only a long, narrow trail of wet stones leading to a larger crack in the floor where the runnel had made its final escape.

Azerick pulled out the loose stone in the wall where he secreted whatever coins he managed to earn or steal, but upon gazing at the empty niche, he remembered that he had given the last of them to Bran. His stomach ordered him to get moving with a growl that would brook no disobedience. He left through the warehouse entrance and headed for one of his favorite market squares.

The square was at a large intersection where many of the city's workers, both private and governmental, crossed through on their way to work. Bakers and other food venders crowded into the square, often coming to blows for the best corner to put up their stalls, alternately shouting out the quality and low prices of their victuals and condemning the cost and inferiority of the morsels sold by their competitors.

Azerick tried to blend in with the crowd and position himself next to one of the more crowded displays, but every time he insinuated himself into a cluster of people, they immediately gravitated away from him. He felt like a beekeeper moving toward a hive with a smoke pot, constantly driving the bees away from him so he could collect the valuable honey. That was all well and good for a beekeeper, but Azerick needed the crowd to stick together for him to filch a bit of food to eat.

When his stomach rumbled powerfully once again, he decided he was going to just have to do a snatch and run, hoping the proprietor would not see him or care enough to raise too much of a fuss. His luck was off today; he could feel it. The way things were going, the crowd would resume their normal pressing mass the moment he struck, which would allow a watchman or the baker to grab him and beat him.

Azerick's stomach ordered him to stop whining and get down to business. He walked casually toward the stand where numerous freshly baked loaves of bread were stacked on the table and sticking up out of baskets, filling the air of the market with their mouthwatering aromas. His stomach ordered him to move with haste.

Azerick sidled up to the table, ready to grab a large round loaf of black bread when the baker looked right at him. "What are you doing here? Why did you have to pick my booth? Go on, take the bread and be gone with you. Nobody's going to want to come to my stand now, defiler."

The street rat looked at the baker in confusion then glanced over his shoulder as the crowd moved away muttering.

"Beware death's shadow."

"Do not let his shadow be cast upon you or you will die".

"All die who get near him. We may all die now."

"What are you people talking about?" Azerick shouted.

"Cursed! He is cursed to lose everyone he befriends."

"I am not cursed! What are you talking about?"

"His family is all dead, friends all dead. He is cursed, cursed by the hand of Sharrellan."

"He is the hand of Sharrellan, delivering her touch of death to all who get near."

"I am not cursed! I am not the hand of death!" he shouted, but the crowd drew away from him and continued their droning.

Azerick grabbed the loaf of bread from the table, casting a glare at the baker and everyone around him. He half expected the baker to change his mind and demand that Azerick pay for the bread, but his face had gone purple, black splotches stood out against the plum-colored flesh, and his tongue protruded, swollen and blackened like a plague victim.

The street rat threw down the loaf and ran. The street-clogging populace parted like the water at the bow of a swift-moving vessel to let him pass.

"Beware death's shadow, beware the hand of Sharrellan," the people's mantra continued, following him, chasing him like a swarm of relentless bees trying to drive him away from their hive, their chanting a mimicry of the bees' angry buzzing.

Azerick found himself near the docks and burst into Peg's shop, not knowing where else to go. "Peg, what is going on around here?"

"Now why did ya have to come back here, lad?" Peg asked as his face purpled and black splotches began spreading across his visage. "Hasn't old Peg treated ya right since he met ya? Ain't he done nothin' but help ya?"

"Of course, Peg, I know you have. What's wrong?"

"Then why'd ya come back and kill me? Look at me, boy. Already your foul curse is on me. Ya killed me, boy. Ya killed me sure as sure. Go on now and let me die in peace."

"No, Peg," Azerick wailed, "I did not want you to die! I did not mean to!"

"Meaning don't mean nothin' when you're dead. Go on now, I can't hardly talk no more," Peg slurred around his swollen, blackened tongue.

Azerick ran from the store and sprinted down the harbor front past the long piers and moored ships until he saw a ship with someone he recognized shuffling about on the deck.

"Bran!" Azerick called out as he ran the length of the long dock. "Bran, you haven't left yet. I don't know what is going on. Everyone is acting strange and dying. I think the plague has come to Southport. We need to get out of here."

His friend turned toward him, his face already showing the signs of death. "It's no plague, Az. It's you, you are the plague. I was too slow. Everyone on the ship is dead already. I suppose it doesn't matter now anyway. Andrea is long dead, killed by your curse when she met you, just like the rest of us."

"No! I did not kill her! It's not my fault!"

"Yes, it is. Do you know why she was out the night the slavers took her?" Azerick shook his head. "Her father put his hands on her again. He did that sometimes when he was really drunk. Just his hands. They fought, and she ran off even though she knew it was dangerous."

"No, no, no," Azerick moaned, not wanting to hear it.

"You could have kept her safe, Az. You knew what it was like for her, but you kept your nice, safe little haven all to yourself. You were safe from the depredations of the city above. You let her die. Your selfishness let her die."

"It is not my fault!" Azerick vehemently denied. "I could not keep her safe! I could never keep those around me safe! They all died: Mother, Father, Jon and the others; they all died."

"Now you begin to see. Everyone around you dies. Your family died because you are cursed, and Andrea died because you were a coward, because you were too much of a coward to try to keep her safe. Better to let others take her. That way you wouldn't feel the weight of responsibility. Your conscience could be clear. She would be dead, but you could deny culpability. But you know the truth. You know it was your fault."

Azerick barely heard Bran's last words. His own thoughts were echoing inside his head too loudly for him to focus upon his friend. *I could not keep her safe! I could never keep those around me safe! They all died: Mother, Father, Jon and the others; they all died.*

"They all died because I did not keep them safe. I may not have been able to save Father, but I should have been there for Mother, Jon and the others, and Andrea," he said, talking to himself as he left Bran behind.

Azerick awoke in a cold sweat, somehow knowing it was not the nightmare that woke him. Someone was coming. He heard the trapdoor hidden beneath the burned-out timbers of the tanner's shop open then a sudden cry and the thump of a body hitting the stone. He sprang out of bed, grabbed his knife, and prepared to defend his home. If the gods cursed him, then his enemies would suffer under the spell of his shadow as well. He would make certain of it.

CHAPTER 20

Half a dozen men surrounded the trapdoor in the burned-out remains of what appeared to have once been a tannery. All six men were slavers and normally would have been hunting the streets for valuable targets on this moonless night. Instead, they had followed Kaleesh, one of their own who claimed he knew where one of the men, or boys as it turned out, lived. The man in charge of the slave ring had put out a very sizable reward for the capture of whoever it was that had cost them a fortune by freeing their last shipment of slaves and making them all look foolish.

Kaleesh had been with the group that had chased the boy into the squatters' district before losing him thanks to the help of what many thought was the thieves' guild. Kaleesh had not gone back to the warehouse, now rendered useless by the infiltrators' knowledge of its existence. Instead, he had stuck around the dilapidated ward hoping to find where the boy had gone to ground.

Kaleesh was an experienced thief out of Bakhtaran and knew they had chased the young intruder to his warren like hounds running a fox back to its den. It was as much luck as skill that led him close enough to the hidden entrance to let him spy the street rat sneaking away the next day. The boy was cautious and far from inept, the fact he was still alive testified to some measure of skill, but he was not a real thief like Kaleesh was.

The swarthy-skinned, hook-nosed Sumaran knew there was no need to follow the boy throughout the city, although he easily could have without detection. It was simpler to wait for the boy, who used far less caution than he should have, to return and pinpoint the location of the trapdoor for Kaleesh.

Kaleesh considered ambushing the lad inside his own home, but he could not be certain if there were others living inside. He was confident the boy was not a member of the local guild despite their apparent interference. Still, entering another's lair by oneself was unwise, so he decided to let a few of his closest cohorts in on the plan. He would take half the reward and split the remainder between the others. It was still very profitable, much more so than if he had foolishly told the entire company. Telling the boss directly was even more foolish. The thieving bastard would have simply ordered everyone down the hole and not paid out at all.

"The way in is under here," Kaleesh told his group. "Raheem, you go first and we'll follow you down.

Raheem lowered himself into the dark hole, climbing down the metal rungs of the ladder bolted to the stone wall of the shaft. He had only descended a few steps when the ladder rung pulled out in his hand. Raheem's stomach lurched with the terrifying sense of falling. He reached out desperately to grab onto another rung as he plummeted into the darkness, but his weight pulled the slick rung out of his hand.

The slaver did not know what struck him when he hit the floor below, but his entire body convulsed and contorted as waves of agonizing electricity created by the magical ward Azerick had managed to reproduce coursed through his body.

Kaleesh heard Raheem's body strike the ground and was glad he had decided to let the fellow Sumaran be the first to descend. He had never liked Raheem and figured that if the boy trapped his lair, as he himself certainly would have, then let Raheem find the first one.

"Be careful and watch for more traps," Kaleesh told the others.

Jonah went next, followed by Kaleesh and the others. Jonah climbed carefully down the ladder, reaching with his leg when he came to the missing rung. The next step was slick and coated in grease or animal fat.

Jonah supported most of his weight with his arms until he was able to get his feet firmly on the next step and avoided touching the slick rung with his hands. He saw where the missing rung slipped into a slot in the sides of the ladder. It let a person step on it without incident, but the moment they leaned back it slid right out of the slot. The bar itself dangled from a stout cord against the wall just a few inches in front of his face.

He was only two rungs from reaching the bottom, just three feet above where Raheem lay, when the step moved. The rung only shifted a fraction of an inch, but that was enough to pull the cord that disappeared into a crack in the wall, which pulled the trigger of the crossbow hidden behind it. The slap of the cord striking the steel bow heralded the death of Jonah. The former slaver dropped the last few feet, landing atop Raheem with a quarrel protruding from his side just below the armpit.

Bah, two men dead and they had not even reached the den's floor! The gods only knew how large the place was. It could cover half the damn city for all he knew. The first flickering doubts began to fill Kaleesh's mind. Maybe he had better go back and tell the others? No! It was just one street rat; he was certain! They would just have to be more careful.

"Now the rest of you watch what you're doing!" the Sumaran hissed up the shaft.

Kaleesh grabbed the sides of the ladder with his hands and the inside of his feet, slid the rest of the way to the floor, and then motioned the others to follow him the same way. One after another, the three men slid to the bottom and joined the Sumaran in the gloomy passage, looking warily for signs of any more traps.

Kaleesh could hear the men's fear in their breathing as they all stared up the dimly lit passage. A luminous fungus grew on the walls, adding a small amount of bluish light to the dim, yellow light of an oil lamp with its wick turned down, placed at what appeared to be a four-way intersection perhaps thirty yards ahead.

"Death awaits all who enter here," an eerie voice whispered down the passage. "Flee! Run while you can, body thieves, you vile purveyors of flesh, run!"

Kaleesh's men looked ready to do just that until he froze them with a glare promising a knife in the back of the first man to flee.

"It is just a boy playing tricks with you," he growled at his men. "I know who you are, boy! I know your face! It is you who had better run if you can!"

Laughter, more disconcerting than the eerie whispers had been, filled the dank passage. Only Kaleesh's unspoken threat kept the men behind him from running away and fleeing back up the ladder.

Azerick watched the first man who attempted to climb down the treacherous ladder strike the ground, landing on the ward he had created. The narrow passage behind the wall hid far more traps, ready to unleash their hidden death upon anyone unfortunate enough to find their triggers. After the second slaver set off the crossbow and dropped atop his associate, Azerick's fear at the intrusion became anger then a grim sort of amusement.

When the dark-skinned man threatened him after hearing his spooky warning, Azerick could not help but laugh at the fear the man tried desperately to conceal. His friends were even worse at hiding their emotions than their leader was. He could smell the sweat rolling off their normally pungent bodies. Fear sweat had an altogether different odor to it than the stale stench of poor hygiene.

Azerick watched through small holes in the wall revealed by simply pulling out stones not mortared in place. He saw the swarthy man take the lead and move like a man who knew something about the art of thievery and trap setting. His movements reminded him of the way the guild thieves moved: carefully and precisely, spotting and avoiding the trigger plates that would spell his death.

It was obvious this man was too skilled to trip any of the traps hidden along the floor, so Azerick was going to have to take a more direct course of action. When Kaleesh stepped past another trigger plate, Azerick simply pulled the trigger on the crossbow himself. With speed and agility that shocked Azerick, the man dropped to the floor as the bolt clattered off the wall just above his head.

Cursing, Azerick grabbed the handle of a short spear and thrust it through a murder hole in the wall, stabbing the man directly behind Kaleesh low in his side. Azerick drew the spear back and stabbed again as the man cried out in pain but was silenced by the second thrust piercing his left lung. The other two men behind him shouted out in terror and turned to run despite Kaleesh and his threats.

Before they could move, Azerick was already tugging on a rope near the bottom of the wall that ran through a pair of pulleys before disappearing again into the ceiling. The tether pulled the stoppers from two clay jugs filled with lamp oil. The oil poured through the cracks in the ceiling and rained over the two men at the rear of what was left of the raiding party. Slipping in the oil, the two men turned and sprinted back toward the metal ladder.

"Stop, you fools, or he'll kill you both!" Kaleesh shouted at the fleeing men, but his words fell on deaf ears.

With their shoes soaked in oil, climbing back up the ladder was proving difficult. Shins banged into the metal rungs as their feet slipped, but fear lent strength to their arms and they managed to pull themselves up. Just below the empty space where the slip-bar dangled, a square hole appeared in front of the lead slaver to reveal an angry pair of hazel-green eyes lit by the yellow light of a lamp.

The eyes vanished as quickly as they had appeared. Azerick thrust a flaming brand through the opening in front of him, igniting the intruder's oil-soaked clothing. The slaver emitted a terrible keening as his garments burst into flames. In his terror, he released his hold on the ladder and fell right onto his partner desperately trying to clamber up the ladder past him, setting his own combustible clothing aflame.

Both men fell screaming as twin flailing balls of fire, landing in a writhing, screeching pile upon the corpses of Jonah and Raheem. Kaleesh pressed his hands over his ears in an attempt to block out the horrible screams the men made as they flailed about on the floor for one or two agonizing minutes before they finally fell still.

Kaleesh's nerves were worn to their breaking point. He knew he could not flee. The hell-spawn of a boy would not let him. He would not leave this place alive unless he killed him. He focused his thoughts and knew he could do this.

"Do you think you have won, boy? Those men were all fools, but I am no fool! I am of the Faslum fee Sariq, the most feared group of thieves and assassins in all of Sumara! I will not fall for your tricks! I will find you, and I will gut you. To the abyss with the reward!

Delivering your corpse with the skin flayed from your body will be my reward! Do you hear me, boy? I am Kaleesh, and I swear this to you!"

Kaleesh ignored the deranged laughter reverberating from behind the wall and echoing through the passageways. He knew where the boy was hiding now, and that would allow him to avoid his tricks and traps. Then he would find him and drag him out of his little cubbyhole.

Kaleesh was so wrapped up in his thoughts of vengeance, he almost missed the obvious trigger plate just below his hovering foot. Kaleesh smiled and extended his leg beyond the trap, marveling how those other fools would probably have stepped right on the thing that was so obvious to his darkness-attuned eyes.

His world exploded in a brilliant flash of pain as his foot fell through the floor. What had looked to be solid stone was nothing more than fired clay, painted and weathered to look exactly like the stone surrounding it. Kaleesh's foot dropped through the shattered clay cover and tripped the spring-loaded jaws waiting beneath. Steel teeth pierced his soft flesh and grated against the bone, but it was inaudible over his cries of agony. The slaver looked through tear-blurred eyes as the boy emerged from the shadows of the passage ahead like a cold and remorseless wraith coming to exact its revenge.

"Who are you?" Kaleesh shouted past the tears of pain.

"I am the hand of Sharrellan, and you are caught in my shadow," the boy said as he scooped up the curved sword Kaleesh had dropped.

Kaleesh stared in horror as the boy's shadow, dimly cast by the flickering lamp just ahead, draped itself across his piniored form. He let out one final scream before the boy drew back the blade and swung it forward with all his might, silencing him for all eternity.

Azerick stared emotionlessly at the head that rolled to his feet, staring up at him wide-eyed with a look of horror permanently etched upon its face. He tossed the sword aside and began the grisly task of dragging the six corpses to the sewer entrance of his lair, one by one, and tossing them into the filthy water where they would probably find their way into the harbor in a few days, less if it rained heavily.

"At least my financial situation has improved," Azerick said to himself as he stared at the small pile of coins and valuables laid out on the table in front of him.

"You want me to be the hand of Sharrellan, the reaper's shadow?" Azerick shouted at the ceiling and the gods supposedly living far above. "I will be your hand, goddess of death. I will be your hand against everyone who threatens me or those close to me! I will send you so many vile, tainted souls you will have to open another circle of hell to keep them all in!"

Outside, high above the city of Southport, the low rumble of thunder echoed across the dark, cloudless sky.

CHAPTER 21

It was easier to recreate the ward the slaver had destroyed than it had been that first time, but such protection had thus far proven unnecessary. It had been several months since the failed invasion of his home, and if anyone else knew where he lived, they had apparently decided to leave him be.

That did not mean that Azerick did not face any struggles. He owed money to the thieves, and his food supply was running short. Azerick scanned the crowd milling about the merchant district's market. He was looking to pick a mark out of the hubbub that may provide him with the means to buy a meal or two and pay his taxes to the guild.

There, Azerick thought to himself. A doddering old man in flowing robes. His disarrayed hair, scruffy beard, and mismatched shoes made him appear like a vagabond without two coppers to rub together. Nevertheless, his robes, although a little worn and giving clear evidence of what he had for breakfast, were of a good-quality material.

Azerick liked marks in robes because robes were loose, flapped in the wind, and were easy to slip his quick hand and nimble fingers into to pinch a purse. The young sneak thief plotted out his working area once again, now in relation to his target's location and movement along with his escape routes.

The old geezer's path would take him right by a fruit and vegetable stand. Azerick strolled through the market square, browsing the diverse items displayed on the various counters and tables like a casual shopper perusing the day's wares.

Most market sellers kept a keen eye out for thieves and pickpockets and could spot the amateurs of lesser skill and quickly run them off.

Azerick knew how to blend in and dress for each job and location. He wore clothes of, if not good quality, at least passably better quality than your typical street urchin or beggar. He always wore the best he could steal or buy depending upon which option was readily available.

Stealing them had the highest profit margins but it was harder to steal clothes than a quick bite to eat off a food stand. However, Azerick would buy them on the rare occasions he could afford them, considering them a good investment. He also kept his hands clean and his hair groomed. People did not look at you as closely if you did not look like you just crawled out from under a dung heap.

Azerick paused in front of the produce stand, acting as though he were looking over the fresh fruits and vegetables as the old man meandered up to the same stand. The old man smelled of pipe smoke and strange spices and mumbled to himself constantly as he browsed the little side street shops.

This is too good to be true, Azerick thought to himself.

If Azerick had not been so hungry, his inner voice probably would have reminded him about things that appeared too good to be true; they usually were, and people who leapt at those kinds of opportunities fell into a pit with dirty wooden stakes at the bottom of it.

Unfortunately, times had been tough lately. Azerick had not made a decent score in quite a while, and the local thieves' guild was breathing down his neck to pay his taxes. In fact, they were getting downright aggressive in their collection attempts, and Azerick was sure to pay in bruises, or worse, if he was careless enough to let them catch him.

As soon as the old man was a few feet from the produce stand, Azerick picked up a round, yellow-green piece of fruit and looked to be examining it more closely. As he was inspecting it, it "slipped" from his grasp and rolled toward the old man in robes. With an exclamation of surprise, Azerick made a swift lunge after the wayward citrus and toward the old man. With his head down, one eye on the rolling fruit and the other on the man's belt pouch, he bumped hard into the robed figure.

As one hand scooped up the escaping fruit, the other hand deftly liberated the man's pouch with a quick cut of the fastening strings using a small, razor-sharp blade affixed to the inside of his index finger. The coins in the pouch did not make so much as a single clink as Azerick transferred his catch from the old man's belt to a pocket inside his own worn but clean, short cloak.

"I beg pardon, good sir!" Azerick said as he held up the fruit to display the reason for his clumsy jostling. Azerick felt a moment of giddy pleasure at the flawless execution and success of his endeavor.

His thrill of success turned to fear when a hand wrapped around his wrist and held it fast. Fright gave way to pain when a paralyzing jolt shot through his arm and all the way down to his toes. His hand spasmed, crushing the piece of fruit into a pulp. The gnarled fingers of the old man let loose their grip and Azerick flew backward and lay in a most undignified sprawl on the cobbled square. Azerick could only moan as he lay there, his arm stuck out stiff as a board with sticky juice running down its length and dripping off his elbow.

The old man bent down, reached into the inside pocket of the thief's cloak, and retrieved his purloined purse while Azerick could only lie in the street, twitching, with the sticky juice from a now well-pulped citrus fruit running down his rigid and extended arm.

The old man looked down at the prostrate form of the young thief, his eyes sparkling with mirth under his bushy, grey eyebrows. "Boy, if you plan to have a long life in your chosen profession, then I strongly recommend you heed this one piece of advice: never rob a wizard."

With a dry chuckle and his sage advice, the old man, or wizard Azerick now knew, went on his way whistling a jaunty tune. Now the little voice that was usually so adept at keeping Azerick one step ahead of trouble rang quite audibly in his head about jobs that seemed too easy.

"Now you remind me," Azerick muttered to himself.

Azerick was just beginning to regain voluntary control of his arms and legs again, glad to be able to make his escape before someone got it into their head to call the Watch, when the momentarily forgotten proprietor of the stand loomed over him.

"Now who do you think is going to pay for that ruined piece of fruit you got in your fist?" he demanded.

Azerick breathed out slowly and closed his eyes. "Help me to my feet, good sir, and I am certain we can resolve this like gentlemen without the Watch, I pray."

The vendor was a large man, accustomed to the rigors of fieldwork by the look of the obvious strength in his arms. He was dark-haired, barrel-chested, and a cotton apron hung from his thick neck and belted around his waist. He easily pulled the wiry, would-be thief to his feet. It was only by a great force of will that Azerick was able to keep his feet under him and stand unsteadily before the glowering farmer on wobbly knees.

"Well, sir, it seems I owe you for this piece of produce of yours. However, I am in a bit of arrears at the present time. If you will tell me at what hour you close down your stand, I shall return to assist you in loading it into your wagon so you might be off back home. I hope that will be sufficient to work off my debt to you."

"If I let you out of my sight now, you'll just run off, and I'll be out of a sale and still be loading my cart myself. I'll probably never see you again, unless you try to rob another wizard in this square!" said the big man, letting out a loud guffaw.

"Sir, I assure you, despite the occupation I have chosen, or which chose me for that matter, I am a man of my word and will return here promptly to make amends for the damage to your goods."

"Well," the farmer pondered, "if I call for the Watch, you'll just run off or they'll arrest you. Either way, I'm not getting my money, so I guess I'll trust you to your word. You be back here an hour before the sun sets and you can help me load up for the day. And if you don't show, well, I still got a good story to tell over a mug of ale tonight!" The vendor let out another good bellow of laughter and clapped Azerick on the back hard enough to set him in motion out of the square and away from the laughing eyes of the other patrons and vendors.

All Azerick could think about as he walked back toward his home hidden beneath the buildings and streets of the old industrial district, was the shame of everyone's eyes on him and their humiliating laughter at his failure.

Oh, I will be very careful of robbing a wizard again, very careful indeed. This is not over by a long shot. I will have my revenge, wizard. I always get my revenge.

The old wizard likely thought his show of power and embarrassing the young thief would put enough fear into the typical petty cutpurse and street urchin. Ordinarily, he would likely have been correct in his assumptions. However, Azerick was no ordinary street thief. At least he did not think of himself as such.

The problem with trying to intimidate Azerick was that nothing seemed to cow or scare him. Many had tried and nearly all had failed. Azerick was, to all appearances, completely incapable of experiencing real fear. It was not that he was immune to it or oblivious to its effects. The problem was that his mind instantly transformed any fear a particular situation may cause into anger.

Instead of suffering the quaking effects and indecision fear would normally bring on, he became angry with whatever or whoever dared to try and frighten him. That anger triggered an incredibly powerful sense of determination and stubbornness that would push him to cross the Great Desert to exact revenge for any harm to or severe wounding of his pride.

These thoughts of revenge so occupied his mind that he let his street awareness waver, yet another thing he would not have allowed under normal circumstances. Had he not been so preoccupied, he most certainly would have spotted the three guild thugs before they took notice of him, and easily avoided them.

"Well, well, what have we here?" snarled the obvious leader of the group.

"Hugo," sighed Azerick, "not now. I'm having a really bad day."

"That's too bad, because it's about to get a whole lot worse," Hugo replied as he launched a strike at Azerick's head.

Azerick easily ducked the clumsy but powerful swing and struck Hugo twice in the stomach with a quick blow from each fist. The big youth let out a whoosh of expulsed air as he backed up a step. Carrot overcame his moment of surprise and let loose with an attack of his own. Azerick blocked the punch and delivered two quick jabs and a right cross that rocked his assailant on his heels and left a broken nose and a stunned look in his eyes.

Azerick was about to charge between the two punks and make his escape when the third boy, Rolly, made a running slide toward him and executed a leg trip. Azerick went crashing face down toward the cobbles. Only a quick, last-second twisting of his hips kept him from landing on his face and prevented serious injury.

Hugo and Carrot both recovered from their assault in those precious few seconds and started laying in with a series of kicks to Azerick's legs and side. Azerick protected his vitals as best he could with his arms and twisting motions, but enough blows got through that he was taking a significant beating.

After a few moments, Hugo decided he had made his point and he and his cronies ceased their assault. "Faralynn says if you don't pay your taxes real soon I get to take care of you myself." The gleam of cruel anticipation in Hugo's eyes left little room for doubt as to the pleasure he would gain from causing Azerick a great deal of pain.

Faralynn was the local chapterhouse leader who collected taxes and tithes from all thieves working in the area in which Azerick unfortunately found himself. He had originally worked within Andrill's district, but Faralynn's rise to power over the past year had redrawn the lines, which put the young street rat within the powerful and unforgiving hands of one of the most dangerous, and only female, guild leaders in the city.

Hugo and his friends laughed at the implied threat and gave him one more good hard kick to the ribs as they left Azerick curled in the fetal position on the street.

"You and your moronic friends just got a permanent entry on my list, Hugo," Azerick muttered as he picked himself up off the filthy cobblestones.

As soon as he regained his feet and his breath, Azerick once again continued his trek home, taking the time to design two plans of payback for his wounded body and pride, but this time he kept more alert to his surroundings.

No, best to focus on one plan at a time, he thought. Azerick devoted his full revenge-filled thoughts to the wizard. Hugo could wait a bit longer he reasoned. Azerick had never had magic used against him before. It instilled a sense of powerlessness while in its grip, and that made him feel, not scared, but certainly disconcerted…and angry.

Hugo and his friends had been a pain and an annoyance for the past several years. Azerick guessed that made him about sixteen or seventeen years old now. He had stopped keeping track some time ago.

That started Azerick thinking about his life before the streets and the one, or ones, who occupied the top of his revenge list: whoever set up and killed his father. He probably could have asked Andrill for help in getting information about his father's murder, but he still owed the man a debt and was not about to increase it. It was hard enough just surviving right now.

Azerick picked his way through a dilapidated warehouse with half its roof caved in. He looked around carefully before entering a large crate covering the trapdoor beneath it. He reached down and lifted several planks to reveal the entrance. This allowed him to grip the opposite floorboard. When he pulled, a whole section of the floor pivoted up to reveal a passage with ladder rungs built into a stone shaft.

Azerick barred the trapdoor from inside and began his descent. He carefully avoided the rungs designed to cause a slip, make a bell ring, or worse, launch a spike into the belly of the one unfortunate enough to trip it.

He settled himself into his abode, his stomach singing to him in a rumbling baritone, and once again started to think of his past, back nearly five years to a time of safety, comfort, and happiness. Those thoughts, as he waded back upstream in the river of time, took him once again to those days of happiness but also to the most horrifying and dreadful moments of his young life. He thought back to the cause of his whole purpose of being: revenge against those responsible for his life and the loss of his family, fine home, and education. His education had been the most important thing in his life aside from his parents.

CHAPTER 22

By the time Azerick came out of his reverie, it was nearly time to go back to the 'market square of shame,' as he now referred to it, and make good on his debt. He was a man of his word after all. Integrity was one of the few things no one could ever take away. It could only be willfully surrendered.

"Well, as I live and breathe, whoever would have guessed a street rat would keep his word and do some honest labor?" the produce merchant commented as he watched Azerick approach his cart. "I really didn't expect you to show up, boy. Might be some hope for your character yet."

"Rest assured, good merchant, that my character is just fine as I see it."

Azerick spent the next half hour moving and stacking the crates of fruits and vegetables so the farmer could safely cart them back to his farm. It was not terribly difficult work, and he was finished in fairly short order.

"You owed me a debt, boy, but I'll thank you for your service anyway. Here, take these as a token of my good character," he said and handed Azerick a small bag with a few apples, pears, and a gourd.

"Payment is not necessary. I owed you for what I damaged, and my labor made us square."

"Nonsense, boy, I know you're hungry, and now you don't have to worry about stealing a meal tonight. That makes me feel well enough that we're still even if you accept it. A man, a boy even, needs to know what it feels like to receive compensation for honest work. Perhaps if more thieves and street urchins knew that feeling then they would be more prone to doing honest work instead of trying to take the easy road and just steal it."

"Yes, sir, thank you," he replied and walked away, not wanting to argue with the man who obviously knew nothing about living on the streets if he thought it was an easy life.

Azerick did not think anything about his life had ever been easy since his father's death. He did appreciate the food. He was not particularly interested in trying to filch a loaf of bread or a small wheel of cheese today. His earlier exploits still stuck in his craw, and he just did not feel up to it.

Tomorrow, however, is another day, he thought as he made his way across the city yet again and crept back into his bolthole.

Azerick spent the next week plying his usual trade, nicking bites to eat, lifting purses, avoiding Hugo and his crew like the plague, and burglarizing the occasional home when he was really desperate for money. He stuck mainly to the middle and upper-middle-class homes of merchants. He never pulled off another caper as lucrative as the one that had made him enough coin to buy his precious alchemic set. Such had been an act of desperation and his situation, as bad as it was right now, did not warrant the possibility of spending several years in prison.

His gift to his friend Bran had absorbed the remaining gold he had made from that run and now he was having a hard time making his payments. He was at least two weeks past due and needed to make a decent score soon before the guild got tired of leaving the collection job to those three idiots and sent out some real thugs to finish the job. He could always pawn his alchemic set back to Azeel, but he immediately discarded that as an option. He would have to burgle another house and soon. Nothing as risky or elaborate as before, but something he could hit quickly and with minimal risk. Maybe he would start casing some likely places tonight.

"Or maybe they will just have to wait a bit longer," Azerick muttered to himself as he spied a familiar old man in robes striding up the street.

He looked around for some way to create a distraction that would break the old wizard's attention long enough for Azerick to get in and out quickly. Once again, the fates supplied the perfect means. Hugo and his motley little band were across the square, likely scoping out a mark or two as well. Azerick's quick mind went to work and formulated a plan in seconds.

He threaded his way through the crowded streets toward his three nemeses, scooping up a fresh lump of horse dung along the way. When he came within range, he shouted at the three thugs to gain their attention.

"Hey, Hugo, I got all the taxes you're worth right here."

As soon as Hugo looked up at him, Azerick flung the fresh dung at Hugo's broad face with the accuracy of a champion archer. The filthy ball of manure hit Hugo right in the mouth with enough force to peel back his puffy lips and shatter the dung ball into dozens of tiny projectiles that caught Carrot, Rolly, and a few unlucky bystanders in its expanding spray.

"Kill him!" Hugo screamed, spitting out bits of horse dung.

Azerick took off like an arrow launched from a bow with the three hoodlums in pursuit. He ran through the crowds as fast as he could without knocking into any of them and slowing his escape. His path of flight intentionally took him on an unerring course toward the old wizard who had so humiliated him previously.

Within moments, he caught sight of his target, ducked his head, and ran full tilt into the old man. White wispy beard, boy, and stained robes rolled into an uncontrolled tumble onto the cobbled street.

"You!" the old, coarse voice shouted in surprise as recognition of his assailant sparked in his mind.

Azerick spared a glance behind him with a look of fright, scrambled to his feet, and ran off into the crowd. Hugo, Carrot, and Rolly continued their pursuit through block after block of streets and alleys before Azerick eventually lost them by ducking into a printing shop and running out of the back door before his pursuers were able to turn the corner and spy his escape route.

Azerick ran several more blocks before slowing down to a nonchalant walk and admiring the purse of coins he had snatched from that old fool of a wizard. He had just turned the corner out of an alley and onto the street, eyes on the coin pouch in hand, when he bumped into someone strolling down the sidewalk.

"Pardon me, sir," Azerick said as he moved to his right to let the person pass.

"Pardon I will not give you, boy," came the coarse grumble from the man.

Azerick looked up to see who impeded his passage and saw stained robes, a wispy unkempt beard, a craggy, lined face, and sparkling eyes filled with both amusement and malice. He could only gape as the old wizard plucked his stolen property from the thief's hand and secreted it back into his robes.

"I told you before, boy, it's decidedly unhealthy to steal from a wizard."

The old man then started mumbling words in a language Azerick did not understand and waving his hands in front of him in an odd but obviously intentional pattern.

Before Azerick realized what was happening, he felt a great force against the entire left side of his body lift him off his feet and fling him through the air. The young thief sailed across the plaza and was dumped unceremoniously into a large fountain where several women were washing clothes and bathing small children. He landed with a great splash as women grabbed their wash and children and retreated from the sudden spectacle. Water filled his mouth as he yelled a curse before coming up and regaining his feet.

"You sorry, old, goat-bred bastard, this is not the last of this, I swear!" Azerick shouted indignantly from the middle of the fountain, his clothes dripping and his soaked hair plastered to his head.

"Boy, you must be the stupidest, most hardheaded, or just plain foolish thief who ever cut a purse. Whichever one it is, it is most assuredly impeding your ability to learn and make wise decisions."

The old wizard's hands started their rhythmic gesticulations once again. The water around Azerick started to excite into a roiling froth. Before he could move, another great pressure enfolded him in its embrace. This time he was able to see the cause. A large fist of water crushed him in an unbreakable grip then lifted him high into the air and slammed him back down into the pool. Some people in the crowd cried out in fear while many others actually applauded the show as the young man was lifted up once again, coughing to expel the water from his lungs. Back and forth, the watery fist tossed him about like a terrier shaking a rat. The animated fist lifted him up then dunked him hard to the left then raised him back up and slammed him to the right. Over and over the cycle repeated itself.

After what seemed an eternity, Azerick finally found himself dumped at the wizard's feet, sodden and expelling water from his lungs with great fits of coughing.

"Now, boy, what do you have to say for yourself? Have I managed to get through that great thick head of yours?"

"This is not over, wizard," Azerick gasped and coughed the water from his lungs. "I would kill you one day, but that would be a mercy. No, there will be no easy death for you. I will humiliate you. I'll make a mockery of you before all who would call you friend, I swear it!"

"By the gods, boy, what will it take for me to drive this lesson into that muddled mash of porridge you call a brain?"

"Death, old man! You'll have to kill me before I will ever submit!"

"It's fortunate for you I have too high a regard for one's life, even for one as angry and hardheaded as you are, to grant you exactly that, even though you have given me plenty reasons to justify it. Most of my order would not be so gracious. Count yourself fortunate, but know that even I have a limit as to the amount of foolishness I'll brook!"

With that last warning, the old man disappeared into the applauding crowd. Azerick was still trying to get his wind back when three shadows darkened the area around him.

"Will you fancy that, Carrot? Here he is all nice and clean while we smell of horse crap," Hugo said in a deceptively amused voice. "Let's help our friend up and walk him home."

"Here you go, friend. Up on your feet, let's get you home," Carrot said to Azerick as he and Hugo lifted him from the ground.

Still out of breath and exhausted from the magical trouncing he had just received, he was barely able to form a protest and even less able to resist them as they carried him away from prying eyes. They carted him into the alley and dumped him onto the cobbles before rifling through his pockets and cloak and finding the small coin purse he kept tucked in his shirt.

"This will do for a start, but it's far short of the taxes you owe," Hugo said as he counted the coins in his hand before dropping them back into the pouch. "This is to remind you to have the rest by tomorrow."

All three began planting kicks to his back, sides, and arms. Azerick thought they were finished until Hugo said, "And this is for hitting me in the face with horse crap!" and began kicking him once again.

This round the kicks lasted twice as long. He was almost certain they were going to make good on their frequent threats to kill him this time, but just as he was about to black out, Hugo issued him one more threat then all three left him lying in the alley's gutter bruised, bleeding, and aching over every inch of his body.

Azerick lay there for over an hour, promising to inflict a great amount of pain on each of them for every kick they gave him. Through sheer force of will, he was able to drive himself to his feet and hobble home. It took him nearly two hours to cross the city and make it back to the safety of his lair where he lay down on his pallet. He thought he had the necessary reagents to brew up something for the pain and speed his healing, but that would have to wait until tomorrow.

Azerick had neglected to turn his large hourglass, so he had no idea how long he slept. He awoke many times during the night as each movement sent fresh amounts of pain coursing through his body. He shuddered and winced as he sat up and was surprised to find that he was actually in more pain this morning than he had been last night.

The pain was still as acute as it was before, but now a significant amount of stiffness had set in to accompany it. So much pain filled his young body as he stood up that he nearly lost consciousness. Floating motes of light filled his vision while a wave of dizziness threatened to spill him onto the floor.

Azerick fought back the pain and vertigo and crept over to his alchemic set. He sifted through the glass jars of ingredients and found what he needed. He had made pain-relieving and healing aids frequently and knew their manufacture by rote. He ground blood moss, cristholis seed, and willow bark with the mortar and pestle, lit his oil-fueled burner, and set his retort to boil water. He poured in the mashed ingredients and set one of the small hourglasses to time the brewing cycle. He made his way to his little stove, kindled a fire, and set water to boil for some tea. He was soon sipping his tea waiting for his blessed potion to finish.

Once it was completed, he poured it into his drained teacup and drank the bitter concoction down. It was still so hot that it scorched his mouth and throat, but he scarcely noticed it over the rest of the pain.

In a few minutes, Azerick felt well enough to make something to eat. He dug through his depleted larder and came up with enough to make a stew that would last him a few days. He set a large kettle of water to boil then added chunks of vegetables, salted beef, barley, oats, and just about whatever else he could find. The healing draught would cause him to burn his food at a greatly accelerated rate, and he would need the stew to keep the potion effective and maintain his strength. He did not even wait for the stew to finish cooking before he ate a bowl of it then crawled back into bed. Every time he woke up for the next several days he would wolf down a large bowl of stew then fall back asleep.

After nearly a week of bed rest and healing draughts, Azerick was ready to go back out. He had to go out whether he was ready or not. He was out of stew, and every bit of food he had in his larder had gone into its making.

Azerick was still stiff and ached where several ribs had been cracked or broken, but he was able to move relatively freely. He just had to ensure he took extra pains to avoid Hugo and the two testicles. That is what Azerick liked to refer to them as, right and left testicle with Hugo being the dangle in the middle.

While Azerick spent the week recovering, the city was abuzz with word of a great festival thrown in honor of the Academy's millennial anniversary. There were to be large feasts, acrobats, and brilliant magical displays for the nobles and lesser folk alike. Men dug massive roasting pits on the great parade field that normally hosted knightly tournaments and other displays for citywide attendance.

The duke had pledged to serve five hundred sides of beef, pork, and mutton. There was also going to be a private feast held at the Academy with the duke, nobles from across the kingdom, and the entire staff of the Academy as well as all the students. The students would be served in a dining hall separate from the nobles, but the duke swore to visit during the dinner to address them all and give them accolades for their diligence and contributions to the kingdom.

A festival of this scale would create an untold number of opportunities for a wide range of nefarious activities, but Azerick chose a very specific target. He snuck onto the grounds of the Academy the night before the ceremony, figuring there may be tighter security if he waited to infiltrate the grounds on the day the nobles and the duke would be arriving.

He slept the night in the loft of the stables, hiding from the stablehands behind bales of hay or under piles of loose straw. He stayed in the loft until the next evening, watching the horses and fancy coaches as the city's elite arrived. Drivers parked the expensive coaches in the square in front of the stables after they delivered their precious cargo to the front steps of the Academy and safely tucked the horses away in the numerous stalls.

The stables were huge and could accommodate at least a hundred horses by Azerick's quick count. The enormous structure was partitioned in two, the forward section used to house the mounts belonging to the students and staff. The back, and much larger portion, was for the Martial Academy's training mounts. Few guests stabled horses for tonight's feast as any noble of worth had arrived by coach. It was unbecoming to ride horseback to an event as elaborate as the one being held this evening.

As Azerick began to descend from the loft, he came across one of the many rats typically infesting such places and lured it to him with a bit of food. He caught it up and dropped it in a hard leather satchel he kept slung over one shoulder.

This should prove useful, he thought.

Azerick exited the stable and was questioned only once by one of the stablehands. He simply showed his furry captive to the groom and said the Academy had hired him to exterminate as many rats as he could lest one run across the shoe of one of the many prestigious guests and besmirch the cleanliness of their hallowed grounds.

He scanned the rows of parked carriages until he found one to his liking. A boy, probably a page, dressed in his master's livery stood eating an apple next to a fine coach. He was about Azerick's age and size but lacked the hardness he had achieved through his harsh life on the streets.

"Ho there," Azerick called to the boy.

"Who are you, and what do you want?" the boy demanded.

"I just came to look at the carriages and thought maybe you would let me take a look inside one."

The boy looked at Azerick and sniffed. "I think not. You are likely to leave a stain and an ill scent upon the upholstery."

"Come on. Look I'll give you a silver piece for just a peek. I won't even step inside or touch anything, I promise," Azerick said as he held up the shiny piece of silver.

As the page reached for his promised reward, Azerick let the coin slip from his fingers. When the boy bent to retrieve it, Azerick clouted him hard behind the ear with the blackjack he had made from a leather pouch and a fistful of small, lead balls. The boy fell to the ground at Azerick's feet in a crumpled heap. He grabbed the boy under the arms and dragged him into the carriage. A minute later, Azerick emerged from the coach wearing the fancy livery of the page, leaving the real page securely bound and gagged on the floor of the coach.

He walked through a set of stone arches and crossed the well-manicured lawns before reaching the main Academy building. He let himself in through a postern door and found the kitchen. Azerick grabbed up a serving tray, ate a couple of the snacks, and swept out into the dining hall.

A cacophony of sounds coming from several harps, lutes, and a harpsichord as well as the tuneless droning of dozens of nobles and Academy members filled the hall. Azerick made his way around the long, brightly polished tables while serving the morsels off his tray. The nobleman, whose livery Azerick wore, flagged him down to get him some wine. The man did not even look at the imposter long enough to see that he wore a different face than the one who had brought him here. The only thing the rich man saw was his colors. The wealthy never see the face of the lesser people who serve them.

Azerick made several rounds about the tables, listening and learning the names of those in attendance. He found the old wizard who had humiliated him twice and served him, leaning over his shoulder with his silver tray, and was once again invisible while standing in plain sight. He learned his name as well—Magus Allister. Armed with this knowledge he began to execute his plan.

Azerick went back to the kitchen and found a tray with a silver dome used to keep the contents warm. He also found a flagon of wine into which he poured a quantity of extremely spicy red sauce. He served the wine to Lord Answorth Bronwyn, Lord Mayor of Groveswood and the covered silver dish to his wife, Lady Tabitha Bronwyn. Groveswood was a town east of Southport. It was a relatively small town but boasted a long and proud history. Many wealthy merchants and minor lords sought its mild weather, shaded groves and gardens, and peaceful surroundings, building summer manors and often moving there permanently in their retirement.

"My Lord and Lady, Master Allister begs you to try a special vintage as well as a rare treat he deems only a palate of your character deserves, but please wait until I inform the magus that it has been delivered before you indulge. He wishes to make a toast of it and witness your delight."

"Of course, please send the magus our warmest regards," Lord Bronwyn commanded without even looking over his shoulder at the imposter who served him.

Azerick skirted the back wall, circling to the far side of the room to the table directly across from the Bronwyns to where the wizard sat. He bent down and spoke softly into the old wizard's ear.

"Master Allister, Lord and Lady Bronwyn wish to raise a cup to convey their deepest appreciation for your diligent service to the Academy and the excellent tutoring you have provided the many children of the kingdom's upper class."

Azerick ducked back into the shadows as Magus Allister gazed across the table and raised his goblet in salute to the Bronwyn's' kind words. The lord raised his cup, and his lady gave the wizard a nod and a smile. Lord Bronwyn brought his wineglass to his lips and sipped as his wife lifted the cover on the silver serving dish.

Both lord and lady let out a scream, one of shock and pain as the fiery spice burned a trail from his lips to his stomach, the other of horror when the large black barn rat ran down the table as soon as its shining, silver prison was lifted.

Cries went up from the ladies seated at the table as they jumped up, several falling backward over their chairs as the furry, black streak raced across plates and turned over wineglasses. Serving boys, pages, and kitchen staff chased after the fleeing rodent swinging serving trays and wooden spoons, driving it from the dining area.

The crowd was starting to settle down as Lord Bronwyn stopped choking enough to point an accusing finger at the magus. "What is this, sir? You dare try to poison me and frighten my wife into an early grave! Is this your idea of a joke?"

"My Lord and Lady, please, I have no idea what has happened," the flustered and confused wizard replied. "If this is indeed some kind of hoax, the guilty party will be found and dealt with, I assure you."

The master of the Academy stepped up to offer his reassurances to the Bronwyns. "My Lord and Lady Bronwyn, please accept my sincerest apologies. Everyone, please be seated. The excitement has passed. Let us get on with the banquet. I offer all of you my deepest apologies. It appears that someone, likely one or more of the spirited students, sought to play a cruel jest on us old stuffed shirts. You know how children are. I am sure the rest of the evening will go splendidly."

The music picked back up as the well-dressed crowd returned to their seats and resumed their conversations, many starting to have a laugh at the excitement. Azerick continued to keep an ear to the conversations hoping to discover another chance at creating further mayhem.

The evening wore on with no more excitement until he chanced upon some hushed words coming from a dimly lit alcove, words promising of a midnight rendezvous and a secret tryst in the garden. Azerick watched from behind a fluted pillar as the conspiring pair returned to their seats. The man was middle-aged and sat next to a hatchet-faced woman who always looked to have just bitten into a lemon. The pretty, younger woman took her seat next to a great fat man dressed in flamboyant silks.

Azerick retreated to the kitchen and fetched another pitcher of wine, then returned to Magus Allister, and filled his cup, deftly mixing in a fine powder. He watched as the man with the sour-faced wife excused himself from the table followed several minutes later by the pretty woman with the fat husband.

Azerick trailed the woman out of the hall and into one of the gardens. Sticking to the shadows, he heard a whispered call, a short squeal of delight, and giggling. He followed the sounds of a man and a woman taking their pleasure to a darkened little alcove surrounded by creeping ivy and rosebushes. As the amorous couple frolicked in the garden completely unaware of the voyeuristic eyes on them, the young thief reached through the bushes and absconded with a piece of the woman's underclothes. He crossed the grounds of the garden looking for the living quarters of the teaching staff. As he searched along the halls, a man in a well-made but plain robe accosted him and demanded to know his business.

"Young man, what are you doing here? These are the personal quarters of the magi."

"Please, sir, Master Allister bid me fetch a scroll he had set out that he wished to show to Duke Ulric, but I have gotten turned about and have forgotten the directions to his quarters."

"Bah, I don't have time to play tour guide to some boy too simple to follow instructions. I have a great deal of work to do."

"Please help me, sir, lest I be turned into a newt or some such. I do not wish to be a newt," Azerick pleaded in his most pitiful voice.

"Take those stairs up to the third floor. His is the room on the right at the far end of the hall, and see that you do not get lost or you may well get something worse than being turned into a newt," the man warned.

Azerick sprinted up the stairs, taking two steps at a time, to the third floor and ran down to the end of the hall. The door was a simple wooden one with a typical lock. He was about to take his lock picks to it when he felt the same queer sense he had experienced from the fancy jewelry box at the manor house he had robbed.

At least there are no dogs or guards this time, he thought.

Azerick closed his eyes and concentrated as he had before in the mansion. The emanations from the door felt stronger, cleaner, somehow better constructed, but lacked the malevolence of the jewelry box. The jewelry box had been dangerous, possibly deadly. He felt that if he set this ward off it would likely do little more than alert the owner or perhaps give him a good jolt. He did not know how he knew that, but he was certain his assumptions were correct.

It took far longer to manipulate the energies of this ward than the last one, and a magical ward is what he knew it to be now, but he finally got it to release its hold on the door. His practice in creating wards of his own had paid off handsomely. With the ward taken care of, he went to work on the lock with his picks, which took far less time to undo than the ward had.

Azerick crept into the wizard's chambers. The room turned out to be far smaller than he would have expected of a wizard of the Academy. A bed was near the window, with a large trunk at the foot. A desk sat facing the wall under the only other window in the room while a large bookcase filled with books, powders, and small knickknacks stood against the wall opposite the desk. A small alchemic set rested on a table next to the bookshelf. He looked around the room for something to steal and selected a book titled *"Elementary Magic"* and a large crystal from the bookshelf. He stashed both items in his shoulder satchel, darted back out of the room, and ran back to the dining hall.

The mischief-making thief cut through the gardens once again and caught sight of the two lovers making their way back inside. Azerick ran back through the door leading to the dining hall ahead of the couple and spied the old wizard coming up the hall from where the privy was located.

Still enjoying the fruits of your wine, eh wizard? Azerick chuckled to himself.

As the old man strode past, Azerick dropped the pilfered undergarment into one of the silk robe's large pockets. He then cut through the kitchens, once again grabbing a wine pitcher, and walked briskly into the dining hall.

"Here, My Lord, let me fill up your cup since you are still here. I thought you had gone out to the gardens with your lovely wife," Azerick said.

"My wife went to the gardens, you say?" the fat man asked.

"Yes, milord, a few minutes before Magus Allister excused himself saying something about having to show someone his wand. Do you think he means to give us all a magic show? Though it did sound to me to be a private showing. Oh well, here they both come now."

The couple exchanged angry whispers while the fat man glared at Magus Allister. He stood up, threw his napkin down, and waddled around the table to confront the wizard.

"Magus Allister, I would know to where you disappeared and what foul business you have perpetrated," he demanded.

"Sir, with all due respect, where I went and what I did is none of your affair," the wizard replied, his face coloring with both embarrassment and irritation at the man's effrontery.

"It is when your affair is with my wife! Show her your wand indeed!" the fat man shrieked.

"Sir, I assure you I have no idea of that which you speak," the wizard replied, his face getting nearly as red as the jealous husband's.

Leaning against the wall, Azerick cleared his throat and pointed at the wizard's pocket. Quicker than Azerick would have thought possible, the fat man thrust his hand into the big pocket and came up with the silken undergarment belonging to his wife.

"Explain this, sir!"

"I, I, I cannot," the old man stammered.

"Now, Peter, certainly you do not think I would betray you with this...ugh...old man, do you? I would never stoop so low," his wife said.

"What precisely is the level that you would stoop to, my dear?" the man asked.

Azerick thought it time to make his escape and head back home, feeling that his work was mostly complete.

CHAPTER 23

He was still running on the excitement of the evening and knew he would not get to sleep anytime soon. He stayed up for a couple of hours reading the book he had stolen, finding it of great interest. He hoped he would be able to keep it when this was all over. It contained a detailed explanation of magical theory and even a few minor cantrips and spells.

He read over them and knew that with a little time he could decipher their meaning and possibly cast them. Much like the magical wards he had unraveled, he seemed to have an almost natural understanding of the mystical words. Azerick studied a few of the minor spells and was able to make sense of the writings and meaning after a couple of hours of study. He eventually grew tired, but instead of placing the precious book in his bookcase, he laid it gently on the floor at the intersection of two passageways just up from the main room in which he slept and lived.

The next morning, he awoke and went back out into the street, this time actually searching for Hugo and his friends. It did not take long, and Azerick cherished the look of surprise on Hugo's face when he called him over.

"I couldn't get you any coin, Hugo, but I have something that should be worth at least as much as I owe," Azerick said and produced the crystal he had stolen from Magus Allister's room.

"What is this? What do I want with some piece of glass?" Hugo demanded.

"It's crystal not glass, and it is said to have magical properties."

Hugo looked at Azerick out of the corner of his eye. "What kind of magical properties?"

"I don't know, I'm not a wizard, but I'll bet someone schooled in magic will pay you well for it."

"All right, street rat, but next time, you better have real coin," Hugo demanded, then punched Azerick once in the gut, and stalked off admiring the reflected sunlight thrown off by the crystal.

Azerick caught his breath as the thugs walked away laughing at his distress. Once the three left, he went off in search of food to restock his larder. By noon he had a couple of small sausages, a fist-sized wheel of cheese, and two loaves of bread. Now that he was assured of having a decent lunch, he made his way back home to enjoy his repast.

He crept into his dwelling with more stealth than usual, looking and listening for any signs of an intruder. He checked each of his many traps as he slinked down the passageway, but all were still functional and ready. He spread out his fare, set some tea to brewing, and waited for it to come to boil.

A wavering aura of light illuminated the gloomy chamber then filled it with sunlight. Azerick shielded his eyes with his hand and squinted at the sudden brilliance coming from a few yards up the passage from his chamber. A black, silhouetted form appeared, created by the sunlight streaming in from what appeared to be a hole in the air leading directly to the streets of the city above.

"Boy, we have a great deal to discuss before I decide what manner of punishment I shall inflict upon you," came the deep, rumbling threat of the angry magus.

"I believe it is best that we call the game a draw rather than escalate the war to greater levels," Azerick replied.

"You think this a game, do you? I shall dispel that notion from your mind."

The wizard stared down at the floor ahead of him where the book of magic rested, lying in the dust. "Not only do you dare to steal my book, but you then defile it by carelessly tossing it to the ground! Not surprising to find you are an illiterate little savage."

The wizard seemed even more incensed about his book lying on the ground than anything else Azerick had inflicted on him. Magus Allister took several steps forward and bent down to retrieve his precious tome.

A flagstone shifted under his soft-soled foot, and mortar and dust flew into the air as a powerful spring pulled a rope from under the false grout that hid it. Pins holding the rope securely out of sight sprung out from between the stones securing them in place as they could no longer bear the force of the heavy counterweight dropping from behind the wall.

The wizard felt a sharp pinch around his ankles and found the world turned upside down as the rope went taut. He swung back and forth, twisting round and round as he dangled at the end of the rope holding him aloft. Heavy cloth covered his eyes and he bared his buttocks as gravity pulled the hem of the robes down over his head.

"I had a mind to be merciful, boy, but now I will truly make you rue the day you ever crossed me!" he raged.

Azerick heard the wizard start making the strange mumbling sounds and hand gestures he had the day he conjured the huge watery hand to grasp and dunk him repeatedly in the fountain. Azerick sprinted across the room and into the passage in the blink of an eye, a slender willow rod in hand. He swung the switch, interrupting the wizard's casting by laying a great red welt across his exposed, wrinkly buttocks.

The wizard let out a great howl as fiery pain lanced across his sensitive posterior. "Damn you, boy! I have had quite enough of this foolishness, and I will suffer no more abuse from you. Now let me down this instant!"

"I think not, wizard. You are under my control, and we will come to terms before I decide to let you go."

"You think that it is so easy to trap a wizard, do you, boy?" Allister queried with a chuckle. "I'll show you what it means to have a dragon by the tail."

Before Azerick could even think of raising his switch for a second strike, the suspended wizard whipped his hand in a rapid gesture and spoke a single word. Azerick found himself unable to move as if he had been turned to stone.

A shimmering wave like the heat reflecting off the desert sand limned the wizard. Another string of words and gestures turned the wizard right-side up, floating a foot off the ground, the rope no longer wrapped about his feet.

"Whip me like a disobedient mule, will you?"

The willow rod flew from Azerick's grip and moved as if wielded by an invisible hand. He felt fire erupt again and again as unseen red welts rose across his backside.

"Now, boy, I'm going to release you, then we are going to sit down and have a talk like civilized gentlemen. I know that may be a difficult part for you to play, but I expect you to do your best, and I will tolerate no more of your foolishness."

Azerick found he had regained the use of his limbs and shot the wizard a glare before walking over to the table and sitting down. Fresh pain lanced across his whipped backside, but he would not give the old man the satisfaction of showing any sign of discomfort. Allister took a seat across from him and studied his face for a moment.

"Tea's done, would you care for some?" Azerick asked his guest.

"So long as it agrees with me better than the wine did last night," Allister said, lifting an eyebrow in accusation.

Azerick merely smiled and poured the tea into two plain cups.

"That was quite a performance you put on. The tainted wine, the rat, nearly getting me in a duel for a lady's honor."

"I try my best at whatever I do."

Magus Allister got up and studied the books on Azerick's bookshelf then inspected the exquisite alchemic set resting on the crude table. He revised his opinion that the boy was illiterate.

"That's quite a set you have there. Do you know how to use it?" the magus inquired.

"I have been able make it suit my purposes, and yes, it is quite nice, isn't it? I was surprised to see such shabby equipment in the quarters of a powerful mage like yourself."

"It serves me well enough, but you have brought up the very point I wished to discuss with you. My door was warded to give me a warning and an unfriendly greeting to anyone who opened it that had no business within, and I would know how you managed to get past it."

The magical portal leading to the surface expired, throwing the room into a gloomy dimness. Azerick lifted the glass off the oil lamp sitting on the table and rubbed the wick between his forefinger and thumb. A small flame kindled between his digits and set the wick alight. He returned the glass flute to the top of the lamp and trimmed the wick.

"How did you do that, boy?"

"I read your book and followed the instructions. It was not any more difficult than creating or unraveling your little magic traps, easier even since the book gave good instructions. Really, if that's all there is to magic, then you have had a lot of people fooled for a very long time."

"No, there is a great deal more to magic than what you have read in that book. The spells you saw were of the lowest order, little more than what any street-corner charlatan could conjure up. But still, to have cast even those cantrips without any instruction from a real mage is remarkable."

"Remarkable, that's me in a nutshell."

"Yes, why didn't I see it before?" the old wizard mused, peering intently at the young man seated across from him with his wizard's sight and seeing for the first time the powerful aura surrounding all wizards. "You have the gift, boy, and a strong one at that, I think. Still, there is no way you should have been able to get past my ward. Granted, I didn't put much thought or effort into it. I did not think I needed to, but even my most minimal work should have been more than sufficient to keep you out."

"What do you mean I have the gift? What gift?"

"You have the gift of magic in you. Contrary to what you may think, not everyone who can read can just pick up a spell book and cast spells. A person must have some amount of natural talent to do what you did, and even then would normally require a great deal of training."

"So what do you want of me now? I assume you're not going to kill me otherwise you would have done it already."

"I'm no more a killer than you are, boy, rest easy on that. I have a mind to take you with me back to the Academy. I'm certain I can talk the headmaster and the council into granting you a scholarship."

"I'll have you know I've killed men before, so this better not be a trick of some kind."

"Perhaps you have, boy, but there is a line between being forced to kill to survive and cold-blooded murder, and I don't see a murderer in front of me. Do I, boy?"

"No, I don't feel anyone ever died by my hand without good cause, but I'll let the gods be the judge of that."

"Oft times they're the only ones who can. Now pack up what you want and we will be off, assuming you want to go, that is. I think the Academy will suit you far better than the streets, no matter how comfortable your home is. What do you say?" the magus asked.

Azerick considered his options for several minutes while the old mage waited patiently. He had always wanted to attend the Academy, but as a scholar not a wizard. He felt like this was his home, a place where he felt safe. But for how long? How long could he keep his lair a secret? He still had to run the streets to survive, and there lay the greatest danger: the danger of being caught as well as that presented by the guild thieves. All it took was for him not to pay his tax before they got tired of trying to collect and made another example out of him.

"I took a crystal from your desk too. Did you know that?" Azerick asked.

"You mean this crystal?" Allister held it up for Azerick to see. "Of course I did. I keep a close eye on all my possessions."

"What happened to the people who had it?"

"They'll likely think twice before receiving stolen goods again, particularly magical ones. I gave them a lesson similar to the one I gave you. Last I saw, they were hanging by their breeches from a bronze statue of a mounted knight," Allister said with a grin.

"So it was magical after all?"

"No, but they told me some street rat told them it was when he gave it to them as some kind of payment. I assumed that you expected me to find it and therefore would not have given it to someone you liked. To tell the truth, I didn't like the looks of them anyway."

"All right, I'll go with you," Azerick said.

Once Azerick packed away his alchemic set, books, and some clothes, Magus Allister conjured another portal to the outside. Azerick could see the streets and the sun through the window or doorway the wizard had created.

"What is that?" Azerick asked, looking at the thing in front of him with a skeptical eye.

"It is a magical gate. One end is here and the other is on the streets above."

"It looks like it opens just above us in front of the warehouse. Why not just have the other end open on the Academy grounds?"

"There is a pretty strict limit to how far apart the two openings can be," the wizard patiently explained. "The Academy would be much too far away for this kind of spell."

"I heard wizards can teleport to anyplace they want. Why not teleport us there?"

"Teleporting is a risky thing, much too risky for any living thing, particularly if you don't have a fixed, properly prepared place set up to teleport to. Even then, the odds of all of you ending up in the right place, or even the same place at the same time, are not good enough for even the most experienced wizards to hazard. Now let's be on our way before this thing wears off. It is not as easy to create as I make it look. It's enough to make a man tired and hungry, even a man as experienced as me."

Master and new student stepped through the magical gate and emerged onto the street. The wizard came to a stop and briefly closed his eyes while Azerick stumbled, dizzy and disoriented.

"Try and stand still, boy, and focus on a fixed object. The feeling will pass in a few seconds."

Azerick did as he was told, and true to his word, the dizziness passed and they continued on their way, the wizard toting the alchemic set, Azerick carrying the worn bag full of books, clothes, and a few personal belongings.

CHAPTER 24

The Academy stood as the apex of human achievement, where the best of their society received the finest education in the kingdom. It was not for street rats. Through the insistent sponsorship of Magus Allister, Azerick was granted a scholarship to attend. The first time he had come to the Academy, he had seen very little of the grounds during the day, but now he took the time to examine it in all its splendor.

The Academy was actually three separate schools. One section was dedicated to the study of magic, one instructed students in martial training, while the other taught purely scholarly pursuits to the nobles and the wealthiest of Valeria's citizens. Martial training included tactics, small and large-scale troop movements, mounted combat using swords, bows, lances, and all manner of martial weapons. The Martial Academy also boasted an archery range, tilting lanes, a large field to practice maneuvers, and a stable. It produced the kingdom's finest officers and elite military units.

The Magus Academy had its own practice field as well where the students could cast far-flung and hugely destructive spells. The buildings and towers were all alabaster white. Several towers came to a point, sheathed with red, fire-baked clay tiles. Domes made up of dozens of huge hexagonal panes of glass capped two of the Magus Academy towers and were used as observatories. The two glass-domed towers housed the largest telescopes in the kingdom and were used to study and track the moon and the stars.

The three schools maintained their own dining halls, training grounds, libraries, dormitories, and classrooms. The only part of the campus they shared was a large park separating the three schools called "the commons." The campus was comprised of three massive central buildings where the students from each school took their meals, attended classes, studied in the library, and were housed.

Allister showed Azerick to his room and got him settled in. A staff member issued him bedsheets, a pillow, and blankets as well as two robes that served as the Magus Academy uniform to wear as long as he was on Academy grounds. He was trying on one of the robes when another student entered the room.

"Oh hi, I didn't know I had a roommate this year. I didn't have one last year. I hope you don't snore. I hope I don't snore! I'll apologize now for snoring since I don't know if I snore or not. I'm usually asleep when I'm sleeping, so It's hard for me to say whether I do or not," the new boy spouted out nervously.

"Okay," Azerick said, drawing out the word in confusion. "I'm Azerick, and you are?"

"Oh sorry, I'm Franklin, but my friends call me Rusty."

"Because of your hair?" Azerick asked.

Rusty was tall, a good six inches taller than Azerick was but probably weighed twenty pounds less and had a headful of bright red hair.

"No, it's because it takes me a little while to get the hang of things after the summer break…and winter festival break, and spring festival break, and just about any break in school longer than a week. Sometimes my spells don't go right after I have a break in study, and I set things on fire. When that happens I tell them it's because I'm rusty, so everyone started calling me Rusty."

Rusty talked fast and in a nervous fashion, his eyes constantly darting around trying to look at everything at once. "So what's your favorite sphere? Mine's fire!"

"Sphere? I don't know what you mean."

"You know, sphere, element, like fire, water, earth, wind, or astral."

"Oh, I don't know. I don't have one yet."

"Really? How long have you been studying? I've never seen you at the Academy. Where were you apprenticed before?"

"This is my first time here or anywhere. I've never studied magic before."

"You've never studied before? At your age? How did you get in here then?"

"Magus Allister sponsored me. When did you start studying?"

"Most of us start at around six or seven years old. Man, I've never heard of anyone starting the Magus Academy at your age. The Martial Academy maybe, but it's going to be hard for you to catch up. You should be an apprentice by now, perhaps even a journeyman if you were really good. I'm an apprentice myself, but I hope to graduate to journeyman by the end of the year. You start out as a novice, but don't worry, I'll help you so you don't get stuck with the kids too long."

"Thanks, I appreciate it."

"What does your father do? He must be pretty important to have enough influence to get you into the Magus Academy at your age."

"He was a ship merchant, but he's dead now. Magus Allister saw me do some things, and I guess it impressed him enough to get the rules bent for me."

"Well, that's good, and he's a pretty powerful wizard around here, so you must have something going for you. Let me help you unpack."

"Okay, thanks."

Rusty showed Azerick a small bookcase, a table, and a desk where he could set up his things, and Azerick began unpacking.

"Whoa, where did you get that alchemic set?" Rusty exclaimed when Azerick began setting it up on the table.

"I bought it in town."

"You must have had quite an inheritance to buy a set like that."

"I had some money, but it's mostly gone now."

"It looks like it's been used. Did you use it?"

"Yeah, I made a few things with it."

"You said you never studied before. What did you make?"

The question made Azerick hesitate for a moment. "I made potions that would help a person sleep, ease pain, speed healing, and a type of really flammable oil."

"Wow, that's pretty high-level stuff. Where did you learn how to brew them?"

Azerick showed him his book on alchemic theory and practice as well as the book on magic Allister had let him keep. He showed off the few cantrips he had learned from the book to Rusty.

"And you learned all that just from the book without any help? I learned those spells in my first couple years, but I would never have been able to do it without a real magus to teach me. No wonder Magus Allister brought you here."

"I just hope I can learn enough not to embarrass myself. I'm still not sure if I'm really cut out to be a wizard or not. I think I would like to be though," Azerick said.

"I'm sure you'll do fine. You probably won't even be in the baby class that long."

"The baby class?"

"Yeah, that's what some of the kids who have been here a while call the novices, mostly just the jerks, not me. They act like none of them ever started at the beginning and just instantly advanced to apprentice or journeyman."

"Are there a lot of jerks in this school?"

"There's a few. Mostly it's the wealthy kids from old families who think they're better than everybody else. My father is one of the ministers of finance for the duke, but our money and family doesn't go back that far. He was just an accountant for some moneylender until about ten years ago, and then he got the ministry position. That's how I was able to get into the Academy. You have to kind of watch out for them. They like to gang up and pick on the younger kids and those whose family doesn't have much influence."

"I can take care of myself, but thanks for the warning." Azerick went to place his book back on the bookshelf and stepped on the hem of his robe. "How can anyone stand to wear these things? There's no way you could fight in this without wrapping yourself up and falling." Azerick cursed as he kicked at the bottom of his robe.

"You don't have to wear it if you don't want to. It's only required for graduation and formal occasions. Most people wear whatever they want. Some wear the school robe, and some wear fancy ones made of silk and have all kinds of ridiculous patterns on them like they're already some high magus or something. I think they look like idiots."

"I can imagine."

Azerick pulled off the cumbersome robe and changed back into his charcoal and hunter green outfit replete with short cloak. It was not the richest-looking clothing, but it was still in good shape. He and Rusty continued talking for another hour or so and became fast friends. Late that afternoon, a bell tolled from across the common.

"What's that for?" Azerick inquired.

"That's the dinner bell. C'mon, I'm starved."

The two wizards-in-training raced down the stairs and entered a large hall filled with benches and tables. They got in line and were served with the best-looking assortment of food Azerick had seen in a long time.

"Look at this food!" the former street rat exclaimed.

"Yeah, kind of an army chow deal here, but it's not too bad," Rusty replied, being far more accustomed to eating a richer fare.

Azerick was soon gorging himself and drinking fruit juice. The food made him feel better than he had in a long time. Rusty was doing most of the talking since Azerick was far too busy putting food into his mouth to get any words to come out of it. Midway through his dinner, he felt a tingling at the back of his neck, his street sense alerting him to someone at his back.

"Hey, Rusty, what are you going to set on fire this year? Maybe this time it will be your hair, not that anyone would notice," came a snide remark from behind Azerick.

"What do you want, Travis?" Rusty asked, looking ill at ease.

Azerick looked over his shoulder at the newcomer. He was about Azerick's age, dressed in a fine robe of blue silk with the cuffs and hem bordered in black. Strange designs and sigils sewn into the silk with silver thread adorned it. Of course, he was not alone; bullies never are. He was backed up by three more richly dressed, but not quite so gaudily, boys about the same age.

"You bringing in strays now, Rusty?" Travis taunted, looking down his nose at Azerick.

"Do you have some kind of problem with me?" Azerick asked as he got to his feet.

"I have a problem dining with peasants whose only business here should be mucking out the stables," Travis sneered.

"Azerick, just ignore them. You don't want to get into it with them."

"Yes, stableboy, you don't want that, I assure you."

"You should be glad I'm here. I did just come from the stables, and you should be happy to know that I gave your mother a good brushing and a nice bag of oats. I heard she was a good ride, but I'm not sure if they meant under a saddle or under the sheets," Azerick fired back.

"You...how dare you! I'll kill you!" the enraged young man sputtered as he withdrew a wand from his robes and pointed it at Azerick. "Take back those words this instant, or so help me I'll kill you where you stand!"

"Azerick, do it, take it back!" Rusty cried in panic.

"Pfft, with a stick? You're not even holding it properly. Here, let me show you how to use it."

Travis glanced down at his wand, and in that split second, Azerick's hand snaked out in a flash and snatched the rod way. Travis looked up, about to demand his property back when Azerick struck out and slapped him hard across the face with it. The bully, now on the defensive, raised a hand to cover the stinging welt already beginning to form on his face only to receive its twin on the other side by an equally swift backhand blow.

In an attempt to retrieve his wand, Travis lunged at the commoner who had dared strike him. Azerick ducked a shoulder and drove him back into two of his friends standing behind him. The third member of Travis' gang rushed forward. Azerick turned and lunged for the table, scooped up the heavy wooden tray, and cracked it across the boy's forehead.

The boy flew backward into a pair of spectators seated at the table behind him, knocking them over onto their table and upsetting their trays. The rich boy and two of his cohorts were back up and charging. Azerick jumped onto his table and was ready to defend his high ground when a booming voice resounded across the dining hall.

"That is enough!"

Azerick and all four of his tormentors found themselves suspended above the tables and benches. Travis continued to curse and threaten him. Azerick reached down, scooped up a baked potato, and hurled it, striking him between the eyes.

"I said that was enough! What is the meaning of this?" demanded a man in robes.

"Magus Morgarum, he stole my wand and hit me with it—twice. He also hit me in the face with a potato, shoved me, and hit Thad in the face with a tray. He must be thrown off the grounds immediately!" Travis demanded.

"The headmaster decides who attends this school, Apprentice Beaumonte, not you. What do you have to say for yourself?" he demanded of Azerick.

"I was just defending myself."

"We'll see about that." Whatever force was keeping them suspended ceased and sent all five plummeting to the floor and onto tabletops.

The five students soon found themselves standing before Headmaster Dondrian. He wore the typical wizard garb Azerick had seen most of the other mages wear about campus. His robes were a rich silver with mystic symbols and runes stitched in black silk thread. He was mostly bald, what hair he had was in a two-inch strip running from one ear and wrapping around to the other, and starting to grey at the temples. His lips were a bright red like someone had created them by slashing a blade across solid flesh and carried a sheen due to his constant habit of licking them. He sat quietly during each boy's telling of the events within the dining hall until he felt he had heard everything he needed to hear.

"Young master Azerick is here at the request of our own Magus Allister. Regardless of his background or social standing, you and the other students will afford him the same courtesies as every other student. I will not tolerate hazing of any student for any reason whether they are new or of a lesser social class," Headmaster Dondrian calmly chastised.

"Yes, Headmaster, I'm sorry. We were just having fun with a new student is all, and I guess we got carried away. What about my wand?"

"You know wands like that are dangerous and expressly forbidden to be owned or possessed by students. I will give it back to you when you return to your home for spring festival. You and your friends may go. Azerick, please stay here a moment."

Azerick steeled himself against the rebuke he knew was coming and prayed they would not throw him out of the school on his first day.

"Azerick, as I told the other boys, you are here at the request of, and as a personal favor to, Magus Allister. I hope you realize how great an opportunity he has granted you."

"Yes, sir, I do."

"Then you must conduct yourself as such. You are not on the streets anymore. You are attending one of the most prestigious institutions in the kingdom, and you will conduct yourself appropriately. Your actions are a direct reflection not only upon yourself but also upon the man who argued quite strongly for your presence here. Do you understand?"

"Yes, Headmaster."

"Then you may go, and remember what I said."

I'll remember what you said, but if you think I'm going to let a bunch of puffed-up nobles run roughshod over me you are sorely mistaken. Academy and Allister be damned, Azerick fumed as he stalked down the stone halls of the Academy.

He had just entered the hall leading to his room when Travis and his friends stepped out of an alcove, blocking his path.

"Don't think this is over, peasant. You made a big mistake and a powerful enemy. If you knew who my father was, you would know they can never throw me out of the Academy, but they'll toss your low-born butt right back into whatever gutter Allister dragged you out of."

"I really don't care who your father is. If I'm pressed, I'll defend myself. It would be a whole lot better if you just left me alone."

"Better watch your back, poor boy," Travis warned as he and his friends walked away.

"I can't believe you did that!" Rusty exclaimed when Azerick entered the room they shared. "That was the most incredible thing I've ever seen, stupid but incredible. No one has ever stood up to them like that before."

"It wasn't that big of a deal. I've faced a lot scarier guys than them before."

"Still, you better watch out. They pick on almost everybody. With what you did to them today, and being poor, they're going to be after you."

"I'll be careful. I'm not afraid of them, but I don't want to get kicked out of school either. It has been a dream of mine almost as long as I can remember. Travis said no one could kick him out of the Academy. Why can he get away with so much?"

"His father is Duke Ulric's cousin. I don't know what that makes him, but whenever he gets in any kind of trouble, his father is able to fix it and he's back in a day or two. Eventually, they just stopped punishing him for most things, but don't worry, I'll help you keep an eye out for them as best I can. Will you show me your alchemic set?" Rusty begged.

"Sure, I'll show you how to make that super-flammable oil. I call it dragon's breath. Luckily, I still have a little of the distillates left otherwise we'd be spending the entire night watching the base ingredients cook."

Azerick used the few ingredients he had remaining to make a small batch of the combustible mixture and showed it off by setting it alight in a small vessel the size of a shot glass. The glass got so hot it shattered, and the liquid flame spread out on the plate on which it was sitting and continued to burn, causing the metal to glow orange before finally consuming itself and going out. The two boys stayed up late into the night as Rusty told Azerick about the school and classes, and he taught Rusty a little about life on the street.

CHAPTER 25

A zerick awoke with the rising of the sun. Rusty did not wake until the first morning bells started ringing an hour later. The dining hall was filled with chaotic chatter but became more directed when Azerick walked in. Hundreds of eyes followed him and Rusty as they took their morning meal. They had about an hour to themselves after breakfast before the first class started, so Rusty gave Azerick a quick tour of the grounds before leaving to attend his classes.

Azerick's first day of school consisted of taking a multitude of tests to determine what he was proficient in and what classes he would have to take to catch up. He scored well in reading, mathematics, alchemy, and basic history and was placed in those classes with students near his own age.

However, he had virtually no education regarding the history of magic, magical theory, the principles of magic, or applied magic and would have to be placed in classes with other beginner students. This meant he would be sitting in class with children half his age, and that thought made him feel more than a little awkward.

The first day of class, he proved to be something of a distraction. The younger children were unable to contain their sniggering and seemed to pay far more attention to the older boy in their midst than to the teacher. Azerick, however, paid strict attention to all of his instructors, wanting to absorb as much knowledge as quickly as he could.

It took only a few days for Travis and his friends to find out he was in a class with the younger kids. They often found him in the hall between sessions and went out of their way to mock him. Azerick ignored their jibes and taunts for the most part. Mere words were not sufficient to cause him distraction or risk jeopardizing his attendance.

Azerick had hoped by ignoring them they would grow bored and give up trying to provoke him, but it went on for the next several months until one day they came into the classroom while the instructor was out. They had never followed him into the classroom before, and he fell ill at ease.

"Listen up, you little twerps, and peasant. It's going to be winter festival soon, and you know what that means and what will happen if you don't bring us what we want," Travis announced and left with his entourage in tow.

All the younger children started talking and grumbling about how mean Travis and his friends were. Azerick turned to one of the boys in his class. "What were they talking about?"

"Those mean boys make us bring back all of our candy from winter festival and give them almost all of it. If we don't, then they' tease us and make our lives miserable. I wish we were as big as them, then we could beat them up and they couldn't take our candy," said Gerard, clenching his small fists.

Azerick knew this had nothing to do with candy. It was about power and tribute. It was about recognizing authority and grooming those beneath you to stay subservient. It was how the few hundred guild thieves were able to oppress and extort the thousands of homeless and shopkeepers. The school was his home now, and the young people in this classroom were his extended family. He had seen what happened when thugs were left unchecked, and he would not allow it to happen again.

Azerick stood up and turned to the class. "Listen up everyone; you don't have to be big to defend yourselves. I have fought people a lot bigger than me and won. What you need to do is find strength in your numbers. I know if you all work together you can defend yourselves against them and any bullies you come across."

"But they're really big and mean, and they know more magic than we do. We can't fight them," one of the girls cried out.

"Have you ever seen anyone get chased by bees before?" Several kids nodded. "Bees are small, so why do you run from them?"

"Because they can sting you, and there are usually a lot of them," Gerard said.

"Exactly, just like there are a lot of you, and I can teach you how to sting them just like those bees."

"How?"

"This is our home, and it will be our battlefield. We know the terrain, and we can prepare it to our advantage. Travis and his thugs fight for power and sheer pettiness, but we fight for our home and our friends, and that makes us more dangerous than any threat they try to levy."

Azerick explained to the younger students what he had in mind. He worked with them over the next several days, practicing what they needed to know in order to defend each other against Travis and any other people who picked on them. They snuck out to the training grounds during free time and had secret meetings and practice sessions in the school's many unused rooms and corridors.

Azerick returned to his room after one of his after-class practices and found Rusty already there. He flopped down onto his bed and draped his arm across his eyes in hopes of relieving the headache he felt coming on.

"Are you going to the winter festival tomorrow, Azerick?"

"I guess so. It should be a nice change of pace, and the fresh air will help me clear my head," Azerick answered.

"How are your studies coming along? Still having trouble with some of the spells?"

"Yeah, the cantrips were easy, and I picked up on some of the lower-level wizard spells, but anything even a little tougher than those I just don't seem to get. I understand what they are trying to teach me, but it just does not make any sense to me. I'm starting to think Magus Allister was wrong about me," Azerick lamented.

"I'm sure you'll get it. Some people get hung up for a while then everything just kind of clicks and they take off again. You have already learned more in the last four months than I did in my first year."

"I hope you're right."

It bothered Azerick a lot that he may not be cut out for the Magus Academy after all. He felt like he was letting down Magus Allister. But the old wizard assured him he was doing just fine and that he had faith in him and his potential. The old mage came by to check on him from time to time and even tutored him when he was having trouble with a particular spell.

Despite his reassuring words, the roadblock Azerick seemed to have reached concerned Allister. Ordinarily, he would not have considered this a problem given Azerick's lack of experience. Nevertheless, he had been learning so quickly in the beginning, and being able to disable the ward he cast on his door he had expected him to come along much faster.

Maybe I am just expecting too much this soon, the wizard thought.

Rusty and Azerick went out the next day to the winter festival. Since Azerick had no money, Rusty bought them pastries and grilled sausages they ate on a stick. They watched jugglers, acrobats, and men walking above the crowd on stilts ten feet high throwing candies and sweets to the children below. Twice Azerick saved Rusty's coin pouch from a couple of petty cutpurses. After the second attempt, Azerick convinced Rusty to let him carry the money.

As the day started turning into evening, the thousands of people crowding the streets began to flow like a river; a massive current of bodies pushed inexorably toward the docks where the fireworks were going to be lit and a few of the Academy wizards would be throwing up some of their own visually impressive spells. The river of humanity forced the two young wizardry students along like flotsam, helpless to go anywhere but where the current guided them.

They were able to get a respite when a few people broke from the herd and carried them into a side street where they could catch a breather away from the tight confines of the populace. Their relief was short-lived when Azerick saw who it was.

"Look here, boys. The street rat got himself a girlfriend," Hugo taunted.

"Hey, Carrot, you didn't tell us you had a sister," Rolly added.

"Couldn't be my sister, she'd whore herself out to beggars before she'd be seen with a street rat," Carrot replied.

"You owe us money, street rat. Now pay up and we'll only bust you up a little bit," Hugo promised.

"I'm not working the streets anymore, Hugo. I don't have to pay your guild's tax anymore."

"You don't get it, do you? Once a street rat, always a street rat. You're on my streets right now, and you'll pay your tax. I seem to remember you owing me some silver from the last tax you didn't pay. Not to mention bustin' Carrot's nose again. By rights, I could take your ear just for that." Hugo produced a rust-marred but sharp knife.

"Give him the money, Azerick, it's okay," Rusty pleaded, clearly frightened.

"Not going to happen, Rusty. Remember what you've been taught."

"Better listen to your girlfriend, rat, and give us the coin."

"I have a better idea. How about I show you a magic trick?"

"What kind of magic trick? This better not be some kind of trick or you're really gonna get it."

"Just watch," Azerick said, rolling his eyes at Hugo's moronic statement.

Azerick moved his hands in a swirling and reaching pattern, and a glowing nimbus of coruscating colors began trailing his motions like the streaks of light following behind fireflies.

"Wow, would you look at that, Hugo! What's he doin'?" Carrot asked.

"I don't know, Carrot, but I don't like it. What are you doing, street rat?"

The three thugs standing in front of them may not have had a clue what was happening, but Rusty did. He choked down his fear and started casting a spell of his own. A shimmering aura, that would help deflect blows as if he were wearing armor, surrounded his body.

A brilliant rainbow of colors erupted from Azerick's fingertips straight into the faces of the three hoodlums. Carrot stood as still as stone, his eyes rolling back up into his head until only the whites were showing; Rolly dropped to the ground and lay motionless.

"My eyes! What did you do to my eyes? I can't see!" Hugo cried and lashed out with his knife.

Hugo blinked rapidly and lunged at Azerick as Carrot came out of his momentary stupor. Azerick grabbed Hugo by the wrist as the thug blindly flailed at him with the knife. Hugo cried out once again, and the knife fell from his nerveless fingers and dropped to the ground as

Azerick sent an electric jolt coursing down his attacker's arm much like Allister had done to him when they first met, only to a lesser degree.

The moment Hugo resumed his attack, Carrot's eyes rolled back down as he shook off his stupor and charged at Rusty. Rusty brought his hands up, shouting out arcane words, and fire leapt from his fingertips onto the top of Carrot's head. As his wooly hat and red hair burst into flames, Carrot let out a screech of terror so high-pitched only girls under the age of ten could usually hit such a note.

Hugo clambered halfway to his feet, grabbed the awakening Rolly under one arm, and tore off out of the alley in a lurching, shambling stumble after the fleeing, flaming Carrot. The crowd parted almost like magic when the screeching Carrot broke out of the end of the side street. Many onlookers pointed and clapped thinking it was part of the show. Azerick and Rusty ran out of the other end and back into the street, the crowd of people thankfully thinning now as most had already made their way to the docks. The two companions slowed once they were free of the crowds and caught their collective breaths.

"By the gods, Azerick, I can't believe that just happened!" Rusty shouted, his hands on his knees, gasping for breath as they came to a halt.

"You did well, Rusty. I've been fighting those three for years."

"I set a guy's head on fire!"

"Yes, you did. Congratulations, Rusty, you fought off your first bad guy using magic."

"Wow, my dad's never gonna believe this."

CHAPTER 26

The next day, Azerick sat in the classroom with his much younger classmates. The tension of anticipation filled the air as the children looked at one another. They did not have to wait long before the source of their anxiety made its appearance. Travis and his friends strolled into the classroom wearing contemptuous sneers on their faces.

"All right, kiddies, time to give it up. Let's have it," Travis demanded.

Azerick had gone over this with the kids. They all agreed that if they were going to stand up to their tormentors, they would have to initiate the rebellion themselves and not rely upon him to defend them.

"We're not giving you anything. It's ours, so leave us alone," Gerard stood and said defiantly.

Travis and his friends laughed at the young boy who glared at them so boldly. Azerick looked around the room at the frightened faces of the other children and knew he would have to provide a little motivator to get them to back the brave boy.

"You heard him, Travis. They're not going to let you push them around anymore, so why don't you leave them alone?"

"Do you think he can protect you, is that it? Even if his casting ability wasn't pathetic, he's still outnumbered four to one. Now give us the candy, or you know what's going to happen," Travis warned.

From somewhere across the room a girl stood and said 'no.' Another child stood as well with a cry of 'no,' followed by a chorus of standing children all shouting 'NO' with anger gleaming in their defiant eyes.

"It looks like you are the ones who are outnumbered now, Travis."

"Do you really think a bunch of novices can take us on? You're going to pay for this, peasant," Travis threatened and looked around the room, glaring at the children who dared to defy him. "Then you will all pay, worse than before."

"Do it," Azerick said in a quiet but firm voice.

The shouts and chanting of young voices filled the room, and brilliant lights erupted into the faces of Travis and his fellow extortionists. Small balls of electrical energy stung them from a dozen different sources. Azerick added his own spell to those of his diminutive allies, and the floor beneath the bullies' feet was too slippery to stand on. All four bullies' fell to the ground when they tried to escape the numerous stinging attacks.

Azerick shoved a writing desk at Travis. It slid across the slick floor and slammed into him, knocking him back down as he tried to get to his feet. Other children started hurling books, quill and scroll cases, and anything else they could get their tiny hands on to enact their revenge against the boys who had tormented them for the last two years.

Azerick and his miniature minions broke off their attack and bolted from the room en masse, heading for the stairs before Travis and his cohorts could regain their composure.

"Get up and go after them, you idiots," Travis commanded, slipping and crawling toward the door. They managed to make it out of the classroom, gained the hallway, and bolted after the fleeing novices as Azerick and the younger students bounded down the stairs.

The squad of children ducked into a room at the bottom of the steps as Azerick drew upon the last bit of arcane power he could muster. He repeated the same spell that had caused Travis and his gang to lose their footing in the classroom and waited at the bottom of the steps. He could hear the pounding footsteps coming down the stairs in pursuit and watched as the four poured out onto the landing above.

"You're dead, gutter filth!" Travis shouted at him as the boys surged down the stairs after their quarry.

The charge turned into a tumult as they stepped upon the sabotaged steps below and tumbled into a heap at Azerick's feet.

"Now!" Azerick shouted at his troops.

The children came running from the room and fell upon their attackers with a vengeance. Tiny feet kicked out at the struggling, tangled mass of bodies while others bombarded the prone forms with opened bottles of ink.

"Stop this, stop this at once! Break it up!" came the command of Magus Lillis Bauer, Azerick and the children's instructor.

She waded into the chaotic mass of children, pulling and pushing the younger children off the bruised, ink-stained, and humiliated group lying on the floor. She dispelled the slippery effect coating the stairs with a simple command and gesture, grabbed Travis and Azerick by the upper arm, and proceeded to frogmarch them upstairs.

"The rest of you follow me to the classroom so I can get this sorted out," she ordered the students.

She dropped the arms of the two apprehended boys as she surveyed the damage to her classroom, her mouth hanging open in disbelief. "What have you all done to my class?"

"They attacked us, all of them, on his command!" shouted Travis.

"They came here to bully and extort the younger students. I just told them to defend themselves."

"Nonsense, Travis is from a very influential family and would never have to stoop to something so far beneath him. Let us go see the headmaster and see what he thinks of your slander," Magus Bauer said. "The rest of you children are to clean up this mess before I return."

Once again, Azerick found himself before Headmaster Dondrian. However, this time he was not alone. Seated to the right of the headmaster was Magus Allister, a severe and disapproving look upon his countenance. Magus Bauer stood behind the miscreants as they awaited judgment.

"Now tell us exactly what happened," Headmaster Dondrian said.

Travis stepped forward before Azerick had a chance to explain and began to speak. "Sir, my friends and I had gone to visit the younger pupils to see how they enjoyed the festival and to ask if they found the men on stilts who were passing out candy. We also thought to offer them some tutoring, but when we asked, Azerick attacked us. I guess the younger kids got caught up in the excitement. Maybe they thought it was a game or something, and they started casting cantrips and throwing things at us."

"Azerick, did you incite the younger pupils to attack Travis and his friends?" the headmaster asked.

"Yes, sir, but…"

"Did you cast an offensive spell at them?"

"Yes, sir, but…"

"Did Travis or any of his friends attempt to take anything from the other students?"

"They were going to."

"Are you an augurist, Azerick?"

"No, sir, but…"

"Then you cannot tell me what they *were* going to do. So, on your command you incited several students to attack another student without provocation." Headmaster Dondrian looked at Travis. "Did you or any of your friends cast an offensive spell or retaliate against any of the other students in any way?"

"No, sir, we didn't cast any spells or hit any of them. They're just little kids, and Azerick was hiding behind them where we couldn't get to him to try and make him stop," Travis said, once more using half-truths.

Azerick clenched his fists and his anger grew as he saw the inevitable conclusion being wrought by Travis' skillful lies. "Headmaster, they told the kids to make sure they all brought in their candy a few days before the festival, or else."

"I was just telling them to look for the stilt walkers because they give out candy, and I didn't want them to miss it," Travis replied.

"Ask the other students, they'll tell you they were bullying them and taking things from them," Azerick insisted.

"Of course they will. Azerick is older and they are very impressionable. They look up to him and he uses that to confuse them into mistaking our intentions so that he can remain in control. He's a dictator and he's drunk on power. He saw us as a threat to his position. That's why he attacked us."

"I've heard enough," Headmaster Dondrian said. "Azerick, you will be moved to an age-appropriate class immediately. You will just have to make an effort on your own to catch up. You will also clean the stables every day after class for the next month. Travis, you and your friends are not to go into the novices' classroom or living area again. Is that understood?"

All of the boys replied it was and were marched out of the headmaster's office. Azerick paused outside the door to collect his thoughts while Travis and his friends went on their way and Magus Bauer returned to her students.

Azerick started wondering if this was all worth it. Life was almost easier on the streets. He was answerable to no one there; all he had to do was survive. But was surviving living? He loved the feeling of the magic coursing through him and from him when he cast even his meager spells. How much more exciting would it be once he learned to channel even greater power? Would he ever learn how? He loved magic, but the way they were teaching him just felt unnatural, like trying to write with his off hand. He heard snickering coming from behind the headmaster's closed door.

"I'll be honest with you, Dondrian, I rather enjoyed seeing that brat, Travis, put in his place. And by a group of first and second year novices at that," Azerick heard Magus Allister chuckle.

"The boy certainly has leadership skills and the ability to use what he knows to its maximum potential. However, I am concerned as to his progress."

"I think he has made terrific progress considering the short length of time he has studied."

"Normally I would agree, but when put into perspective, your description of his abilities and the speed at which he learned what he knows now, there just does not seem to be any further progression of a measurable quality."

"I'm sure it is just temporary. Many students get hung up until they discover their own rhythm and method and not just the mechanics of casting we teach them." Magus Allister wished he felt as confident as he sounded. In truth, he was completely stumped at his young protégé's lack of improvement.

"I hope you are right. My reputation is on the line every bit as much as yours, you know. And if he keeps causing trouble with the powerful families of the students, it is going to be very hard to continue to shelter him without good reason."

"Give him more time. We will put him in class with his friend and other students his own age. Perhaps that will help him come along. By the way, did you hear about the incident young Azerick and Franklin got into during the festival?" the magus asked, a small grin spreading across his wrinkled face.

"With the street thugs?"

"Indeed, a nice bit of magic use there, I should say."

"Is it true Franklin set a man's head on fire?"

"That's what I heard. Fire always was his forte, you know. It's surprising he was able to compose himself enough to cast it successfully. Like the novices, it would seem his friend's presence was enough to give him the confidence he needed."

"A born leader," Headmaster Dondrian mused. "If he ever does come fully into his power, he will certainly be a force to be reckoned with."

Azerick slowly made his way back to his room, pondering the words of Magus Allister and the headmaster. He decided to take his punishment and continue his studies. He would work harder and study more to learn everything he could. Learning had always come easy to him, and he would not buckle under pressure the first time a subject actually challenged him.

Rusty was brewing up some concoction in his alchemic set when he walked into the room. Azerick had told him he could help himself to it as long as he was careful not to damage it.

"What are you working on?" Azerick asked his friend.

"Well, I was working on the pain potion you made before, but I couldn't get it right, so I'm making cocoa instead. Want some?"

"Thanks, I could use it."

"You look a bit out of sorts. Is everything okay?"

"Remember what I told you Travis and his friends were going to do?"

"Oh yeah, I forgot. What happened?"

Rusty was rolling on the floor laughing when Azerick described the pandemonium that ensued and how the novices dominated their older and more experienced foes.

"Now I have to muck out the stables every day after class, but on the bright side they're moving me to the apprentice's' class, so you can help me."

"That's great! I'm sure together we can get you past this block and have you casting new spells in no time."

Rusty showed Azerick to his new class the next morning. All of the students were around his age, which made him feel a bit more comfortable until Travis and his friends walked into the room. They shot hate-filled glares at Azerick from their desks a few rows over.

The teacher came in and started his lecture on magic fundamentals. Azerick was able to comprehend most of what the teacher was talking about and felt confident in his new class. However, his next lesson was in applied magic where he would actually have to practice and cast his spells.

No matter how the mages explained it to him, he just could not seem to apply what they taught him. Travis laughed at him as many of his spells went awry or just fizzled out with no effect at all.

He had far better results in his next class. His face lit up the moment he entered the classroom full of glass beakers, stone mortar and pestles, and alchemic glassware of every kind. Azerick already knew most of what the magus was teaching, so this time it was Azerick helping Rusty with his coursework and laughing at Travis' mistakes.

Today's project was to make a thick red smoke used to obscure movements in battle, signal others, or just for putting on displays. Azerick and Rusty burst into a fit of laughter when the magus had to clear the classroom because Travis used skunk moss instead of red creeping moss and filled the room with a noxious green cloud.

"This, boys and girls, is why it is important to know your ingredients by sight, smell, touch, and taste instead of just relying on the bottle's label," Magus Morgarum instructed.

Azerick liked Magus Morgarum, his alchemic instructor, from the start. He was a short pudgy man who always wore a friendly smile. It was obvious he had a passion for alchemy and enjoyed passing on his knowledge to his students.

Azerick continued his day attending history, writing, and mathematics classes, all of which he excelled in. Only the applied magic course was holding him back, but that was the most important class to him, and his incomprehension bothered him. He was embarrassed at every failed spell and mistake he made. He dwelled on this as he made his way to the stables to start working off his punishment.

The stables were just as he remembered them, although the first time he was here he had not bothered to notice how much waste the horses produced. One of the stablehands who had been told to expect him gave Azerick a shovel, showed him where to start shoveling, and where to dump the wheelbarrow when it was full. He could hear the other stablehands working at the far end of the stables and started scooping the horse dung into the wheelbarrow.

Azerick was pushing his fourth load toward the huge pile behind the stables when his wheelbarrow shifted and spilled out onto the stable corridor floor. With a sigh, he righted the cart and bent down to shovel up the mess.

As he leaned over his shovel, the entire pile exploded upwards, pummeling him with the semi-hard dung balls. He turned toward the sound of great fits of laughter and saw Travis and his friends pounding their knees and pointing at him. Azerick impotently hurled a horse apple at the group as they walked off still laughing. He was glad to be finished for the day and headed back to his room.

"Oh phew!" Rusty cried out as the dung-spattered Azerick walked in. "What happened? Did you haul the dung in your arms or what?"

"It was Travis. He did something to make my wheelbarrow tip, and when I bent over to scoop it up the whole pile blew up in my face."

"Oh man, I wish I could have seen that!" Rusty said, bursting out laughing. "That's a good one."

"Hey! Whose side are you on?"

"Yours, of course, but you have to admit it was pretty funny."

"Yeah, I guess you're right," Azerick chuckled. "I just hope they're happy with their revenge and leave me alone now."

CHAPTER 27

He kept a wary eye out, constantly looking over his shoulder for Travis and his ilk. Once, when his cart tipped on him, he hoisted his shovel and ran down the stable looking for any sign of ambush but did not finding anyone other than the confused stablehands. He wrote it off as just an unbalanced load and paranoia. As he put away his shovel and cart, he could hear the unmistakable sounds of steel clashing on steel and followed the din toward the Martial Academy's individual training ground.

He peered into a large courtyard where dozens of boys and young men were watching several groups of padded students practice their melee skills. The weapons master was shouting instructions as each student tried to bash through the other's defenses with dulled blades. Azerick thought of Ewen, his old fighting instructor, and hoped he was still doing well. His thoughts took him back to the pleasant memories of the old salt's friendly insults and instructions. He had not realized how much he missed his martial training until now. His reverie was broken a moment later.

"Hey, you, what are you doing here?" shouted the weapons master now stalking toward him.

"Me?" Azerick stammered, pointing at himself.

"Yes you. Are you a student here?"

"No, sir, I mean yes, sir."

"Well, which is it, yes or no?"

"I'm a student at the Magus Academy, sir," Azerick explained.

"Magus Academy! This is where real men learn to fight, boy. They don't just wiggle their fingers at people. These boys fight, sweat, bleed, live, and die by their own skill or lack of it. They don't just wave their arms and hurl lightning bolts at people. Go on back to your books, boy, and leave the fighting to real men."

Azerick turned his back on the weapons master and stalked off humiliated and angry, laughter from the fighters rolling off his hunched shoulders.

I do not belong with them, I do not belong with the mages, and I do not really belong on the streets either. So where do I belong? he thought as he walked back to his room.

For several weeks, it seemed that Travis had decided they were even and Azerick had no more run-ins with the group of snobs other than a few snide remarks and insults. Every day after class, he continued his chore of mucking out the stables and snuck over to the practice grounds at the Martial Academy to watch the students spar. He was careful not to allow anyone to see him, but occasionally someone spied him watching and sent him off.

Spring festival, with the accompanying spring break, was upon them. All of the students went home to their families for two weeks of vacation and celebration. Azerick decided he would stay at the Academy and practice his spellcasting, not that he had anywhere else to go. Today, he was in his room practicing when someone knocked on the door.

"It's open."

Magus Allister with his familiar grey, scruffy beard and food-stained robes stood framed in the doorway then entered the room.

"I hope I'm not intruding," the old mage said.

"No, not at all. I'm just practicing my casting."

"I hear you practice a lot. Is it coming along any better now?"

"Not really," Azerick answered. "I have learned one or two new things, but nothing really harder than before."

"That is unfortunate. I really thought you had it in you to be something special, in wizardry that is. I am not saying you lack for special talents. You are clever and creative and are able to use what little you know to accomplish quite a bit. I was sure I saw a real spark of magical talent in you, is all. It really has me stymied. I am not often wrong in that regard."

"Are they going to make me leave the Academy?" Azerick asked in a tight voice.

"I don't think so. You show great leadership skills. It may be they will transfer you to the Martial Academy, or the Scholar's' Academy, if that suits you more. Would you like that?"

"I guess it would be better than leaving the Academy altogether, although it's not what I really wanted. I wanted to be a wizard. I like magic, and everything I read and what little I can perform seems right, but it just feels like I'm going about it the wrong way."

"The headmaster is going to make his decision after spring festival. I'll see what I can do to have you transferred to—" He looked toward a scratching sound near the ceiling. "What the devil is that?" Allister exclaimed, looking up at what appeared to be a large metal spider with a bunch of feathers coming out of the back of its thorax instead of the usual bulbous abdomen.

The construct's body, not including the feathers, was about the size of a man's hand and it clung to the ceiling by its eight metal legs, swishing its feathered rump back and forth.

"Oh, that's just a toy I made to help keep the spiderwebs off the ceiling and do some dusting. Rusty used to burn the webs off, but last time he set his pillow on fire and I feared for my books."

"How did you make it? What powers it? How long does it stay animated?" Allister inquired, rapidly firing off questions at the surprised apprentice.

"I collected a bunch of scrap metal from the Academy blacksmith, had him make me a few things I couldn't shape myself, put it together, and infused it with one of my minor spells," he explained as if the entire concept was no more spectacular than cooking oatmeal.

"But animating objects is very powerful magic. Runes must be inscribed, and it takes very high-level spells to create even the crudest of golems," the old magus asserted.

"I read about golem creation when I was thinking about making it, but like you said, even this simple thing was way beyond my ability to make that way. So instead of permanently animating it like a true golem, I just used ink to write the commands on its body and infused the metal with a spell. I figured all magic is energy, so if I cast a lingering spell onto it and tied it into the construct's form it could use the spell as a temporary energy source instead of a permanent enchantment. I use a light spell to power it since it is one of the easiest and longest lasting spells I know. It will keep going for about a day before I have to replenish it."

"But it shouldn't work like that. A light spell is a light spell. That would be like using it to start a fire. It is light, and that is all it can ever be," the old wizard insisted.

Azerick just shrugged his shoulders not really understanding or caring how it worked just that he was able to do it.

"This changes everything, lad. When the headmaster hears of this, I'm certain he'll let you stay. I will insist on it. We will figure out why you have a problem with the higher spells eventually. Maybe you are a specialist, an artificer, although even they need to be able to learn the powerful enchantment spells and rune inscribing. I just don't know right now, but I'll get to the bottom of it, I promise you."

Once Magus Allister left him alone, Azerick decided to go for a walk around the Academy and think about what the wizard had said. Could he be an artificer? Could he be one of those rare wizards able to craft items and imbue them with powerful enchantments? The idea did not sound half-bad. He enjoyed studying his engineering book and making things with his hands. Truly gifted artificers commanded a great deal of respect and were often asked to make things of wonder and power for kings and nobility.

Azerick heard the sounds of striking objects. He looked around and saw that his wanderings had taken him back to the martial training grounds. A young man a few years older than Azerick was swinging away on a practice dummy in the large, sand-covered courtyard. The young fighter saw Azerick watching him, turned, raised his sword in acknowledgement, and started walking toward him.

"Hey there!" he called out to the student wizard.

"I'm sorry; I wasn't paying attention to where I was going. I'm leaving," Azerick said, not wanting any trouble.

"That's okay, I don't mind. Weapons Master Zorbrun isn't here, just me. My name's Alexander, Alex for short," the young man said and extended his hand.

"Mine is Azerick."

"I've seen you quite a few times watching us. Are you interested in fighting with weapons?" Alex asked.

"A little. I did some training when I was younger, before I came to the Academy. In fact, if my casting doesn't get any better soon they may transfer me over here."

"Better than being kicked out, I suppose, unless your heart's desire was firmly set on being a wizard," Alex said, mimicking Azerick's exact thoughts.

"I liked the idea, and I can cast a few spells, but I liked weapons training too, so it wouldn't be the end of the world if I was transferred. It would be better than constantly making a fool out of myself at the Magus Academy. So why aren't you gone like everyone else for spring festival?"

"My family is away on business, and I don't care to stay with my relatives much. They look down their noses at me because I'm my father's bastard. My mother died giving birth to me, so he took me in but shoved me off on the Academy as soon as he could. How about you? Why are you still here?"

"I don't have a family. My mother and father died a few years ago, so I decided to stay here and practice too."

"I guess we're a bit of a pair then, aren't we? You want to do some sparring? Maybe I can teach you a few things in case someone jumps you and you can't get a spell off," Alex offered.

"Sounds great, let's do it."

Alex got Azerick some padded armor and a dulled sword. The two boys squared off and began exchanging blows. Alex was by far the stronger and more experienced of the two, but he complimented the young wizard's skill while suggesting improvements. By the end of the match, both students were tired but Azerick was the sorest, having received several bruises from the other's sword. Azerick had only managed to land two hits and those likely would not have proved lethal or even incapacitating in a real fight unless they turned septic and his foe died of infection.

"I'll be here tomorrow if you want to go at it again," Alex offered.

"Sure, that sounds good, but next time I would like to try the staff."

"I'm not much for staff work. It's more of a farmer's weapon than a fighter's, but I guess it's only fair to give you the advantage if you know how to use one. I'll see you tomorrow."

Azerick bid him farewell and walked back to his room, his spirits buoyed by making a new friend and enjoying the feeling of practicing with a weapon again.

He spent the next morning practicing his spells before heading to the weapons yard after lunch. There was only one cook left on the grounds, so he made a sandwich out of some pork and cheese. He wrapped a second one up in cheesecloth and set out for his weapons training appointment. Alex was already there warming up when he arrived. Alex had missed lunch since no one bothered to ring the bell for meal call and he took the offered sandwich with thanks. Once he finished eating, they set up for their next duel.

"Don't you want to put on your armor before we get started?" Alex asked as he grabbed up his staff.

"No, I'm going to try without it."

"Pretty confident with the staff, are you? We'll see how you feel after I give you a few more bruises."

The two fighters went at it, their staves sending clacking echoes across the courtyard. Alex was obviously not nearly as skilled with the staff as he was with the sword, and Azerick's preference for the weapon put them on nearly even footing in the fight. However, Alex was still bigger and a more experienced fighter, and he managed to slip a blow through Azerick's defenses, but instead of feeling the satisfying slap of wood against the younger boy's ribs, his staff was deflected slightly and bounced off with a dull thump that was hardly even noticed by his opponent.

"What the...?"

Azerick took advantage of Alex's momentary distraction and slipped in a blow of his own, smacking the young man's side with a satisfying crack. Alex let out a grunt of surprise and pain and tried to bring his defenses back online, but Azerick had momentum now and took full advantage of it.

The younger student thrust, swung, and swept the ends of his staff at his larger foe and pushed him back on his heels into a defensive withdrawal. Azerick was finally able to overcome Alex's defense and landed a solid thrust into his midsection. The young fighter doubled over with a great gasp of breath before Azerick hooked his heel, flipped him onto his back, and pressed the butt of his staff to his throat.

"I yield, I yield," Alex cried out laughing with whatever breath he was able to get. "Not a bad job for a spell slinger. Speaking of which, I should have landed that blow to your side. What did you do?"

"I cast a spell that gives me the same protection as a decent set of armor without the restricted movement."

"Isn't that kind of like cheating?"

"It's a skill I happen to possess. I don't think it is cheating any more than your advantage in size and skill."

"I guess not, but next round I think I'll go back to my sword. What about you?"

"I'm sticking with my staff. I was never much for sword work."

Alex retrieved his training sword while Azerick caught his breath and waited. Once Alex was ready, they squared off again. The next match went similarly to their first day with Alex giving Azerick tips and landing bruising blows even through his magical armor. Unlike their first bout however, Azerick was able to get a few good blows in himself as his increased skill at the staff compensated a bit for his foe's much better sword handling. By the end of the day, bruises covered both of the exhausted students.

They kept up their sparring matches for the rest of the spring break. Both boys took great delight in honing their skills, but it was obvious that Azerick made the most improvement in his fighting skill. By the end of the two weeks, their bouts often ended in a draw, neither one able to dominate the other.

Azerick was enjoying a quiet day of reading in his room when Rusty busted into the room. Spring break was nearly over and Rusty's entrance heralded the last of his quiet time alone. As much as Azerick was glad to see Rusty and continue his studies, it also meant dealing with Travis and his frustrating failures again.

"I'm back. Did you miss me?" a smiling Rusty asked.

"I'm not sure. Who are you again?"

"Very funny. So what did you do while I was gone? Did you go to spring festival?"

"I went one day with Alex, but I stuck around the Academy the rest of the time."

"Who's Alex? I'm gone for two weeks and you trade me out for a new best friend, huh?"

"He's in the Martial Academy. We sparred almost every day."

"Oh no, and a metalhead at that! You, sir, are a vile fiend!" he cried as he flopped onto his bed.

"You will just have to get used to sharing me, so you best get over it. Restricting the pleasure of my company to just one friend reeks of selfishness of the highest magnitude, and I'm far too giving a person for that."

"Well, I guess I can't hold it against you too much considering what I did while I was on holiday," Rusty said with an air of mystery. "Well, aren't you wondering what I did?"

"No, not really."

"Oh you have turned evil, evil and vile. Well, I'm going to tell you anyway. I met a girl," Rusty said, practically bouncing around the room.

"A girl, really, where?"

"At spring festival, of course. Her name is Colleen, she has long blond hair; she's beautiful, smart, and she smells great."

"Wow, she sounds great. So how did she lose her eyesight?"

"What do you mean? I didn't say she was blind."

"Well she must be blind if she's going out with you."

Rusty threw his scorched pillow at Azerick. "She thinks I'm quite charming, thank you!"

"I'm sure you two will be quite happy together as long as you don't set her pretty, long blond hair on fire," Azerick said and threw Rusty's burnt pillow back at him.

"The pillow was an accident, and the only person's hair I set on fire I did on purpose," Rusty fired back.

"What about that time in applied magic class when you thought a flaming crown would look good and you pronounced yourself the fire king?"

"Setting my own hair on fire doesn't count, occupational hazard."

"What about in alchemy class when Magus Morgarum..."

"All right, all right, you made your point. I am not going to set her hair on fire, and I have learned a new quenching spell to put out any fires I may accidentally set."

"Now that may well be the most brilliant thing you have done yet."

Rusty and Azerick continued to catch up, Azerick telling him about his sparring, Rusty telling him about his walks and stolen kisses with Colleen.

CHAPTER 28

Far too soon it was back to class as usual. Travis and his friends were all huddled around a desk carrying on what must have been a very amusing conversation. When they caught Azerick's eye, they laughed even harder and whispered amongst themselves before Travis stood up and turned toward Azerick.

"Hey, Azerick, I was wrong to call you a peasant before," he said.

Azerick was less surprised by his pronouncement than he was worried about what horrible thing he might follow that statement up with, knowing it was unlikely someone as spoiled and cruel as he was had had some kind of major personality change over the holiday.

"It seems I gave you far too much credit and insulted peasants everywhere by giving you claim to such a high status," he continued, turning and looking at the other students in the classroom now that he had everyone's attention. "It seems that our good friend Azerick is not so much a peasant as the son of a whore!"

Azerick jumped up from his seat, his face burning a brilliant shade of red. "Shut your mouth, Travis, or I swear I'll kill you!"

"Yes, that is quite enough, young man!" Magus Florent demanded, but Travis continued.

"I was at my father's shipping house when I overheard him and one of his ship's captains talking about a whore who lived above an inn in the common quarter with her son *Azerick*. Apparently, she was not that good though. Her last customer cut her up like a piece of beef ready for the stew pot!"

The world narrowed in Azerick's eyes, and the only thing he could see was Travis' laughing face. His skin began tingling, and tiny arcs of electricity limned his body. A curtain of white-hot fury blotted everything out as he extended his arm and let loose a scream of rage. Deep within his subconscious, he grabbed at those silver strands of energy he had used to create the magical wards. Azerick tore at them with his mind and twisted them into a form shaped purely from his unbridled fury. The world went dark, and he sensed nothing more than a distant, dull sensation of falling and the floor rushing up to meet him.

For Rusty and everyone else in the room it was a different scene altogether. Most of the teenage students were appalled at the filth spewing from Travis' mouth and their eyes turned toward Azerick in pity. Azerick's scream of rage filled their ears a fraction of a second before an intense light, a horrendously loud crack, and the smell of ozone filled the room.

Azerick dropped to the ground unconscious, blood leaking from his nose and ears. Travis was down and not moving, and his friends crawled around on the floor moaning pitifully. The lightning had blackened the wall behind the tormenting boys and blasted off a large section of the plaster and stucco. Students started screaming once they overcame their momentary shock.

"Someone run to Magus Morgarum and have him bring healing potions, the best he has, quickly now!" Magus Florent commanded.

Several students ran to the alchemist's classroom to summon help. Magus Florent bent down to check on Azerick first and found he was still breathing. She then checked on Travis. He was breathing, but it was shallow. His shirt was in tatters, and he had a horrible burn across his chest where the electric bolt had grazed him. Had it hit him square, it likely would have burned clean through him and ended his young life then and there.

Magus Morgarum ran in on the heels of the students who had summoned him and took in the damaged room and the students lying on the floor. He pried open Travis' jaws and poured a purple liquid down his throat from a slim metal vial. He then administered a dose of the healing draught to Azerick before checking on the conscious but moaning students caught just outside the path of the powerful bolt.

Azerick awoke in a strange bed. He glanced around and saw several other beds, but no one else occupied them. He looked over and found Magus Allister sitting in a chair next to his bed.

"I see you are awake, good. How do you feel?" the old wizard asked kindly.

"Terrible. My head hurts, and I'm really thirsty and hungry."

"Not surprising on both accounts. You are thirsty because you have been unconscious for two days, and your head hurts because you cast a spell well beyond your ability."

"What do you mean? What did I do?"

"What do you remember?"

"Travis was saying things about my mother. I got really angry, furious, my vision got real narrow, and all I saw was red. I remember grabbing at the Source and doing something with it, but I do not know what exactly. Then I blacked out and woke up here."

"Do you remember feeling anything else just before you passed out?"

"I remember touching something but not with my hands, more like my mind. It felt like I had fallen into an icy river."

"That was the flow of magic, the Source. As of yet, you have been taught how to dip a finger into the Source and draw upon its power. This time, you reached into the flow hand and fist and channeled a great deal more energy than you have learned to handle. You released that energy in the form of a lightning bolt against Travis."

"Magus Allister, I'm so sorry! I didn't mean to. I don't know how I did that!"

"I think I do, and if I am right, which I am certain I am, then I owe you a great apology, but we'll talk about that later," Magus Allister promised.

"Is Travis all right? I did not mean to hurt him, at least not kill him. No, that is not true. I wanted to kill him, but only because I lost control of my temper. I don't want him dead now, you have to believe me," Azerick begged, fearing they would cast him out of the Academy and possibly put him in jail.

"I do, lad, don't you worry. He's going to be fine. His family took him home for a few days to rest."

"What are they going to do to me now? Will I be kicked out of the Academy?"

"Travis' family is quite upset and has a significant amount of influence, but given the situation, I think things will be all right. Several of the students, as well as Magus Florent, have come forward and given testimony that you were provoked most cruelly. There are factors in this you do not yet understand, but I will explain it all later. Get some rest now, and I'll have someone bring you something to eat and drink."

The kind old wizard left Azerick alone to his thoughts. A woman in white robes came in shortly afterwards with some food and watered-down wine. He ate everything, drank two glasses of the thin wine, and fell back into an exhausted slumber.

Azerick opened his eyes and found himself standing by a swift-moving river, but instead of water it looked like it was made entirely of liquid silver with an iridescent sheen.

You have finally awakened, came a disembodied voice. From where, Azerick could not tell.

He spun around in a circle looking for the source of the voice. "Where are you? Show yourself!"

I am here, same as you are.

"Where am I?"

You are where you are supposed to be, where you need to be.

"Who are you?"

Who are you? the voice echoed.

"Is this some kind of game?" Azerick demanded.

If it was, do you think you would be winning or losing?

"What are you?" Azerick shouted, growing impatient and angry at the voice's wordplay.

What are you?

"I'm an orphan, street rat, and a student of magic! Happy now?"

Are you happy? Which of those titles makes you happy? Titles are merely words, descriptors, not who or what you are. They do not define you.

"What am I then, since you seem to have all the answers?"

The only answers I have are within you. What you are is what you choose to be.

"Are you me? Are you my own voice, the voice of my mind?"

I am part of you, a part you are just now beginning to discover. Whether I become you, you become me, or you become something else is entirely up to you.

"You said I had awakened. What do you mean? I was in bed at the Academy, so I must be asleep, not awake. Unless this is a hallucination," Azerick argued.

No, you are awake. For the first time in your life, you are awake. You are finally seeing clearly, seeing what is real. However, you must choose if you will stay awake or go back to sleep and live the life as the person you came here as.

"What will happen to me if I go back to sleep?"

You will be an orphan, street rat, and a student of magic—for a time.

Azerick realized the voice was talking in metaphors. He needed only to figure out the meaning. "What happens to me if I stay awake? Who am I then?"

You will be what you are meant to be, what you need to be.

"What happens?"

Everything will happen.

"How do I stay awake?"

Touch the Source, let it fill you, body and soul, and become one.

Azerick looked at the luminescent river and its swift-moving current flowing over the horizon. He listened to the rushing flow of energy for the first time and realized it was calling to him like the voice of a long-lost loved one. He heard his mother's and father's voices in the flow, inviting him to become part of it. It was beckoning him home. He walked slowly to its bank in an almost hypnotic state. He felt his feet slip into the edge of the flow. It was warm and comforting. He imagined this was what it felt like to be in a mother's womb: safe, loved, and protected.

The river of energy flowed just above his waist as he trailed his hands in its sparkling current. The ground beneath his feet vanished, and Azerick's head slipped under the roiling tide of energy as it swept him along its length. He fought for the surface and gasped for breath when his head broke through to the air above. He coughed out great mouthfuls of the prismatic substance before he was swept under again, pulled down deeper and deeper in its depths.

He held his breath as long as he could and fought for the surface, but the Source was not going to release its prize this time. It held him in its deep embrace until spots began to form and stars exploded in his vision. It was trying to kill him. It was a trick. He had tapped into power mortals were not supposed to touch, and he was going to pay for that sacrilege with his life. His starving lungs forced his mouth open and he inhaled the Source, taking pure magical energy into his lungs, filling him and killing him.

CHAPTER 29

Azerick fell from the bed gasping. The large spots blacking out his vision slowly dispersed as he looked around the room. He was still in the infirmary and still in his bed, or next to it rather. Azerick looked toward the window and saw the sun had not moved much since Magus Allister's visit. He climbed back into bed and thought about his strange dream. Was it a dream, or was it a vision?

At first, he thought the voice was the one claiming to be the goddess, Sharrellan, but it did not hold the same sort of malice and underlying malevolence. Was it the Source speaking to him? Why would something that was supposed to be an inanimate source of power and creation speak to him? Did it speak to all wizards eventually? Did it mean that whatever was blocking him from accessing higher magic was gone now?

The confused, young mage did not know and fell asleep while pondering the meaning of whatever it was that had happened. Azerick just hoped this time there would be no new voices. It was getting rather crowded inside his head as it was.

Azerick's sleep was pleasant and undisturbed this time. He awoke the next morning shortly after sunrise. An attendant brought him some milk and oatmeal with honey to break his fast. He ate ravenously and felt some strength flow back into his body. Magus Morgarum waddled in shortly after Azerick's second helping of oatmeal. Azerick had even managed to talk the attendant into getting him a honey cake and was licking the sticky remnants of the treat off his fingers when the alchemic instructor came to check on him.

"How are you feeling this morning, my boy?" the friendly magus asked.

"I feel great actually. Better than ever."

"Good, good! That was a very close call, you know, for everyone. Most mages who channel power that far beyond their skill are not so lucky."

"I'm really sorry, Magus. I didn't mean to."

"I'm sure you didn't. I will have to let the headmaster know you are awake and feeling well. He wants to have a word with you, as you may expect."

"I figured he would," Azerick said with a slump of his shoulders.

"I'm sure everything will turn out just fine. If it means anything to you, you have my support, and I will recommend that you stay here at the Academy. You are one of my best pupils, you know."

"Thank you, Magus Morgarum, I appreciate it."

"Not at all, Azerick. Your clothes are over in that closet. Best get dressed while I go talk to the headsman, um, headmaster that is," he said with a wink.

Azerick found his clothes in the small wardrobe next to his bed. He had just finished dressing when Rusty came running into the ward.

"It's about time you woke up," Rusty said and punched Azerick in the shoulder.

"Yeah, well, I figured I couldn't hide out here forever."

"That was quite a performance you put on. It's been pretty nice in class without Travis."

"He'll be back soon, I'm sure."

"Yeah, too bad you didn't nail him with that lightning bolt. That was incredible! I never saw anyone lower than a journeyman cast a lightning bolt before. It made my hair stand up."

"Yeah, but it almost killed me, you dummy, so don't expect a repeat performance for a while. Here comes Magus Allister. I have to go. We'll talk later."

"Okay, good luck."

Azerick followed Magus Allister out of the infirmary and up the stairs of the headmaster's tower. He stepped through the door when the old mage opened it for him and walked into the large office he was far too familiar with. The room was full of people. The headmaster sat behind his desk, Magus Allister took a seat to his right, and Magus Florent sat to his left. Next to Magus Florent sat Magus Morgarum, beside Magus Allister sat Magus Bauer; no one was smiling.

"Please take a seat, young man," Headmaster Dondrian instructed, gesturing to the wooden chair in the center of the room. "I trust you know why you are here?"

"Yes, Headmaster, because of the accident in class," Azerick replied nervously.

"Accident? You nearly killed four students," Magus Bauer waspishly accused.

"Lillis, please, we are here to find out what happened and decide what we are going to do about it. Let us not jump to judgment too quickly," Magus Allister politely chastised the sour mage.

Magus Bauer sniffed loudly and turned her head.

"Now, Azerick, we know what happened. What I want you to do is tell us what was going through your mind at the time. Did you see or feel anything strange just before it happened?"

"Travis was saying some really horrible things about my mother, and I got angry, really angry. Everything kind of went dark. I felt something though, now that I think about it. It was strange, kind of like the feeling I get when I channel the Source, only it was stronger, cleaner. I didn't know how to cast that spell, so I just made it do what I wanted."

"Azerick, have you ever cast a spell without being taught, or used magic without knowing it?" Magus Allister asked.

"I don't think so, Magus, not that I know of."

"Do you know what a magical ward is?" he asked.

"It's a magical protection spell," Azerick answered.

"Correct, and as you know, the only way you can get past a ward, with few exceptions, is with magic. Have you ever encountered a ward before?"

What is he doing? Is he trying to get me in even more trouble? "Yes, sir, twice," he answered, figuring honesty was the best thing right now.

"Will you tell us about those incidents please?"

"The first time was almost three years ago. I found a warded jewelry box."

Magus Bauer interrupted with a snort. "Found in someone else's possession I would wager. The boy obviously has a history of criminal behavior, and for that reason alone he should be removed from our prestigious institution and jailed."

Allister ignored her with a sidelong glance and continued his questioning. "How did you know it was warded?"

"I was just about to open it when I felt a strange energy emanating from it. I studied it with my eyes closed, and I could see and feel the energy surrounding the box. It felt dark and angry like it was just waiting to release its power onto someone."

"Then what did you do?"

"I studied the way it was made, how the different strands of energy were sort of woven together to form the ward, and I just kind of unraveled them."

His pronouncement startled the wizards sitting in attendance, and they began muttering amongst themselves, scarcely able to believe such a statement from someone so young and inexperienced.

"And when was the next time you encountered a ward?"

This was the question Azerick was most worried about answering. The old wizard already knew what he had done, but he did not know how the rest of the mages would react on finding out about his invading the Academy several months ago.

"It was on the door to your room, sir. I undid that ward just as I did the other one a couple years ago. It was a little harder, but it was not as scary or evil-feeling as the other one."

The wizards all started talking at once, each one trying to raise his or her voice over the other. The meeting, or trial, or whatever it was, broke out into a verbal tumult. The headmaster banged a small, stone statuette on his desktop and called for order.

"Azerick, do you recall ever having used magic before coming here and not simply unmaking it?" the headmaster asked.

Azerick shifted uncomfortably in his chair. These things were his secrets, and he despised revealing his secrets. He took a deep breath before answering.

"When I was trapped in the sewers by thugs, I made a light, and later I made several wards by copying the one I had found."

"That is quite an impressive feat for one so young and with absolutely no training at the time. Your studies must be going very well with having such a natural affinity for magic," Magus Allister continued.

"No, sir, actually I have been having a hard time with my casting and learning anything more than the most basic spells."

"And why do you think that is?"

"I'm not sure. The lessons just don't make sense to me. It doesn't feel right," Azerick answered, frustrated that he could not explain it better.

The old mage stood up and walked over to Azerick, placing his hand on the young man's shoulder. "It seems we have done young Azerick a great disservice in more than one way. It is now clear he is not responsible for what happened in the classroom or to those students who were injured."

"Ridiculous! Who is responsible for it then?" Magus Bauer demanded.

"You are. You all are," a terse reply came from the far corner of the room.

A fit, middle-aged man stepped out from the shadowy corner of the room. He was tall, topping six feet, and broad shouldered. He sported a sharply trimmed goatee turning grey at the sides of his chin. His eyes were dark brown bordering on black. He wore black pants, a white shirt with ornate lace cuffs, a red vest made from the skin of some scaled creature, and a voluminous black cloak with a red silk lining. Mystic symbols and sigils sewn into the cloak with purple silk shimmered with obvious power. Azerick guessed him to be in his late forties.

"Master Devlin, thank you for joining us today. Would you please explain what you mean by that?" Headmaster Dondrian requested.

From the looks on the faces of the gathered wizards, with the exception of Magus Allister and the headmaster, his presence came as a surprise.

"You have a boy you claim is highly creative and not lacking in intelligence, can undo the wards of established wizards, nearly kills half his classmates with a spell only a practiced spellcaster should be able to manage, and yet fails to learn anything beyond the typical novice spells. It should be obvious even to cookbook spellcasters like yourselves what the problem is. You are trying to teach wizard spells to a sorcerer!" Master Devlin proclaimed.

A collective gasp arose from the mouths of the wizards in attendance, and once again Azerick found all eyes in the room turned to him.

"I'm a sorcerer? What does that mean?" Azerick asked.

Magus Allister explained in a soft voice. "It means we were trying to make you into something you are not. Most people with an intelligence as astute as yours can learn some very basic spells, little more than tricks really, even if they lack the true gift of magic. What confounded us all was the fact that your aura showed a strong propensity for channeling magic. What we failed to see was that you possess a spirit that runs directly counter to wizardry. Simply put, you cannot be a wizard, we cannot teach you, and you cannot learn to become a wizard. Who you are, your very nature, simply will not allow it. It would be like teaching a horse to fly."

"Does that mean I have to leave the Academy?"

"No, I have asked Master Devlin if he would take you on as his apprentice, and he has been generous enough to accept you if you wish to stay. You will remain at the Academy, reside in your own room, but Master Devlin will teach your applied magic and magical theory classes. Please know that sorcerers are very rare, and we are all quite proud to host your instruction here at the Academy. However, if you would prefer not to apprentice under Master Devlin, we will find you a position at the Martial or Scholar's' Academy."

"Yes, where the next student who hits you with a sword at the wrong time catches a fireball in his face and you both die a horrible death," Master Devlin said in a sarcastic tone.

"Master Devlin, please," the old wizard begged, then faced Azerick again. ""Whatever polite social graces our guest may lack, he is correct. You do run the risk of losing control of your power again. In fact, the older you get, the more likely it will happen unless you are able to learn some control on your own. It is possible. There are hedge wizards and a very few sorcerers out there who have done that very thing. However, it is not a path I would recommend."

"I want to go with Master Devlin. Wizard or sorcerer, I know I am meant to wield magic."

"Very well. Master Devlin will take you to where you will begin your instruction. You may go now," Headmaster Dondrian said, dismissing him.

Without so much as a nod to the assembled wizards, Master Devlin opened the door and rushed Azerick out of the room. They walked in silence down the stairs of the headmaster's tower, across the main hall, and up the stairs of another tower where he was ushered into a round room similar in size and shape to the headmaster's office. It contained almost everything a student and magus would require.

There was a bookshelf with several books lining the shelves. Azerick could tell they were a new addition since they were about the only thing in the room not covered in a thick layer of dust. At the far wall, a large desk sat facing the door and a smaller desk stood opposite it about ten feet away. A table rested against another wall near a shuttered window which Master Devlin opened, letting in some much-needed fresh air. Across the room from the window, an archway allowed passage into another room.

"Take a seat, boy," the sorcerer commanded and pulled out the chair from behind the desk but chose to remain standing himself. Devlin paced about the room, hands steepled under his chin. "Tell me what they have taught you thus far so I have an idea of how much damage they did."

"Um, I learned several cantrips, verbal, somatic, and reagent requirements for several novice spells and a few apprentice spells, even though I have not been able to cast any spells above novice yet, and none without great difficulty and problems. I learned about the history of magic, magic fundamentals, and alchemy; and I am good in math, writing, and engineering. Oh, and I can also animate simple constructs by powering them with basic spells for short periods of time."

The last statement actually got a reaction from the dour sorcerer in the form of raised eyebrows. "You have a reasonable level of education, which is good. I can't abide a dullard. I have not the time, patience, nor inclination for such. Remember what you learned about magic fundamentals, but do not attempt to use anything they taught you about magic. That information is for the sake of knowledge itself. As for your education in applied magic, forget everything you learned completely. It will do you no good. Worse yet, it will keep you from learning what you must about sorcery."

Devlin clasped his hands behind his back, turned, and stared down at his new apprentice. "I am what you shall become: a sorcerer. I am impatient, intolerant, and rather brusque. I lack a certain political tact some people are apt to call rudeness, and I make no apologies for it. I am a hard taskmaster, and you may not like my methods or demeanor, but I assure you that you will learn. You are the only student I have, so you gain the benefit of having my expertise and pleasant disposition all to yourself. You may ask your questions now."

"You called the mages in the headmaster's office cookbook spellcasters. What did you mean by that?"

"I meant to insult them, as I often do to my great pleasure, but I suppose you are looking for a more specific answer to your question. What do you know of sorcerers?"

"Nothing, nothing at all. I thought they were the same as wizards, just called something different."

"I will forgive your ignorance and your insult this one time. No, wizards and sorcerers are quite different, although to the ignorant what we do may look the same. It all has to do with the way we tap into the Source. You do know what the Source is, don't you, boy?"

"It is the source of all magic, where we draw on the energy to power our spells," Azerick answered.

"Correct. The greatest difference is how we gain access to the Source. I call them cookbook casters, because like a baker or scullery maid using a cookbook to create a meal, anyone with a touch of magical proclivity can pick up a spell book and cast any spell they find in that book if they are given enough time to prepare, assuming they have the appropriate amount of skill of course. A sorcerer literally creates his own spell so has no need of written instructions."

"So if sorcerers don't have spell books or instructions, how do they learn their spells?"

"Each sorcerer casts his or her spells differently. You have to determine the most efficient way to access the Source and bend it to your will in a way that works best for you. I can give you basic instructions in how to form castings and draw upon the Source, but you will have to learn how to form the actual spells yourself. Learning new spells is a very time-consuming and arduous task, but once learned, your affinity with the Source makes you a power to be reckoned with.

"Wizards must recreate each spell form the exact same way every time. Centuries ago, some clever men and women with a rare aptitude found a way to channel and shape the Source into a spell. Because they are essentially cheats and frauds, those formulas cannot vary. The Source is like a room with an infinite number of doors. Wizards must be given a very specific key to gain access to the spell lying just beyond those doors. A sorcerer makes their own keys and can therefore open any room within the Source's vast labyrinth given enough time, assuming of course that they possess the requisite skill. It is this instinctive ability that makes us so powerful. Make no mistake, when a general goes into battle, he will take a battle-trained sorcerer over a wizard every time. The amount of sheer destructive force a powerful sorcerer can lay down is a truly awesome thing. We don't just know magic, we are magic."

Azerick absorbed this information and ran it all through his mind. "Master Devlin, I am ready to begin as soon as you are willing to teach me."

"Very good. You show enthusiasm without a childish, flippant attitude. We will start in the morning. You will study under my tutelage in place of your applied magic class…and history. I need to bring you up to speed, and this is more important than learning about old, dead wizards. I will see you tomorrow. You may go."

Azerick returned to his room, nervous about the sudden change in his life, but the knowledge of his failures in magic not being a result of his ineptitude buoyed his spirits.

Rusty was still in class, so he had the room to himself. He sat in solitude for a time pondering everything that had happened recently. He thought of the mysterious and frightening vision or dream he had had. He considered what it would mean to be a sorcerer. He stretched out his hand and tried to touch the Source with his mind.

He felt the strange tingling sensation course up his arm until it suffused his entire body. It came to him much more easily than it had when he tried to touch it the wizard way. He started moving his hand, shaping the energy from the Source into a specific purpose with his thoughts and will. He called out a word of power purely on instinct and felt the deep pleasure controlling and releasing the magical energy brought him.

"Hey!" Rusty shouted as he came through the door.

Azerick opened his eyes and saw that he had set Rusty's blanket on fire. Both boys rushed to the bed, folding the blanket up and snuffing out the flames.

"At least I only set my own stuff on fire," Rusty complained.

"Oh really? I didn't realize Carrot was wearing your hat."

They both laughed at Azerick's jest and the small accident that left a large scorch mark in the middle of Rusty's blanket.

"Well, at least it matches your pillow now," Azerick teased. "Seriously though, I'm sorry about that, I didn't mean to cast anything. I was just testing something out."

"Like sorcery? I heard all about it! Everyone is talking about it all over the school!"

"It's not that big of a deal. I just hope I can do better with it than I did before."

"Are you kidding? You are the first sorcerer to attend this school in over a hundred years!"

"What about Master Devlin? Where did he learn if not here?"

"I heard he studied in a city somewhere out in the Great Desert," Rusty whispered as though he were telling a great secret.

"That would explain the tan," Azerick said only half-joking.

Rusty grinned. "Tell me everything about being a sorcerer, and I'll share all the school gossip about you."

Azerick rolled his eyes. "What are we, an old married couple?"

"Only if you treat me right. Now start talking."

CHAPTER 30

The next morning, Azerick and Rusty answered the call to breakfast with their usual enthusiasm, even managing to trip each other and roll down half a flight of stairs. They sat at their table eating with a few other students who were naturally curious about Azerick's newfound abilities and bombarded him with questions. He answered them as best he could and was in the midst of trying to explain the difference between a wizard and a sorcerer when a familiar voice spoke out.

"I bet you think you are pretty special, don't you? You are still a peasant and the son of a whore no matter what they call you here," Travis said, his voice filled with scorn.

"Leave me be, Travis!" Azerick warned as he stood and faced his tormentor.

Azerick could see the red marks where his lightning bolt had burned Travis across the left side of his face and some of the exposed skin on the faces of his friends.

"Or what? Do you think I'm afraid of you because of some freak accident? Your whole existence is a freak accident. I can call on magic that can kill you whenever I want. This isn't over between us, you can count on that!" Travis caught the eye of one of the magi in the dining hall and walked away, leaving his threat hanging in the air like a dark cloud.

"Don't worry about him, Azerick, he's all talk," Rusty tried to assure him.

"No, he's not. He will do something when he thinks he has the upper hand. I hurt him, and even worse, I humiliated him in front of people. Inside every thug, bully, and person of power lies a very fragile ego. He won't let this go. He can't."

After breakfast, Azerick climbed the steps of the tower where Master Devlin would begin teaching him sorcery. The fluttering in his stomach increased as each step took him nearer to the unknown. Master Devlin was an intimidating teacher, and having to start all over, learning a new form of magic, was an emotional mixed bag.

"Take a seat, boy, and we will begin," the sorcerer instructed as soon as Azerick walked into the room. "Your training is going to be significantly different than what you may have been used to. For one thing, there is very little you can learn from books. For another, I can only tell you what you must do and very little on how to do it. Sorcery is unique for each sorcerer. That is one reason wizards fear us so much. Most wizardry is rather generic, and with experience, you will be able to recognize what a wizard is going to cast as he begins to form the weave, because wizards cast their spells much the same way no matter what spell book they prepared them from. With that knowledge, you can defend against it and brace yourself for its effect. Because a sorcerer channels and shapes his spells in a manner of his own devising, it is much harder for a wizard to know what is going to be unleashed upon him until the spell is cast."

"I think I cast a spell yesterday using sorcery. I reached out and touched the Source completely on my own without any sort of instruction. I could feel it in my mind and in my hand. I thought about what I wanted, shaped the energy from the Source into a form, and released it. I didn't actually mean to cast anything, but I did set my friend's blanket on fire," Azerick added sheepishly.

"That is a good start, and it gives me faith that you will be more trainable than I had hoped. It was very foolish though. You know nothing of sorcery yet, and even the smallest spell, when it goes awry, can cause serious harm. You must not release any more spells unless I am instructing you to do so."

"Yes, sir, I won't. But how will I practice outside of class?"

"I want you to get comfortable channeling the Source and shaping it, but you must learn to let it go, to let the spell's energy dissipate without actually unleashing it. The first thing you must learn is how to tap the Source in the way that is most efficient for you. Some sorcerers grab it as if they are wrestling a wild beast. They use brute force to bend it to their control. Others reach out to it gently, as if they are trying to catch a soap bubble in the palm of their hand. You must discover what works best for you. Now, try it, reach out and seize it, and make it yours.

Azerick stretched out his consciousness and felt the turbulent force of the river-like Source. It threatened to sweep him away when he tried to grasp it fully. It pulled at him and tried to break away from his grasp like an animal that did not want to be caught and tamed. He grabbed it and held on with all his concentration, but when he tried to shape it in any way, it slipped from his grasp.

"It keeps pulling away from me. The harder I try to hold it the more it resists me."

"Then come at it from a different direction. Sorcery has no place for quitters. If one method does not work, try another until you get it."

Azerick reached out once more, this time easing his will gently into the flow. He touched the energy with a hand that existed only in his mind. Gently, he tried to hold onto the Source and pull it toward him, but it slipped away again the way a leaf floating in the water will drift away from your hand when you try to grab it.

He shook his head to clear his thoughts and tried once more. He thought back to how he had touched the Source the day before in his room. Azerick reached out gently but firmly, holding onto the Source as if it were a physical substance. Once he had it in his grasp, he molded it as if it were made of clay instead of trying to hammer it into shape as if it were stone or steel.

The Source bent to his will with an eagerness that surprised him. He knew with certainty this was his destiny; this is who and what he was. Azerick knew now he could never be anything else. The young sorcerer pulled more and more energy to him, shaping it, commanding it. He was drunk on the power he channeled as it flowed around and through him. At this moment, nothing else existed: no school, no death, no magus, only him and the Source. It made him invincible.

He found himself staring up at the angry red face of Master Devlin. "Control yourself, boy! You must command the power, not the other way around. The Source will devour you in an instant if you let it. It will destroy you and everyone close to you if you let it control you. Do you think that little lightning bolt that got away from you was horrible? A sorcerer could lay an entire village flat if he were stupid enough to let the Source have its way with him!"

"Yes, sir, I'm sorry. I didn't know what was happening. It just felt so…" Azerick tried to explain as he pulled himself up off the floor.

He felt the right side of his face stinging and looked at the thick book in his master's hand that he had used to bludgeon his pupil back to reality.

"You are capable of channeling great power, but you are not yet able of controlling it. You must remember that at all times, or it will consume you. In many ways, an inexperienced sorcerer is more dangerous than a master is, not just to an opponent, but also to himself and innocent people around him. Now, compose yourself, try again, and remember what you did before, both the right and the wrong."

Azerick did as he was instructed, tapping into the source, holding it, forming it, controlling it, but not letting it carry him away again. By the end of the week, several of the minor spells he had known as a wizard he was able to cast as a sorcerer. He was amazed at the difference and ease with which they came to him. He was able to cast nearly twice as many spells now before fatiguing himself to the point he could not draw from the Source without rest.

Azerick had just finished his afternoon session with Master Devlin and decided to go and watch the Martial Academy students in the sparring field. He was eager to tell Alex of his unexpected progress. He crossed the commons and stole up to the entrance of the practice field, trying to keep out of sight. He watched the students strike and defend with their weapons and shields with a bit of jealousy. As much as he loved magic, he still longed for the feel of simple melee combat, the exertion and concentration it required, and the satisfaction of feeling one of his blows finding its target.

The hawk-eyed weapons master caught Azerick spying on his training and stalked over to berate him once more. "I thought I told you this area was for fighters, not for bookworm spell hurlers. How would you like me to throw you to one of my wolves and let him chew on you a bit? Maybe a few bruises will help you learn your place!"

"I would like that very much, Weapons Master," Azerick replied, refusing to shy away from his scowling face.

"Don't you get smart with me, boy! Wizard or no, I'll take you right out in the middle of my yard and beat you black and blue!"

"Weapons Master, I've sparred with him before during spring festival. He's not bad. Will you let him practice with us?" Alex asked, coming to his friend's rescue.

"You think you can look a man in the eye and take his life with honest steel and not some wizard's trick, boy?"

"I know I can, Weapons Master," Azerick replied confidently.

"I'll have no wizard's tricks on my field: no illusions, no fire, or magic attacks of any kind."

"Yes, sir, just a spell that grants me some protection no different than if I was wearing armor, if I may."

"As long as it isn't unduly advantageous and it doesn't spark or have any offensive tricks to it, I'll allow it. See, I know about you wizards and your tricks!"

Alex gave Azerick a wink and a clap on the back as the drill instructor led him into the yard to choose a weapon. He chose a staff from a rack after testing the balance and weight of a few different ones.

"A staff is a peasant's weapon, but I guess that is what you wizards like to tote around as well. Who wants to show this little wizardling how real men fight?" the trainer asked.

Everyone in the practice yard raised their hand and clamored for the privilege of showing off for the weapons master, except Alex who just stood with his arms folded and a knowing grin on his face.

"Dirk, why don't you do us the honor of teaching this whelp the difference between a battlefield and a classroom," the weapons master said, choosing a large boy about two years older than Azerick.

Dirk strode arrogantly out into the center of the yard to the applause of his classmates. He was bigger and older than Azerick but not as big as Alex was. Azerick cast his armor spell and stepped out to meet his opponent amidst the catcalls and jeers of the melee students.

"This match goes until one yields, is incapacitated, or killed," the weapons master explained.

Azerick was sure he added the threat of death for his benefit in an attempt to frighten him. If that was so, it didn't work. The weapons master stepped back and the two fighters did the same. He then gave the signal for the bout to begin.

Azerick and his sword-wielding opponent circled each other slowly. Dirk swung his blade in a lazy manner, taunting the younger Magus Academy student along with the crowd. Dirk was not taking this fight seriously. He knew wizards were soft and weak with no martial training at all. He was seconds away from being shown the error of his ways.

Dirk thrust forward with a lazy jab. Azerick, instead of executing another simple parry as he had been doing thus far, whipped the end of his staff up sharply, forcing the dulled blade up over Dirk's head. Pivoting to the left, he swung the end of his staff and struck the older boy in the side near his kidney. Dirk arched his back in surprise and pain and Azerick pivoted again, this time to the right, and struck him a blow to the stomach that doubled him up. He then took a half step back and brought the end of his staff down upon his opponent's back, knocking him to the ground.

At the crowd's howl of outrage, Azerick stepped back to allow the fighter to regain his feet and his breath and looked over to his friend. Alex shrugged, still standing with his arms crossed and his smile just a bit wider.

"Enjoy your momentary victory while you can, wizard. I'm ready for you this time," Dirk said as he regained his feet.

"I'm not a wizard, I'm a sorcerer," Azerick clarified.

Dirk just gave him a confused look and charged in swinging. Azerick parried each blow, giving ground as he fought off the larger, stronger boy's attack. Dirk jabbed forward with his blade and tried to skewer him. Azerick blocked the thrust and threw the blade far to the outside, half turning his attacker around. He spun behind him in the opposite direction, which placed him squarely at his opponent's back. Azerick stabbed out hard and sent Dirk to the ground once more with a jab to his left kidney.

The injured fighter lurched forward from the blow but riposted with a vicious backhand swing that would have taken Azerick's head off if he had not ducked and had the sword not been a dulled training blade. Azerick crouched under the desperate swing and jabbed the end of his staff into Dirk's sternum, taking all the wind from him. Dirk measured his length in the sand and dirt of the training ground and desperately tried to draw in air.

The fallen warrior rolled onto his back, and Azerick placed the butt of his staff lightly under his vanquished foe's throat just above the rib cage. Still lacking the breath to form words, Dirk tapped the weapon touching his throat three times as an act of submission. Azerick extended a hand to his opponent and helped him to his feet.

"You fight pretty well for a wizard," Dirk gasped out, his hands on his knees in an effort to hold himself up.

"Sorcerer," Azerick corrected again.

"You fight damn well no matter what you call yourself," the gruff weapons master said. "I won't tell any man no who wants to learn to fight. Where did you learn your staff skills? I know they don't teach that stuff in the Magus Academy."

"I studied under a master named Ewen when I was younger, then it was mostly what I taught myself and learned in the streets."

"That explains it. The streets are a tough master, but you learn quickly or you die. Trust me, I know. You bring yourself back anytime. I want to see you here regular like though if you're serious about learning how to fight like a man."

"I will, sir. I'll be here every day if I can."

Alex and Azerick got nearly an hour of free sparring before the bell signaling the end of classes began to toll. The melee students began dispersing, and Azerick said his farewells before returning to his school. As he walked past the stables, Travis and his friends burst out of one of the stalls where they had been lying in wait, grabbed him, and forced him back into the empty pen.

Realizing that trying to push four other boys was futile, he grabbed one by the shirtfront and yanked him in the direction they were pushing, pivoted, and threw him headfirst into the stable wall where he slumped down to the straw-covered floor.

The other three young men shoved him up against the same wall a fraction of a second later and started raining blows on him with their fists. Azerick cowered, ducked, and dodged as best he was able, even snaking out and connecting with a few quick jabs of his own, but their greater numbers soon brought him down. After he slumped to the floor, all four boys launched a few extra kicks before stepping back. Travis pulled out his wand and threatened him once again.

"I told you we weren't done, peasant. This is just the beginning. Did you think I would forget about what you did to me? Every time you start to feel comfortable or safe, I will remind you that you are not welcome here. Do yourself a favor and leave the Academy, or I will kill you. Maybe not today, maybe not tomorrow, but someday I will do it. I can take you out any time I want to, but I won't do it right away. I want you to be afraid. I want you to wonder if today is the day I end you until I decide to actually do it. Think about that every time you see me and live in fear."

Azerick pulled himself up off the ground as soon as they left and dusted the straw and dirt off his clothes before going back to his room. If Travis thought he could scare him, he was sorely mistaken.

"What the heck happened to you?" Rusty asked as he walked into the room.

"I was sparring with the Martial Academy guys after class."

"Are you crazy? Those guys are all psychotic killers who love to bash each other's brains in for fun."

"I did fine with the sparring. It was Travis and his friends who gave me all the bruises."

"Are you all right? You should go to the infirmary then tell the headmaster."

"Pfft, I've gotten hit harder by the floor falling out of bed. Those guys are amateurs. Try getting beat up by Hugo and his cronies. They may be as dumb as horse droppings, but they know how to work a guy over. Besides, you know the headmaster cannot, or will not, do anything about it. I can handle it myself. What is that wand he likes to threaten people with?"

"I heard him say it was a wand of magic bolts, like the spell most of us learn early on, only more powerful."

"Sounds unpleasant. I may have to do something about that sometime."

Azerick avoided the troublesome group as best he could by keeping a wary eye out and varying his route when he traveled the halls just as he did on the streets. However, he still had to go to class. In alchemy class, he sat down with a glass beaker full of a caustic liquid only to find that his chair was an illusion. He fell flat on his backside and spilled the substance all over him, which ate large holes in his clothes.

He returned the favor by switching the labels on some of Travis' component jars. When he set his mixture over a flame, it started to bubble and expand, releasing a noxious odor that ended the class for the day.

Over the next few weeks, an all-out battlefront of pranks erupted. One of Azerick's potions blew up, covering him, Rusty, and Magus Morgarum in a pink-tinted dye that took nearly a full week of scrubbing to remove. Of course, Magus Morgarum was clean the next day: a feat he did not feel inclined to share with his two sabotaged students.

Azerick found a good illusion spell in one of the library spell books. With Rusty's help, he cast an illusion over Travis that made it appear as though he were wearing no clothing. The effect was only visible to those more than five or six yards from the source of the spell, so neither Travis nor his friends were aware of the image. He looked not only nude, but also tragically underdeveloped in the manhood area and slightly overdeveloped in the breast area.

Travis and his friends crossed the commons and walked into class followed by the stares, giggles, and catcalls of every student they passed. By the time the group had made it to class, Travis was livid at not knowing why everyone was staring, pointing, and laughing. He looked at his robe, asked his friends if they saw anything wrong, and demanded to know what everyone was staring at. It was not until Magus Florent saw through the illusion and dispelled it that he became aware of the prank.

Travis repaid Azerick by making it appear as if the landing atop a flight of stairs was larger than it really was. When Azerick stepped toward what he thought was the top of the stairs, his foot fell through the illusion and he tumbled the entire way down, breaking his elbow and wrenching his knee, which had to be mended with a healing draught.

Azerick retaliated by sending one of his small constructs through Travis' window late one night. The automaton skittered across the ceiling and hung above the sleeping mage's bed. The construct looked like a spider, but its bulbous abdomen was a bladder filled with a sticky substance, which it released onto its unsuspecting target as he slept.

Travis awoke when the automaton poured the honey-like goo onto his head and shoulders. When he leapt from the bed, the construct released its hold from the ceiling and dropped down onto his pillow where it crawled under it and exploded. The pillow burst into a cloud of feathers and down, effectively tar and feathering him.

Weeks would pass before another strike and retaliation erupted. This cycle continued for the rest of the year. Sometimes, Travis and his friends were able to corner him alone and pummel him, after which Azerick would stalk them individually and administer a beating of his own. Azerick knew this could not continue. Something would eventually have to give in order to produce some sort of treaty or deliver a final, decisive blow. He only hoped Travis' anxiety was as great as his own.

Azerick stuck to his melee training as best he could, getting in three or four days of practice a week with the Martial Academy students. Both his magical and martial skills were developing quickly, and by the year's end he had nearly caught up to most of the students his age in the Magus Academy and could hold his own with his staff against many of the Martial Academy fighters.

He stayed at the Academy during the summer when most students went home to their families for two months. Master Devlin took advantage of the extra time to work him even harder in his studies. From sunrise to sunset, he pushed Azerick at a grueling pace, forcing him to learn as much as he could.

"Now, I want you to cast a spell at me. Tap the Source, form your spell, and release it at me," his master instructed.

"You want me to actually attack you? I can't. What if I hurt you?"

"There is little fear of that, Azerick. You may be clever, you may be skilled for one with as little training as you have had, but I'm certain my shield will protect me from anything you can muster," Master Devlin responded with a laugh.

Azerick did as he was told, feeling rather foolish at his presumptuous thought. He called the power into himself, formed it, and was preparing to launch a stream of magical bolts when something interrupted him. He felt the power slip from his grasp as an object smacked him in the middle of his forehead.

"Now tell me what just happened," his tutor said.

"You hit me with something, and it made me lose my hold on the Source," Azerick answered, rubbing at the red spot on his forehead.

"No, you allowed an external force to break your concentration. That will get you killed in a fight. You must not let anything break your focus: not pain, not sounds, nor fears. If your own mother or child is being burned to death and their screams assail you mercilessly, you must block all of that out, or you are of no use to anyone, not even yourself. Now try again."

Azerick began his casting once more, and again his master struck him with a small bag filled with dried beans. On his third try, he successfully sent three luminous missiles at his master. His spell struck, but the protective magic Devlin used to shield himself easily dissipated it.

"Good, now try again. As you become more focused, the method I use to distract you will get harder."

Azerick was able to work past the distractions on most of his successive castings until his instructor hit him with the flat of a book across the shoulder. Azerick was soon too fatigued to continue casting and was still distracted by the book bashing. Master Devlin had him go through the motions of casting without channeling the Source until he could perform the movements and words without error. His master finally dismissed him for the day, battered and bruised, but with more confidence.

Azerick found Master Devlin hard and unfriendly but a good teacher. He set a pace he knew Azerick had to work hard at but was able to maintain, albeit barely. He didn't allow his student to slack off one bit, making him repeat lessons over and over until he got it.

Azerick was also able to find someone to spar with to practice his staff skills on occasion. By the time Rusty and the rest of the students returned, he felt as though he had completed another entire year of school, which was not far from the truth.

His concentration was now sufficient that he could form and cast a spell without interruption, even when Master Devlin jabbed him in the thigh or shoulder nearly hard enough to draw blood. Azerick accepted his training without complaint, which he was certain pleased and impressed his teacher even though he knew Master Devlin would never say as much.

The young sorcerer was a little concerned when Devlin informed him he would need to build his concentration to the point he could take an arrow or a cut without losing focus. Azerick hoped his master would not take his training to that level, but he was not certain given Devlin's methods thus far.

Rusty and the other students returned to the Academy and he and Azerick spent the day catching up. Azerick told Rusty about his studies and the spells he had learned, which impressed his friend quite a bit. Rusty told Azerick about his summer and how he and Colleen had shared kisses by the fountain at his home.

Travis and his goons wasted no time in harassing him once they returned. Azerick had hoped the petty rivalry would pass now that he had established himself at the school, but it seemed only to make Travis hate him even more. The pranks and fights went on week after week, month after month. Azerick developed something he liked to call a sundering spell. He used it in class to weaken the legs of Travis' chair so that it broke apart when he sat down. Travis caught him in one of the lesser-used hallways a short time later, and he and his friends proceeded to punch and kick him.

"Remember what I said, peasant. One day I'll be bored of you, and then you are finished. I'll tell you this much; this is the last year you will be attending this school. I suggest you leave on your own, but if you persist in this stubbornness, I will make you. Dead or alive, you will leave this school."

"I'll take your suggestion under advisement," Azerick answered.

His remark earned him a few more kicks before they left him lying in a darkened alcove. It was hard to keep away from such places, as the Academy was filled with innumerable shadowy halls and recesses from which to launch ambushes. The Academy was huge, but it boasted only a few hundred students. He read in one of the history archives that it had an attendance of well over a thousand several centuries ago, but for the last few hundred years, fewer people were being born with the talent to become wizards, and sorcerers were nearly extinct in the northern lands. Azerick picked himself up and limped back to his room.

"Got you again, huh?" Rusty asked.

"Yeah, I have to give them credit; they are getting better. I think Hugo would even let them tag along with him and his pals."

"This can't go on, you know. Something has to be done to end this."

"It will. When one of us is dead it will be over. In fact, Travis said this was the year I could leave on my own before he killed me."

"You have to go to the headmaster and have him put a stop to this. Travis *will* kill you if he gets the chance and get away with it too!"

"I will just have to make sure I don't give him the opportunity then," Azerick said with confidence.

"How are you going to do that?"

Azerick pulled Travis' wand from his sleeve. "It will be a lot harder for him to kill me without this."

"How did you get that?"

"I swiped it when they jumped me."

"When he finds out you took his wand he will kill you for sure,"

"He won't find out, I'm going to make sure he gets it back."

"If you're going to give it back, why did you bother taking it in the first place?"

"Remember his chair leg?" Azerick asked as he began casting his sundering spell on it.

"Do you think it will work?" asked Rusty.

"I think so, although it is harder to set on a magical item. I can feel it resisting me. Ah, there, got it. Well, time to go put this back where I found it."

With his work done, he limped back down the Academy halls until he found the site of his most recent fight and carefully placed the wand behind a pedestal supporting a bust of some long-forgotten wizard.

"Where is my wand?" Travis demanded the next morning at breakfast.

"I don't know what you are talking about, Travis," Azerick replied.

"I know you took it. You must have taken it when I was pummeling you yesterday."

"Did you try looking for it there? Maybe you dropped it."

"You better hope I find it, peasant, or I swear you will not live out the week," Travis promised before stalking off toward the site of their latest battle.

Azerick waved at Travis' back. "Good luck with that."

CHAPTER 31

Winter festival came and went with something resembling an undeclared ceasefire. Azerick had to wonder whether Travis had given up trying to drive him off or if this was the lull before the storm.

"Azerick, did you hear?" Rusty asked excitedly.

"Hear what?"

"We're going to have a big ball before the summer break! I'm going to bring Colleen so you can meet her."

"That's great, Rusty. It sounds like fun."

"You don't seem too excited. What's the matter?"

"I don't have anything to wear to something like that. It will make it even more obvious that I don't really belong here."

"I have lots of clothes. You can borrow some of mine. You're not as tall as I am, but they should be fine with a bit of hemming," Rusty offered.

"Thanks, Rusty, but I insist on wearing my own underwear. I've seen what you do to yours."

"Very funny, maybe you should just go in your underwear then!"

Azerick and Travis rarely crossed paths before summer's start, but instead of appreciating the relative peace, their seeming reduction of hostilities only set Azerick's nerves more on edge. With the day of the ball upon them, he tried to forget about his anxiety. Rusty gave Azerick a white silk shirt with a crimson crushed velvet doublet and black trews with a red embroidered pattern down the outside of each leg. Rusty wore a brilliant yellow shirt with lace cuffs under a royal blue doublet and a pair of blue trews with gold thread embroidery.

"Wow, you almost look like a gentleman," Rusty teased.

"Be careful, I have a reputation to protect."

They made their way to the formal banquet hall where the Academy had set up for the ball. Rusty went to find Colleen amongst the huge crowd of girls invited to attend from an all girl's school. The ball was open to all three branches of the Academy, which made for a rather good mix.

Azerick went to the long table covered by dozens of trays of small finger foods and two massive crystal punch bowls. He reached for a glass and the large ladle resting in the crystal bowl at the same time another hand grasped for the handle.

"Oh, pardon me, sir," begged a delicate feminine voice as the hand withdrew.

"No, please, it is I who must beg pardon from a fair maiden," Azerick replied using charm he did not know he possessed. "Please, allow me to get that for you."

"Thank you kindly, my gallant sir," the young woman replied with a giggle.

Azerick filled the proffered glass with the fizzy, slightly-fermented beverage before filling his own.

"My name is Azerick, by the way."

"Pleased to make your acquaintance, Sir Azerick, I'm Loranna," the lovely blond girl answered and offered her hand.

Azerick gently took her hand by the fingertips, bent at the waist, and brought his lips to within a whisper's brush of contact.

"Which school do you attend here, Sir Azerick?"

"I am in the Magus Academy, Lady Loranna."

"Oh pooh, let's drop the formals shall we, Azerick, I find it so tedious. I hope you don't think me too presumptuous."

"Not at all, Loranna. I thank you for your forthrightness. Formalities are something I am definitely not used to."

"So you are a wizard then?"

"Basically. I'm actually a sorcerer."

"A sorcerer? What does that mean?"

Before he could answer, the appearance of the last person Azerick wanted to see tonight interrupted them both.

"Forgive me for my tardiness, Lady Loranna, but there are so many people here. Fortunately, your beauty glows like a star amongst the blackness even in this crowded room. Let us be away from here. You are far too noble to be conversing with a peasant," Travis said with a viperous tongue.

"Sir Azerick was very much the gentleman."

"I once saw a play where a man played a very convincing King Thomas, but I assure you he was no royal. A commoner in velvet is still a commoner," Travis explained in his most pompous voice, guiding Loranna away with a little push to the small of her back.

She glanced briefly over her shoulder with a look of apology on her face.

"How dare you presume to speak to my date, peasant?" Travis hissed once Loranna was out of earshot.

"We were just talking, Travis. Let it go."

"Insult me again with your presence at your peril. Remember what I told you at the beginning of the year. Time is almost up."

"Yes, you have been promising my death for quite some time now, haven't you? It seems to me you are all threat, or you would have done something more than a few childish pranks and weak drubbings," Azerick shot back, sounding bored with all of the blustering.

"You will regret this night, peasant, I promise you," Travis hissed then stalked off after his date.

Azerick knew he should not have pressed him, but he was tired of putting up with the constant threats. Besides, Master Devlin had declared that his skills allowed him to advance to the rank of journeyman, and Azerick was confident he could defend himself against Travis and maybe even his friends too.

"Hey Azerick, this is Colleen. Colleen, this is my best friend, Azerick."

"Pleasure to meet you, Azerick," Colleen greeted and performed a small curtsy.

"The pleasure is mine. Rusty talks about you all the time. You are very lucky. Rusty is a good man."

"Oh, I'm the lucky one, Azerick, believe me," Rusty insisted.

"I know; I was just trying to be polite. She is far too pretty for you."

"Very funny, true, but funny."

"We're going to go dance; you should find someone to dance with too," his friend suggested.

"I will. I may even steal Colleen from you for a dance or two," Azerick promised as Rusty led his girl away.

Azerick did manage a few dances, but mostly he just walked around, speaking briefly to a few people who had heard of the sorcerer and were curious about him. He thought about his studies and Travis' threats. He knew this was not the place for him, but he needed to continue learning under Master Devlin's tutelage.

He decided to get away from the noise and the crowd by taking a walk in the enormous garden behind the Magus Academy's main building. He was enjoying the cool evening air when a muffled cry a short distance away broke the tranquility of the garden. Azerick threaded his way through the maze of hedgerows until he reached a small clearing. Even in the wan moonlight, he could clearly see the look of surprise on Travis' and his friends' faces.

Azerick took in the scene and deduced what was happening. He saw Loranna pinned under Travis' weight with his hand covering her mouth, her dress torn, and tears streaming down her face. Travis' friends were a short distance away, whether as voyeurs, lookouts, or simply waiting their turn he knew not and cared even less.

Fury, like the fierce rage he had felt that day in class when he had nearly killed Travis, inundated his body.

"Get him!" Travis commanded.

The three young men charged the interloper. Azerick raised his hand, and in the blink of an eye, sent three magic bolts flying from his fingertips, one lancing into each of the attackers.

Azerick took advantage of their shock and pain at being hit by the bolts to cast a couple of defensive spells on himself. The familiar shimmer of magical armor surrounded him while the second spell produced a near-invisible globe of defensive energy to block or reduce the damage from lesser spells.

He heard Travis command Loranna not to move. The weight of the threat, as well as her own terror, kept her pinned in place. All she could manage to do was sit up and scoot backward until her back pressed against a hedge, her wide eyes looking on in terror. Travis joined the fight just as his friends regained their feet.

"You have no chance, peasant. Leave now, say nothing of what you saw, or I will kill you. I may even be generous enough to allow you to stay in this school," Travis offered.

"If you were really certain of your chances of beating me, you would not bother to try and make deals. It is not in your character to deal when you can just take. What's the matter, Travis, did you not study your little recipe book today? I guess you figured you were man enough to rape a girl with just your scumbag friends to help you that you didn't need to prepare," Azerick deduced. "Here's a deal for you. Go tell the headmaster what you did and tried to do, leave this school, and never return."

"Are you joking? Do you know who my father is? I can do anything I want, take anything I want, and no one can do anything about it. Like I told her, no one is going to believe anyone over my word, especially when I have three witnesses who will corroborate anything I say."

"You're wrong. I can, and I will, do something about it if no one else will."

"Then you can die here," he snarled and began casting.

Azerick saw Travis and all three of his friends reach into their pockets, pull out what he could only assume was a reagent of some kind, and begin casting. He prepared a retaliatory strike of his own. Travis completed his spell first, and Azerick braced himself for the impacts of the arcane bolts.

His shield stripped the magical projectiles of much of their power, but what got through was still excruciatingly painful. He maintained his focus and completed his spell an instant before the other three student mages. He sent another spread of bolts to strike each one again. Being unshielded, they took the full force of each bolt. Coupled with the pain of the first salvo Azerick struck them with, their concentration was broken, and each one lost control of their impending spells, and the gathered energy dissipated harmlessly into the air.

This new source of agony was too much for them, and they toppled to the ground, writhing in pain. Travis was already partway through another casting when Azerick started to prepare his next spell. He knew Travis would launch his next assault before he could finish. Azerick spared part of his focus to try to ascertain what spell his foe would hit him with next.

He recognized the weave before Travis was halfway through finishing it. Azerick braced himself for Travis' second salvo, knowing that he could not dodge the attack. He was struck by two more bolts, feeling fortunate once again that he had the foresight to cast his ward no matter how minimal the protection. He bore through the pain again and advanced on his nemesis, hand outstretched before him. Travis must have known he could not prepare another spell in time even if he had one ready, which he did not, so he drew his wand, ready to release its fury.

"Give it up, Travis. Stop now. You will not even be able to utter the command word to trigger the wand you think makes you so powerful. Your friends took two bolts each and look at them. I have three ready to release on you without a thought, and you are unprotected. You might live, but you might not. I nearly killed you before. I am in control of my power now and will not hold back."

"The only reason you beat me was because I wasn't prepared. If I had known I would have to fight you tonight, I would have beaten you!" Travis seethed, his face flushing a deep crimson.

"You mean all four of you *may* have. That is the only way you have ever beaten me. It takes four of you so-called nobles to take on one peasant."

"I can beat you! Meet me tomorrow night when I am ready if you are not a coward. You can even have her," he sneered, looking at the weeping Loranna.

"You want to duel? Fine, then it is over. If I win, you leave me alone forever. If you win, I'll leave the school."

"Fine, meet me behind the wooded hill at the far side of the Martial Academy's maneuver training ground."

Travis pulled and kicked his friends to their feet and stalked off defeated. Azerick went over to Loranna and helped her stand. She fell into his arms, clutched the front of his doublet, and buried her face into the crushed velvet, sobbing.

"It's all right, they're gone. They can't hurt you now."

"I don't understand; he was so polite and such a gentleman. He was a noble. Why would he do that?" she sobbed.

"A person is not born with true nobility. I have seen more nobility in a man without the coin to buy bread than I have seen in some of the wealthiest and highest-born people of this city."

"Thank you for saving me. He called you a peasant and that your mother was a, was a...but you are the gallant one. He is just a pig dressed in silk and velvet!"

"Come, I will walk you back to the ball."

Azerick escorted Loranna to the main hall and left her with friends while he went to contemplate what to do next. Thankfully, he did not run into Travis or his group while walking the halls. He decided he would talk to Master Devlin about what had happened. He climbed the familiar stairs to his master's rooms in the tower, rehearsing in his mind what he would say.

He reached the top landing and was about to knock on the door when he heard voices coming from the other side. He paused, not intentionally eavesdropping but trying to decide whether he should interrupt or not. What he heard from the snatches of conversation he picked up made him hesitate and listen.

"There are several pieces as of yet unaccounted for. Your assistance in helping my patron locate and possibly retrieve these artifacts would be greatly appreciated," an unfamiliar voice said from beyond the door. "I brought all of the information we have on the one piece we have secured as well as what little we have gleaned as to the whereabouts of some of the rest. Sadly, it is not much, which is why we have chosen to approach you. Your knowledge of Sumara may be key in their discovery."

"It is my understanding that trafficking in artifacts of power is highly illegal in your kingdom, is it not?" Azerick heard Devlin ask.

"The king is bastard born and unfit to sit the throne. Your kingdom has a rich history and a proud lineage in its leader, and we ask for nothing less."

"What you say is true. I assume compensation for such a risk is equally great?"

"My patron is very generous in rewarding those who are successful, but very intolerant of those who are not."

Azerick could not believe what he was hearing. His own master was betraying the king, betraying him, and with the same people he was certain were tied to his father's murder. Azerick fled down the stairs as fast as he could go, his mind reeling from the implications of what he had just heard.

Azerick stopped at the foot of the steps as anger pushed away the surprise and hurt of betrayal. *I will go back and kill them both or die trying!* he thought and turned around to make good on his threat.

He paused and forced himself to focus just as his traitorous master had taught him when casting spells. Losing his focus now would get him killed as sure as a lightning bolt to the head, and that is what he would get, or worse, if he tried to challenge Devlin. He knew he would never be able to overcome or even surprise the powerful sorcerer.

Perhaps I should flee the Academy. No, I will learn everything I can from Master Devlin. I will watch him, and maybe I can get some answers from him. But could he still study under him knowing he was linked to the people he wanted dead? He decided to wait and give it more thought. Acting rashly would only hasten defeat. Besides, he had a duel tomorrow, and he would not let Travis say he was a coward by not showing.

He went back to his room. Rusty had not returned, and Azerick figured he was probably canoodling with Colleen somewhere. He lay down on his bed and went over everything in his mind before falling asleep.

CHAPTER 32

Azerick woke at the sound of the morning bell calling everyone to break their fast. Rusty was on top of his bed, snoring away, the smell of Colleen's perfume still clinging to him. Azerick was hungry, but instead of eating with the rest of the students, he snuck through the kitchens and pilfered a couple of rounds of bread, cheese, and smoked meat. He was sure Rusty would appreciate something to eat when he woke up and found he had missed morning meal call. It was still more than either of them could eat, but he felt the need to be prepared.

Rusty was still asleep when he returned to his room with the bundle of food. He decided to wait until Rusty awoke so they could eat together, maybe for the last time. He busied himself with brewing up some potions. It would take most of the day to make what he wanted, but there were no classes today so he had time. It would also help keep his mind occupied. He knew Travis would not fight alone and that his friends would jump in as soon as he looked to be losing.

Azerick was not confident he could beat all four of them without using his strongest spells, and that ran the real risk of killing someone. He had no apprehension about killing a man if he deserved it like those men in the thieves' guild who killed Jon and his family, but these were just school bullies. Travis probably deserved to die for what he had attempted with Loranna, but it was not his place to be the judge and executioner for every crime committed in the city.

Rusty was finally beginning to stir and mumbled out Colleen's name once with a smile on his face while still half asleep before regaining full consciousness.

"Hey, lover boy, are you hungry?"

"I'm starved. Dancing works up an appetite."

"Almost as much as the after-dancing activities, I would wager."

"How did you know about that?" Rusty asked guiltily as his cheeks flushed a bright red.

"You just told me," Azerick answered.

"What are you cooking up?" Rusty asked, looking at the liquids brewing in the alchemic set and helping himself to some of the food Azerick laid out.

"Just something I may need later. So how was your night with Colleen?"

"It was fine, great I mean, you know…" Rusty replied, stumbling over his words as his face attained an even brighter shade of red than normal.

"Rusty, I just want you to know you have been a good friend, the best friend I ever had. If I have to leave sometime and not come back, I want you to have the alchemic set."

"What are you talking about? Where are you going? I can help if you are in trouble!"

"There is just something I have to do, and it may take me away for a while, that's all. I don't want you to get involved."

"But you are my friend, and friends help each other," Rusty insisted.

"Not with this. This is personal. You need to stay here and finish your training, marry Colleen, and raise a family."

"How did you know we were talking about getting married?"

"You just told me—again. Man, Rusty, you are terrible at keeping secrets."

"You won't tell me what is going on, will you?"

"No, I can't. This is something I need to deal with on my own."

"Just be careful, okay. Whenever you finish what you need to do, I'll be here for you if you need anything," Rusty promised.

The two friends clasped wrists and finished eating. Azerick went back to work on his potions while Rusty busied himself studying his spell book. Later in the day, Rusty took his leave to go and meet with Colleen. Azerick finished his potions and poured the contents into steel vials, six in all, which he stoppered with corks and sealed with wax. These he slipped into special pockets he had sewn inside his cloak.

Once outfitted, he left the main hall and crossed the commons, stopping by the training yard to borrow a staff from the weapons rack. Fortunately, they did not bother to lock up the staves like they did the bladed weapons. He then threaded his way through the wooded area of the huge maneuver training field, pausing at the top of the hill to prepare his defensive spells before walking down to meet whatever fate awaited him.

"I'm surprised you actually showed up, peasant," Travis sneered.

"And I'm not the least bit surprised to see you brought your friends to help save your miserable skin," Azerick replied, looking at the three other young wizards standing with him.

"Don't worry about them; they are just here to congratulate me when you fall."

"Let's do this then."

Travis motioned to his friends to back away and give them room. The three fell back about fifty feet and off to the side of the clearing that made up the dueling ground. Travis began drawing in the Source, forming a weave with the strands of energy and muttering the words to a spell.

Azerick reacted instantly, drawing in his own power to form his attack at the same time. Travis must have prepared his defenses ahead of time as well, Azerick surmised, as he realized his opponent was forming an offensive spell.

Azerick completed his spell first and launched three dagger-shaped, brilliant bolts at Travis. A spellcaster could shape the visual appearance of many of their spells as a method to personalize their castings. All three bolts should have struck Travis in the chest, but an invisible shield harmlessly dissipated them.

Such total protection from his spell should not have been possible given Travis' skill level. His ward could protect him from some of the damage, but only a wizard of much higher power could negate it entirely. This unexpected revelation caused Azerick a great deal of concern.

Travis released his own stream of bolts that looked like small glowing skulls. Both bolts pierced Azerick's shield, which bled off some, but not all, of their power, and struck him in the chest. The blow burned like mad, but Azerick maintained his focus and launched another, stronger spell at his nemesis. A green, arrow-shaped bolt sprang forth from his outstretched hand, but whatever force was protecting his target turned his spell aside once again.

Travis completed his next spell, laughing at Azerick's seemingly impotent casting. Travis hurled a large ball sparking with electricity. Azerick tried to dodge the crackling orb but was caught a glancing blow on his shoulder as it sailed past. Even with the minor protection of his shield, agonizing pain lanced through his body.

Azerick now realized that Travis was wearing some kind of enchanted device protecting him from the spells he had thrown at him thus far. Blinking the sweat and pain-induced tears from his eyes, Azerick prepared his most powerful spell, hoping it would be strong enough to pierce whatever protection he had purchased.

It was the most complex spell Azerick knew, and the time it took to cast was such that Travis was able to launch another pair of skull-shaped bolts at him before he completed it. Once again, the young sorcerer ground his teeth in pain and concentration, willing himself to focus on his casting.

Azerick thrust his hand out and shouted the arcane command to release the gathered power. The clap of thunder set his ears ringing as the smell of ozone produced by the lightning bolt filled the air. Travis was hurled back and sent sprawling as his ward failed to fully protect him from the spell's deadly force.

The young sorcerer spun around to face Travis' friends, knowing they would interfere now that their leader was down. They were already casting when Azerick turned to face them, and he knew he could not complete his spell before all three struck. He doubted he would be able to withstand the barrage of all three students' spells.

Azerick was forming his attack even though he knew it was probably futile when a gout of flame sprang from the tree line a few yards to the side of Travis' three friends. The flaming lance of fire stretched from Rusty's hands and shot between the young mages, burning all three. They dove and rolled in the dirt trying to smother the flames from their burning robes.

"What are you doing here, Rusty?" Azerick shouted in surprise and relief.

"Saving your butt from the looks of it."

Rusty covered the three young men on the ground as Azerick turned back to face Travis. Travis had recovered from what should have been a mortal blow, holding his wand out before him.

"Put the wand away, Travis, and admit defeat," Azerick demanded.

"No, I have you now. You'll never be able to get a spell off before I kill you."

"Don't do it, Travis, or you will be sorry. I promise you."

"You lost, peasant, and I'm going to blast your friend too, right after I kill you," Travis swore as he uttered the command to unleash the wand's power.

Azerick dropped to the ground as Travis triggered his wand. A massive explosion ripped through the air as the wand exploded, releasing all its stored energy in one mighty blast due to the sundering spell Azerick had cast on it previously to weaken its structure. The force of the uncontrolled discharge crashed over everyone in the clearing, blasting leaves from the surrounding trees and sending Rusty and the three other students flying through the air. The concussive wave washed over the prone sorcerer, rolling him away from the epicenter of the explosion.

When the dust cleared, the young men climbed unsteadily back to their feet, ears ringing, and looked around in shock at the damage the exploding wand had caused. All of the trees surrounding the clearing had been stripped of their leaves. At the source of the blast, the ground had been laid bare of all grass leaving nothing but dirt, blood, and Travis' ruined, unmoving body. The five students slowly walked up to the corpse, and all knew he would never move again. The arm that had been holding the wand was simply gone, and his face and chest were shredded and blackened from the blast.

"You did this. You knew what would happen! I heard what you said and saw you drop to the ground just before his wand blew up!" one of Travis' friends shouted.

"I didn't know it would be so powerful. I thought it would just break," Azerick tried to explain.

"You killed him! It was murder, and I'll see you hang for it!" another shouted.

"I would be very careful with who you threaten right now. Do you think this is the first man I have killed?" Azerick asked, his eyes full of menace.

The three wizards decided to run instead of challenging the dangerous sorcerer.

"How did you know I was here, Rusty?"

"I knew you were going to do something that would probably get you killed, so I waited for you to leave then followed you here."

"I wish you hadn't gotten caught up in this, but thanks for your help."

"What are you going to do now?"

"I have to leave. I knew that before I came out here," Azerick replied as he walked over and pulled his packsack and staff out from behind a tree.

"They are going to ask me what happened, you know. What do you want me to tell them?"

"Tell them the truth."

"Did you know that was going to happen when you sabotaged his wand?" Rusty asked looking at the corpse.

"No," Azerick replied, shaking his head. "I really did not know that would happen. At least not nearly that bad, but I am not sorry for it. He was going to rape a girl last night, but I stopped him. He would have cheated in order to kill me tonight as well, so he got what he deserved. I probably saved a lot of people from his predations."

"But you were already packed, ready to leave," Rusty pursued, doubt creeping into his voice.

"I knew I would not be returning to the Academy no matter what happened here tonight. There are other things going on I cannot talk about."

"All right, Azerick, you are my friend and I trust you. Keep yourself safe. You know I am here if you ever need anything," Rusty promised as he embraced his friend.

They parted ways there in the clearing. Rusty went back toward the Academy, and Azerick headed off in a different direction, both wondering if they would see the other ever again.

Rusty moved at a sedate pace, his mind feeling as though it were in a fog as he desperately tried to come to terms with what had happened and what he should do about it. A troupe of Academy instructors, led by the friends of the recently deceased Travis, intercepted Rusty as he walked slowly back to the school.

"There he is, Headmaster. He saw that street rat kill Travis!"

Rusty started at the unexpected shout and saw Travis' trio of friends leading Headmaster Dondrian, Magus Allister, Magus Florent, and Magus Bauer toward him at a rapid pace. Magus Bauer looked furious and ready to flay the skin from someone. Magus Florent and Allister looked concerned, while the headmaster just looked confused.

"Franklin, what has happened? Where is Azerick?" the headmaster asked, winded from the swift walk.

"I don't know where he is. As to what happened, that's a long story, but Travis is dead and they were part of it," Rusty said, pointing at the three who had brought the teachers.

"Take us to Travis and where it all happened," Magus Allister said.

Rusty led the group back the way he had come and into the small clearing. Nothing had changed in the last half hour. The massive blast had scorched the ground clean of grass and shrubs, the nearest trees were bereft of much of their foliage, and Travis lay strewn about a large area in so many pieces it would take days to recover most of the bits for burial.

"By the gods," Allister rumbled, looking on in disbelief. "I think we had best get back to your office, Dondrian, and discuss this further. We will need to contact the boy's father."

"As well as the magistrate," Magus Bauer added in her own shrewish voice.

"Indeed," the headmaster replied, heaving a sigh. "This is a most distressing situation with little chance of it coming out well for anyone involved."

EPILOGUE

Several dark-robed figures sat around a large stone table in high-backed chairs of ancient design. The light was poor, barely illuminating the grey, featureless walls of the dusty, stale chamber.

"Ulric is taking too long to secure the armor, and with it, the throne," one of the figures said.

"The length of time is not unexpected. Dundalor's armor was scattered throughout the known world a millennium ago. We knew it would take time to recover."

"But what of the delay to our own plans for the king and the kingdom?"

"We are not ready to move right now anyway. The king still commands forces that are loyal to him. If Ulric ultimately fails, we want enough of our own people in place to make the coup as bloodless as possible, at least to the citizens. Jarvin and his ilk are another matter."

"How much longer shall we allow Ulric to ready himself to make his bid for the crown before we must write him off as a failure and move in ourselves?"

"Not long, another year, perhaps two will give us enough time to judge Ulric's chances of success or failure and shore up our own position in the interim."

"What of the recent reports of the dead rising?"

"Fanciful tales from peasants most likely, but we can use it to our gain regardless of their veracity. Casually spread the word that it is the result of having a bastard sit the throne. After all, the king represents the land, and if his blood is impure, it surely taints the land as well."

"Very well, gentlemen, all glory to the sun god.

"All hail Solarian," the dark cabal intoned in unison.

To be continued in:
THE SORCERER'S TORMENT
Book Two of The Sorcerer's Path

FROM THE AUTHOR

I hope you enjoyed this tale and will try my other works. Feel free to look me up on Facebook! You can also check me out on my website http://brockdeskins.com/ where I write serial fiction, free for your enjoyment, and answer questions!

Author page:
https://www.amazon.com/Brock-Deskins/e/B005M6VQ1O

Facebook:
https://www.facebook.com/brocksbooks/

Twitter:
@brockdeskins

PLEASE REVIEW MY BOOKS (Especially if you liked it). Customer reviews are the primary means of enticing others to purchase them. I am dependent upon the sales of my books to earn a living that will allow me to continue writing stories that I hope bring you some measure of entertainment. Thank you for your support.

OTHER BOOKS BY BROCK E. DESKINS

The Sorcerer's Path is an epic fantasy series.

The Sorcerer's Ascension: Torn from a life of comfort and luxury, his family destroyed by political intrigues and aspirations, a young boy must quickly grow into a man before the deadly streets of Southport devour him. Follow Azerick through a page-turning adventure that pits him against thieves, thugs, murderers, and men of power that will stop at nothing to achieve their goals.

Azerick must fight just to survive, but for him survival is not enough. A hunger to avenge the wrongs committed against him burns deep within. But that is not all that lies within the young man. There is a power waiting to be unleashed that may be the key to achieving the justice and security he seeks--if it does not destroy him first.

The Sorcerer's Torment: Azerick flees The Academy but quickly falls prey to powerful beings that use his skills and power for their own amusement. What these creatures do not understand is the power of the young sorcerer's will and the lengths he will go to for vengeance. Despite becoming a prisoner, Azerick finds his first true love, but can he keep it?

The Sorcerer's Legacy: Azerick has found himself a home and tries to settle down. He takes on an apprentice and tries to put all the death and desire for vengeance behind him. But when the Rook finds him, Azerick is once again pulled back into Ulric's schemes. Knowing that all he has worked toward and everyone close to him is in danger as long as these schemes are ongoing; Azerick decides to put an end to it, once and for all.

The Sorcerer's Vengeance: After narrowly avoiding being killed in his own bed by the land's most feared assassin, Azerick leaves his school behind to find out who sent him and to put an end to the threat once and for all. Azerick's search will take him to the very pits of the abyss and back to unleash hellish fury upon those that threaten him.

The Sorcerer's Scourge: With the siege broken and Ulric dead, Azerick can finally relax, study his magic, and run his school in peace. Unfortunately, Jarvin's reign is far from uncontested and the true usurper decides to make his move. Jarvin escapes with help from an unlikely source—a vampire named Landrin who still clings tenaciously to his own humanity. While Azerick and a large force from North Haven race to save the king in exile, evil forces are preparing to unleash a nightmare upon the kingdom that may well destroy them all.

The Sorcerer's Abyss: Now the master of the Fifth Circle of the abyss, Azerick is challenged by another demon lord for supremacy. Azerick must face this threat as well as his innermost demons, all the while searching for a way to escape his hellish prison.

Ellyssa fears she is going insane as she plagued by nightmares of her capture and enslavement. Deciding the key to saving herself lies in the total destruction of the object of her fears, she embarks on a crusade to find and kill the slaver, Captain Jake, and eradicate the slave trade.

Ellyssa's nightmares and battles spill out onto the streets of North Haven and gains the attention of The Academy. Fearing Azerick's school is turning out rogue wizards, The Academy decides to hunt down and destroy the rogue and place the school within their control.

The Sorcerer's Return: Azerick has come back from the abyss in order to try to unite all the races against the return of the old gods who seek to destroy them and subjugate the few they allow to survive a brutal purging. However, fighting ancient gods may be the least of his troubles as he battles to save a fractured kingdom, a brilliant son traveling a dark path, and the splintered soul of his own humanity.

The Sorcerer's Destiny: Brutally purged of his demonic influence, Azerick continues the struggle of uniting the kingdom to face the coming of the Scions, ancient gods banished by the mortal races during the Great Revolution two thousand years ago. The fallen gods' prison is crumbling, and Azerick is powerless to stop them from breaking free and enacting their cataclysmic vengeance upon the world.

The humans must ally with the other races in a final battle against impossible odds while their entire world crumbles to the ground and is trod beneath the feet of an unstoppable foe. How can they set aside their distrust of each other when they fear the very person trying to save them?

Rise of the Order: Banished to the abyss after helping defeat the Scions and saving the world from eternal darkness, Azerick languishes in perpetual misery as Lord of the Fifth Circle. The denizens of his hellish realm view him as a usurper and outsider. The chaotic creatures form an alliance with one goal in mind: destroy Azerick Giles, but Sharrellan stands in their way.

A powerful spell tears through the demonic planes, and when the dust settles, the dark goddess is nowhere to be found. It is up to Azerick to return her to her seat of power, but he has a price: return him to his mortal form and send him home.

Back home, a vast empire is on a crusade to conquer the world, and it has set its sights on Valeria. Their goal is to unite the world under a single banner, eradicate the spawn infestation unleashed by the Scions, and replace the gods who they feel have forsaken them with their mystical rulers.

Can Azerick save the dark goddess from the clutches of her demonic subjects and become mortal once again? Will he have the power to protect his people from The Order if he does?

Descent Into Chaos: The Order has arrived in force, and the fate of Valeria, and perhaps all the world, is poised to come under their iron-fisted control. Azerick and Daebian are forced to flee Southport and make a contentious alliance when King Miles capitulates to the invaders. Reduced to insurgent warfare, Azerick and his allies attempt to battle The Order's vastly superior forces in a series of hit and run strikes, but the enemy legions may not be his biggest threat.

Princess Sylvian Attar, daughter to The Order's godlike emperor and empress, has taken a personal interest in Azerick. Herself a powerful sorceress, Sylvian hunts Azerick in hopes of removing Valeria's legendary hero from the battlefield thus sapping her enemies' will to fight. Azerick decides there is but one course of action he can take against this unstoppable foe. It was time to inject a little chaos into The Order.

Brooklyn Shadows is a modern-day vampire tale. Full of action and snarky dialogue, Brooklyn Shadows is an enjoyable read for anyone who enjoys the supernatural underworld and butt-kicking vampires.

<u>**Shrouds of Darkness**</u> (Brooklyn Shadows Book 1) Leo Malone has been a vampire for the better part of the twentieth century. Once a prominent Sherriff (vampire cop), he now earns his living as a private eye and occasional bodyguard for anyone that requires some serious protection. Leo is hired by the daughter of a mob accountant who has gone missing.

The fact that her father is also a werewolf has Leo following a trail of grisly murders that will lead him through a web of intrigue and conspiracy involving his fellow vampires and the local werewolves that make New York their home, all the while trying to keep one particularly determined cop off his back and himself out of jail. Leo is not some pretty-boy vampire that all the girls ogle over, but a hard-eyed, remorseless killing machine who does not take crap from anyone.

<u>**Blood Conspiracy**</u> (Brooklyn Shadows Book 2): While dealing with the aftermath of the failed vampire council coup, Leo discovers that the modified Cure has fallen into the hands of a black ops government project designed to create vampiric super soldiers. When the inevitable happens, the off-book Homeland Security operation forcefully enlists Leo to help them resolve the situation. Worse yet, he has to work not only with an antagonistic werewolf named Meat, he is reunited with his hated creator, Lesile.

<u>**Primacy of Darkness**</u> (Brooklyn Shadows Book 3): Jack the Ripper, sadistic madman of old London, once thought long dead, has returned

to New York in an effort to quench his thirst for blood and mayhem. When the city's vampire enclave finds itself insufficient to deal with a madman of Jack's caliber, Vincent, the enclave head, enlists Leo Malone to put the maniac down before he reveals the existence of vampires as he throws the city into the throes of chaos and terror. Leo soon finds that Jack is not the only monster with which he must contend. A ghost from his past has also seemingly crawled from its grave and seeks to put an end to him and the rest of his kind.

The Transcended Chronicles is the story of an outlandish young man as he goes from being a troublesome youth to one of the kingdom's greatest secret agents. Blessed (or cursed) with an amazing ability to both fight and abuse his body with every conceivable vice known to man, Garran Holt is either the kingdom's greatest hero or its biggest embarrassment.

<u>The Miscreant</u> **(The Transcended Chronicles Book 1):** Garran Holt is a troubled young man. Unable to tolerate his self-destructive ways, his mother sells him into indentured servitude as part of a work crew building King Remiel's new trade road. When mercenaries sent to disrupt the road's construction attack his work camp, Garran discovers an inner power capable of turning him into a warrior of unparalleled ability. When the leader of his work crew recognizes Garran as being one of the transcended (a fighter able to slip into the swifter currents of time), he is trained as an agent, one of the kingdom's elite spies. Crude, abrasive, and deeply committed to destroying himself with drugs, alcohol, and debauchery, Garran might be the kingdom's only hope against falling to The Guild, the powerful trade cartel bent on becoming the true and undisputed power in the land.

<u>The Agent</u> **(The Transcended Chronicles Book 2):** The Guild rules the kingdom through their puppet monarch, and Garran must race to save the last living heir to the throne before the powerful syndicate's assassins complete their extermination of anyone who could oppose them. Garran and Prince Adam Altena struggle to find allies in hopes of rescuing Adam's sister, who was forced to marry the usurper in order to prevent even the thought of rebellion, and raise an army

capable of defeating The Guild. With The Guild now in control of Anatolia's powerful army as well as their legion of mercenaries, their future is grim. How can a disreputable agent and a deposed prince convince their neighboring rulers to oppose The Guild, an organization that has had them cowed for decades?

Empire of Masks is an exciting and explosive new series that takes place in the world of Hedon and takes you across the land of Eidolan where ships sail through the skies and men and women wage war with magic, swords, muskets, and cannons.

<u>Highlords of Phaer</u> (**Book one of Empire of Masks**): Born a slave, descended of kings, Jareen Velarius just wants to provide the best life he can for his family, but Eidolan is a realm that challenges even the most stalwart of souls. Caught between his masters and those brave or foolish enough to strike against them, Jareen struggles to reconcile his role as a dutiful slave with that of a man who desires to be free. His goal: to return his people to a life stolen by the highlords more than a millennium ago.

Auberon Victore, sorcerer, alchemist, son of a powerful overlord, and Jareen's master, creates an alchemic compound he is certain will change the world; he just does not know how. Jareen sees it for the weapon that could break the sorcerers' iron grasp wrapped around the necks of every lowborn in the empire. It will change the world, but not in the way his master desires.

Across the Tempest Sea, a mighty storm has raged for a thousand years, keeping a terrible, long-forgotten enemy at bay, an enemy whose cruelty knows no bounds. Only the perpetual storm and their fear of the sorcerer highlords keep the Necrophages from returning to Eidolan and cloaking the empire in death and darkness. But the tempest is waning, and the dissidents' freedom may well come at the cost of their total destruction.

<u>Nightbird:</u> The Great Revolution ended the highlords' tyranny two hundred years ago, but the legacy of that epic war, and that of the principal architects' descendants, lives on. With the highlords' death and their taking magic, as it was once known, to their graves, Eidolan

fell into a time of darkness and its cities lived in isolation. However, some people, dubbed arcanists, discovered a new form of magic and the airships returned to the skies, rejoining the cities in trade as well as conspiracy, but a new darkness, more dreadful and deadly than any they faced before, is coming.

Kiera is a fifteen-year-old nightbird, one of many who flit about after dark, stealing whatever they can find in order to survive. She lives on a derelict airship in the poorest part of the city with Wesley, a young man who plies his trade as an escort to wealthy older women, and his little brother Russel, an autistic savant who communicates only through sign but who could secretly be the most powerful techno-arcanist the empire has ever known. Deep in debt to the underlord Nimat, Kiera dives into evermore dangerous schemes that put her at the heart of a secret war that could spell the destruction of not just the city, but the very empire.

Kiera is caught in the center of several factions on the brink of war. When she can no longer tell friend from enemy, there is only one side she can trust—her own.

Mourningbird: A creature of darkness lurks in the shadows of Velaroth, wearing the skin of its victims, and grips the city in terror. Dorian, a Necrophage bent on sowing chaos and paving the way for his people's invasion, has declared war on the humans of Eidolan, and there appears to be no one capable of stopping him.

Kiera's world is shattered by those who hold power, and she is forced to seek an ally. The nightbird is coming into power of her own, but can she stay alive long enough to seize it? Russel's behavior has taken a turn for the worse, and his actions have drawn the attention of those who would use his amazing talents for their own gain...and everyone else's loss.

The battle for Velaroth, and perhaps the world, has begun. Who will win? Who will live to mourn the dead? Will there be anything left for the victor to claim as their prize?

Standalone books

The Portal is a fun and exciting story of some less than popular teenagers that accidentally open a portal to a mystical land during one of their role-playing games. Drew, a dour and anti-establishment teenager, is pulled through and captured by evil creatures lying in wait on the other side. Now it is up to his friends and older brother to rescue him, but who will rescue Drew's captors from him?

Amelia (Battle for Ardentia): Amelia is a precocious, ten-year-old girl with a powerful imagination. In her alter-ego guise of a demi-goddess warrior princess, Amelia fights against a powerful demonic sorcerer named Romut and his horde of monsters in a never ending series of battles to protect the people of her imaginary world. However, the true battle strikes home when Amelia is diagnosed with a brain tumor. Now Amelia must fight not just the evil living in her imagination, but for her very life.

ABOUT THE AUTHOR

Brock Deskins was born in a small town located in rural Oregon. At age twenty, he joined the army and served as an M1A1 tank crewman, dental specialist, and computer analyst. While in the military, he became an accomplished traveler, husband, and father of three wonderful children. His military career completed, attended college to brush up on his skills as a computer analyst and gain new skills as a writer. Brock received his degree in computer networking and is now devoting his full time and limited attention span to writing.

BIBLIOGRAPHY

THE SORCERER'S PATH
The Sorcerer's Ascension
The Sorcerer's Torment
The Sorcerer's Legacy
The Sorcerer's Vengeance
The Sorcerer's Scourge
The Sorcerer's Abyss
The Sorcerer's Return

The Sorcerer's Destiny
Rise of the Order
Descent Into Chaos

BROOKLYN SHADOWS
Shrouds of Darkness
Blood Conspiracy

THE TRANSCENDED CHRONICLES
The Miscreant
The Agent

EMPIRE OF MASKS
Highlords of Phaer
Nightbird
Mourningbird

OTHER BOOKS BY BROCK E. DESKINS
The Portal
Amelia: Battle for Ardentia

Curious about other Crossroad Press books? Stop by our website:
http://crossroadpress.com
We offer quality writing
in digital, audio, and print formats.

Subscribe to our newsletter on the website homepage and receive a
free eBook.